The Redcap
A Sam McKay Novel

K.M. Hardy

Picaty Press—Tooele, Utah
ISBN: 978-1-7367346-0-5
Library of Congress Control Number: pending
Title: The Redcap: A Sam McKay Novel
Author: K.M. Hardy
Digital distribution | 2021
Paperback | 2021

This is a work of fiction. The characters, names, incidents, places, and dialogue are products of the author's imagination, and are not to be construed as real.

Dedication

To my darling husband, kids, Gran, and my mom: thanks for being my biggest fans!

Also to my professors RW and SH: thank you for all that you taught me.

Prologue

Sunday, May 21, 1998
Aberdeen, Scotland

" **A**ch, donnea be too hard on yerselves, boys. Ye couldnea have known wha' the bitches really wanted," Callum MacWood jested. He downed his third shot of Irish whiskey and looked to his cousin, Thomas McFarland, and his mate next to him. Haunt 49 was particularly crowded that evening, but it was of no matter to the musician; he quite enjoyed the feeling of beautiful, curvy women rubbing up against him. Thomas and his big friend, not so much.

"Haud yer wheesht, Callum," Thomas slurred over his fifth round of whiskey, "Helen's the love of me life, and I'll no' sit here and listen to me own cousin drag her beautiful name through the mud."

"Ye've only known her two bloody days, ya nyaff!"

"I love her!" Thomas roared. Standing up from his barstool, he tried to take a menacing step towards Callum, only to have his leg give under him and send him to the ground with a loud crash.

The busy pub erupted in soft laughter from the bristly blond giant's clumsiness before turning their attention back to their own drinks and mates as Thomas picked himself back up and sat down wobbly on the stool again.

Callum laughed and snapped at the bartender, "Oi! Another round fer me an' my mates, lad!"

"No' for me, and I think he's plenty pissed." Thomas' enormous companion said sternly.

"Ach, me kin can handle another round, aye?"

"Aye!" Thomas boomed and held out his empty glass.

"Course ye can! Come on, Sammy! Le' me get ye another ale!"

Sampson Angus McKay turned his full, fiery attention to Thomas' irritating cousin and growled, "My name is Sam, and I said no' for me."

The towering six-and-a-half-foot man had hardly said more than five words strung together to Callum for nearly the entire three-day weekend; the sudden growl frightened him more than he wanted to admit. But, despite the giant's gruff, intimidating stature, his soft brown eyes made it easier for Callum to summon any courage he had as he retorted, "Ach, fine! Donnea ge' yer panties in a twist, mate! Jus' two, lad."

The bartender filled the empty glasses and went back about his business.

Sam had decided he'd had enough of Callum's manner and stepped away from the bar, his nearly empty glass of Guinness still in hand. The people in the crowded pub seemed to sense how angry the giant, black-haired man was and quickly stepped out of his way as he headed towards the outside terrace. He eyed the thinned crowd until he spotted an empty seat in the corner that was mostly clear and well-hidden. He purposely walked over.

Despite the warm and wonderful sunshine that day, Aberdeen was still barely coming out of the spring thaw, and the nights would drop to a temperature that made anyone freeze if they weren't used to it. The pub, smelling of sweat and beer, was warm, so Sam appreciated the briskness as he cooled down both his body heat and his temper. He was also ready for a break from Callum's band, The Blue Selkies.

Sitting on the cold metal chair, nursing the last of his ale, Sam pondered over the events of the previous three days that had led him to the position he was in: confused, angry, not to mention in significant trouble with Captain Glowery, his superior at Rosneath, Helensburgh's police force. He'd never been put on probation from any job before, not once in his life. But earlier that day Aberdeen's police came to his hotel to question him, and it was revealed that he was partially responsible for the robbery that had taken place at the Kirk of St. Nicholas church the night before. His supervisor was called, and he had been reprimanded over the phone and told to stay away from the village's headquarters until the matter had been sorted out. He was told two weeks, but he knew that the paperwork alone would take that long, if not longer. He'd only been made detective a week before; it was a hell of a way to start off his new career.

Sam started to wonder if he should have taken up Thomas' cousin's offer of another drink after all as he angrily swallowed the last of his ale in a painful gulp.

"How di' I no' see wha' she was up to?" He pondered aloud. "How the hell di' she do it?"

***

Friday, May 19, 1998

It was early afternoon when Sam and Thomas drove into the bustling heart of Aberdeen at Callum's invitation.

"Ach, Christ, big man!" Thomas wailed. "Ye couldnea have driven *any* slower?"

"The speed limit is in place for a reason, ye nance," Sam rolled his eyes.

"Yer a Detective now, Sam, even if we did ge' stopped, ye could always flash yer badge."

"Aye, bein' dishonest is a fantastic way t' start m' new career."

"Dishonest is an ugly word, why no' say ye were testin' the boundaries of yer jurisdiction?"

Sam chuckled. "Away and boil yer heid, we're here now."

"Aye, and no' a moment too soon. We've only an hour to check into the hotel and meet my cousin a' the pub!"

"Remind me why I agreed to come along t' this? I donnea even like grunge music."

"Aye, anno, bu' yer my best mate," Thomas smiled. "An' besides, Callum said he can ge' us into the pub withou' a cover charge an' a discount on the drinks! Jackie never does tha' a' *his* pub, tha' alone is enough reason to come, no?"

Sam smiled and nodded, "Aye, I suppose yer right."

With so many people walking through the streets, Sam felt like he was practically smashing the brakes of Thomas's rusty old Hillman Imp through the floorboards.

"Ach, easy there!" Thomas insisted. "Donnea break Hillary, now!"

"I'm amazed this piece of shite hasnea broken down once durin' the three-hour drive here."

"Watch yer tongue, man! I'll no' be havin' ye disrespect this classy lady."

"Then perhaps ye could ask yer cousin why he'd be so daft to book a gig in such a crowded place? I cannea drive without fear of hittin' someone."

"Well, unlike bein' the police, a musician has t'go where there's lots of people. And considerin' the tourist season is startin' t'pick up, The Blue Selkies are more likely t'get a gig here than anywhere else besides Glasgow."

Sam felt relieved when they spotted the hotel where they had reservations. The next three days, they were supposed to be at the bar every night to show support to Callum, with the promise of discounted drinks, which was really the only reason Sam was fine spending his time in such a crowded city for three days. He'd worked hard studying for the last month to pass the exams to be a detective in their home village of Rosneath. When he'd told Thomas that he had the next three days off, he'd been invited along for this spur-of-the-moment adventure of drinking and music. Despite arguing that he'd rather hear music and drink at Jackie's and skip all of the travel, Thomas had insisted the trip would be fun and ultimately convinced Sam to come. After the long, cramped drive, Sam was grateful to get out and stretch his legs for a while. He parked and retrieved the overnight bags from the back of the car, and the two of them walked in.

Taking one look inside of The Green Globe hotel, Sam had to let out a low whistle; it was certainly posher than he was accustomed to, which led him to assume that Thomas' cousin's band was doing better than scraping by, if they could afford to book a few rooms there and give Sam and Thomas a room for free. On one side was a medium-sized sitting room with three floral couches facing a fire roaring away in the fireplace, and to the front was a grand staircase that flourished out at the bottom underneath a sparkling chandelier. On the other side of him was the front desk that had a wall of old-fashioned keys hanging on pegs behind it with a door next to it.

"No' bad, eh?" Thomas waggled his eyebrows.

Sam rolled his eyes and followed Thomas to the front desk where a bell sat, and Thomas wasted no time in ringing it for the attendant.

The moment the bell sounded, a short, curvy woman with dirty blonde hair, wearing a form-fitting pink skirt emerged from the door and smiled at the two of them. "Good afternoon, lads. Ye checkin' in?"

"Aye, there should be a reservation under Callum MacWood for a suite for Thomas McFarland?"

The woman glanced down at her book before looking to Sam. "And will ye be stayin as well, sir?"

"Aye," Sam nodded.

She smiled and fluttered her eyelashes, "Well, the suite was reserved for only one. Bu' ye seem like such charming lads, I can let it go."

"Thanks, love," Thomas brought his bristly blonde stubble cheeks up into a suggestive smile.

Retrieving a key from the board behind her, she kept her eyes on Sam and paid no attention to Thomas. "Of course, I'm happy t' help. Number 15."

Sam took the key with an amused smile. "Cheers."

Thomas, ignoring his hurt pride, picked up his bag and followed Sam up the stairs and down the hallway to number 15. The suite had one giant bed, a sitting room with a long couch, a bathroom with a claw footed tub and a divan, as well as a small table for two with an electric tea kettle and two floral cups perched perfectly on saucers.

Thomas turned to Sam and smiled devilishly. "I'll fight ye for the bed."

Knowing he was completely serious but not in the mood to create a disturbance for the other guests, Sam laughed and shook his head, "N'thanks, I'll jus' take the couch."

"Alrigh'!" Thomas beamed and threw his bag on the bed before heading towards the door again. "Come on, big man, Callum's playin' a' Haunt 49 tonight. I's a good twenty minutes from here so we bes' be on our way."

Sam barely had enough time to deposit his own bag on the couch before Thomas was already out the door again.

The twenty-minute walk through the crowded stone city barely took fifteen for the two large men. Before they knew it, the sun had set, and there was a line of people stretching around the side of the building that was Haunt 49.

Paying no mind to the crowd, Thomas walked up to a wide, angry-looking man that was the bouncer at the door and said confidently, "Thomas McFarland and Sam McKay, we're guests of the Blue Selkies."

The ornery man glared and looked down at his clipboard; for a moment Sam wondered if they were going to be sent to the back of the line, but then he snorted, unlatched the rope, and allowed them to pass.

"See?" Thomas smiled back at Sam excitedly. "Tol' ye!"

But Sam could barely hear him as the loud and edgy guitar music blasted through the air; he had to resist the urge to cover his ears. Everywhere he looked, he saw bodies of women wearing halter tops (that showed off more than they were intended to cover) jumping and grinding together with men in ratty t-shirts and jeans. The male lead singer was practically screaming into the microphone to be heard over the absurdly loud guitar, bass, and drummer in the background. Sam couldn't understand one word of the lyrics, though he was certain he heard the words *sex, love,* and *madness* more than once. A few times he felt a pair of feminine hands rub along his arms and back as he and Thomas waded through the crowd towards the bar. It was only when one of those pairs of hands tried to turn him around and pull him down for a too-close-for-comfort dance that he had to tell the woman they belonged to "no thanks." He continued on his journey to the back.

Finally, the song ended, and the lead singer yelled into the microphone, "Everybody havin' a great time?!"

The crowd erupted in screams and shouts in response.

"Us too! We're havin' lo's of fun! Well, we need t' take a pish, bu' the Blue Selkies will be back in five minutes!"

The crowd screamed again as the musicians removed their instruments, hopped off of the stage, and waded through the crowds of women throwing themselves at them to the bar at the back.

"Oi, Thomas! Over here, ye giant bassard!"

Thomas and Sam turned their heads to the source of the voice, which Sam confidently assumed belonged to Callum. Sure enough, the drummer stepped forward, and he and Thomas wrapped their arms around each other in a growling bear style hug.

"Ye made it!" Callum shouted.

"Aye, no thanks to me mate here! He drives slower than granny did!" Thomas roared a laugh and gestured to Sam, who was sitting calmly at the bar sipping on a pint of Guinness. "Callum MacWood, meet Sampson McKay!"

"Good t'meet ye, Sammy!" Callum smiled and offered his hand.

"Jus' Sam, an' you too," Sam called above the crowd as he shook the drummer's hand. "Cheers for lettin' me tag along with Thomas."

"O'Course! Any mate of Thomas' is a mate of mine! Now help yerselves to the bar, lads! Jus' put i'tall on me tab! We gotta' ge' back up there in two minutes, bu' we'll talk again on our next break, aye?!"

"Aye!" Thomas beamed and turned back to the bartender, "Give me yer finest Scottish whiskey over ice!"

"Sorry, mate! All out! I only go' Irish whiskey left!" the barkeep yelled.

"Perfect!"

Like magic, a glass was produced from thin air with three clear ice cubes sitting in it and then finished with the dark, caramel colored liquid that came nearly to the top. Thomas swallowed all of it in one gulp and roared in delight.

"Easy, pal!" Sam said, "The night's still young!"

"Aye, and I'm gonna' dance some of it away!" Thomas laughed and abruptly turned towards the crowd, only to accidentally crash into a woman that was standing right behind him. "Ach, bollocks! I'm s—"

When Thomas stopped talking and stared at the woman he'd so clumsily bumped into, Sam watched the situation curiously.

"I'm so sorry, lass," Thomas apologized emphatically. "Allow me t' help ye with tha'."

"Ach, t'is alrigh'," she replied sweetly. "Cannea come to a crowded pub and expect to no' ge' yer drink spilled on ye."

Thomas seemed to barely hear a word she said as he looked over her and took in everything he saw: nearly as tall as him, flaming red hair, and blue eyes. Sam curled his lips up in amusement to see his friend so utterly smitten.

"Ye alrigh' there, big man?" The woman asked with concern.

"Wha's yer name?" Thomas blurted out.

She giggled. "Helen McHugh."

"Helen McHugh, ye are so beautiful. May I buy ye another drink?"

Thomas' blunt approach made Sam choke on his drink, but that wasn't nearly as big as a shock as Helen accepting the offer.

"Aye," she smiled. "I'd like tha'."

"Wha'll ye have?"

"Rum and coke."

Thomas turned back to the bar and shouted to the barkeep, "Two rum and coke!"

Sam had to stop himself from laughing; Thomas normally hated sweet alcohol, but as he and Helen danced and drank together, it was apparent that he was too smitten to care. It was very amusing to witness.

The music started to get too loud for his liking, so Sam refilled his ale and walked to a quieter, less crowded section of the pub to enjoy it. Standing in a shadowy section of the corner, he just watched the people around him curiously. If he didn't know any better, he'd have thought he'd stumbled into a free-for-all orgy. Having enough of the obscene rave before him, he rolled his eyes and took another drink when he noticed a woman sitting alone at a small table in the corner. While most of the women that night had hardly any clothing on at all, what intrigued him was her modest, yet form-fitting jeans and a red short-sleeved turtleneck that seemed to compliment her pale skin. Strawberry blonde hair pulled up in a pony tail, martini glass in her hand, she stood out like a sore thumb compared to the rest of the patrons. She bobbed her head to the music as she sipped her drink, appearing not to have noticed Sam at all. With hardly anyone else around, he allowed himself to look at the attractive woman for a few moments, until she seemed to sense he was admiring her and looked directly into his gaze. Keeping his demeanor calm, he coolly raised his glass to her and offered a smile. She reciprocated with her own smile and a wink before raising her own glass to him and taking a sip.

From out of nowhere, another woman that was wearing a skirt so short it barely covered her backside began to dance next to Sam. Doing his best to be polite, he bobbed his head along to the screaming music but tried not to engage her too much.

"Wanna dance, big man?" She purred loudly.

Sam shook his head. "N'thanks, lass."

"Awe," she pouted and pushed her chest out. "Bu' i's a crime t'let a lady dance alone."

Sam gulped. "Wha' a meant to say was I'm no' a very good dancer."

"Well, yer in luck, I'm an excellent teacher."

Sam felt another hand wrap around his arm and turned to see the woman in the red turtleneck lean over and take his glass of ale away from him.

"Thanks for holding my drink, sweetie."

Her American accent was a surprise, but Sam was more than relieved that she was giving him an out from the uncomfortable situation. He cleared his throat and played along. "Ach, no problem, luv."

"Sorry it took me so long, there was a long line for the bathroom."

"Tha's alright," he nodded and smiled down at her.

She stood up on her toes to give him a kiss on the cheek. Out of the corner of his eye, Sam could see that the poor woman in the short skirt had turned a few shades of red and very quickly disappeared into the dancing crowd before she could embarrass herself any further. Relief flooded him when she was out of sight, and he turned back to his savior and smiled, "Thanks fer tha'."

"No sweat," she smiled.

"For a moment, I thought I'd have t' fight her off for the rest of the night."

"Well, I wouldn't hold it against her," the American woman giggled, "I thought about coming over myself once or twice, she just beat me to it."

Sam could feel the back of his neck getting warm at her playfulness; taking back his glass, he quickly took a drink of his ale and said, "I'm Sam."

"I'm Mary."

"Nice t' meet ye, Mary."

"You too, Sam," she winked at him for the second time. "If you need to be saved again, you know where to find me."

The way she swayed her hips as she walked back to her little table had Sam captivated. Instead of leaving the conversation where it had ended, he found himself following her. "I dunno wha' kinda men ye're used to, lass, bu' a gentleman always thanks a lady properly. Can I buy ye another drink?"

Mary smiled. "Why not? Apple martini please."

Sam had to hold himself back from sprinting to the bar as he went to retrieve her order before carefully carrying the glass back through the raving crowd. Taking a seat next to her, he clinked his glass with hers. "Slàinte."

"Cheers," she agreed and took a delicate sip of the neon green liquid. "So, would I be wrong in guessing that this really isn't your scene?"

He scoffed, "Is tha' obvious, eh?"

"Well, I mean the red around your ears when that woman started gyrating on you didn't give you away or anything."

Sam nearly choked on his drink, and Mary stifled a giggle. He quickly regained composure and cleared his throat. "Alrigh', how abou' a more comfortable topic such as last names?"

"I'll tell you mine if you tell me yours."

"McKay."

"Winter."

Before Sam could reply, the familiar voice of his travel companion boomed loudly through the crowd. "Good on ye, big man!"

Thomas, his arm wrapped around his new close female friend, walked over, and the two of them took a seat at the table with them. Beaming, he gestured back and forth between the four of them, "Sam, this is Helen McHugh. Helen, me best mate Sam McKay."

"Lovely t'meet ye," the blue-eyed redhead said sweetly.

"Aye," Sam nodded, "Same. An' this is Mary Winter."

"Hi," Mary smiled.

"Yer American?" Helen asked.

Mary answered with a giggle. "Guilty."

"Wha's an American doin' all the way over here, lass?" Thomas asked.

"Aye, and alone at tha'." Helen nodded.

Thomas continued his assault of questions, and Sam swallowed nervously, afraid that his friend would scare the poor woman off before he'd even had a chance to ask her for her number. "Are ye travelin' with some friends?"

Mary didn't appear to be bothered by the barrage of questions and stated simply, "No, I'm actually here on business."

Sam, intrigued by her answer, interjected, "Wha' business is it tha' ye do?"

"Well, I'm an apprentice to a Renaissance Era historian. He was supposed to make this trip but came down with the flu about a week ago, so the museum sent me in his place."

Thomas and Helen's eyes grew wide, seemingly very impressed by her answer. Sam was, too, and he answered, "Really? Donnea be offended, bu' ye seem awful young t' be given an opportunity of this magnitude."

"Oh, I'm not offended at all," she answered with a smile. "I agree with you, actually. But my boss told me he has complete faith in me, and this trip gives me a chance to prove myself to him and the museum."

"Wha' exactly are ye here for?" Thomas asked.

"We've been trying to follow the whereabouts of a certain noblewoman, and the research we've uncovered suggests that her final resting place would be here in Aberdeen at the Kirk of St. Nicholas."

"Anno tha' church!" Helen said excitedly.

"Oh, really? I'm supposed to go tomorrow and see if I can find her headstone and take pictures of it. But, unfortunately, Mapquest doesn't have a clue where Aberdeen is in the world, let alone how to get from one place to another in this city. I've been asking around for directions to St. Nicholas, but unfortunately, I'm not great with Scotland's language barrier. It's amazing that I've been able to hold a conversation with you guys for this long."

The group laughed.

Helen took a sip of her rum and coke, and her eyes perked up. "Well, I can help ye, if ye'd like! I'd be happy t' take ye to St. Nicholas' church tomorra'."

"Would you?" Mary exclaimed with relief.

"Ach, course!"

"Oh, thank you, Helen! You're a life saver!"

Helen then turned to Sam and Thomas, a mischievous glint in her eye, and continued, "In fact, why don't you lads come with us? If yer still gonna' be in town, tha' is."

"Oh, we'll be in town fer the whole weekend!" Thomas blurted out happily. He turned to Sam and said, "Wha' do ye say, big man?"

Sam chuckled to himself, "Aye, i' does sound fun."

"Wha' time are ye supposed to be there, Mary?" Helen asked.

"At 4:00 p.m. I'm supposed to get the official tour and history of the Kirk before beginning my search of the headstones."

"Four o'clock is perfect!" Thomas boomed, "We'll meet with you ladies and take ye out for lunch a' one o'clock, then we'll head over t' the church and help Mary find her mysterious headstone!"

"If i's alright with Mary tha' we tag along," Sam said and looked over to her.

"Oh, I'd love it!" She answered emphatically, "After all, it's not every day you make new friends in a new country. And I'm supposed to fly back home on Sunday anyway, so we only have the one day to spend together."

"I's settled, then," Thomas answered excitedly. "We'll meet fer lunch a' one in front of The Green Globe hotel, and after tha', Helen'll lead us to St. Nicholas' fer the tour."

"Thank you all, so much," Mary smiled at them, "I've only been here a day, and I'm already loving Scotland!"

The group kept talking and laughing well into the night until Mary began to get tired, citing jet lag and needing some real rest so she could be at her best the following day. Sam agreed, though he mostly was ready to get away from the screaming music for the evening. The two of them left together, while Thomas and Helen insisted they wanted to stay and enjoy the music longer. Sam could tell that, really, neither of them wanted to say goodnight just yet. Mary's hotel was fifteen minutes away, so he stayed with her until a taxi arrived and said goodnight before heading in the other direction to his own lodgings. When he arrived, he made himself as comfortable as he could on the couch that wasn't nearly long enough for his tall frame and drifted off, decidedly happy that he had come to Aberdeen after all.

Sam and Thomas were up with the rising sun; while Sam ate his porridge quietly, Thomas couldn't seem to stop gushing about Helen: her meadow-flower-blue eyes, beautifully flaming red hair, swearing up and down that she was the love of his life. Eventually Sam had to tell him to shut up and eat when other hotel patrons were complaining about all of the noise being made. The morning seemed to pass very quickly, and before either of them knew it, it was time to meet the girls in the lobby. While Thomas fussed about with combing his hair, trimming his face, and spraying on some of the hotel's flowery smelling cologne, Sam felt perfectly comfortable in a red polo shirt with his jeans and a sweater jacket. As amusing as it was to see the bristly blond giant fuss over a girl, he was starting to grow impatient at Thomas's vanity.

"Ach, ye nance, if ye put on anymore of tha' bloody perfume ye're likely t' turn the lady off!" Sam groaned.

Thomas growled in reply, "Haud yer wheescth, i's cologne! And I jus' want'a make a good impression fer Helen."

"If ye didnea scare her off las' evenin', then i's highly unlikely ye'll make a bad one. Now will ye come on, already?"

Thomas relented and followed Sam out the door and down the stairs of the hotel where they were both pleased to discover the ladies waiting in the sitting room for them. Thomas, of course, only had eyes for Helen, and Sam had to admit to himself that if he thought Mary was attractive the night before dressed down for an evening out, she was gorgeous in black slacks with a turquoise blouse that complimented her fair skin. And without the smell of beer and cigarette smoke to mask it, her heady, fruit scented perfume wafted to his nostrils, and he felt a little intoxicated from the scent.

"Ye look stunning," Sam blurted out before he could stop himself.

Mary giggled. "You clean up pretty good yourself, I like the jacket."

"Thanks," he chuckled. "Hungry?"

"God, yes. I'm anxious to try some of the fish and chips I've heard about."

"Well, I cannea say I know Aberdeen's bes' Chippys, bu' I think we'll make do."

Mary laughed, picked up the suitcase she had next to her, and slipped her arm into the crook of his elbow. Sam swallowed hard, and the two of them headed to the door when they both realized they were alone and looked back at their companions.

Thomas and Helen appeared to be lost in each other's eyes, and Sam had to clear his throat to get their attention. Thomas offered his arm to Helen (who took it enthusiastically), and the group of four walked off together to the closest restaurant where they enjoyed large portions of fish and chips accompanied with a lot of laughter.

Once everyone ate their fill, they all crammed into Thomas' rusty Hillman Imp, and Helen guided them through the city on Union Street until they reached the Southern Boundary gates of the Kirk of St. Nicholas. The gate alone had an intimidating aura to it, as it was comprised of tall grey stone pillars with iron gates in between each of them. Looking through the black iron, the group could see lush green grass and trees, which seemed to give the stone city of Aberdeen a tranquil feeling. In the middle of the grounds, which were heavily peppered with historical headstones and monuments, sat a beautiful stone cathedral with a clock tower and gold-trimmed plated glass windows. The chill in the air didn't stop the trees along the grounds from producing their spring pink blossoms, which only added to the building's foreboding beauty. Despite being in the middle of the city, surrounded by activity and tourists, even Sam had to admit he felt a sense of majesty at the historic site.

Mary was the first to speak. "Wow, how beautiful."

"Aye, t'is," Helen agreed.

Thomas ruined the moment when he pointed to a sign hung next to the gate that said, "Closed until June 1 for Renovations."

"It appears we have a problem, ladies."

"Oh, no," Mary lamented. "How can that be? My boss had this appointment set up for months."

Noticing a buzzer and speaker at the front of the gate, Sam walked over to it and assured her, "Well, now, hold on. Le's see wha' we can work out."

He pressed the buzzer, and a moment later a flat voice answered, "I'm sorry, but we are currently undergoing some renovations and tourists are no' allowed on the premises."

Mary quickly stepped over to the speaker and answered, "My name is Mary Winter, I work for Dr. Harold Murlock. Am I speaking with Father Giles?"

"Aye, m'dear, I'm Father Giles. I believe I had corresponded with Dr. Murlock regarding the Kirk of St. Nicholas' closure and informed him tha' we would have to reschedule his research."

"Father, Dr. Murlock has been sick with the flu for a few days now and has been unable to check any of his messages. I've been sent in his place. I didn't know about the closure, but I have all of the paperwork here. I just need to take a quick look-"

"I'm sorry, lass, bu' I cannea make any exceptions fer tourists no matter the reason. There is simply too much debris and dangerous materials around a' the moment."

"I promise, Father, I only need a brief tour and to look at a few of the headstones here on the grounds."

"Then ye'll have t' come back in June, m'dear."

They heard a click as the priest abruptly ended the conversation. Sam looked to Mary, who was anxiously pulling at her sleeve.

"I came all this way for nothing," she said softly.

"Ach, I'm sure yer boss will understand the mix-up," he tried to reassure her.

She scoffed, "I doubt it. The thing about historians, Sam, is really all you have in this line of work is your reputation. And if I go back without so much as a peek at what I was sent here for then that will be the end of mine. Not to mention, it will put a hold on our research because we won't know whether or not the noblewoman we're looking for is here or not for another month, which puts the permits to come excavate and do further research on hold for longer. They can take months, if not years, to get approved as it is. Dammit, how am I going to explain this?"

Sam couldn't help but feel sympathetic to her plight; he understood completely what it was like to want to make a good impression on someone who was willing to take a chance on one so young. Clearing his throat, he said, "Well, if there's anythin' I believe, i's tha' no matter how hard things get, ye have t' try."

He rang the buzzer again but was met with silence that time. So, he continued to ring it over and over until finally the priest answered again, "I've already tol' ye, no visitors durin' renovations. Now please leave the buzzer be."

"Father Giles, my name is Sam McKay. I'm a Detective in Rosneath. We'd like t'have a look around, please."

They were met with silence, and Sam began to wonder if he should ring the buzzer again when they saw the doors to the church open, and a pudgy-faced bald man donning priest robes walked through the large grounds towards the gate.

"May I see some identification, constable?" Father Giles asked in a much less friendly tone than before.

Sam retrieved his wallet and produced a badge as well as his ID card. He hid his smug smirk when the priest opened the gate.

"Will ye take full responsibility for this young lady should any harm come to her?" Father asked and glanced over at Mary.

"Aye, father."

The priest continued to stare at her for a few moments, his eyes scrunched together in a peculiar way.

"Is there a problem, Father?" Mary asked sweetly.

The Priest shook himself out of his trance and continued. "No, sorry. Detective, will ye also take full responsibility should any damages befall the Kirk of St. Nicholas durin' yer visit?"

"Aye, father."

The man sighed, "Verra well, jus' the two of ye then?"

"No, there's fo-" Sam turned around and realized that sometime during the encounter, Thomas and Helen had slipped away completely unnoticed. He stopped himself from laughing and nodded, "Aye, father, jus' the two of us."

The priest moved to the side and allowed Sam and Mary to enter before locking the gate behind him. "If ye'll quickly follow me, I'll give ye a brief tour of the church and then I can give ye one hour t' explore the grounds."

"Tha' doesnea seem like verra much time, father."

The pudgy man sighed. "Two, bu' no more. Understood?"

"Absolutely. Lead the way, father." Sam smiled.

The priest turned around and began walking back to the doors of the church with Sam and Mary only a few steps behind him.

Sam looked down to Mary, who was smiling brightly at him.

"What luck, you're a cop, too! Thank you so much, Sam." She whispered.

"Ach, no problem. Di' ye happen t' see which way Thomas and Helen went?"

"No," she giggled. "Think they went off to get to know each other better?"

"Tha's one way of sayin' it," he chuckled along with her. "I'll be' ye a pint when we run into them again, Thomas' hair will be completely unkempt."

"And Helen's shirt will be buttoned wrong," she added.

"If the two of ye will follow me, please, and I shall give ye the quick history of the Kirk."

The Priest's clipped tone caused Sam and Mary to hush themselves with a smirk, and they followed him as he very quickly walked through the lush green grounds and back to the church.

"As we're out amongst the grounds, we'll start with some facts here: The graveyard of the Kirk surrounds the church on three sides: the North, the South, and the West, with the highest proportion of table stones on the South and the West sides. As I'm sure ye're aware, the East side is left bare as when Christ returns, he shall split the Eastern Sky and the dead shall rise from the grave t' meet him. Bu', peculiarly, the graves on the grounds of the kirk dinnea follow the standard Christian pattern of the stones facing the east."

"Why is that, father?" Mary asked.

"Ye can ask on June the First, lassy. Now, t' continue, the monuments in the cemetery date back as far as the 17th century."

"Tha' explains why mos' of these headstones are hard t' read," Sam said aloud.

"Indeed," the Priest answered. "Among some of the most notable burials here a' the Kirk are Alexander Dingwall Fordyce, a British Naval officer and a Whig Politician, an' Sir Alexander Anderson, a Scottish advocate and politician who was viewed as one of the major forces tha' molded the city of Aberdeen."

The priest opened the doors of the church, and Sam and Mary followed him inside. The dark wooden pews and the stone walls facing a blue stained-glass window with white doves held Sam in awe. Were it not for the electric chandeliers, he thought that he'd been transported to medieval times as he looked around the dim church.

The Priest's voice brought Sam's attention back to the present. "The Kirk was named after St. Nicholas, who's major miracle was rescuing some sailors in a storm, an' tha's largely due t' the church's proximity to the sea. The earliest mention of a built church on this Kirk is in a Papel Document of 1151 Anno Domini. I's also the ancient burial place of the Clan Irvines of Drum Castle, known as the Drum Aisle."

"Wonderful," Mary beamed. "The Noblewoman I'm looking for was an Irvine."

"Indeed," the Priest answered. "T' continue, during Medieval Scotland, t'was one of the biggest churches, along with St. Mary's in Dundee. The building was enlarged in the 15th century, and many tapestries and various art were collected durin' the time period. Many pieces still hang in the church today."

"Anyone I might've heard of?" Sam asked.

"Most notably would be the hand-embroidered tapestries of Mary Jamesone, the daughter of George Jamesone, who was known as the Van Dyke of Scotland. Most of her work is located here. There are, in fact, a number of pieces of late Medieval Art and 17th century woodwork tha' are preserved on site in the Chapel of our Lady of Pity, otherwise known as The Vault. The Kirk of St. Nicholas also retains a larger number of Medieval effigies than any other Scottish Parish Church, although none of them are in their original burial positions."

Sam could tell the brief tour was coming to its end when they approached the western doors; the Priest turned to them and said shortly, "The las' bi' of information I can tell ye is tha' there is an East and West church on the Kirk. In 1874, a fire destroyed the East church, which contained nine fine bells, one of which was high and thick and 1.2 meters in diameter named Lowrie. In 1887, to commemorate the Victorian Jubilee, the church was rebuilt and thirty-six bells tha' were cast in Belgium were installed. However, because the tunin' of the bells was poorly done, the bells were again replaced in 1950 w' forty-eight bells made by Gillett and Johnston, a clockmaker and bell foundry based out of Croydon, England."

"Verra' interestin', father," Sam said cheerfully. "And thank ye fer allowin' this young lady to do her job."

"Of course, an' I hope ye will remember t' leave a donation on behalf of yer visit as ye explore the cemetery."

"Oh, of course," Mary smiled and quickly produced a twenty-pound note.

The Priest took it and added, "Remember, I can only le' ye look fer yer headstone for another hour and a half. After tha', I must ask ye t' leave. Understood?"

"Absolutely," Mary nodded. "Thank you again, Father Giles."

The pudgy-faced chaplain nodded curtly, opened the doors for them, and slammed them shut as soon as Mary and Sam were outside of the church again.

"I was told that all Scots, especially priests, are extremely friendly," Mary voiced aloud.

"Ach, donnea le' him make ye feel otherwise, he's jus' havin' a bad day, i's all."

"Well, I've only got ninety minutes to find my headstone, so I better get going."

"We shoulda' asked him where the Irvines would be located in this giant labyrinth."

"Yeah... you don't think he'll answer any more questions, do you?"

"I wouldnea bet on it," Sam chuckled. "Come on, we'll tag-team. Wha's the name of the lady yer lookin' for?"

"Lady Agatha Irvine of Galloway: she was born in 1618, and we think she died around 1690."

"Alrigh', well I'll take the end row, and ye take this one, and we'll meet in the middle, aye?"

Mary nodded and began to walk down the row of headstones while Sam walked up the stone pathway to the end of the section. He carefully looked at each headstone and monument he passed for Agatha Irvine or Lady Agatha, anything resembling her name. Many grand monuments still stood beneath the trees and the names were easy to read, some of which had shriveled flowers that had been placed on the ground by (he could only assume) various distant family members before the Kirk had been closed.

He had just started the second row, when he had to study a tiny, faded headstone that could have been mistaken for a rock. He squinted his eyes until he was able to make out the words "Joseph Rinaldi, born and died May 16,1689." Worn away from the centuries that had passed, Sam suddenly felt humbled to be standing on the grave of an infant who appeared to have been forgotten. On the side of the tiny grave were the parents' headstones. The child's parents apparently had died the very next day. Sam immediately felt a sense of sorrow for the young family; he studied the graves for a moment longer and could swear he felt a cold chill run through him. As with all headstones, the reasons behind why the parents and the infant had died were not mentioned, but the way the little family's final resting place was situated together, Sam could almost guess: The infant had died in childbirth, and the mother and father from grief.

Bowing his head, Sam softly mumbled, "I'm so sorry."

Shaking himself out of his melancholy, he continued walking along the path and read each name on the hundreds of headstones that surrounded him, but the more he walked, the more he felt as though he was walking through a very tragic portion of history. Most of the names he read gave him the sense that the deceased resting beneath the stone had been fortunate enough to live a long, healthy life. But every time he came across one that belonged to a young child, he felt a reverent sadness come over him. Eventually he and Mary came together again in the middle of the first ground.

"You have any luck?" She asked.

Sam shook his head. "You?"

"No, not yet. Hey, are you alright?"

Sam attempted to hide his gloominess by snorting. "Aye, I'm fine."

Mary eyed him curiously, and he could tell his rouse had not worked. She gave him a gentle smile. "You would think with how many graves, both official and unofficial, that I've seen, I wouldn't be as affected every time I see someone else's history. But I am, I get it."

"I donnea know how ye can do it. T' me, death is personal."

Mary turned and began to walk to the next plot, and Sam followed her.

"Is that why you became a cop?"

"No' quite," Sam smiled. "I've wanted t' be a constable since I was a young lad at 15."

"You've never wanted to run off and become famous or anything like that, huh?"

"Wha' is it with ye Americans' obsession w' bein' famous?" He teased.

Mary poked his arm in retaliation but couldn't help but laugh her agreement. "It's true, we are."

"No, me father is a grocer back home. He always taugh' me t' enjoy the little things an' tha' there's nothin' wrong with a simple life. He always says: 'Never think ye're above anyone, Sampson. In the end, we all face the Lord's judgment.'"

"He sounds like a smart man," Mary smiled. "What about your mom?"

Though Sam expected the question, that didn't stop him from bristling at the mention of the woman he despised. Clearing his throat, he answered, "Me mother's gone."

"Oh, I'm sorry for asking. I didn't know that she died."

"She didn't, she jus' left."

Mary gaped at his answer. "What?"

"Aye, when me brother was a wee infant. I was only seven at the time."

"I'm not trying to be nosy, but do you know why?"

"Nope," Sam shook his head flippantly, "me da' doesnea talk abou' her much. Truthfully, I never ask. I jus' remember standin' a' the door, watchin' her ge' in the car, an' drivin' off."

"Wow… pardon my French here, but what a bitch."

"Aye."

"What about your younger brother? What does he do?"

"Josh is a bi' of a hell-raiser," Sam chuckled. "Bu' when he does work, he delivers groceries on behalf of me da' an' step-mum."

Mary chuckled. "My older sister would regularly tell people that I was a thorn in her side."

Sam nudged her. "Tha's our job as the oldest, t' remind our younger siblin's wha' pains in the asses they are. Heaven help me when me baby sister ge's older."

"You have a sister, too?"

"Aye, me' da' and step-mum had wee Hannah three years ago." Sam withdrew his wallet and withdrew a picture of his baby sister to show Mary.

"Awe, she's so cute! I bet she just melts your heart."

"Aye," Sam chuckled. "Tha' she does."

The two of them continued to walk and talk together as they wandered through the labyrinth of headstones; having company and much less morbid conversation certainly made Sam feel much happier about the search. Before either of them knew it, they were at the southern gate again and still had not found the headstone of Lady Agatha Irvine. Before Sam could suggest they take one more look around, Father Giles appeared and informed them their time was up. Promptly escorting them both to the gate, Mary practically jumped when the iron bars slammed shut behind them.

She sighed, "Well, I guess my boss and I will have to go back to the drawing board."

"Do ye have any other leads t' look at while ye're in Scotland?"

"No," she shook her head, "Dr. Murlock was so certain that Lady Agatha was buried here, he didn't give me anything else to go on. Guess I'll be flying back home empty-handed tomorrow."

Before Sam could respond, a car honked behind them, and the two of them turned around to see Helen and Thomas in the Hillman Imp.

"Oi! There ye two are!" Thomas said casually. "We though' we lost ye!"

Sam and Mary looked at each other with a knowing smirk.

"We've been right here doing research," Mary answered. "Actually, we wondered if we had lost *you.*"

Sam had to hold his chuckle in as Helen shifted about the car, nervously adjusting her blouse, and Thomas ran a hand through his disheveled hair.

"Ach, com'on!" Thomas answered. "I's almost time t' see Callum's band again!"

Sam turned to Mary and asked, "Ye wanna come? Have one more nigh' in Scotland t' remember us by?"

"Why not?" She winked.

Once everyone was situated as comfortably as possible, Thomas drove them back to the hotel as quickly as he could, and the four of them walked to Haunt 49 together.

Once again, the pub was filled with people dancing to the screaming music of The Blue Selkies; Sam and the others had to push their way through the crowd to the back, where they barely managed to find an open table. Ordering a round of drinks and a pizza for them all to share, the four of them laughed and ate and drank well into the night.

Around 11:00 p.m., Mary turned to Helen. "Come on, let's go dance!"

"Aye!" Helen agreed happily before turning to Thomas, "Ye comin'?"

"Aye!" Thomas nodded enthusiastically.

Helen then turned her attention to Sam and asked, "Wha' about you, big man?"

"Ach, n'thanks," Sam shook his head.

"Com'on, Sam," Thomas nudged him. "Ye cannea leave a lady dancin' alone!"

Sam rolled his eyes at the familiar comment but was saved by Mary.

"That's alright, guys. If he doesn't want to dance, he doesn't have to."

"Thank ye," Sam nodded.

"It's not his fault he's too chicken," she added, earning laughter from Thomas and Helen and a mocked hurt expression from Sam.

Before he could retort, Mary had bounded into the crowd with Helen and Thomas right behind her. Through the wisps of cigarette smoke, Sam watched the three of them dance and laugh heartily to the screaming guitar. Sam had to admit to himself that he felt awkward sitting at the table alone just watching them. It was when a slower song came on that Helen and Thomas broke away to dance with each other exclusively. Mary accepted the advances of a tall stranger who started to dance with her. Sam felt a slight pang of jealousy stir up in him. Then the stranger put his hands on Mary's hips, and she wrapped her arms around his neck before sending Sam a purposeful wink. Deciding that he'd had enough of her obvious torment, Sam shook his head and took another sip of his ale before he stood up and walked over to Mary and the stranger.

Holding out his hand to her, he growled, "Sorry, I'm late, darlin'."

"That's okay, honey," she smiled innocently. "This nice man was kind enough to keep me company until you got here."

Sam towered over the stranger, who quickly threw his hands up in defeat and slinked away into the crowd as Sam pulled Mary closer. Placing his hands on her hips where the other man's hands had been, he smiled inwardly to feel her wrap her arms around his neck in return. The two of them began to sway to the words of The Blue Selkies' love song.

"So, ye're a scholar and a tease," Sam said to her.

"I don't have the slightest idea what you're talking about," Mary answered coyly.

The two of them laughed and continued their intimate dance until the music began to pick up again. Sam decided to stay and continue dancing with Mary, despite the crowds of people invading his personal space. He refused to say it out loud, but he was having fun.

About an hour later, Mary wiped her forehead with the back of her hand and shouted, "I think it may be time for me to go back to my hotel!"

"Ye gettin' tired already?!"

"Early flight!"

"I'll walk ye out!" Sam turned to look for Thomas and laughed to see his friend and Helen standing in the middle of the dance floor with their lips locked on each other's.

"I'm pretty sure they'll be fine!" Mary laughed along with him.

"Aye! Come on!"

Leaving the crowded bar, Sam and Mary walked outside and tried to flag down a taxi when Mary realized she had left her suitcase in Thomas' car, so the two of them walked back to the hotel to retrieve it.

Suitcase in hand, Mary turned to Sam and smiled. "This trip has been incredible. Thank you, Sam."

Before he could respond, she leaned up and kissed his lips. Sam's whole body instantly got warmer from her chaste gesture, and he wrapped his arms around her to deepen it, to which Mary responded by placing her hand on his cheek and holding him there as her mouth danced with his.

When they finally withdrew from each other, Sam took a deep breath of air; if it weren't for Mary standing in his arms and helping him stay upright, he was sure he would have tripped. "Christ!"

Mary whispered. "So, your place or mine?"

He opened his eyes wide at her brazen question. "Pardon?"

"Oh, come on, you really want to play coy right now?"

"Ye're a forward lassy, aren't ye?"

"You're just now getting that?" She winked and leaned up to kiss him again.

Despite the chilly air, Sam couldn't deny how incredibly warm he felt from Mary's advances, and a deep moan escaped him. Unable to resist, he answered her in between each passionate kiss. "Well… we are a' my hotel… an' yours is a' least fifteen minutes away, righ'?"

"Mhmm," Mary agreed. Kissing him once more, she leaned back and seductively whispered, "Lead the way."

Sam didn't know what time it was, only that it was dark out, and he and Mary were alone in the hotel room, entwined under the mess of sheets. Though he was breathing as though he'd just run a marathon, he lay on his back with a giddy smile plastered on his face while Mary leaned over him and ran her fingers across his chest.

"You should smile a lot more," she stated.

"Wha'?" He asked, completely confused by the random comment.

Giggling, Mary leaned down and placed a chaste kiss on his lips, "I just mean I haven't really seen you smile all weekend. You're cute when you do."

"Huh, I'll keep tha' in mind. Perhaps if ye give me more reasons t'smile, it'll stay." Flipping the two of them over, he leaned over her and began to kiss her neck.

"Mmmm," she teased. "As much as I would love to accept that challenge, I really do need to get going."

"Wha' time's yer flight?"

"At nine out of Glasgow, I've got to get my bags and hail a taxi."

Sam reluctantly released her as she left the bed and began to pick up her scattered clothing. When she turned to her left to retrieve her bra, he was face to face with a peculiarity high on her hip: a nasty red scar about the size of a cricket ball with the word *Memento* tattooed on it.

He lightly ran his hand over it and asked, "Wha's tha'?"

After looking at what he was referring to (though he got the feeling she knew exactly what he was referring to), Mary said simply. "Exactly what it says: a memento."

"This looks like a burn mark. Were ye in an accident?"

"No, not really," she answered and quickly pulled her pants up over her hips, effectively hiding the mark again.

When she turned her back to him, Sam could tell that the matter was closed for discussion. As she finished getting dressed, he leaned back against the pillows and yawned, "I donnea suppose ye like me enough to leave me yer number?"

Mary chuckled, "With a fourteen-hour time zone difference? When would we have the time to talk?"

"Then how abou' an address, and I'll drop ye a line? Maybe email?"

Suitcase in hand, Mary leaned over him and smiled. "Why don't we leave this with a 'Maybe I'll see you again, sometime?'"

Before she could leave, Sam gripped the back of her neck and brought her down to him for one last kiss, so passionately charged that it left them both panting.

"I dinnea think ye were a one nigh' stand woman."

"Trust me when I say that it's better for you that I am."

"Why's tha'?"

"Because you like me too much," she answered with a wink.

He furrowed his eyebrows. "Wha' an odd thing t'say, especially to a naked man."

Giggling, Mary gave him one final peck on the lips and said, "Go to sleep."

She stepped away from the bed and sauntered towards the door, leaving Sam wanting her even more by the way she swung her hips at him. When the door closed behind her, he collapsed back against the pillows and sighed. He couldn't sleep now if he tried, not without a cold shower to stop the burning Mary left him with. Ripping the sheets off, he walked over to the posh washroom and didn't come out again for a long time.

The bright morning sun started to creep over Sam's eyes, and he squinted when he heard the door to the hotel room shut. Turning over, he chuckled to himself to see Thomas walking in with bags under his eyes and his clothing crumpled.

"Ye had a good nigh' with Helen, then?" Sam teased.

Instead of an enthusiastic reply, Thomas' face turned sour.

"Ye alrigh'?"

The bristly blond answered by dropping onto the couch with his face squashed into the pillow.

"Oi, big man, wha' happened?"

"I dnmph tkbit," Thomas answered with his face covered.

"Wha'?"

Thomas lifted his head and growled, "I said I donnea want' talk abou' it."

Sam rolled his eyes and shook his head. Fishing his underwear out from under the bed, he stood up and started to get dressed. "Well, come on, we bes' ge' some breakfast."

"Ye go on withou' me, I'm stayin' here."

"Do ye want me t' bring ye back somethin'?"

Thomas shook his head and shoved his face back in the pillow as a response.

Sam ignored his temper tantrum and left. Making his way down the stairs of the hotel, he noticed two police constables talking with the curvy hostess behind the counter. He couldn't help but overhear their conversation:

"Aye, I remember seein' the lassy las' night."

"Was she stayin' here as a guest?"

"No, bu' she came with one of our guests. In fac', tha's him." The curvy woman pointed to Sam.

The two constables, a very gruff, short man and a tall and skinny woman, turned to face him as he reached the bottom of the stairs.

Confused but calm, Sam furrowed his eyebrows and asked, "Can I help ye two, Constables?"

"Are ye Sampson McKay?" the man asked.

"Sam McKay, aye."

The woman held up a photograph of Mary. "Do ye know this woman, sir?"

"Aye," he nodded. "May I ask wha' this is about?"

"Were the two of ye together a' the Kirk of St. Nicholas yesterday?"

"Yes."

"Did ye tell Father Giles of the Kirk tha' ye're an Investigator from Rosneath and tha' the two of ye needed t' have a look around?"

"Yes, I did."

The two constables shared a quick side glance before the smaller one said, "Mr. McKay, we need to ask ye to accompany us t' the station."

Sam suddenly felt trapped; though he was a brand-new Detective, he knew how this routine went, and his involvement certainly didn't look favorable, especially if the constables decided that he was a threat. But he knew that the best thing that he could do was cooperate, so he allowed the constables to escort him to their car, and they drove to Aberdeen's Police station.

After turning over his wallet, badge, and giving the officers all of the information they needed to check his background, he was seated in a blank, white-walled room, waiting for whoever it was that he could hopefully get answers from. He sat in the cold metal chair for a long time and stared at the two-way mirror, knowing full well that there was someone behind it watching him, and he crossed his arms.

Finally, the door opened and a middle-aged woman in a black suit walked in. "Detective McKay, I'm Detective Rose Addair."

"Mornin'," he nodded, relieved at the use of his title. "I donnea suppose ye can extend me a professional courtesy an' tell me wha' is goin' on here?"

The detective ignored his question, took a seat across the table from him, and placed a tape recorder on the table. She pressed the record button. Leaning her elbows on the table and folding her hands together, she kept her gaze trained on Sam. Though he concentrated on keeping his outward appearance calm and unmovable, he couldn't help but feel intimidated by her piercing stare.

"For the record," she spoke loudly, and clearly, into the recorder. "I's Sunday May 21, 1998, lead Detective Rose Addair questionin' suspect Detective Sampson Angus McKay of Rosneath, Helensburgh's Police Force."

Sam bristled at the word 'suspect'.

"Detective McKay, wha's yer business here in Aberdeen?"

"I'm here on holiday with a friend, Thomas McFarland. We came t' support his cousin, Callum McWood, an' his band The Blue Selkies."

Again, the photograph of Mary was laid in front of him, and Sam felt more than suspicious. "Ye know this woman?"

"Aye, I me' her a few days ago a' Haunt 49, the pub. Her name's Mary Winter, she's American, an' she came t' Aberdeen on behalf of her work."

"And do ye know her whereabouts now?"

"She said she had an early mornin' flight t' catch out of Glasgow. I assumed back t' America."

The detective leaned back in her chair, crossed her arms and legs, and looked Sam directly in the eye. "Where were ye las' night, Detective?"

"A' the pub until around midnight."

"Was she with ye?"

"Aye."

"Until midnight?"

"No, we left the pub together an' wen' to my hotel where yer constables retrieved me from. The Green Globe."

"And wha' were the two of ye doin' a' the hotel?"

Sam narrowed his eyes in disbelief at the middle-aged woman, but he answered her unabashedly, "Shaggin'."

"Di' she ever tell ye she was returnin' t' the kirk?"

"No, I tol' ye she said she had an early flight to catch back t' America, an' she had t' ge' goin. She left around 2:30 a.m. Now will ye please tell me wha' the hell this is all abou'?"

The unflappable woman tilted her head to the side and continued to stare at him; knowing that she was sizing him up, Sam didn't break their gaze. Their staring contest seemed to last forever, until she relaxed her posture and answered him. "Las' night, there was a break-in a' the Kirk of St. Nicholas. Many pieces of artwork were stolen from the kirk's vault."

"Okay," Sam shrugged his shoulders. "So wha's tha' go' to do with me?"

"She tol' ye her name's Mary Winter?" Detective Addair asked as she pulled out more photographs and laid them on the table in front of Sam. In all of them, he instantly recognized Mary's face, but her hair was different in every single one: long, short, or medium, and black, red, brown, or bleached blonde.

Sam's mouth went dry. "…Who di' I ge' mixed up with, Detective?"

"She's had many names, many identities, and in every city she's been in, there's a robbery an' her face is always somewhere in the crowd. Do ye recognize any of these photos with her? Have ye seen anyone else tha' looks like this?"

"No, the woman I was with ha' dark blonde hair."

"Well, Father Giles of the Kirk said he recognized this one—" the detective pointed to the short brown-haired Mary "—Said he recognized her as a tourist he helped months ago."

Sam's mind flashed back to the day before at the gate when the Priest was staring at Mary in a funny way. "Christ, tha's why he was starin'. He though' he recognized her."

"Aye, he couldnea give us a name, bu' we were able t' find out she'd been callin' herself Isobel Carey. An' las' night, a witness saw two individuals leavin' the Kirk a' 3:30 a.m., her an' a very tall man whose face was shadowed. How tall are ye, Mr. McKay?"

Sam slumped back in his chair and sighed. Wiping his face with his hand, he answered, "I'm 6'6", Detective."

"An where were ye las' nigh' a' 3:30 a.m.?"

"In my hotel room, sleepin'."

"Can anybody corroborate yer alibi?"

Sam shook his head, "No, I was alone after Mary left; my friend Thomas didnea ge' back until this mornin'."

Detective Addair leaned onto her elbows again. "Mr. McKay, di' ye have anythin' t' do with the theft a' the kirk?"

"No," Sam answered emphatically. "Detective, I swear to ye on my father's life tha' I had nothin' t' do with this."

"Well, Detective McKay, this mystery woman has never been seen with an accomplice before. An' yet, here, we see she's go' one. Why do ye think tha' is?"

"Because she used me as an alibi an' a patsy," Sam growled but quickly tried to regain his composure. "An' I fell for it like a complete nance."

"Well, if tha's true, then ye won't mind me askin' for yer shoe size, will ye?"

Sam looked at the Detective, "Thirteen, an' I can confirm tha' I was a' the kirk yesterday a' 4 o'clock in the *afternoon*."

"Will ye submit to givin' us yer shoes for our forensics team? T'won't take bu' a minute."

Though Sam knew that there was already so much evidence piled against him suggesting that he was the shadowy man with the crooked woman Mary the night before, he knew better than to resist what the officers needed and decided to trust that the truth would pan out for him. He nodded his head.

"Good, ye'll be makin' our jobs much easier." Detective Addair pressed the stop button on the recorder, stood up from the table, and walked to the door. Turning around again, she gestured for Sam to follow her. "Do ye have somewhere t' stay, Detective McKay?"

"I'll be a' the hotel for another night, then I'm supposed t' go home t' Rosneath."

The two of them walked down the hallway of the police station until they came to the same desk where Sam had checked in his badge and wallet. Without prompt, he immediately sat down on the closest bench, removed his shoes, and gently placed them into the evidence bag the detective held out to him.

"Thank ye, Detective," she said flatly, "I'll be back in a moment, if ye'd like t' make a phone call, ye're welcome to."

Before he could even say "thank you," the Detective walked around the corner of the desk and disappeared behind a door. Turning to the phone on the corner of the desk, Sam picked it up and called his father's house.

"Hallo!" said a cheery, baby voice and Sam smiled.

"Hallo, Hannah," he cooed into the phone with a smile on his face.

"Sam!" The little girl screamed into the phone loudly, "I miss ye!"

"I miss ye too, lass. Can I speak t' daddy?"

"Okay."

Sam heard the phone hit the table; for a moment he feared that Hannah had accidentally hung up on him, until he heard a low rumbling voice in the background.

"Hallo?" Jeremiah McKay answered.

"Dad, i's Sam. I'm no' hurt, bu' I'm a' Aberdeen's Police station."

"Christ, boy, are ye alrigh'?"

"Aye, I'm fine, there's jus' been a misunderstandin'. I jus' wanted t' tell ye before Glowery did."

"Ach, I appreciate tha', son. Is there anythin' we can do?"

"No, bu' I migh' no' be back tomorrow nigh' after all. I'll let ye know when I know anythin'."

He heard his father take a deep breath before answerin', "Aye, alrigh'. Good luck, son."

"Thanks, dad."

Sam hung up the phone just as Detective Addair walked back through the door. She handed him his shoes.

"Yer Captain wants ye to call him once ye ge' back t' yer hotel. Thank ye again for yer cooperation."

The cold woman left Sam confounded as she strode away; whatever it was Captain Glowery wanted to speak to him about, he knew it wouldn't be good.

He got back to the Green Globe around four o'clock, and sure enough, when Sam called his captain, he was given more than an earful. He'd only been promoted to Detective a week before, and inadvertently assisting a burglary was not the way he wanted to impress his superior. Captain Glowery yelled into the phone, and Sam had to hold it away from his ear as he took the reprimand. When the phrase "thinkin' wi' yer bloody prick an no' yer head" was made, Sam's blood began to boil. But he kept himself calm and answered with, "Ye're absolutely righ', sir. I wasnea thinkin'." It was then and there the Captain informed him he would be put on probation for two weeks, until the final results from Aberdeen's Forensics team were in, and the situation could be smoothed over.

"Yes, sir. Verra well, sir." Sam growled into the phone, and he heard the other end of the line slam onto the receiver. Sam gently replaced the hotel's corded telephone back onto the receiver and ignored the hostess' dirty looks as he walked back up the stairs to his hotel room.

Tired, angry, and feeling very hungry (which did nothing to improve his mood), he walked past the still-sulking Thomas (who hadn't moved from the couch the entire time he was gone) and collapsed onto the bed. He didn't get to rest for long when there was a loud pounding on the door.

"Oi! Wake up, ye bampots!" Callum's voice yelled through the door. "Tonigh's gonna' be our busiest night! If ye want a seat, ye bes' come with us!"

"Away an' boil yer heid!" Thomas muffled yell came from the pillow.

"Ach, we're gonna' ge' some dinnar first! Come on, lads!"

"Enough, Callum! We'll no' be goin' out tonight!"

"Wha' the hell's wrong with ye?" Callum persisted.

Sick of the back-and-forth yelling, Sam marched over to the door and ripped it open, "If the two of ye plan t' argue like ol' maids, then we bes' no' involve the rest of the inn!"

Callum slunk past Sam and walked over to his depressed cousin. "Oi, wha' is it, big man?"

Thomas refused to answer, so Callum tried a different tactic. "I know wha' ye need: t' ge' pissed! Com'on, I'll buy ye all the whiskey ye can drink t'night!"

With the promise of free alcohol, Thomas stood up from the couch and walked towards the washroom. "Le' me relieve m'self before we go."

Chuckling, Callum turned to Sam. "Wha' about ye, Sammy? Would whiskey make yer troubles disappear?"

"I's Sam," he grunted, his stomach growling loudly. "No, I need food."

"Come on, lads, dinnar and drinks are on me!"

Hours later, sitting in the cold metal chair on the outdoor terrace of Haunt 49, Sam angrily swallowed the last of his ale. Looking at the bottom of the glass, he debated on going to get it refilled when Thomas came staggering out of the bar, his arm around Callum.

"Oi, Sammy—I mean Sam, can ye keep an eye on 'im? We've go' another set t' play," Callum huffed.

Before Sam could answer, Callum practically dropped his drunk cousin on the table in front of him and ran off for the stage. Sam pulled another chair over from a vacant table and helped Thomas into it.

"Wher's m'whiskey?" Thomas slurred.

"Ye've had enough, pal."

"No' yet... I can still see Helen, standin' there in front of me."
Thomas pointed his finger to a woman at the other end of the
outdoor terrace.

Sam looked to where he was pointing and was surprised to see
none other than the woman herself that appeared to have broken his
friend's heart. She was standing with some other ladies and slowly
sipping her rum and coke. She appeared to be sad. As if she could
sense them watching her, Helen turned her head. When she saw
Thomas, her posture turned stiff. Sam grew curious.

"I need another drink s' I'll stop seein' 'er." Thomas added.

Sam watched Helen carefully for a moment before he cleared his
throat, "Alrigh', pal, jus' sit tight. I'll be back in a moment."

Leaving Thomas to lay his head on the cold table, Sam made his
way through the crowd over to Helen. The closer he got to her, the
more curious he became. Her eyes were puffy and red, a clear sign
that she had been crying. And while the people surrounding her were
dancing to the music, she wasn't even swaying. When Sam reached
her, she didn't hesitate to meet his gaze.

"Is this the part where ye tell me I've hurt yer best mate, an' I'm
nothin' more than a vicious bitch?" she asked.

Sam gave her a tiny smile and shook his head, "I cannea have an
opinion on wha' I don't know. He didnea tell me anythin'."

Helen nodded her head appreciatively. "Thank him fer tha'."

"Ye can thank him yerself. I donnea think it'd be too far-fetched t'
say tha' ye love him jus' as much as he loves you."

Helen looked away from Sam and back towards Thomas. She
heaved a dramatic sigh.

Sam cleared his throat and continued, "Look, i's no' my business
wha' happened between the two of ye tha' caused such a row. Bu' if
I know anythin', i's tha' no matter how hard things ge', ye have to
try. Especially if two people really want to."

Helen looked back to Sam and smiled, "I remember Thomas
sayin' ye love to say tha'."

"I believe it, too. If ye wanna fix it, go fix it."

"I can't, he... he mus' absolutely hate me."

"He'll forgive ye for wha'ever ye do, trust me. Come on." Sam
gently took her elbow and led her back through the crowd to the big,
bristly blonde man who was close to passing out. When they got to

the table, Sam pulled over his chair for Helen just as Thomas looked up.

Tears started to flood Thomas' eyes when he saw Helen; grabbing her hands, he blurted out, "Helen, me bonnie darlin'! I'm so sorry! I promise, I'll never ask ye t' marry me again!"

Sam had turned to leave but stopped himself as soon as he heard his friend's confession. Stunned, he turned around and demanded, "Ye asked her t' marry ye?! Ye donnea even know her, ye daft bampot!"

"I know I love her!" Thomas shouted.

Before Sam could argue further, Helen chuckled and turned to Sam. "I's alrigh'; I said no. I tol' him if he cannea slow down, then we bes' no' be seein' each other."

"Smart lass," Sam muttered under his breath.

"I love ye, Helen," Thomas continued, "I'm sorry fer pushin' ye, lassy. I promise t' slow down."

"Aye, an' I promise t' talk to ye bettar, luv," Helen added.

Thomas grinned wildly and leaned forward to kiss Helen. She reciprocated his enthusiasm by quickly crawling into his lap.

Taking that as his cue, Sam turned away from the love birds and walked through the busy crowd towards the door of the pub. Though he was smiling at being able to help his friend, he'd had more than enough drama for the weekend. Unable to stand the music long enough for one more pint, he decided to just go back to the hotel and see what was on television for the remainder of the evening. By the way Thomas and Helen were making up, he was sure he wouldn't have to give up the bed again for their last night in Aberdeen.

Sam walked into the lobby of the Green Globe and started for the stairs when he heard a familiar voice call him.

"Detective McKay?"

He turned to see Detective Addair in the sitting room. Tired, he sighed, "Ye have more questions for me?"

"No, I came t' tell ye tha' yer footprints were no' matched a' the crime scene."

He instantly felt relieved. "Tha' was fast. I appreciate ye takin' the time t' tell me in person."

"I also wanted t' tell ye tha' we found the man tha' matched our description: tall, bulky, an' dark."

"Who was he?"

"Jus' a poor homeless soul. Actually, he came to the police force an' insisted we were lookin' fer him."

Confused, Sam furrowed his eyebrows. "Wha'?"

"He confirmed tha' the woman we're lookin' for paid him 100 quid t' stand on the corner with her, jus' needed t' stay out of the light so no one could see his face. He was carryin' a message for ye, too. Said the lassy tol' him if he met anyone named Sam to say this word: memento. Do ye have any idea wha' he's talkin' abou'?"

Sam bristled: he knew perfectly well what it meant. He saw Mary or Isobel's—or whatever her name was— burn mark, so she burned him in return.

"Detective?" Addair probed again.

"No, I'm sorry, I don't."

Detective Addair eyed him for a moment longer before she relented. "A' any rate, ye're off the hook now. I'll inform yer Captain Glowery tha' ye were very cooperative an' to no' be too harsh with ye."

"I appreciate tha'. Goodnight, Detective Addair."

The middle-aged woman nodded curtly and left without another word.

While Sam felt a great sense of relief that his innocence had been successfully proven so quickly, he still felt bitterly angry at how easily he'd been duped by the American woman. Ignoring the pointed looks the hotel's staff were giving him, he marched up the stairs towards his hotel room, intending to take a long shower, hoping to clear his head. Standing under the streaming hot water, he vowed to himself to never let anyone trick him that easily ever again.

Chapter One

Monday, April 20, 2021
Chicago, Illinois

Elena Juarez adjusted the paper grocery bags in her arms as she rooted through her small purse for her key card. Uptown Chicago's Natty Towers apartments were close to the water, making the wind even more frigid as it bitterly blew against her. She was getting on in years, which just made her cold all the time. But the freezing air also made her teeth chatter painfully.

"*Bons céus acima,*" she whispered to herself. "So cold!"

Before she could find the card to get in the Towers, the young doorman Victor Donkirk opened the door.

"Good morning, Mrs. Juarez," he smiled.

"Good morning, Victor," Elena reciprocated. Victor was always polite to her and loved hearing her native Portuguese (as he made a point of telling her once). She thanked him with an emphatic, "*muito obrigado.*"

"No problem at all. How was Brazil?"

"Warm," Elena sighed and the two of them laughed.

"I bet. Do you need any help carrying these up to Mrs. Matheson's place?"

"No, no, I've got it, now. I found my key just as you opened the door."

"Well, let me at least get the elevator for you." Victor raced ahead of her to press the up button and then the button for the fourteenth floor when Elena was inside. Once she swiped her key card into the slot next to the penthouse number, the elevator dinged in acceptance, and the doors began to shut. "Have a good day, Mrs. Juarez!"

"You too, *gentil senhor,*" she answered just before the doors closed. Relieved to be out of the cold, she leaned against the back wall as the elevator soared to the top of the Towers. Though she already missed her sister Maria, she was positive she missed Brazil's warm sun even more.

Elena's employer, Annabelle Matheson, had given her the last week off to spend with her sister; with the previous year's pandemic interrupting her plans to go and visit in 2020, Annabelle had been gracious and insisted that Elena reschedule her chance to see her family as soon as travel bans were finally lifted. The week had been wonderful; for the first time in years, she could see her sister, not to mention there was no longer a threat of hugging her for fear of the disease being spread. After what felt like years of being quarantined, returning to normal activities was such an exhilarating privilege. And it had ended all too quickly. Tears were shed when Elena left for the airport on Saturday evening, by both Maria and Elena. But she had promised Annabelle she would only take one week off, even though the kind old woman had insisted she could take longer. Elena refused because she worried about her sweet employer.

Annabelle Matheson was an 85-year-old wealthy widow; her husband had died of complications from pneumonia twenty years before, leaving her and their two children and five grandchildren behind. Ten years later, David and Lisa Matheson (Annabelle's children) had hired Elena to work as a live-in housekeeper, personal grocery shopper, and also to make sure Annabelle didn't miss any doctors' appointments. Elena loved working for the kind old woman, and they became fast friends. Going to Brazil when neither of Annabelle's children were available to stay with her had worried Elena. But Annabelle insisted, "I can get on just fine without you for one week. I'll be right here when you get back." Elena had made sure to prepare a week's worth of meals for her employer as well as have any emergency phone numbers she might have needed ready at a moment's notice. Satisfied that she had done everything she could for Annabelle for seven days, she allowed herself to relax and went on her vacation.

Once the elevator reached the fourteenth floor, the doors opened and Elena was greeted with a strange concoction of smells: one was faint but revolting, and the other like burned plastic. It made her want to retch. She quickly walked through the hallway and set the groceries and her purse on the dining table before searching through the large penthouse.

"Annabelle?" She called, but there was no answer. "Annabelle, it's alright. Sometimes these things happen, I'll clean it up. There's no need to be upset. Come on, *pobre mulher,* where are you?"

The old woman wasn't in the kitchen, the three bedrooms, or the two bathrooms. Walking past the dining room to the other end of the apartment, Elena looked into the living room and screamed.

Annabelle Matheson was lying supine on the floor; her eyes were wide open, a look of terror molding her wrinkled features, and her throat slit from one ear to the other. Blood soaked her clothes and the floor surrounding her body.

Elena crossed herself in terror. *"Ai meu Deus!"*

She ran back to her purse for her phone, hysterical and hands shaking, and dialed 911.

"911, what is your emergency?" A male voice answered.

Elena sobbed into the phone, "Please, please come quick! Mrs. Matheson, Annabelle Matheson, she's dead!"

***

Cleveland, Ohio
Saturday, July 17, 2021

Belinda Copper was in her office reviewing reports when the office phone rang.

"Director Copper," she answered.

"Good morning, Ma'am," answered the familiar, cheery voice of Agent Evan Dower, "I'm sorry to interrupt, but there's an Edward White here asking to speak with you. He's insisting that he knows you."

Belinda's eyes opened wide upon hearing the familiar name. "Yes, I do know him. Have someone escort him to my office immediately please, Evan."

"Yes, ma'am, he's on the way."

Belinda wasn't too worried about making a certain impression, as her office was always kept neat and tidy. After tucking the documents on her desk away, she walked around her desk and adjusted the two guest chairs to face each other just as there came a knock at the door.

"Come in."

A young agent opened it, and in walked Edward White: Belinda's friend and, at one point in their lives, her lover. He was wearing a grey tweed three-piece suit and carrying a black suitcase. His hair's bright whiteness only made his surname ironic to her now, but it matched his well-trimmed goatee and made him look sophisticated.

"Belinda," he smiled as he walked into her office, his arms outstretched.

"Edward," she smiled in return and walked into his embrace. She noticed a very tall, unfamiliar figure standing next to the agent, but the way he held himself suggested that he was private security. "And who is this?"

"Oh, forgive me. Belinda, this is Isaac Porter, my head of security."

"A pleasure to meet you," she nodded.

The tall man simply nodded in reply.

Turning back to the agent, Copper said, "Thank you, Zina."

The young agent nodded and walked away.

"It's alright, Isaac, I'm sure I'll be safe in here," Edward nodded to his guard.

Without a word, the imposing figure closed the door, leaving Director Copper and her old friend alone.

Edward stepped back and looked over her appreciatively, "You look incredible. I love the white hair, it suits you."

She smiled and reciprocated the compliment. "And you look just as dashing as ever."

"Only with a few more wrinkles around the eyes," he chuckled before he leaned in to give her a friendly peck on the lips. Looking around her and taking in her office, he added, "I knew nothing would ever stop you from making it to the top."

Belinda scoffed, "I wouldn't consider being the Director of Cleveland, Ohio's FBI office 'the top.'"

"No? Well, I do. Being in charge has always suited you, Belinda. And it doesn't matter what size the district is, it's how you handle the weight of the responsibility. And like always, you wear the weight with grace."

"You flatter me with your compliments, Edward. Please, make yourself comfortable. Would you like a drink?"

"Yes, thank you." he sat in a guest chair on the other side of the Director's desk. "Do you still buy only Hennessy XO?"

4

"Of course." Director Copper reached into the cabinet next to her desk and retrieved a teardrop shaped bottle three-quarters full of the amber liquid and two glass tumblers. Filling both glasses half full, she handed one to Edward and took a seat in the other guest chair next to him. "I've yet to find a better brand of cognac. How are Fiona and Charles?"

"Doing well: Fiona has just finished her residency at Weiss Memorial and has been offered a position in the maternity ward."

"Is she still dating that boy from the university?"

"No, no. That ended some time ago. She's decided she wants to focus on her career as a prenatal doctor before settling down with her own family. And Charlie owns his own salon in San Francisco. He called me last week to tell me he has an appointment with a hot new movie star."

"How exciting for him. Anyone I know?"

"I forget the name, but I know they were in a couple recent superhero movies. Charlie's very excited."

"You must be very proud."

"I am," he smiled. "The both of them are happy and doing well."

"And yourself? How goes the life of a real estate mogul and Chicago's historic connoisseur?"

"Oh, you know, keeping the modern world at bay so that we don't forget the past is a battle that is never over."

"'A battle,' hmmm? So that's why you now have personal security."

Edward chuckled, "You'd be amazed at how dangerous the historic landmark business can be, not to mention busy. But I did find the time to write an autobiography that's about to be published."

"How exciting," Copper smiled and took a sip of her cognac. "You'll have to send me a copy."

"I'll do better than that and hand-deliver a first edition," he winked.

Chuckling, Copper set her drink down. "So, what prompts this visit?"

White took a sip of his own drink before he leaned his elbows onto his knees. "Well, Belinda, I wish I could say that I was in town on business and wanted to see an old friend. But I'm afraid I've come here with a purpose."

"Personal?"

"More like acting on behalf of. What do you know about a woman named Annabelle Matheson?"

"I remember seeing her name in the news a few months back. She was rich, a philanthropist of sorts, found dead in her apartment."

"She was also a patron to the society, and a dear friend of mine. It's been months since her death, and I recently learned that it's been declared an unsolved cold case."

"Well, that tends to happen when a case goes without a lead for some time, Edward. And you're here to ask me to look into it, is that it?"

"As a matter of fact, yes." White withdrew a file from the briefcase he'd placed on the floor next to him and handed it to her. "This is everything a little bird was able to get for me from the Chicago PD. I'm afraid I don't know what it all means, but I gather that it's not much."

Copper accepted the file and began to skim over the slim contents. "Not very much, at all. How did you know her?"

"We met at a fundraiser for Chicago's Historical Society twenty years ago. Her husband had unfortunately passed away a few months before, leaving her with an enormous fortune. Apparently, he was a big history buff, and she had decided she wanted to use her money in a way that she could remember him. Through conversation, we learned that we both graduated *summa cum laude* from Harvard: she in 1957, I in 1975. We shared some of the same ideals and became friends."

"How close of friends?"

White smiled slyly, "Jealousy is not in your nature, Belinda."

She chuckled, "I'm only trying to get a complete picture of your relationship, Edward."

"Completely platonic; she would invite me over for tea with her children and grandchildren on occasion, and we would discuss politics, business plans. I even helped her children get good deals on their first houses. As a patron, she would attend meetings at the society on occasion, but nothing further than that, you have my word."

Copper finished looking over the details of the case before she looked up again. "I have an acquaintance at Chicago's FBI office that owes me a favor. I can have him look into this for you."

6

"If I wanted Chicago's FBI to look into this, I would have asked them to," he smiled, "I'm asking you, because I trust you more. And I know you only hire people that will get the job done."

"It's out of my jurisdiction, Edward. And besides, I'm sure you're aware that things are not at rest in Chicago right now."

"I know, between the hatred towards the police and what's going on in Gangsterville, I know this is terrible timing. But please, Belinda. Annabelle's children, David and Lisa, deserve answers for who killed their mother. And you just said that you have an acquaintance that owes you a favor, right?"

Copper sighed. "Alright, I'll see what I can work out, and I'll let you know immediately. If he's alright with it, I have just the team for the job."

"And you'll let me know what you find?"

"As often as I can, Edward."

"I just want to be in the loop."

"And you will be as much as possible. I can't promise you everything, but I will promise you to tell you everything that's relevant. Alright?"

Edward smiled and took another drink of the cognac. "Thank you, Belinda. I knew I could count on you."

***

A few miles out from the shore of Cleveland, in the middle of Lake Erie, Sam McKay and his son Oliver were in a small aluminum fishing boat eating their ham sandwiches. Two fishing rods were situated on both ends of the boat with their lines cast into the water. They'd been out on the boat since 5:00 a.m. that morning, but it was already 1:00 p.m., and neither of them had much luck catching any fish yet.

"Come on, Dad," Oliver whined as he adjusted the obtrusive orange lifejacket, "the fish just don't want to bite today."

Sam looked at his fifteen-year-old son and chuckled, "They donnea want' bite because ye keep scarin' em' off with yer mewlin'."

Oliver rolled his eyes but continued, "I don't even like fishing. You couldn't at least let me bring my phone?"

"Ye've never been fishin' before; ye cannea say ye donnea like somethin' ye've never done. An' t' answer yer question, no, cause then ye would've spent all this time playin' some stupid game rather than focus on catchin' a fish."

"I like boating on the waves. Can't we just turn on the motor and go for another spin like we used to?"

"Aye, sure we can. An' then we'll have nothin' t' show fer this trip, an' yer mother will think I le' ye run off with those wee trouble makers ye call friends."

"I already told you, Dad, I haven't seen any of those guys since I finished my time at the center months ago. Not that you or mom has given me a chance to get into trouble anyway since then."

"I'm glad t' hear our efforts in co-parentin' are workin'. Besides, this is our las' day on this trip before ye go back t' yer mum's fer the week."

"Yeah, yeah, yeah, one week at your apartment and one week at mom's house. Don't you guys care that you're invading my privacy?"

Sam scoffed, "I asked yer granda' the same question when I was yer age, an' ye know wha' he tol' me? He said 'Privacy is a privilege, Sampson. Ye have t' earn it.' When ye earn it, yer mother an' I will give ye the privilege."

"And when will that be?"

"When ye've earned it."

Oliver opened his mouth to argue further, when his fishing pole started moving against the side of the boat. The boy dropped his sandwich and picked up the rod before it was pulled into the water. "Dad! Dad, I've got one!"

Sam set his own sandwich down and quickly scooted over to Oliver. He wrapped his hands around the boy's. "Alrigh', reel 'er in slowly. Ye donnea want'a go too fast, or ye might lose 'er."

"How can you lose a fish that's on the hook?"

"She may no' have swallowed the hook enough. Don't fight the fish, son, jus' be gentle. Com'on, reel 'er in. Tha's it…"

Oliver followed Sam's instructions and reeled in the line slowly, giving little pauses in between each reel, until the two of them started to see a golden shimmer beneath the surface.

"Tha's it, tha's it!" Sam praised. He turned around and grabbed the fishing net on the floor and slowly lowered it into the water, as Oliver brought the fish in closer.

"Geeze! It's fighting hard!" Oliver gritted as he struggled to reel in his line.

"Ye can do it, com'on!"

The olive-golden fish was finally brought close enough to the boat, and Sam swept the net under it before pulling it inside the boat. "Well done, lad! Ye did it!"

Oliver beamed at the prize he'd caught as Sam untangled it from the net. "What is it? What did I catch?"

"Looks t' be a Walleye."

"It's huge!"

"Aye, I'd say abou' 19—20 pounds! More than enough for dinnar tonight."

Oliver's head jerked up. "Wait, we're gonna' eat this thing? With the head and the guts and..."

Pulling the hook from the fish and setting it in the cooler on the floor, Sam laughed heartily, "Well, we haf'ta clean it first. I promise ye it won't be watchin' ye eat it."

"What do you mean 'clean it'?"

"Cuttin' off the head, cleanin' out the guts, and gettin' the filets off. Tha's the part we eat."

"And... you're gonna' make *me* clean it, right?" Oliver winced.

"Relax, son, I'll be teachin' ye how. Anyways, ye love fried fish. Wha's so different abou' this?"

"Well, I've never had to catch and kill my own fish before I eat it."

"Then this'll be a good experience for ye," Sam laughed and reeled in his line. "I'll tell ye wha', we'll take one more spin around the lake. Then we'll head back in. Deal?"

The relief that showed in Oliver's eyes made Sam want to laugh. Once all of their fishing equipment was secure in the bottom of the boat, Sam started the outboard motor, and the small fishing boat cruised along the water. Oliver would sometimes stick his hand in the passing waves and splash a little back at Sam, who would laugh and splash some right back at the boy. When they got closer to the docks, Sam slowed the boat down, and they puttered into the marina. Sam instructed Oliver to stay with the boat while he retrieved the truck and trailer. In no time at all, the two of them had everything packed up and ready to go. With Oliver buckled in the front seat, the cooler with the only catch in his lap, Sam pulled the trailer out of the water, and the two of them headed back to Oliver's mom's house.

Meredith Staton had never liked being in the outdoors much, and it boggled Sam's mind that she had kept the boat. She had gotten everything in the divorce, and he fully expected her to sell it when he was deported. But she didn't, and he was strangely grateful that she hadn't. When Meredith had asked what his plans with Oliver were for the week, and Sam had told her he'd had a fishing trip planned for the two of them, she offered him use of the boat as she "never got around to getting rid of it." Sam supposed that somewhere in the back of her mind, she intended to use that favor as leverage. But rather than question her motives, he accepted the offer and thanked her graciously.

Once they pulled into the drive of the grey house with white trim, Sam and Oliver set to work unloading the boat and putting everything away. They had barely put the fishing equipment in the shed behind the house, when Meredith walked out of the bright red front door and greeted them.

"Did you guys have fun?"

"I caught a Walleye!" Oliver answered excitedly. "Dad thinks it's twenty pounds!"

"Wow!" Meredith opened her eyes widely. "Well, don't think you're coming in the house smelling like *that*."

"Ach, he jus' needs t' wash his hands, Meredith. I's nothin' more than a little lake water on him."

She sighed. "Fine, but take your shoes off at the door."

Oliver handed the cooler to Sam and ran to the house.

Meredith turned back to Sam. "Hey, you need to turn on your phone. Derrick called me and said your boss has been trying to get ahold of you all morning."

Curious, Sam retrieved his phone from the glove box of the truck; he made it a point to turn it off whenever he and Oliver were together for an outing. As soon as it powered on, he saw that he had four missed calls and one voicemail from Copper.

"Mus' be important."

"Do you need me to take Oliver a little early?"

"Aye, I think I do. Thank ye, Meredith."

"Of course," she smiled sweetly. "Just take off your shoes, too."

"I'll only be a minute," he whined.

Rolling her eyes, Meredith answered, "Ugh, fine. Just don't get any fish guts on my floor."

Sam chuckled and walked past her to the house. Oliver emerged from the kitchen with two sodas in his hands.

"Here, Dad," Oliver smiled as he handed one to him.

"Thanks, son. Listen, I have t' go. Somethin's come up at work. Ye're gonna start the week with yer mum a little early, alrigh'?"

The smile on Oliver's face disappeared quickly. Turning his attention to his soda, he mumbled, "Yeah, okay."

Not wanting to leave his son feeling upset, Sam placed his hand on the boy's shoulder and added, "Hey, di' ye have fun?"

"Yeah, I guess."

"Well, then next weekend, you and me will be out on the lake fishin' again. I promise."

"Yeah, okay. Bye." Oliver turned and walked into the kitchen.

Sam sighed and called out, "I love ye, son."

The boy didn't answer.

Turning back to the door, Sam looked at Meredith. "Ye have tol' him wha' my job requires, haven't ye?"

"I told him that your job is important, and sometimes you can't be around for everything," she said simply.

Sam bristled at her answer. "Di' ye have t' make it sound like I donnea *want* to be around fer everythin', when I really do?"

"You know that's not what I implied, Sam."

"Ye could've fooled me."

Meredith rolled her eyes, "Look, I'm not in the mood to fight with you. Will you drop off his stuff later today before you have to go do whatever new case it is?"

"Aye, I will. An' I'll call ye when I know wha's goin' on. We'll work out a plan between me an' Oliver then."

"Okay," she nodded, "Be careful, Sam."

"Aye, ta," he answered. Getting into his truck, now detached from the boat trailer, Sam listened to the voicemail as he pulled out onto the street.

Copper's voice was level yet firm as he listened to her message. "McKay, I have a special assignment for you and your team to look into. Get back to the office, pronto."

He shook his head and sighed, knowing it wouldn't be an easy one. After calling her back and telling her that unless she wanted the office to smell like Lake Erie and fish, he would need to get cleaned up first and would be there as soon as possible. Copper answered with a "Fine, just be quick," before hanging up on him. Rolling his eyes at her last word, he drove back to his apartment.

Chapter Two

It was nearly 2:00 p.m. by the time Sam walked into the FBI office in Cleveland, Ohio. His faithful team waiting at the door, they followed him to the conference room where Copper was no doubt waiting for them. Derrick Rivera was Sam's short, Latino-American partner. He'd helped Sam with his private operation as well as solidified getting Sam a position as an asset of the FBI. Despite Rivera's hot-headed nature rivaling his own, Sam considered him not only a partner but a good friend. Julie Russell: fiery red hair and a drive to match. She was beauty, brains, and skill all rolled into one as she'd proved during her time in SWAT before her career took a sidestep. When Sam met her, he'd taken her under his wing and given her the chance she needed to prove she was far from being out of the game. And Simon Abler: African-American, tall and lanky with thick rimmed glasses. Practically a genius with computers since birth, the boy had gotten into trouble trying to stop animal abuse when he was discovered; he knew more about computers than Sam would ever be able to learn. The four of them could bicker and argue just as well as they could solve crimes together, but no one would ever be able to tear their family unit apart.

Walking into the conference room, Copper was already there and seated at the head of the table. Sitting next to her was the ever-cheerful and optimistic Evan Dower. Though the Director's irritated cat-like demeanor hardly ever changed in the year Sam had known her, he couldn't help the feeling that she was particularly anxious. She had a stack of files directly in front of her; before he could ask what was going on, Evan had already begun his usual excited gushing.

"I didn't get the chance to say anything, but you four did an amazing job with the bomb squad last week! Everyone, even on the news, is praising you as heroes! I mean, just by the way you—"

"Thank you, Evan," Copper said sternly, "But we have another matter to attend to, at present."

"Yes, of course. Sorry, ma'am," Agent Dower answered, folding his hands together in embarrassment.

Ever quick to get straight to the point, Copper turned her attention back to the team and stated, "I'm sending you to Chicago to investigate a murder that's gone cold."

"Serial?" Rivera asked.

"At the moment, it appears not to be."

"So, what's so special about it?" Julie asked next.

"I'm going to level with all of you: A friend has asked me for a favor, and I'm cashing it in. He wants this case solved."

The team of four didn't react beyond a blink. Taking their seats, Copper continued while she handed each of them a file. "Annabelle Matheson: age 85, found dead in her apartment with her throat slit."

"Her throat was slit?" Simon asked. "That's pretty dramatic. Doesn't that usually mean the attack was personal?"

Sam looked over the file in front of him. "'Says here there was no sign of rape or any sexual trauma, bu' there was a burn mark found on the carpet near the body. Robbery gone wrong?"

"Well, if it was, Chicago PD hasn't been able to find anyone that fits the bill so far," Evan answered. "She was a widow, loved by her children and grandchildren. Everyone who met her seemed to love her, as she had no known enemies."

"Bu' this is a pretty strange random act of violence. Who found her?"

Rivera spoke next. "According to the PD's notes, she was found by her maid, Elena Juarez. She said she was out of the country during the time of death. Her alibi checked out; she's not a suspect."

Copper set the copy of her file down and stood up before addressing the team. "That may be, but for the time being I want you to retrace all the steps made by the Chicago PD: double check every alibi, interview every detective involved, dig deeper into everything Mrs. Matheson was involved in. And one final note: I want to be kept in the loop. Everything you find, you report it back to me."

"Does the Chicago office know we're coming?" Julie asked.

"Yes. Greg Bronson is the Director. He's assured me that you're welcome to use his facilities."

"When d' we leave?" Sam asked.

14

"I told him you'd be there by morning. You've got your pick of the company cars to drive in, so go home and get packed. If you run into any trouble, Agent Dower will make sure that you're taken care of."

Her over-eager puppy smiled, "Anything you guys need, I'll get it for you."

"Let me know when you get there." Copper made her final statement, gestured for Evan to follow, and the two of them left the conference room without another word.

Once the door had closed behind them, Simon rolled his eyes, "Well, okay then. So, we're being taken away from our regular jobs of investigating the impossible to look into the murder of one old woman that could easily be handled by the local police? Yeah, this is going to go over well."

"Seriously," Julie agreed, "the Chicago PD won't like having another agency on their turf, let alone an out-of-state one."

"Let's not forget how happy the FBI boys will be when a bunch of out-of-towners come into their house," Rivera added.

Sam interjected. "We'll worry abou' those bridges when we come to 'em. Fer now, le's go ge' packed an' meet back here in an hour."

Everyone nodded and left. An hour later, they were piling into a black SUV with their suitcases. While Sam took claim to the passenger's seat (so he could continue to read the case file during the trip), Rivera, Julie, and Simon played rock-paper-scissors to see who would get to drive. Rivera won and slid into the driver's seat with a smug grin. Julie and Simon groaned as they got situated in the backseat, and Rivera began their five-hour journey. Stopping only once for a bathroom break and some dinner, the team arrived in Chicago and got checked into a motel around nine o'clock that night.

The following morning, after a very bare motel breakfast, the four of them loaded up and drove towards the FBI Chicago headquarters. Two tough-looking agents greeted them at the door in the underground garage before taking them to the elevators and up to the thirteenth floor.

"The Director's office is at the end of the hallway," one of them said curtly.

"Thank ye," Sam answered.

The agent snorted, and the elevator doors shut.

The four of them followed the hallway, but none of them missed the dirty looks they were getting from the other agents on the floor. The whispers and glares made the walk seem longer, but finally they found themselves in front of a dark wooden door with a plaque on it that said: "Director."

Sam knocked.

"Come in," a feminine voice answered.

Sam and the others walked inside and were greeted by a petite, freckled woman sitting behind a desk in the foyer before another door.

"Identification, please?" She asked politely.

Everyone produced their badges, and Sam answered, "We're from the Cleveland office, Belinda Copper's house. Director Bronson is expectin' us."

"Yes, you're right on time. My name is Heidi, I'm Director Bronson's assistant."

Simon chuckled, "Like, you're the Moneypenny to his M?"

Sam turned and shot him a scolding look, but the young lady held her own in her response. "Yes, you could say that I take care of most of the paperwork and handle all of the visits for the director, which includes sifting out the crazy ones that will likely waste his time."

Rivera snorted, Simon looked at his feet abashedly, Julie smiled at the young woman proudly, and Sam chuckled appreciatively.

"Now, then, if you wouldn't mind, I need you to hand over your weapons before I can let you in to see the Director."

"Wha' for?" Sam asked.

"Because the Director doesn't know you, nor does he trust you. And, truthfully, neither do I." Heidi held out a basket to the four of them and waited. Although perturbed, everyone did as they were asked and took their guns out of their holsters and placed them, carefully, into the basket. As soon as they did, the young lady smiled, "Thank you. He'll see you, now."

She knocked on the next door and a croaky voice answered, "Come in."

Heidi allowed the four of them through, where they all saw a thin, balding man with a hooked nose sitting behind a desk. Wearing a tan suit and looking at them with a cold stare, Bronson reminded Sam of a headmaster he knew when he was a child. But the spacious windows behind him did the job of giving him the important appearance that an FBI Director should possess.

The man stood up and walked over to them, stopping in front of Sam. "You must be Agent McKay."

"Aye, tha's me," Sam answered. He offered his hand, but the Director ignored the gesture and moved on to the rest of them.

"Agents Rivera, Russell, and Abler, correct?"

"Yes, sir," Rivera nodded. "Director Copper asked us to give you her thanks for your cooperation."

Bronson snorted, "I'm sure she did. I told Belinda we would be happy to look into this case, since it's in *our* jurisdiction, but she insisted that the four of you are more than capable and wouldn't be a bother. I trust that she told me the truth on that?"

"Yes, sir, she did." Julie said.

"Good, I'm happy to hear that. Well, you are welcome to use our facilities as you need, but I must strongly insist that you not get in anyone's way. Here is what you have walked into, agents: There are approximately 2.7 million people in this city, 12.8 million in the state, and all of them are completely unaware that they are in the middle of an underground turf war that my agents are trying to stop."

The group looked at each other quizzically, but Bronson continued. "Are any of you aware of Chicago's sordid gangster history?"

"We know who Al Capone is, if that's what you mean, sir," Simon chuckled. When Bronson shot him a glare, he cleared his throat and looked down at the floor.

"Sicilians, Italians, Irish, Scottish, Russian… they're all the same to me: the scum of the earth using fear tactics to take advantage of the law-abiding citizens in this fine country. My people have found more dead bodies in the last month than have been reported in the last year. These monsters will stop at nothing to get what they want, including murdering the innocent, and the Attorney General has been riding my ass to bring this bloodbath to an end. I'll be frank: the random death of one old woman is not at the top of my priority list when I have a city of three million to be concerned about, but I would have been happy to take over the investigation myself. The four of you just walking into my house is an embarrassment to my authority."

"We understand yer position, sir," Sam answered calmly. "We donnea want' step on anyone's toes; we jus' want' do our job an' solve Annabelle Matheson's murdar. We'll stay out of yer way, an' ye won't even know we were here. Ye have my word."

"Good, I'm glad that we understand one another." The Director walked back towards his desk and picked up his office phone. "I'll have Heidi get your badges in order so you can come and go without any trouble. She'll also give you a tour of the building. If you have any questions, direct them all to her."

"Thank ye, Director Bronson," Sam answered before ushering the rest of the team out of the door.

Heidi was already at her computer working on their badges. The four of them barely got them pinned on before she was off to show them around the facility. They were shown the forensics lab, interrogation rooms, and the computer labs before she led them to their designated conference area: a tiny, closet sized room with a card table and four chairs.

"Please let me know if there's anything else that you need," she said. Just as quickly as she was there, she was gone, leaving Sam and his team alone in the small room.

Simon was the first to speak. "Does anybody else get the feeling that our welcoming party wasn't very welcoming?"

"Well, you didn't exactly give everyone a great first impression with your sexist quip," Rivera answered him.

"That wasn't sexist! That was a compliment! I referenced one of the most notable characters of all time!"

"Apparently not to her. Anyway, we're just four dopes sitting on their resources solving a simple murder while they handle a bloodbath. This is about as welcome as we'll get, so you might as well get used to it."

"Well, at least they didn't throw us in a dungeon," Julie said sarcastically.

Simon opened his trusty laptop. "Well, let me at least see if I have any internet access here... nada. Yeah, this is *definitely* what I'd call being 'welcome to use the facilities.'"

"Enough," Sam grunted. "We're jus' wastin' time standin' around complainin'. Come on, le's ge' t' the Chicago PD an' start with the lead detectives."

The team didn't find the Chicago PD to be any more welcoming than the FBI; the moment they walked through the door, they were met with more dirty stares. Captain Knight barely acknowledged them, until Sam produced the paperwork explaining they had authorization to take over the case.

"What the hell do you feds want with a cold case?" He asked in a demanding tone. "We've got people for that."

Sam wouldn't admit it in front of his team, but he was ready to punch something from all of the lack of cooperation.

Julie answered, "Look, Captain, we're not here to take over your job. We'd just like to ask your detectives a few questions. Honestly, we'd like to work with them to help them solve this case."

Captain Knight puffed up his chest but it couldn't stretch as far as his pot-bellied gut. "Are you saying my guys can't figure it out, little missy?"

"She's not saying that at all," Rivera growled and stepped in between the paunchy man and Julie.

"Captain," Sam interjected, "I donnea wish t' go over yer head, but I'll have no problem doin' jus' tha', if ye keep jerkin' us around like this. If ye cooperate with us, we'll happily give all credit fer solvin' Annabelle Matheson's murder t' the Chicago PD. No one need know we were even here. Alrigh'?"

The promise of an intact reputation seemed to soothe the Captain, and he directed them to the break room, where the detectives who initially worked the case were having coffee.

Sam and the others walked in to see two fit, plain-looking men sitting at one of the three small tables in the break room. Sam noticed an open file and photos on the table in between them as they sipped from their mugs and talked. One had mousy brown short hair and the other's was grey and curly. Upon seeing Sam's team, they stood up.

"You must be the Feds we were told were coming," the brown haired one said. He offered his hand and a friendly smile to Sam. "I'm lead Detective John Darris."

Grateful for the change in attitude, Sam accepted his handshake willingly. "Agent Sam McKay, i's a pleasure."

"This is my partner, Hank Remy."

"How you doing?" The curly haired man said cordially, also offering up a handshake, which Sam also accepted.

"Fine, thanks. This is my team: agents Derrick Rivera, Julie Russell, an' Simon Abler."

"Good to meet all of you," Darris nodded. "Do you guys want a cup of coffee? Or should we just get straight to the point?"

"Actually, I'd love some coffee," Simon piped up, earning a glare from Rivera and Julie. "What? I haven't reached my caffeine intake limit, yet."

Remy chuckled and magically produced a new paper thermos of the black liquid, "Well, I'm afraid it won't be the best coffee you've ever had, but it does the job of keeping you awake."

"Thank you," Simon smiled. "Got any creamer?"

Detective Remy pointed to the table behind him, "Over there, help yourself."

"Finally," Simon smiled to the others, "we found the friendly ones!"

"Wha' can ye tell us abou' the crime scene, detectives?" Sam interjected.

"Nothing much," Remy answered. "Nothing looked out of place, there wasn't any sign of a struggle, and according to the victim's children and the maid, nothing was stolen."

Darris gestured to the table, "We've got the file with all the photos right here. Figured we better refresh our memory before you guys came. Pull up a seat."

Rivera moved another table closer, and the six of them gathered around. Darris handed each photo down to each of them as he talked. "We couldn't find the murder weapon at the scene, but our M.E. says it was a straight edged blade. She said the jagged pulled skin at the end of the cut suggests the knife might have a broken tip or piece missing from it. The alloys she was able to get from the wound say the knife is made from carbon steel."

Sam furrowed his eyebrows. "Some huntin' knives are made with carbon steel."

"And chef's knives, as it turns out," Darris added. "And since both items are sold unregistered, it's impossible to find out who's bought one of these knives. We checked every known associate and suspect connected to Mrs. Matheson, and her daughter has a set of expensive cooking knives that are made of carbon steel. But none of them have a broken tip, and forensics couldn't find any trace of Annabelle Matheson's blood on them. Based on the decay of the body, the M.E. puts her death around Thursday May 18th to Friday the 19th. The maid was in Brazil during the time of death; the daughter was with her husband and kids; and the son was out of town with his family. All of them have been ruled out as suspects. Plus, none of them had motive to kill her."

"She was rich, wasn't she?" Julie asked, "Don't they all get an inheritance when she dies?"

Remmy answered. "They got their inheritance when Mr. Matheson died twenty years ago; he was the one who had all the money. Mrs. Matheson married into it. When he died, his fortune was split up between the three of them. Once the kids turned twenty-one, they got their inheritance. Mrs. Matheson's money was to be donated upon her death, but about a month before she changed that to leaving it to her maid."

"And you're positive about the maid's alibi?"

"She wasn't even in the country at the time of death, and there's absolutely no footage of her from the apartment's security videos during the window. She swore up and down she didn't know that Mrs. Matheson planned to leave the rest of her fortune to her."

"We also checked our database to see if there were any similar cases like this, but we turned up squat," Darris added. "It's crazy; Annabelle Matheson, by all accounts, was deemed one of the nicest people in the world. Who would want to kill an old lady in such a brutal way?"

"Di' Mrs. Matheson have *any* enemies?" Sam asked, "Anyone a' all tha' dinnea like her?"

"According to everyone we've talked to, the woman was a saint: friendly, funny, helped everyone around her. Even the maid insisted she was the nicest employer she ever had. We combed through her financials, but nothing stands out: She didn't have any outstanding debt and has never set foot near a track, if you catch my drift. A nice old lady like that getting mixed up with the wrong loan shark was a shot in the dark anyway, though. Mrs. Matheson didn't even have extravagant tastes to keep up, she regularly donated some of her inheritance to local charities and Chicago's Historical Society."

"Absolutely no known enemies," Sam sighed. "Tha's verra helpful, indeed."

"It says here that she lived in the Natty Towers Apartments in Uptown," Rivera said. "That a nice place?"

"Yeah, pretty swanky," Remmy nodded.

"Swanky places usually have security cameras in their elevators, don't they?"

"Yeah, usually, but the Towers only have one system and it's in the lobby. The doorman doesn't let anybody in without the proper authorization. We subpoenaed the footage of the week of the murder and two months prior, but nothing out of the ordinary stood out. Nobody suspicious, all residents and visitors accounted for. It's honestly unlikely that the murderer just came in through the front door."

"May I have a look at the tape?" Simon asked.

"What for? We just said you won't be able to get anything from it."

"Well, my forte isn't looking at the people on the tape," Simon smirked. "I want to take a look at the electronic fingerprints and make sure nothing was tampered."

"Our tech guys already looked at that, too. It's clear."

"Fellas," Sam interrupted, "Simon's the bes' computer man out there. Le' him work his magic, aye?"

Darris rolled his eyes, and Remy answered, "Okay," in a sing-song voice.

"Di' ye notice anythin' peculiar a' the scene?"

"Honestly, the thing that seemed very random is this burn," Remy answered, handing a photo to Sam. "Our first thought was maybe the perp dropped a cigarette but quickly put it out before the alarm could be tripped. But forensics says that the fire was started with some household stuff turned into homemade accelerant, but it was put out almost immediately."

"Wait… so the killer just randomly decided to light a fire but then changed their mind?" Julie asked perplexed.

"That's about all that we can figure. Mrs. Matheson had a very sophisticated fire containment system in her home. Our best guess is the perp saw it and didn't want to trigger the alarm, so he doused the fire before it got out of hand, and he'd get caught."

"That's very strange."

Staring at the photo of the large, black burn mark on the white carpet, Sam nodded his agreement. "Is there anythin' else we should know, Detectives?"

Darris and Remy looked at each other uneasily. Finally, Darris cleared his throat, "Yeah… a few days before Mrs. Matheson's body was found, dispatch got an anonymous call saying we should go check on her."

"An' ye didn't?"

"They thought it was a crank call, which happens a lot. This is Chicago, guys. It wasn't until she turned up dead that they made the connection."

"Did dispatch say anythin' abou' the caller?"

"Only that the caller was female; she hung up before they could ascertain anything else. Thankfully we were able to get a copy of the call, just in case we find someone to compare the voice to. Again, to be sure, the maid and the daughter were ruled out. They weren't even a 10% match."

"Well, that's something," Julie piped in, "Can you take us to the crime scene? I want to have a look at the building and see if I can find any other ways in."

"Sure thing," Remy smiled at her. "We'll take you there, now."

"Great," Simon added, "You guys go do the grunt work, I'll stay here and do the eloquent work."

***

The Natty Towers apartments weren't too far from the precinct, but the heavy traffic made the drive extremely long. Finally, the detectives, Sam, Julie, and Rivera stopped their car in front of a single, enormous eighteen-story, building next to Montrose Beach. The structure looked to be made entirely out of mirrors by the way the sky and the sandy shore reflected off of it.

Rivera let out a low whistle. "You would think a building this fancy they would have sprung for elevator security cameras."

"Building manager felt compelled to do so now, let me tell you," Darris chuckled.

Sam looked at Julie, who was critiquing the building closely. "Wha' do ye think? Can anyone climb it?"

"With the right equipment, it wouldn't be impossible," Julie said. "But I don't see any way for somebody to climb this without being spotted. At least, not in broad daylight. And there aren't any other buildings close enough for somebody to make a jump."

Sam turned to Darris. "Wha' floor is Mrs. Matheson's apartment on?"

"The fourteenth floor."

Sam turned back to Julie. "Go up t' the roof an' have a look around. Perhaps somebody came in from the top."

"Yup," Julie nodded, and began to walk towards the building's entrance, Sam and the others right behind her.

The young doorman stopped the group. "Hold on. Only residents are allowed in and out."

Detective Darris flashed his ID. "I'm sure you remember us, pal: Detectives Darris and Remy. These three are FBI consultants. This is Victor Donkirk. We're here to look at the crime scene again."

The doorman didn't argue, but coldly allowed them inside. "I suppose you need to be let into Mrs. Matheson's apartment again?"

"That would be helpful, yes." Darris smirked.

"Just a minute, I'll get the super." Victor walked away, and the newcomers had a chance to look at their surroundings.

The lobby of the Natty Towers had dark wood walls sparsely adorned with black and white paintings, creamy white marble floors, and patterned rugs with plush furniture.

"Damn," Rivera said. "You weren't kidding when you said 'swanky.'"

Remy chuckled.

In no time at all, the doorman had returned with a short, older man, the superintendent, who led them to the elevator. Once everyone was inside, the doorman pressed the button for the fourteenth floor, and the super scanned a key card.

"Is tha' key card the only way t' activate the elevator?" Sam asked.

The superintendent looked at Sam curiously (obviously surprised by his accent) before replying, "No, no, it's just required for the top five floors where our penthouses are. You can get to the other floors with the press of a button, but the penthouses need a special key card to get access. Since I'm the super, I have a master."

"An' the master allows ye into every floor, aye?"

"Yup, that's right."

"Anyone else have access t' this key?"

"Just me and the other super."

"How many residents live in the building?" Rivera asked.

"Well, there are approximately six apartments per floor, most of which are occupied, except for the five penthouses at the top of the building. … About 75 families. But the top penthouse has been vacant for some time."

Sam turned to the detectives and asked, "Di' ye ge' a copy of the tenant list?"

"Yes, and we ran a check on everybody, no red flags," Darris nodded.

The elevator pinged, signaling it had reached the 14th floor. The doors opened to crossed police tape, on the other side of which was the foyer into the penthouse.

"I need to ask all of you to wear these, please," Darris said, producing shoe covers for everyone, "We don't want to disturb any evidence, after all."

"Not for me," Julie said before she tapped on the super's shoulder. "I need to get to the roof and have a look around, please."

"Sure thing," the super nodded.

"I'll go with you," Detective Remy offered. "Two sets of eyes are better than one."

"Thanks," Julie nodded.

Sam, Rivera, and Detective Darris exited the elevator.

"Everything's still here," Rivera noted, "Wouldn't the Towers have cleaned and rented out the apartment by now since the case went cold?"

"Mrs. Matheson owned this place, and now it belongs to her daughter. The Towers has talked to Lisa about selling it back to them, so they could rent it out, but she's not having any of it," Darris answered. "I get the impression that as long as her mother's murder remains unsolved, she'll never sell it."

"Lucky break for us."

While Rivera and Darris continued to discuss the details of the forensics so far, Sam looked all around, trying to get a feel for the apartment's layout. At the beginning of the hallway was a door to the coat closet, which Sam decided might just be big enough for someone to hide in. The hallway led to a medium-sized, dark wood dining room table with floor-length windows behind it. To the left of the table was another hallway which led to the three spacious bedrooms and bathrooms. To the right of the table, near the windows, was a door that led to the kitchen, and next to that was another hallway which led to the living room. Somewhat satisfied with his initial walk-through, he headed towards the crime scene. The white carpet in the middle of the room still had an enormous bloodstain on it that had turned brown with time, and not too far away from it was the ugly, black burned spot. But, just as the case file said, nothing otherwise appeared to be out of place or disturbed.

Sam first looked over the oddity: the burn spot. Looking up and all around him, he took note of the fire extinguishing nozzles sparsely located on the ceiling and the fire alarm on the wall not two yards away. As far as he could tell, the dectective's assessment of the perpetrator starting and extinguishing the fire was correct, so he moved on to the blood stain. He crouched down as close as he could get without touching it. Once again, looking all around him, he took note of the blood spatter on the matching white couches and the glass coffee table.

Rivera and Darris walked into the living room.

"Mrs. Matheson was found lyin' on her back, correct?" Sam asked.

"Yeah," Darris nodded, "Her hands were by her sides, too."

"An' ye're sure nobody moved the body? No' even the maid?"

"The maid said she came into the penthouse, walked through the apartment before she found Mrs. Matheson here with blood all over her, and called 911. She was lying on her back with her hands next to her when the maid found her, and she swears she never touched the body."

Curious, Sam walked back into the kitchen and grabbed the nearest sharp knife before going back to the gruesome scene. Without a word, he cut around the enormous stain until he could pull the carpet back. The blood had soaked through the carpet and the padding clear down to the baseboards.

"Well, *somebody* moved her," Sam continued, pointing to the middle of the stain. "If she really died lyin' down, there'd be an outline of the body in the middle of the blood. Bu' look, i's completely saturated. She bled out on her stomach first."

"You think the maid might be lying, Sam?" Rivera asked.

"I think she may have been in shock, and perhaps she donnea remember movin' the body. She could've tried t' revive the old woman while she waited for the police."

"Forensics said between how little Mrs. Matheson was, and with how late the body was found, it's possible that the blood had enough time to spread out under her."

Sam shook his head, "I donnea think so. Most of it would've been lost with the arterial spray, an' her clothes an' the carpet would've soaked up the rest. There wouldnea be enough blood left t' ge' under her t' drench the baseboards with her body in the way."

Rivera turned to Darris. "Is there any possible way this was a suicide?"

"No way," Darris shook his head. "The blood spatter analysis suggests there was something obstructing the spray. And you're wrong about the maid, there wasn't any blood on her clothes when we arrived. If she touched the body, she should've had a little on her somewhere."

The trio heard the elevator door open. The voices of Julie, Detective Remy, and the super were heard walking through the entire apartment before they joined the others in the living room. As soon as the super saw the scene, he began to turn white, and Detective Remy escorted him to the dining room table.

"I don't think anybody came in from the roof, boss," Julie said. "I couldn't find any trace of somebody being up there for months: no tracks, no scratches from any equipment, not even a cigarette butt."

"Alrigh', look around an' see if any of the windows might've been tampered with."

"I just did, these windows are glued shut. There's no way in or out of this place except through the elevator."

"Well, the lack of struggle suggests that Mrs. Matheson knew the attacker well enough to let him or her in," Rivera said.

"Aye," Sam nodded. "Though with how small an' fragile the poor woman was, I donnea think it would've been verra hard t' struggle with her in the first place."

He started to rise from the floor when a tiny sparkle under the couch caught his eye. He pulled his phone out and turned on the flashlight.

"What is it?" Rivera asked.

Sam didn't answer; he moved the phone around slowly and then he saw it: Under the couch, right behind a foot and well-concealed by the carpet, was a black bead that sparkled with the light.

"Somebody hand me some tweezers, gloves, anythin'!" He barked.

Julie ran out of the room and returned a moment later with a set of kitchen tongs and a plastic baggie. Sam took them and carefully retrieved the bead from its hiding place before dropping it into the baggie and sealing it shut. He held it up and examined it carefully: a small black bead in the shape of a teardrop with a broken hook on the end of it, obviously from a necklace.

"Was Mrs. Matheson wearin' any jewelry when she was found?"

"Just her wedding ring, a peculiar antique made with a ruby."

"An' nothin' else? Nothin' w' black beads is missin'?"

Detective Darris shook his head.

Sam called Simon and put the phone on speaker.

"What's up, boss?" Simon answered in his usual perky tone.

"In the lobby footage, can ye make out if anybody's wearin' any jewelry?"

"… Yeah, a little bit. Give me a second, I'll see if I can sharpen this up." Furious clacking noises were heard in the background before Simon spoke again. "Okay, I can see everybody's necks pretty clearly, but I can't tell you what cut of diamonds Mrs. Robinson might be wearing."

"Start lookin' fer black beads aroun' the time of the murder an' send me anythin' ye find."

"You got it."

Sam hung up the phone and held the baggie up to the light. "Well, this shouldnea be here."

Chapter Three

Sam and the others stood around the dining room table with the superintendent (who was still pale and shaking).

"I've... never seen that much blood before," the poor man mumbled.

Rivera walked over with a glass of water in hand. "Here, drink this. It'll help."

Sam sat down in the chair across from the super. "Does anyone in the buildin' keep an electronic record of who opens the penthouses?"

The super shook his head. "No, we're not a hotel, and we don't want to tangle with privacy laws. But our security company might be able to get you something."

"What do you have the security company for, if you don't watch who's going in and out of the apartment?" Remy asked.

"Sometimes the elevator breaks, and I can't fix it, or if somebody tries to break into an apartment, we can lock the building down. But that's never happened before. Victor never lets anybody in the building, unless they're a resident, or he gets confirmation from our residents that they're expecting guests. He's made it a point to know everybody in the building." The super took a shaky sip of the water. "Something like this should have never happened..."

Sam's phone rang. He put it on speaker before he answered. "Wha' have ye go', Simon?"

"You wanted black beads? Well, I found some. At 9:00 p.m. on Thursday, right inside the window of time of death, I've got a clear picture of a woman walking in with a necklace that has some black beads on it. I checked a week before all the way up to after the police arrived just to be safe, but not one other person was wearing any jewelry with black beads on it."

"Fantastic," Sam smiled, "Send me a still shot, aye?"

"Yeah, no problem boss, but before you give me a raise, you should know about the little hiccup. She's wearing a large, round beach hat; her face is completely covered. I tried looking at the different angles from the security cameras, but I can't get a clear shot of her. Heck, I can't even tell you what her hair color is. She's dressed to hide from cameras."

"Well, of course. Why would she want to make it easy on us?" Julie said, earning a chuckle from Detective Remy.

"Other than that, the detectives were right: nothing fishy about this footage."

"Then that means the killer has to be in plain sight somewhere in those tapes," Rivera said.

Sam sighed, "Well, if the doorman really knew e'rybody, then perhaps he might be able to identify the necklace. I's a start."

"Anything else you need me to do, boss?" Simon asked.

"Aye, see if ye can ge' access t' the buildin's security systems an' find out when Mrs. Matheson's penthouse was accessed."

"Ooh, yay!" Simon said excitedly over the phone, earning a chuckle from Julie and the two detectives. "I just need to make some popcorn before I play 'catch me if you can' with computer security drones."

"Abler," Sam said sternly.

"Right, you got it. No popcorn. Sending you the pic, now."

The call ended, and a second later, Sam's phone pinged with a text alert. He stared at the smoothed but still slightly pixilated image on the screen: in the middle of the Natty Towers lobby was a woman wearing blue jeans, a white shirt and coat, and a large round hat that conveniently hid her face and hair. Around her neck was a long necklace that reached her midsection, and it had black beads. He zoomed in on the necklace as much as he could, before the image became too distorted, and held up the baggie containing his bead next to it. He smirked: even to the naked eye, it was a perfect match.

"Ach, bingo. I be' whoever was wearin' this necklace is the same lassy tha' made the anonymous call. Le's see if doorman Victor recognizes these beads."

The group and the super left the penthouse and took the elevator back to the lobby. Victor was standing next to the door.

"Did you find everything you needed, officers?" He asked in an annoyed tone.

Sam lifted his phone and showed the image to the young man. "Do ye recognize this woman?"

Victor looked closely at the phone screen for a few moments. "No, I'm sorry."

"What about the necklace? Or maybe even the hat?" Rivera asked.

Again, the doorman looked at the picture. "Nope."

Detective Darris stepped forward. "Come on, everybody in this building swears up and down that you don't let anybody in without a good reason, or you know them. You're telling me you've never taken a glance at some of their attire?"

Victor scowled at him. "Half of the female tenants that live in this building wear fancy clothes, or jewelry, and even hats that they only wear once, maybe twice. It's impossible to keep track of who owns what piece of jewelry. I look at the faces, not what they're wearing. And I'm sorry, but I don't recognize the necklace. If it was familiar, I would guess it belongs to one of the tenants. But I'm telling you, it's not."

"Alrigh', thank ye." Sam pulled out his wallet and retrieved a business card. "If ye happen t' remember anythin' a' all, call me. Aye?"

"Yeah, sure," the doorman nodded, accepting the business card.

Sam, Rivera, and Julie walked behind the detectives back to their cars.

"Well, it was a good hunch," Darris said over his shoulder. "But unless your computer genius is able to find something, we're back to square one already. I'm just sorry you guys came all this way for nothing."

Rivera scowled at him, "It's not over yet, Detective."

"Aye," Sam nodded, "In fact, when we ge' back t' the precinct, ye boys have a little work ahead of ye: ge' a warrant an' search the whole buildin' fer this hat an' the necklace. Perhaps Victor go' it wrong, an' they do belong t' somebody tha' lives here. We migh' ge' lucky."

"Alright, we can handle that."

"Great. An' when we ge' back, I'd like t' have a look a' the evidence ye've collected."

"Sure, that's not a problem." Remy answered.

"In fact, we'll be takin' it with us t' the office."

The two Detectives postures bristled for a moment. The both of them turned around and Darris said, "Any particular reason why?"

"There's a lot more resources available at the FBI," Julie answered. "Maybe we'll catch something that you missed."

Darris and Remy looked at one another. After having their quick, silent conversation, Remy answered, "Okay, fine."

Back at Chicago FBI Headquarters, trapped in their stuffy little room, Sam, Rivera, and Julie were combing through all of the physical evidence. Simon was in the computer labs where he'd "be of more use." The evidence collected from Annabelle Matheson's body was standard: the clothes she had worn the day of her murder, shoes, scrapings from under her fingernails, all of the photographs taken at the scene of the crime (including of the antique wedding ring that had already been returned to the next of kin), and a stack of paperwork that contained toxicology and blood sample reports. Everything appeared to be in order.

"Other than a few things that were returned to the family, everything's all here," Julie said. "No wonder the case went cold, that woman with the necklace was thorough."

Rivera nodded his head in agreement, "You're not kidding. Every fiber and hair strand has been accounted for. There isn't one speck of evidence that doesn't belong in Mrs. Matheson's apartment. Other than that bead you found, I mean. Somebody at Chicago's Forensics lab is about to get written up, I can promise you that."

Sam sighed, "Well, t'was worth lookin' at."

Suddenly the door burst open, and in ran Simon with an excited grin on his face. "All of you should be *so* happy that I used to work with criminals!"

Rivera scoffed, "I'd hardly call a bunch of egg-heads sitting behind computers and stirring up trouble 'criminals.'"

"The future is now, Derrick," Simon spat at him, "Cybercrime will outdo violent crime one day, you can bet on—"

"Enough bickerin', children," Sam said, rolling his eyes. "Tell us wha' ye found, Simon."

The lanky young man beamed. "Mrs. Matheson's apartment wasn't hacked or broken into, it was either opened by her or by a security key card from the outside."

Julie furrowed her eyebrows. "And this is good news because…?"

"Because at 9:15 p.m., right within the window of the time of death, it was opened by a card that wasn't issued by the apartment complex."

"What are you talking about?" Rivera asked, obviously intrigued.

Simon smiled giddily, "You know how most hotels have magnetic strip cards that they program at the front desk to match the room? The way those work is they put a time limit on the magnetic strip, based on a guest's hotel stay. Once the guest's checkout time comes, the time limit on the strip expires and the key is useless. The key that accessed the apartment is similar to that, only instead of there being a time limit, there's a code limit on it."

Rivera groaned, "English, Abler, English!"

"Wow, you really hurt yourself whenever you have to use your brain muscles, don't you?" Simon huffed. "Think of it as a sort of… electronic bump-key. The code is *extremely* sophisticated; that's why it can only be used once. Essentially, you insert the card into the reading mechanism, and it'll copy the last used key code and therefore give you access."

"So, there's a chance tha' it donnea work if someone accidentally swiped their card in the wrong place?" Sam asked.

"Yeah, it's a total gambit. But with places like those apartments, people rarely mess up their penthouse number so the odds of screwing up your purchase can be minimal."

"How did you catch *that*?" Julie asked, impressed.

"Like I said, you're lucky I used to work with criminals before I was recruited. The code was written by a hacker I worked with a few times named Malcom. He made his reputation off of these keys, selling them to activists who needed access to high-security places. But last I heard, he stopped making them to go legit about four years ago. He has his own internet podcast show now, trying to raise awareness about government corruption and how the pandemic was a ploy."

"Could it be an old purchase? Maybe somebody kept the bump key until they absolutely needed it."

"No way. He told me that he built in a safety feature for that. 'Keeps the customer's coming back,' he said. The key's good for a month, six weeks maximum."

"He's tha' good?" Sam asked.

Simon nodded emphatically, "Oh yeah."

"Can ye contact him?"

"Sure, but he won't talk to just anybody. Honestly, he may not even talk to *me* if he knows I'm FBI."

"Well, it's a good thing that information isn't public knowledge," Rivera said.

Simon nodded, "I'll see what I can do."

He left and closed the door behind him, leaving the three of them alone with the physical evidence again.

While Rivera was carefully putting every piece of the evidence away, Julie turned to Sam. "Since there's nothing to look at here, should we talk to the family again? Maybe see if something doesn't add up with any of them?"

"Aye, it couldnea hurt."

Rivera spoke up, "According to the notes, the son lives in Brighton Park, and the daughter lives in suburban Des Plaines."

"Ye take the son, we'll g' talk to the daughter."

A half hour later, Sam and Julie were walking up the drive of an idyllic orange brick home adorned with green trees and rose bushes.

"All it needs is the tire swing," Julie commented before Sam told her to hush.

He knocked on the door, and within moments it was answered by a woman with dark, puffy blue eyes wearing a t-shirt and jeans.

"Afternoon, ma'am," Sam said calmly. "Are ye Lisa Matheson?"

"Lisa Matheson-Nichols, yes," she nodded. "May I help you?"

He showed her his badge. "We're FBI. Agent Sam McKay, this is Agent Julie Russell. We've taken over the investigation on yer mother. May we come in an' ask ye a few questions?"

Lisa nodded, and they followed her in. She led them to a quaint living room and gestured to the small loveseat beneath the window. "Please, have a seat."

"Thank ye. Mrs. Matheson-Nichols—"

"You can just call me Lisa; my last name is pretty tedious."

"Verra well. Lisa, we donnea want' take up too much of yer time, so we'll ge' straight t' the point. When was the last time ye spoke t' yer mother? "

"I called her the morning before she…" Lisa couldn't finish her sentence before tears began to flow down her cheeks. She whimpered, "I'm sorry."

"S'all right, lass."

She withdrew a tissue from her pocket and blew her nose. "It seems like I'm always carrying tissues around, right now. I never know when I'm going to fall apart."

Sam nodded sympathetically, "Tha's perfectly understandable. We're verra sorry for yer loss."

"Thank you," Lisa nodded. "That means a lot. I'm sorry, let me try again. I called her the morning before she died. I was just checking on her, asking if she wanted to come to dinner. I was planning on making chocolate silk pie for dessert that night, she loves that...loved that."

"Di' she seem out of sorts at all?"

"No, she was happy and normal. She said she appreciated the offer, but she wanted to stay in that night because her hip was hurting. She fell down a year ago. She wasn't really hurt, so she didn't need surgery. It just flared up from time to time. But she would take some Tylenol and a warm soak, and the pain would usually go away. Anyway, I offered to call an Uber Eats for her, but she insisted she'd be fine."

"What about your husband? Did he and your mom have a good relationship?" Julie asked.

"Mike and Mom got along great. In fact, he was the one who found Elena when Mom was having a hard time on her own. My brother David and I wanted to hire someone from assisted living, but she wouldn't have any of that. So, Mike suggested a housekeeper instead, and she was much more open to that idea. He interviewed Elena, checked her background, even went over with her to meet my mom and make sure she liked her before hiring her."

"So, the two of ye paid Elena t' help yer mother?"

"Yeah, we used our inheritance. It didn't hurt our budget."

"What does your husband do for a living, Lisa?"

"He's a public defender. I'm a manager at the bookstore on East Algonquin. We both got time off after mom was found, but Mike had to go back to work a few weeks ago....I'm not really ready to go back yet." More tears gathered at the corners of Lisa's eyes, and she raised her tissue to wipe them away before she dropped her face in her hands.

Her action caused Sam to notice the two rings on her hands: a sparkly silver diamond ring and band on her left wedding finger, and on her right middle finger, a gold ring with a large, bright red ruby the size of a pea encrusted with tiny stones around it. It was obviously the ring Annabelle had been wearing.

"Forgive me, bu' was tha' yer mother's?"

35

"Yes, it is." Lisa nodded and fiddled with the ruby ring. "It's a family heirloom, passed down through my family for generations. My dad gave it to my mom when he asked her to marry him. Growing up, he would always tell us the stories of the curse that surrounds this ring."

"Curse?"

"According to my dad, it all started when this ring was given to my ancestor, Mary, my great-grandmother of 400 years, by her father right before he died. She was only seven at the time. But, according to Dad, it was supposed to go to her older sister, Alison. When she didn't get it, she sought help from a witch, who put a curse on the ring: *Until it is returned to whom it was rightly promised, death will follow all those who possess the ring.* After that, Alison disappeared and was never heard from again. The next person to inherit this ring was Mary's only son, George, who fell in love with the young lady of House Matheson, Elsbeth. Mary apparently didn't like the Matheson clan much and wanted to keep the ring, but George had already given it to Elsbeth when they were married in secret. Shortly after that, George died of dysentery at only 19, leaving behind a 17-year-old pregnant widow. She gave birth to a son, whom she named George, and he became known as The Bastard of the Matheson clan. Elsbeth kept that ring until her dying day, then it went to her great grandson, Bram Matheson. His first wife died in childbirth, and the ring went to his second wife. Bram died only a few years later from a freak accident with a horse. But the ring continued to trickle its way down through my family to my dad, who gave it to my mom....And now it's come to me." Lisa sadly chuckled, "It's almost funny, a lot of tragedy has surrounded this ring. One would almost think the curse was real."

Sam listened to her story intently before he turned his focus back to the ring; despite some tiny faded spots on it, the band looked almost new. He'd seen the ring in the photos of the crime scene, and obviously any trace blood samples that could be collected had been, which accounted for any of the faded spots from chemical tests. But the way it glinted in the light...he couldn't help but feel that there was more to this ring than met the eye.

"Anyway," Lisa continued, "I asked Detective Remy about a month ago if I could have it back, and he said that as long as it didn't seem to be important to the case, it wouldn't be a problem. He assured me that everything was in order when he returned it to me, but I still have the release paperwork if you'd like to see it."

"Please," Sam nodded.

Lisa walked out of the living room and returned just a moment later with the appropriate paperwork, which Sam handed over to Julie. While his partner looked over the documentation, Sam kept his eyes trained on the ring.

"Everything looks good, Sam," Julie concurred. "There wasn't anything on the ring that suggested it was important to the case."

Even though he heard her, Sam kept his gaze on the piece of jewelry. "May I see it for a wee moment?"

Reluctantly, Lisa slid the ring off of her right middle finger and handed over to him.

Sam examined it closely. "Does your brother know ye have this?"

"Yeah."

"And he doesnea want it?"

"No, he's emphatically insisted that I can keep it."

Julie snickered. "He afraid of the curse?"

"He'll never admit it, but I think he is. Mom offered it to David when he proposed to Allie, but he insisted that I could have it when the time was right. Then dad died, and a few years later I met Mike. I told mom she could hang on to the ring. I knew it was the only thing Dad had given her that really reminded her of him. She said she would will it to me when her time came....I didn't expect to get it this way, though."

Sam heard her, but the ancient ring held him captivated. "...Lass, would it be alrigh' if we held on to this for a little while?"

"Why?"

"I'd jus' like t' check an' make sure there was nothin' the Chicago PD missed. Ye'll ge' it back as soon as possible, I promise."

The sorrow in Lisa's eyes was unmistakable, but she nodded all the same. "Okay."

Sam deposited the ring into an evidence bag from his pocket. "I donnea think we have any more questions a' this time, lass. Thank ye fer allowin' us into yer home."

Lisa nodded and walked them to the door.

Julie was driving them back to headquarters while Sam kept looking at the evidence bag with the ring. "You smell something, boss?"

"She said this ring is four-hundred years old."

"So?"

"So, I' should be a little faded, an' the stones should lose a little of the sparkle, bu' the gold band looks new, an' the ruby is shinin' redder than blood."

"Everything probably looks new because it's been polished up. You know that Forensics is very thorough."

"Perhaps, bu' I wanna compare it t' the crime scene photos jus' t' make sure."

***

Sam and Julie were about to walk inside of their little room when Rivera ran up behind them. "Hey, did you guys get anything?"

"Well, apparently there's a curse surrounding this family because of the antique ring. Sam wants to take a closer look at it, but other than that, not much," Julie said. "What about the son?"

"If David Matheson is guilty of anything, it's probably that he didn't visit his mom often enough. He hardly called her; said they weren't that close. He actually mentioned that he didn't want the ring his mom offered him, and that his sister could have it. Is that it?"

"Yup. Lisa told us the same thing: He's secretly afraid of the curse, so she got the ring."

Still holding the baggie with the ruby ring inside, Sam rifled through the collection of crime scene photos before finding the one he was looking for. He held the ring next to the photo under the lamp light, squinting his eyes to see it clearly before his frustration got the better of him. He walked out into the hallway where it was much brighter. Glancing back and forth between the bag and the photo, they both looked exactly the same.

"See?" Julie said, "It's probably just been cleaned, like I said, and that's why it looks so new."

"The stones, maybe, bu' the band looks too new."

"Maybe the band was replaced some time ago and the stones are the real heirloom."

"Lisa seemed t' know everythin' abou' this ring, I think she would've mentioned tha'."

"Maybe Annabelle got it rhodium plated to keep it protected." Rivera said; Sam and Julie looked at him curiously before he added, "What? I know a little bit about jewelry."

But Sam wasn't convinced; he walked back towards the evidence pile and scoured over the paperwork until he found all of the information regarding the ring. He walked with purpose towards the laboratory section of the FBI office.

"Sam, seriously, what are you thinking?" Rivera jogged behind him, his short legs causing him to run to keep up with Sam's long strides.

"I donnea think this is the same ring," he answered simply. "I think i's a fake."

Rivera scoffed. "What in the world makes you think that?"

"Me gut."

Trying to keep up, Julie piped in, "What are you talking about? We've gone over the evidence logs dozens of times, that ring was never unaccounted for except when it left the chain of evidence. And judging by how attached Lisa Matheson was to it, I doubt she ever let it out of her sight as soon as she got it back."

"Do you have any theories on why this ring is fake?" Rivera asked.

"No' yet," Sam grunted. Turning the corner to the labs, he practically yanked the door open. Marching over to one of the lab technicians, he handed him his badge and the baggie. "Can ye perform a test t' see if this is real gold or no'?"

The technician took the ring without question and looked it over. "That test has already been done. You can see the evidence right here with this little faded spot."

"Do i' again, please."

The technician shrugged and placed the ring in a Petri dish. Then he took another empty Petri dish and placed it next to the ring before he retrieved a little bottle.

"What's that?" Julie asked.

"Nitric acid," he answered before he walked to the other side of the room. He returned carrying a tiny sliver of a golden substance. "And this is real gold. I'm going to use it as a control."

"Control?" Rivera asked.

"Nitric acid will pretty much tell you whether any piece of jewelry is real gold or fake gold. If it's real, then the acid won't change the color at all. It'll just get rid of a lot of impurities and make it shinier. If it's fake, it'll change color."

After putting on some gloves, the technician carefully unscrewed the lid of the bottle, pulled out a dropper, and with a very steady hand, squeezed a drop of the liquid onto the control piece. The gold didn't change color. Satisfied, he turned his attention to the ring, and squeezed a drop onto the side of the golden band. The area turned milky white.

"Huh…this isn't real gold, it's plated sterling silver." The technician quickly wiped off the liquid before removing the gloves and handing the ring back to Sam.

Sam smirked, *I knew it!* "Can this test be faked?"

"No, nitric acid never lies. You can possibly cover it up, but you'd have to re-plate the gold to do that. This hasn't been re-plated."

"Are ye sure?"

"Positive," the technician nodded before he turned and stuck his head against his microscope.

"That doesn't really prove anything, Sam," Rivera said. "Again, it could have been traded out for sterling silver a long time ago."

"That ring looks old," the technician said, his head still buried in the microscope. "Sterling silver wasn't used for jewelry until the mid 1900's, and before then it was mostly used for tableware. Gold doesn't decompose. It may get dirty, but it won't decay like other metals."

Sam thrust the paperwork regarding the ring towards the technician. "Can ye verify if the test done previously confirms the ring is real gold?"

The technician sighed before taking the paperwork. He read over it really fast before he came to a certain page and pointed to the results. "It says here a nitric acid test confirms the ring used in the previous test is real gold."

"Then I was righ'," Sam stated, "This isnea the same ring."

Chapter Four

Sam paced around the tiny conference room.

Rivera spoke first. "Okay, so we know that the ring was tested on April 24th, a week after Annabelle's murder. And then, according to the evidence logs, it was given back to Lisa after being deemed "non-essential evidence" on June 22nd. That leaves eight weeks unaccounted for when this ring could have been switched."

"You should have seen how attached to this ring Annabelle's daughter was," Julie replied, "I doubt she ever let it out of her sight since getting it back. There's doesn't seem to be anything fishy about the PD's logs, though. Nobody went anywhere near evidence that wasn't supposed to be there. Or if they did, they weren't accounted for."

"I can't find anything on the evidence room security footage, either. Whoever did this went to a lot of trouble to make sure they wouldn't get caught."

Sam hadn't stopped pacing. "Evidence tamperin' is a serious offence, bu' i's no' unheard of. Bu' the real question is why? Why was the ring switched?"

Rivera rose his hand. "Because if it turned up missing at the crime scene then there'd be a hunt for it."

"Aye, tha's the obvious answer. Bu' it doesnea tell us wha's so special abou' this ring. Look a' the documents: i's estimated worth is no more than $5,000. Annabelle had diamond earrin's far more expensive than tha', bu' they weren't touched. So, again, why? Plus, I'm curious abou' how the mysterious woman with the necklace fits into all of this."

"If this woman turns out to be the murderer, then we could probably assume she was after the ring as well."

"Maybe…"

Julie took the evidence bag and examined the ring. "…You know, I have a friend who works in jewelry. The guy is a connoisseur of vintage fashion. Maybe he could tell us why this ring is so special."

The three of them had to step outside of the FBI office for Julie to get a decent signal on her phone. Once she had one, she placed a call and waited patiently for someone to answer.

"Hi, is Liam available? … Could you tell him that Julie called and she misses his face? … Thank you." She hung up.

Rivera scoffed, "'Julie misses his face?' What grown woman actually says that?"

Suddenly, Julie's phone began to ring with a FaceTime request. She smiled as she answered and the three of them saw the flawless skinned face of a man with a heavily gelled fauxhawk on the screen.

"Oh my God, Julie Russell," he said, "I was *just* thinking the other day how we need to get together for lattes and pedicures. And here you are, calling me. It's a sign!"

Julie smirked, "Hi, Liam."

"How are you, gorgeous girl? Still having secret rendezvous with your mystery man?"

"Maybe, maybe not," she answered nervously.

"Well, why the phone call? You know you're always welcome to come and window shop with me."

"Well, if I wasn't in Chicago, I would."

Liam mocked a gasp, "You went to Chicago without *me*? The home of shopping heaven, The Magnificent Mile, and you went without *me?*"

Julie pouted her lower lip and answered, "I'm sorry, but I'm actually here because of work. I'll make it up to you at Lola's Bistro when I get back."

"Fine, but as long as we order *all* the desserts."

"You've got it," she chuckled. "Listen, I had a question that I know only you can answer."

Liam put his hand over his heart, "Awe, you flatter me. What do you need, sweetie?"

Sam stepped into the camera view and held up the evidence bag with the ring inside. "Wha' can ye tell us abou' this ring?"

Liam suddenly produced a pair of glasses. "Hold it closer to the camera, there you go. Hmmm… it's not new, that's obvious. It's not even vintage. That's definitely an antique. If I had to guess, maybe three-four hundred years old. But I couldn't tell you for certain unless I saw it in person."

Rivera gawked, "Wow, you are good."

"In a lot more ways than one," Liam winked, causing Rivera to clear his throat from the discomfort. "I've seen some pieces from a Renaissance collection that are similar, though. Your best bet would be to talk to Spencer Stewart."

"Who's Spencer Stewart?" Sam asked.

"Only a Renaissance Era historian who has helped to identify antique jewelry and pottery since 1978. He identified an emerald and gold pendant worn by Queen Victoria in a little pawn shop in 1982, and he led an expedition to find a pearl necklace that Louis the XII had given to Mary before he died, which she turned around and gave to her second husband and love of her life. It was the only piece of jewelry her brother, Henry the VIII, hadn't been able to steal from her. And there was another—"

"We get it," Rivera interrupted, "He's the expert. Where is he?"

"Well, you're in luck, spicy stuff. He's the head of the History Department at the University of Chicago."

"Oh yeah? And how come you know about him?"

"Please, any vintage jeweler fanatic knows him. He's never taken me to dinner before, if that's what you're wondering."

Sam couldn't help but chuckle at how uncomfortable Rivera was becoming, but he stopped the flirting and said, "Thank ye for yer time, we'll look into this professor."

"My pleasure. Julie, you call me the minute you get back to Cleveland, you promise?"

"Yeah, I promise," Julie nodded. "Bye, Liam."

"Bye, gorgeous!" He winked before the call disconnected.

"Alrigh'," Sam said, "Le's ge' Simon an' we'll go talk t' this Spencer Stewart."

***

Across town, the team gathered together in front of an enormous building that resembled a cathedral. It had pointed spires on every corner tower and tall, plated glass windows that adorned every level of the sandy-colored building. Lush green ivy scaled the walls clear to the roof; gargoyles perched on every corner of the architecture.

The only modernization was the glass bubble in the middle of the grounds in front of the library that was connected to the lecture hall. The entire campus itself was enormous, and the team had to get directions from a patrolling campus officer. After what felt like an hour-long hike through the grounds and buildings, Sam and the others made their way to the History Department in the central building of the university.

"Anybody else get the vibe that we're walking through a different era?" Simon asked. "Don't get me wrong, it's beautiful. Just…kind of creepy, too."

Julie chuckled.

Rivera laughed, "If this is your idea of creepy, I'm never taking you to see a horror movie."

The inside of the building was just as majestic as the outside. The high stone ceilings had been modernized with floodlights; chandeliers still hung from decorated stone carvings and chains. Enormous portraits of famous attendees of the college hung on the only walls that didn't have stained glass windows. Below the windows, the walls were lined with books, and the floor had hundreds of tables. The air was a mixture of earthy and fresh, perfectly combining the new literature with the old. Though Sam and the others could hear the faint sounds of pages being turned and the scribbling of pencils as the alumni studied and made notes, the foreboding stone seemed to swallow every noise.

Simon gulped and whispered, "See what I mean?"

In the back of the building was a glass door leading to a long hallway. Sam and the others walked through it and were greeted by a young man dressed in a brown tweed three-piece suit, sitting behind a small desk, looking over papers and marking them with a red pencil.

When Sam cleared his throat, the young man looked up. "Are you looking for the lecture?"

"Afraid no'." Sam held up his badge. "I'm Agent McKay, these are Agents Rivera, Russell, an' Abler. We're lookin' fer a Spencer Stewart?"

"Dr. Stewart," the young man pointed out. He stood up and walked around the desk, "And he is in the middle of giving a lecture in his Medieval England Graduate class. Afterwards is European

Culture, and then it's his lunch hour. I can check his schedule to see when he'd be available for an appointment, if you wish."

Rivera stepped forward, "I'm sorry, who are you again?"

"My name is Noah Porter. I'm Dr. Stewart's assistant and protégé," the young man answered, proudly pulling on his suit coat. "After I finish my doctorate program next semester, I'll be Dr. Porter: historian and scholar."

"Good for you, Noah Porter," Rivera said sourly, "But you seem to have misunderstood us: We are FBI agents, and we are in the middle of an investigation and need to speak with Dr. Stewart immediately."

Noah scowled at the four of them. "The Professor hates to have his lectures interrupted, but it ends in about ten minutes. Perhaps you could come back then, and he might have time for you before his next class."

"I think we can wait in the back," Sam answered. "Who knows? Perhaps we'll learn somethin' useful."

Before the young man could stop them, the four of them marched down the hallway towards a room where they could hear a lecture being given.

"Agents, this is unacceptable!" Noah called as he followed them.

Simon turned around and smiled, "Hey, relax buddy. Every college student likes getting a break from class now and then. Even teachers do, too."

Sam spotted a plaque in front of an open door that read Dr. Stewart, History, and walked inside. The classroom was a massive amphitheater: Rows and rows of students were seated and taking notes, if they weren't staring into the pit at a much older, silvery-brown haired man in slacks and a blue button-down. He was pacing around the pit and looking into his audience as he spoke.

"So, as we know, the end of the Great Welsh Rebellions against English power in the early 13th century not only led to the rise in nobility again, but it also created even more problems for the Crown. Can anyone name a few?" A young lady rose her hand and the Professor pointed to her, "Yes?"

"England had lost a third of its population because of the bubonic plague, mostly commoners. And as a result, the nobles felt that they had more right to their claim to the throne, especially because Henry VI was suffering mental breakdowns, and his rule was considered to be weak. The two houses that were most zealous to take the throne were the House of Lancaster and the House of York, which led to another series of wars that lasted for thirty-two years, until all of the male heirs were ultimately wiped out. Because both houses had a rose as their signet, one red and one white, we know this as the War of the Roses. But it should be noted that historians are still unclear today what the main reasons for the wars actually were: whether it was due to social or financial desolation caused by the previous Hundred Years' War, or the bastard feudalism mentality among noblemen."

"Very good," the Professor smiled. "Thank you, Brianna. Yes, to sum it up: The Crown went from one war with most of Great Britain, right into another one within itself. As a result, the Crown's power decreased even more. That is, until Edward IV of House York had claim to the throne. But even then, the war was not over. When did it end?"

"When Henry Tudor won the War of the Roses," a young man shouted.

"Precisely. Henry VII took the Crown away from the house of York, but then turned around and married Elizabeth of York, subsequently ending the conflict between the houses and starting the Tudor Dynasty. Of course, their union resulted in the birth of children, one of which became the next King of England: Henry VIII. As I'm sure everyone in this room is aware, thanks to a certain popular drama series,"—the students chuckled—"Henry VIII was not only known for his six marriages and his ultimate promoting of divorce, but also for appointing himself as the Supreme Head of the Church of England. Because of this, he dissolved convents and monasteries and was ultimately excommunicated."

"Damn! Boy really wanted to play Pope, huh?" another student shouted and earned another chuckle from the assembly.

"Indeed, Jerome, he did," Professor Stewart laughed along. "But we will get into that next week. Until then, I would like you all to study chapter 34 of your textbooks and write a 5,000-word essay with your opinions on how the events of the Hundred Years' War have shaped Medieval England's growth throughout history. Have a good day."

The entire room replied, "Have a good day, Professor," in return and then suddenly the entire arena of students stood up and began to file out of the classroom; Sam and the team had to hug the walls to avoid being trampled. Finally, the classroom was empty other than the silvery-brown haired man at the bottom of the amphitheater packing up his lesson.

Sam walked down to the pit, his team following behind him. "Dr. Stewart?"

The Professor looked up, "Yes?"

"I'm Agent McKay of the FBI, these are Agents Rivera, Russell, an' Abler. We were told ye're an expert in identifyin' antiques."

"Well, I do my best."

"I'm so sorry, Dr. Stewart," Noah said behind them, "I tried to tell them you have lectures all day, but they wouldn't listen."

"It's alright, Noah. They're federal agents; whatever they need takes precedence over my lectures."

Simon turned to Noah and smiled. "See?"

"We'd like for ye t' take a look at a ring an' tell us whether or no' it had any significant value, if ye can."

"Of course. Do you have the ring with you?" Dr. Stewart asked.

Sam handed him the evidence bag and watched the professor closely.

"I don't understand, agents. This is obviously a fake ring."

"How can ye tell?"

"Well, the band for starters. It's plated sterling silver. And the gems are too bright."

"Aye, ye're correct, Doctor. I'm gonna' break the rules an' le' ye in on a secret: The real one was switched with this one, an' we have no idea why."

Dr. Stewart looked at the ring again much more carefully, then his eyebrows began to furrow together. "Noah, would it be possible for you to take over the next lecture?"

"Certainly, Doctor."

"Agents, please allow me to show you my office." Dr. Stewart handed the evidence bag back to Sam, marched up the stairs of the amphitheater, and walked further down the hallway before turning to a wooden door with his name on the front: Dr. Spencer Stewart, History Department. Stewart's office resembled a wing of a museum: There was a massive bookshelf on one wall with a clay pot or mask on every level next to the books. Paintings of historic moments hung all along another wall. In the middle of the room was a simple desk with a laptop sitting on it. The professor walked over to the book shelf, scanned the rows of titles until he came to a large blue leather-bound book. He pulled it out and began to flip through the pages. "Agent McKay, may I see the ring again, please?"

Sam gave it to him without a word, and the Professor held the bag next to the book after he'd stopped on a certain page.

"Dear God...you said this was switched with the real ring?"

Sam was growing more curious by the moment. "Wha' do ye know, Doctor?"

Dr. Stewart turned the book around and showed Sam and the others the page he was looking at: It was a portrait of a man with long hair and a beard, dressed in extravagant gold and grey clothing with a white cloak draping behind him—obviously royalty. His right hand was positioned on his hip while the left rested on the hilt of a sword that was strapped to his hip. And on the left hand was a ruby ring that appeared to match the one in the evidence bag.

"Agents, do you know who this portrait is of?" Dr. Stewart asked, the excitement evident in his voice.

"History was never my strongest subject," Julie answered.

"Ditto," Simon added.

"This is a portrait of King Charles the First of England, painted in 1636. I believe the ring that you are looking for is the one you see in this portrait."

"What makes you so sure?" Rivera asked.

"Allow me to give you a little history lesson," Dr. Stewart beamed. "This portrait that you see here came from the studio of Sir Anthony Van Dyke, a Flemish Baroque artist who was a leading court painter in England after having success in the Netherlands and Italy. With the rise of his fame, he took on many pupils who helped him to produce portrait paintings, as if they were on an assembly line."

"So, everyone wanted a portrait done by this Van Dyke guy?" Simon asked.

"Indeed, and that was mostly due to the fame that the Crown's love of art had brought. King Charles viewed painting as a way to elevate his views of the Monarchy. In fact, he bought a collection that a Duke was forced to sell, in order to bring foreign painters over to England. Van Dyke sent a few of his works to the Crown and was ultimately commissioned by the King."

"Verra interestin', Doctor, bu' tha' dosnea tell us anythin' abou' this ring."

"You're right, I apologize. Well, this portrait that you see here came from Van Dyke's studio, however it was rumored, I would dare say proven, that the portrait itself was done by one of Van Dyke's students: a Scottish painter named George Jamesone. Jamesone's style was so close to that of his teacher, he was known as the Van Dyke of Scotland. Charles the First liked the portrait so much that he gave the very ring off of his hand to the painter."

Julie spoke up, "Sam, didn't Lisa say her ancestors were part of clans? Clans…Scottish, right?"

"Aye," Sam nodded, "Di' this Jamesone have any children?"

"Oh, yes, many. But, unfortunately most of them died. Only one has been confirmed to continue living, a daughter named Mary. He died when she was very young. She actually inherited much of her father's artistic skills in the form of cross-stitching. She made many tapestries in her lifetime."

"Mary," Julie beamed, "The name of Lisa's ancestor! Same name as the daughter of George Jamesone! They have to be the same woman!"

"Perhaps, bu' there's no way t' prove tha' this is the same ring in tha' paintin', is there?"

"I'm an expert in history and artifacts, Agent McKay. Obviously, I can't tell you for certain that this is exactly the same ring without looking at the real one and studying it, but I can give you my best educated guess. There are many stories and rumors surrounding the Scottish artist, but this is the most credible one, which has been noted in many historical accounts. King Charles gave his ring to the artist as thanks for the portrait. George Jamesone was the Van Dyke of Scotland, and, as a matter of fact, the only Renaissance era artist in all of Scotland."

"Doctor, what would you say this ring is worth?" Rivera asked, "Just give us your best guess."

"If the real ring is legitimately the ring of King Charles the first, it's priceless. There are not many people in the world even aware of the existence of this ring, agents. Of those who are, most have assumed it was lost with time, peddled off to a stranger, maybe even dropped in the ocean."

Julie chuckled at the reference.

"So wha' ye're tellin' us is only someone who knew the significance of the ring would go to the trouble of stealin' it?" Sam asked.

"Exactly," Dr. Stewart nodded again.

"Wait a minute," Simon piped in. "Does that mean we're looking for a treasure hunter?"

"I's possible," Sam nodded before he turned his attention back to the professor, "Doctor, can ye tell me if the name Annabelle Matheson rings any bells?"

"I'm sorry, but no," Dr. Stewart shook his head. "Why? Was this hers?"

Sam nodded.

"I've never met anyone by that name, but I can check my contacts and appointments to see if I'm wrong."

"We would appreciate that, Doctor," Rivera said.

The professor rounded the desk and opened up his laptop. Simon walked over and kept his eyes trained on the computer as the man typed.

"...I'm sorry, no. I've never had a consultation with anyone named Annabelle Matheson. I'm looking at my guest lecture logs now and...that name doesn't appear on any of the registries."

"Thank you for checking anyway, Doctor," Simon smiled.

"Aye, we won't take up anymore of yer time." Sam turned towards the door, his team behind him.

"Agents?" Dr. Stewart called before they left. "Just so you're aware: Matheson is one of the oldest clan names in Scottish history, dating back to the 14th century."

"Yeah, we learned that earlier today," Julie nodded.

"Of course, you mentioned that. It's just that you're looking for someone who clearly knew about a ring that had Scottish ties, and it was handed down through a Scottish family. I just thought it might be important to know."

Sam and the others looked at each other quizzically before thanking the professor again and leaving the building. Deciding they wouldn't need the FBI's facilities, they grabbed a pizza and headed back to their hotel.

While Sam kept thinking about everything the professor had told them, Julie and Rivera were studying the evidence photos, and Simon was clacking away on his computer.

"Boss," the young man sighed, "I don't see anyone on the suspect list that even has a history of stealing gummy bears, let alone a known treasure hunter."

"Well, I think the professor's theory of looking for a treasure hunter might be correct," Rivera said. "Annabelle Matheson had a lot of insured jewelry in her apartment, but according to every insurance investigation all of the pieces were accounted for. Geeze, there's even a necklace on here worth $175,000!"

Simon whistled, "That's more than what I make in three years!"

Sam held up the evidence bag with the ring and kept staring at it.

"What are you thinking, boss?" Julie asked.

"The artist George Jamesone... Mary Jamesone... I've heard those names before."

"Well, yeah, you must have," Rivera chuckled. "We all had to learn American History growing up; doesn't Scotland teach Scottish history?"

"War an' political history mostly, rarely art. Unless ye go to Uni fer tha', which I did not," Sam rubbed his chin. "...Simon, do a search on thefts to anythin' George Jamesone related."

Simon typed on his laptop furiously. "...All hail the curious Sampson McKay! It's the craziest thing, there have been six reported thefts of paintings as far back as forty years. Then nothing for almost ten. Recently, starting back in 2002, there are two paintings that have been reported stolen: one in New York, and another in Quebec. No leads on who stole them other than a card left behind with the initials C.W."

"Seriously?" Julie asked incredulously. "The thief actually left behind their card?"

"That happens more than you think, Jules," Rivera said. "The underground world of thieves only knows each other by their codes, methods, or signatures. It's their way of communicating with each other and potential clients who want their services, 'I'm the best because I didn't get caught.'"

"How many paintin's of George Jamesone's exist?" Sam continued.

Again, Simon typed. "A total of fifteen have been officially accounted for by galleries and associations—eight of which I've already mentioned—and another two were recently discovered to be

51

forgeries. But it looks like three more were reported to be destroyed. Get this, all of them were destroyed in fires."

"But not a single fire?" Rivera asked.

"Nope, three different fires in three different places and at three different times. The first one goes as far back as 1983 in Illinois, and the most recent one also happened in Illinois in 2017. All of the investigation reports say they were started with an accelerant of some kind."

"That sounds suspiciously like an M.O. to me," Julie said.

"I agree," Sam nodded. "Wha' abou' unaccounted for paintin's, anyway to track those?"

"Not a chance," Simon shook his head. "If it's not officially documented with the artist in any gallery or association registries, I couldn't tell you where to look."

"Annabelle Matheson obviously didn't know what kind of ring she had. Who's to say how many people in the world are holding on to a painting that's worth a fortune, and they have no idea about it?" Julie asked.

Rivera nodded. "Ironic, isn't it? These associations are supposed to help protect artwork by keeping it accounted for, but by bringing the extra attention, it makes the pieces easier to target."

"One-eighty here, but it's something interesting," Simon added. "There's a gala happening next weekend at the Hyde Park Art Center. One of the exhibits is labeled 'Renaissance Fare.' And it looks like there will be a painting by 'The Van Dyke of Scotland' among the collection."

Sam furrowed his eyebrows and began to pace the room.

"Do you think there's a connection, Sam?" Rivera asked.

"Me gut is tellin' me there might be. Wha' are the odds of paintin's an' a ring belongin' to the verra artist tha' made them all bein' stolen? Perhaps our treasure hunter is after specific treasure."

"So, you think it might be worth keeping an eye on this painting?"

"Aye," he nodded. "In fact, I think it might be worth attendin' this Gala. Perhaps our thief might make an appearance there."

Simon scoffed, "Boss, that's quite a stretch. And tickets to this thing are *not* cheap." "Then I guess we bettar figure out how Evan can convince Copper t' cut us a check," Sam replied before taking an enormous bite of his pizza.

Chapter Five

Hyde Park Art Center reminded Sam of a school more than an art center. Several classrooms and wings broke off from the main halls where various paintings and sculptures were on display. As if standing in the middle of the heavily populated museum wasn't uncomfortable enough, Sam was doing all that he could to stand in the corner and out of the direct heat of the bright floodlights. He had to resist every urge to adjust his bow tie. Despite all of these inconveniences, he was sure to keep the George Jamesone painting (which was the centerpiece of the Renaissance wing) in his peripheral vision.

"You're a hunk in a tux, boss," Julie teased in his earpiece.

"Haud yer wheesht," Sam gritted under his breath. "Damn thing's so bloody tight around m' balls, I could sing soprana'!"

"It was the best I could find," Simon answered, unsuccessfully hiding a snigger. "Evan was only able to convince Copper to give us the ticket money and a teeny bit extra. We had to make due."

"Aye, I get it, bu' why the hell am I the one attendin' this thing?"

Rivera answered, "Because our main focus tonight is anyone particularly interested in the George Jamesone painting. You're a Scotsman. If anybody should have particular interest, it would be you."

"And you need to look like a potential buyer," Julie added. "The tux adds to that."

"Just remember to blend in by tossing a little cash towards the charity. It'll look rude if you don't even participate in the whole reason for this event."

"Aye, I got the check in m' pocket. When it comes time fer the biddin', I'll buy one of these necklaces or somethin'. Jus' feel like a nance."

"I gotta' say," Simon piped up. "I remember seeing all over social media how people were joking that after the virus scare was over, there was going to be the biggest bash combining all of the major holidays and birthdays that we had to miss. Somebody decided to take it a step further by planning a gala to support a relief fund for their community."

"Tragedy brings people together, Simon," Julie answered.

"Oh, I know. I'm just saying, it's also a smart business tactic on the Art Center's part. This party has to be completely packed with people. Pretty ironic after we needed to keep our distance from each other for so long."

"Indeed," Sam interrupted. "An' I need t' look fer one specific person, so I'd appreciate it if ye lo' could keep it quiet an' focus on the cameras while I keep m' eyes open."

Glancing all around the exhibit, Sam carefully examined all of the attendees. There were groups of people talking, admiring some of the different artwork that was on display, and everyone had a glass of something in their hands. Nobody was acting peculiar or otherwise out of the norm. Though he could see the bait from where he stood, hardly anyone had stopped to look at the self-portrait by the Scottish artist. Most of the crowd was more interested in the modern artwork on display or the hand-crafted jewelry pieces that were being auctioned off at the end of the night. Sam began to wonder if attending the pretentious party was a waste of time.

"Relax, boss, we've got eyes all over this place. So far everyone is just talking, socializing, and drinking their expensive cocktails," Simon said.

"Speaking of," Rivera added. "Will you loosen up and get a drink? You are so tense; you look like a security guard. You need to look like a guest."

Like magic, a waiter walked by, carrying a tray with glasses of champagne. Sam took one of the flutes and a gulp of the very sweet, bubbly liquor. *I'd give anythin' fer a scotch righ' abou' now,* he thought to himself and took another gulp.

"I see you have a particular interest in our Renaissance Fare exhibit?"

Sam turned to see a shorter, older woman with shoulder length silver hair, red lipstick, and glasses standing next to him.

"Aye, ye migh' say tha'."

She smiled and offered her hand, "I'm Justine Ingers, the assistant curator of this exhibit. And you are?"

He accepted and shook her hand, "Sampson McKay."

"How are you enjoying yourself this evening, Mr. McKay?"

"Verra well, thank ye."

"I'm glad to hear that," she smiled. "I wondered if you were a member of our fair community, but your accent tells me you're a guest in Chicago."

Sam gulped, "Aye, Chicago's no' me hometown. I'm here on behalf of...someone influential. He's verra much interested in makin' a contribution t' the city's efforts in providin' relief from the pandemic disastar."

"How very kind of him. Is this person anyone I might have heard of?"

"I doubt it, he prefers t' keep a low profile."

"Well, please pass along my and the Center's sincerest gratitude, won't you?"

"I will, aye," Sam nodded.

"Do you have any questions regarding the bidding that I might be able to help answer?"

"No, I think I got it, Ms. Ingers."

"Very well, then. Enjoy the gala, Mr. McKay," she smiled and walked off in another direction, a faint fragrance that reminded Sam of green apples wafting behind her.

Sam exhaled, grateful that the woman had made her exit before she could probe him with more detailed questions.

"Great job, you weren't suspicious at all," Rivera chuckled through the earpiece.

"Shu-up," Sam growled, "The biddin' is abou' t' start. Have ye go' yer contraption runnin', Abler?"

"We're good to go here, boss," Simon said. "Ready for the bug deposit."

Sam carefully waded through the moving crowd towards the portrait of the artist himself. Reaching into his pocket, he felt for the tiny tracking bug Simon had built and removed the sticky covering with his thumbnail. After glancing around to make sure he wasn't being watched, he quickly leaned forward and stuck the bug on the underside of the frame before leaning away just as quickly. No one around him seemed to care, so he walked away from the exhibit and towards the main hall where the bidding was taking place.

"Aaaaannnnnddddd there's the signal," Simon said cheerily. "If somebody tries to swipe the painting, I'll be able to track them!"

"Great," Sam muttered under his breath, "I'm off t' buy a necklace. Then I'm gettin' the hell out of this ge'up."

***

Sam and the team were sitting in their SUV in front of the apartment building that was across the street from the Hyde Park Art Center. Rivera in the driver's seat, Sam in the passenger, and Julie and Simon in the back, they had been sitting there since the event began to disperse around 1:00 a.m., staring at the building, waiting for anything fishy to happen. The time read 3:57 a.m., and everyone but Rivera was doing all that they could to stay awake. Simon had suggested playing I Spy but was told to knock it off after picking something from the security camera feed he had showing on his computer. Other than the cars that belonged to the tenants in the apartments, there was not a soul on the road.

"How in the world do you do this for a living, meat-sicle?" Simon whined. "I can barely keep my eyes open, much less do a sufficient stakeout."

"I told you to take a power nap earlier," Rivera snickered.

"I *did* take a nap earlier, for all the good it did."

"A power nap and sleeping in are two different things, genius."

Simon yawned in reply.

"Four in the morning and still nothing," Julie said. "Maybe there isn't a connection."

Sam reluctantly nodded, "I'm startin' to agree with ye... bu' I want t' give it a few more minutes."

"Should we try driving around to the other side of the building?" Rivera asked.

"No, I donnea want'a risk us scarin' somebody off. Everythin' still lookin' alrigh' in there, Simon?"

"Not a creature is stirring, not even a mouse, boss," Simon answered sleepily. "Even the security guard is sleeping like a baby in his office. And, for the record, I wish I was him right about now."

"I know this place isn't exactly the Met, but you'd think with a few famous pieces in there, they'd at least invest a little towards making sure it's always safe," Rivera said in an annoyed tone. "A sleeping security guard? That's pitiful."

"It's a community art center," Julie said. "They probably got lucky in getting ahold of the pieces they did. Most of what they show here is contemporary new artists or stuff from their student workshops."

"They're not completely without protection," Simon added. "They've got a decent security system that puts the whole building on lockdown if it's tripped. And each of these paintings has an armed trip wire attached to them. If somebody tries to steal one, the wire will alert the authorities and trigger the lockdown."

"Trip wires are for amateurs," Rivera scoffed. "I know it's probably all this facility could afford; I'm just saying that more detailed security would be the thing I'd do if I had expensive art sitting around."

"Hey, shut up for a second!" Simon blurted out and began typing on his laptop furiously.

Sam turned around, intently interested in what the lanky computer genius had found. "Wha' is it?"

"I just saw a blip in the security camera feed… yup! The feed has been hacked!"

Everyone was alert.

"Can ye pull up the real feed?"

"Working on it now, just give me a second. Looks like a standard hacking device that they planted in the building's computer systems; it won't take long…holy crap! Sam, you were right!" Simon turned his laptop screen around and pointed to one box in the corner. Three men in black and ski masks were quietly tiptoeing through the art center until they reached the Renaissance Fare wing. "Should we call Chicago PD?"

Sam shook his head, "No' yet. First, le's see if they're after wha' we think."

The car was deathly silent as the team stared at Simon's laptop; the thieves reached the George Jamesone portrait and gently pulled the painting a few inches away from the wall. Then one of them produced a pair of clippers from their pocket. Sam smirked.

"Okay, *now* we call Chicago PD." Sam turned and addressed each of them, "Simon, ye stay here an' keep tabs on tha' paintin'. Julie an' Rivera, with me."

While Simon whipped out his phone, Sam, Julie, and Rivera climbed out of the car and withdrew their guns before racing towards the building.

"Chicago PD's on their way," Simon said through the earpiece, "And it looks like the Beagle Boys are heading to the back of the building with their loot. You better hurry!"

"We donnea have time t' run to the back of the buildin'. We'll have t' go in through the front an' trip the alarm. Tha'll at least lock down the buildin' an' wake the security guard."

"What are we gonna' do?" Rivera asked, "Pick the lock?"

Before Sam could answer, Julie had already raised her gun and fired at the glass doors three times. The bullets shattered the glass and the quiet night air was filled with the sound of ringing alarm bells. Sam chuckled as Julie jumped over the broken glass without care, and he and Rivera quickly followed her. The three of them raced through the open hallways towards the back of the art center where they could hear male voices arguing with each other.

"Open the door!"

"I can't! It's locked tight!"

"Then break it down!"

Sam and the others rounded the corner with their guns up. "Freeze! Donnea move!"

The thieves tried to scatter; Julie fired her gun again and hit one of them in the leg, Rivera followed one, and Sam followed the one that was holding the painting until they came to a dead end.

"Stop, now!" Sam bellowed over the loud alarm. "Donnea make me shoot ye!"

The thief listened and carefully placed the painting on the ground. Raising his hands, he slowly turned around for Sam to see. Walking forward slowly, cuffs in his hand, Sam sighed in relief to hear the sirens of the Chicago PD in the background. Within moments, the museum was swarming with police officers who quickly took control of the situation. Once Sam and his team had their badges and credentials checked (which they could tell was completely out of spite, given they had met most of the officers the day before), they stood outside of the building and watched as the perpetrators were escorted to the police cars. The neighborhood was already beginning to flood with bystanders and press outlets as one by one, the thieves were unmasked: all three of them male, mid- to late-thirties. Sam paid close attention to the one that he had chased. He had a hunch that he was the leader of the group by the way he carried himself: quiet but unafraid to look the officers in the eye. More than curious to find out more about the thief, Sam almost didn't notice Captain Knight marching over to him and his team. He could tell the pot-bellied man was more than perturbed by the expression on his face.

"How did you know something would happen?" Knight demanded.

"Wow, rude much?" Simon said under his breath.

"We found a connection in th' murder," Sam answered the Captain. "Annabelle Matheson's ring is connected t' the paintin' those bampots were tryin' t' steal."

"And that told you that a robbery would be taking place here?" the Captain scoffed.

"Hey," Rivera argued. "It doesn't matter how we knew; the point is we stopped it from happening."

"Yeah, at the cost of a door! Who the hell destroyed that?"

"I did," Julie stepped forward. "You can relax, Captain Knight, the FBI will cover the damages."

"Of course, it will," the Captain sneered at her. "But who will cover the overtime for my officers? Thanks to you, they'll be patrolling this street up and down for the next few weeks at the Center's insistence! As if law enforcement isn't under enough scrutiny as it is!"

The paunchy man turned and stomped away before any of them could answer. Sam rolled his eyes and turned back to his team. "Make sure those men are taken t' headquarters, I donnea want t' chance tha' whoever switched the evidence catches on t' wha' we've found."

Rivera nodded and walked off towards the police cars. Sam noticed the security guard being escorted out of the building by two paramedics, all the while rubbing his head. Curious, Sam walked over with Julie right behind him.

"When did all of you get here?" the old man asked very groggily. "Didn't the party end just a few minutes ago?"

"Sir, can you tell us what your name is?"

"My name's Bart Creeves, I work the nightshift here," he answered as he was seated in the back of the ambulance.

Sam walked over. "Excuse me, FBI. Mr. Creeves, were ye hit on the head?"

"No, I don't think so. It sure feels like it, though, with how it's pounding."

Sam furrowed his eyes. "Can ye tell us wha' happened when ye started yer shift this evenin'?"

"I finished my walkthrough of the building after everyone had finished cleaning up the gala, went back to my office to keep an eye on the cameras, poured myself a cup of coffee, and then the next thing I knew I was being woken up by these guys." The old man looked at Sam with worry. "Please don't tell the curator I was sleeping on the job. I *never* sleep on the job. I must have just been very tired this evening."

"You didn't hear the alarm?" Julie asked.

"The alarm?" the old man asked in confusion. "You mean somebody broke in?"

Just then, they all heard someone yelling and looked to see a man wading his way through the crowd towards the building. The police officers guarding the perimeter stopped him until he bellowed, "Let me through! I'm the curator!"

Sam walked over. "I's alrigh', fellas. I'll handle him. I'm Agent McKay, sir. Ye say ye're the curator of the buildin'?"

"Sort of," he answered and showed his security card to Sam. "I'm Justin Ingers, the assistant curator. My boss called me when we found out someone had tried to steal one of the pieces from the exhibit."

"Wait, *Justin* Ingers?" Sam asked perplexed, "Were ye a' the party this evenin'?"

"No, I've been feeling a little under the weather so I thought it best if I stay home. You know, with the pande—"

"Do ye have a wife or sister named Justine?"

"What? What does that have to do with the robbery?"

"Answer the question, please!" Sam demanded.

The curator looked shocked at the outburst but quickly answered, "No, no I don't even know anyone by the name of Justine."

Sam turned and bolted into the building; Julie was right behind him. They ran past the officers until they came to the scene where Sam had the standoff with the thief: The painting was gone.

"Hey, you!" Julie asked the forensics experts that were still combing through the crime scene, "Where is the painting?"

"We gave it to the officer after we finished processing it."

"What officer?"

"I don't know her name. Does anybody know the name of the officer that took the painting?"

The other experts all shook their heads and answered no.

Sam turned to one of the nearest cops and demanded, "Find ou' who in yer unit has the paintin', now!"

The officer did as instructed and spoke into his shoulder radio, but his face went pale when everyone responded that they did not have the painting.

Sam spoke into his earpiece. "Simon, where's the paintin'?!"

"What are you talking about, boss? It's still in the art center. You're practically standing on top of it."

Sam looked all around him until somebody shouted, they had found something unusual. Looking over, the expert held Simon's discarded bug in his hand.

"It was attached to this," the expert lifted up a business card, "The only thing written on it is C.W."

"Shit!" Sam yelled. "Tha' woman claimin' t' be the curator! She's C.W., an' she took the paintin'! An' now, we have no idea where the hell it is!"

***

"So, what you're saying is, the only lead you thought you might get is already gone." Even through the phone, Belinda Copper's voice didn't lose any of her authority.

Sam sighed at the director's infuriatingly level but angry tone; after interviewing every one of the staff on duty and getting absolutely no useful information from any of them, Sam, Julie, and Rivera had moved on to interrogating the robbers.

"Well, no' the *only* lead, Copper. We ran the prints on our apprehended thieves an' they're in the system."

"Who are they?"

"Two of them are brothers known as Harley an' Gilbert Franks, recently released from Statesville Prison; their only charge was burglary, sentenced t' four years in 2017. Because of the pandemic, an' their good behavior, they were released in April, six months early. Bu' the one I'm particularly interested in is Aiden Marcus. I think he's the leader."

"What do we know about him?"

"Thirty-seven years old, served time fer aggravated assault, an' has ties t' the Jaimes clan: Chicago's Scottish mob. He's no' a thief, he's an enforcer. Bu' he was the one callin' the shots an', of the three of them, he's the only one tha' doesnea seem t' care tha' he's been caught. No' t' mention, the other two rolled on him, an' said he hired them fer this job. I believe them."

"And what about this mysterious woman at the gala, do you have any ideas on who she is and what she wants?"

"There wasnea any useable prints on the card left a' the scene, bu' I think the fake curator, C.W., an' the mysterious 911 caller are one and the same.

"What makes you so sure?"

"An anonymous tip from a female caller abou' Mrs. Matheson, a mysterious woman bein' a' the crime scene, a woman posin' as the curator an' then an officer? They all have one thing in common: the gender. Wha' are the odds i's *not* her?"

"Well, if you're right, she's doing a hell of a job making us look like a circus. Bronson has already called me to complain that you four are doing nothing short of embarrassing his house."

Sam rolled his eyes but took a deep breath before he answered, "I promise, we're doin' everythin' we can t' find out who she is."

"I'm glad to hear it, McKay, but get this situation under control before Chicago's Director decides to take over our investigation. The Attorney General is riding my ass just as hard as his, and I don't like having my name drawn through the mud."

"Yes, ma'am. I can assure ye, t'won't be."

Copper hung up without another word. Sam walked back towards the FBI's observation room where Simon and Julie were watching a screen that showed Rivera at work interrogating Aiden Marcus.

"What did Copper say?" Julie asked.

"T' ge' the situation under control," Sam rubbed his face; the bags under his eyes giving away how tired he was feeling. He stifled a yawn and looked at their suspect; Aiden Marcus looked haggard by the state of his unkempt beard and hair. The mug shot they'd pulled up from his previous arrests showed him much cleaner and more refined, but not any less menacing. With the state of him, he looked almost like a madman on the loose, despite his emotionless face. "He say anythin'?"

"Derrick's been working him for at least two hours and nothing; he hasn't asked for a lawyer, didn't state his name for the record, he hasn't even coughed."

"And in other news, the lab confirmed that the poor night guard drank dosed coffee, that's why he was out of it all night," Simon added.

Just then, Rivera stood up and walked out of the camera's sight. A minute later, he came through the door of the observation room looking more annoyed than usual. "It's going to be a while before we'll get anything out of him. We can try putting him in solitary, see if that softens him up a bit."

"Do it." Sam turned to Simon. "Di' ye ge' anythin' off the equipment they used?"

"Nope. Like I said before, they did pretty standard stuff: hacking the cameras, and forensics found a bug in the curator's office. But given the fact that the boss man in there chose to hire a couple of amateurs to steal a not-so-high security painting, I really wasn't expecting to find much anyway."

"Wha' about the rest of the buildin's systems? Is there anythin' tha' looks out of the ordinary? Anythin' a' all tha' suggests there was more than these guys after the paintin'?"

"Nothing, boss, and I checked twice. Whoever C.W. is, she's good. I mean like *really* good."

Sam paced the room, rubbing his face. "Aye, she is."

"Let's not forget ballsy," Julie added. "She could have stayed out of the way the whole time she was at the Gala, but she *had* to go up and introduce herself to you. What was she trying to do? Rub it in your face that you can't catch her?"

"Tha's mos' likely it, yes."

Rivera's phone started ringing. "Agent Rivera." By the way his eyebrows furrowed together, Sam was more than curious about what news he had. "...Okay, thanks Remy. The detectives just finished searching the Towers. They found the hat and the necklace we saw in the security feed in the apartment of a Mrs. Violet Winston, and they found the same hat with a bleached blonde wig and the same necklace in a bag stuck in the garbage shoot, only one of the beads is missing from that necklace. Detective Remy said Mrs. Winston is a bleached blonde and about the same build and height as the woman in the video."

Julie gawked. "Are you saying C.W. dressed up as Mrs. Winston?"

"Yup, and she even went as far as to buy knock-off fashion so nobody would think twice about her."

"Geeze, this lady is *really* good!" Simon gushed.

"Yeah, but she messed up this time," Rivera continued. "They found a little blood on the fake stuff, most likely from Annabelle. Forensics is going to take a deeper look to see if there's any other DNA they can match in the system."

"She disguised herself as a resident of the Towers, a curator, an' as a cop!" Sam sighed, "She really is makin' us out t' be fools. Bu' here's wha' ge's me: She stole the paintin' right in the middle of somebody else bein' caught fer the actual crime...which suggests she knew it would be stolen in the first place."

"Considering Marcus's tactics of trying to steal it weren't very sophisticated, I doubt he'd have any idea who C.W. is," Rivera said. "And he doesn't seem like the type to brag about his plans to just anybody."

"Ye may be righ', bu' obviously somebody wants...wha'ever it is, they want enough t' hire both professionals an' amateurs. Perhaps we migh' ge' somethin' off his phone tha'll tell us who's interested. Simon?"

Simon nodded and turned to leave when his phone pinged with a text message alert. "...So, I've got good news and bad news."

"Bad news first."

"Malcolm knows that I'm FBI and has stated I can never contact him again."

"An' wha's the good news?"

"He says in exchange for immunity from any and everything, he's willing to tell me who he sold the bump key to."

"Tell him I'll give him immunity fer the past, bu' no any further illegal activity."

Simon looked uneasy, but he texted back and waited. A heavily pregnant pause hung in the air, everyone could almost hear each other's hearts beating as they hoped for this one lead.

Finally, Simon got another text and he heaved a sigh of relief. "He says you've got a deal... Geeze, for somebody who's never been seen before, this lady thief gets around. C.W. bought the key and had it mailed to a student P.O. box...at the University of Chicago."

"Can ye find out who it belongs to?"

Simon scoffed. "Please, that's child's play." Pulling out his laptop, he clacked away on his computer furiously until a picture of a handsome, well-dressed young man with a big smile showed up. "... It's registered to a kid named Brendan Palmers the Third. His dad is Brendan Palmers the Second, a partner at Palmers and Young law firm in Chicago, which has been around for almost a hundred years. Brendan number three is a senior majoring in Pre-Law, and he's set up to follow in the family footsteps and go straight into the University of Chicago's Law School after graduation...which, according to the institution's records, he was initially denied acceptance for until four weeks ago."

"Sounds to me like somebody greased some wheels for him," Rivera said. "But I don't think his father had anything to do with it."

"All he had to do was deliver a bump key, and he could continue to live up to the family legacy," Julie nodded. "Something tells me he'll try to cite an illegal search charge against us."

"Well, perhaps he'll cooperate if we threaten t' tell daddy tha' he couldnea ge' into law school on his own," Sam smirked.

Chapter Six

Monday

Sam and his team walked through the Cathedral-esque building at the University of Chicago; Simon hacked into Brendan Jr.'s class schedule and learned that the boy was currently in another History course that was being taught by Dr. Spencer Stewart. The team headed over to the college immediately. Walking through the glass doors at the end of the enormous library, they were greeted with the unpleasant Noah Porter, who barely spared them a glance over the stack of papers he was grading.

"I suppose it wouldn't matter if I told you that Dr. Stewart is in the middle of his Witnessing Medieval Evil lecture, would it, agents?"

"Actually, we're not here for him this time," Rivera answered. "We're here to talk to a student of his: Brendan Palmers III."

The immaculately dressed young man seemed somewhat relaxed by the answer. "If you wouldn't mind waiting here, I can go and fetch Mr. Palmers for you."

"Fine," Sam answered. "We'll wait here."

Porter walked towards the classroom and returned almost immediately with the same handsome young man Sam and the others had seen on Simon's laptop. Leaving the boy with the agents, he returned to his desk and the stack of papers.

"Brendan Palmers?" Sam asked.

"Yes, that's me," the young man answered quietly.

Sam and the others flashed their badges. "Abou' two months ago, ye received a package tha' wasnea meant for ye. We'd like t' know who ye gave it to."

Brendan shifted back and forth on the balls of his feet and cleared his throat. "Um...I'm not sure what you're talking about. I get packages all the time from my mom."

"This one would've been small an' thin."

"No, I don't recall anything like that."

"Then maybe you could tell us how you all of a sudden got into law school four weeks ago," Julie said, causing the boy's eyes to widen in alarm.

"I got in through hard work and study."

"That's interesting, because the University of Chicago Law School only has a 15% acceptance rate of straight-A students. According to your transcripts, you're at about a B+ average. That's not quite enough to make the mark, is it?"

"They made a special exception for me."

"Meaning somebody fudged the records for you for just a small favor?" Rivera asked with a smirk.

Brendan swallowed and sweat appeared on his forehead. "Please, can we go discuss this somewhere a little more private?"

Sam nodded, and the group followed the young man out of the building to a bench next to a small pond completely surrounded by lush trees and grass. For a moment, Sam felt like he was back in Scotland. The place was so green and rustic.

"Listen, my dad went to Chicago Law, and so did my grandfather and my great-grandfather. None of them had *any* trouble getting admitted. Do you have any idea how much pressure I'm under to live up to the Palmers name? Not to mention how pissed my dad would be if I didn't get in."

"So ye go' a little help, is tha' wha' ye're tryin' t' tell us?" Sam probed.

Brendan sighed. "Just... promise that you won't tell my dad, and I'll tell you everything. Okay?"

"Tha' depends on wha' ye know abou' the sender."

"I don't know anything, I swear! Look, I'm taking 28 credits this semester and busting my ass doing extra credit for every one of them, but it still wasn't enough. Then two months ago, I go to pick up my mail from my box, and I've got a note that says 'I'll get you into law school' with a number underneath it. I was burned out and desperate, okay? So, I thought, what harm could it do? I called the number."

"An' who answered it?"

"A weird, distorted, mechanical voice. Kind of like Darth Vader's. Anyways, the voice tells me that they'll take care of everything and get me into Chicago Law. All I have to do is look for a certain envelope and deliver it someplace when the time is right. A few weeks later, I get the envelope, and I call the number again. The voice tells me to take it to Mount Olive Cemetery and leave it in a flower basket that's sitting on a headstone with the name Lopez on it. They even gave me directions to get to the headstone. Next day, I get a call from the head of admissions telling me my application was accepted, and I start Law School next semester."

"Do ye still have the numbar an' address?"

"Yeah, sure," Brendan withdrew his wallet and pulled out the slip of paper he'd mentioned with the addition of an address written below. "I thought it might be a good idea to hang onto it, just in case. But the number's disconnected now, I already tried."

"We'll take it anyway," Sam said, taking the paper from the boy, "Alrigh', fer now we donnea tell yer da'. Bu' if there's anythin' ye're no' tellin' us an' we find it, we'll make sure he knows everythin'. Is tha' understood?"

"I swear, man, that's all that I know. If I could think of anything else that might be important, I would tell you. Honestly."

Rivera handed him a business card, "Well, in case you do remember something else, you call us. Got it?"

"Yeah, sure. Can I go back to class, now?"

Sam and the others nodded, and the young man raced away from them and back to the building.

"With how much cover C.W. has taken to keep her identity a secret, I doubt we'll find anything at the cemetery. Hell, she probably just picked Lopez at random," Rivera said.

"Aye, I agree," Sam nodded. "Bu' we're gonna go check it out all the same, maybe there's a security camera tha' gives us a look at'er. An' while we do tha', Simon, I want ye to see if ye can trace the phone."

Simon cleared his throat. "Yeah, judging by Debra Ocean's smarts, it was most likely a burner phone and we're already out of luck."

"Could ye triangulate where it was bein' used?"

"Within a three-mile radius, *maybe,*" Simon sighed, "If I get lucky, I *might* be able to narrow it down to one."

***

Just as Sam, Rivera, and Julie expected, the cemetery proved to be completely unhelpful; the only security footage available was inside of the main building where the caretakers were. The headstone belonging to Mr. and Mrs. Lopez was surrounded by more headstones with unfamiliar names, a Columbarium wall was behind it, and it faced a large outdoor public mausoleum which didn't carry any security cameras either. As they had finished walking the grounds, Simon was able to get a triangulation on the burner phone after all, and their canvass was narrowed down to one mile between East and West Beverly, right smack in the middle of Chicago. After picking up Simon from the motel, the team made their way to the middle of the triangulated spot and parked on a road lined with stately homes surrounded by fences.

"So, what exactly is the plan here?" Simon asked. "Knock on every door and ask if anybody has the initials C.W.?"

"Simon's right," Julie added. "We don't know exactly what C.W. really looks like, she could be anywhere."

"Aye, anno. … Fer now, jus' knock on every house an' ask t' speak t' the owners. Tell 'em ye're performin' a survey t' see if the residents feel comfortable with their police force or no'. If any of them are middle-aged women, write down their name an' address, an' we'll look into them later. Perhaps I'll recognize one of 'em."

"It's a slim idea, Sam," Rivera said.

"Ye go' a bettar one?"

"I guess not. But it's barely after normal work hours; chances are hardly anybody's home yet."

"I'm all for waiting in the air-conditioned car for another hour or so," Simon said, earning a look from Julie.

"Come on, you big baby, being in the sunlight will be good for you," she snickered.

"I'm *black*, Julie, my people were practically born under the sunlight."

Julie laughed before she changed the subject. "Alright, Rivera and I will take East Beverly, you guys take West. Meet back here in two hours?"

"Aye, good luck."

"You, too."

While Rivera and Julie walked towards the south end of the street, Sam and Simon walked to the north corner and began working their way through each house. No one was home at the first two, and the next was a retired old man who kept them occupied for twenty minutes ranting about how corrupt the police were and how his rights were being squashed. The next three were occupied by families who held the opposite opinion of appreciating the police. So far, no one appeared familiar to Sam. Then they came to the last house on top of a small hill. Positioned in the middle of a well-cared-for park consisting of trees and shrubs, the house was grey blue with white trim, complete with a wraparound porch and pillars. It resembled a southern plantation. Although it was enormous in size, it wasn't quite big enough to be considered a mansion.

Sam rang the doorbell next to the screen door. When no one answered, he tried to knock instead.

Simon snickered. "We're off to a good start, aren't we? Two empty homes, three magazine cover soccer moms, and a cantankerous old hippy thinking we're here to spy on him."

"Ye know, Simon, ye complain abou' as much as my son. An' I've found tha' hard work changes his attitude. Should I think of a few chores for ye t' do until yers improves?"

Simon looked down and muttered, "No, boss."

"Verra well, then le's keep at it. We've go' another half a mile of homes t' check."

Just as they starting walking down the long, tree lined driveway, a dark grey Mercedes Benz pulled up. The passenger window rolled down and the driver turned out to be none other than Dr. Spencer Stewart.

"Agents? Is there something I can help you with?"

"Is this yer home, Dr. Spencer?"

"Well, the paperwork says it is, but I'm honestly hardly ever here lately. I've got a pretty full schedule this semester, so I've found it easier to stay in my office and sleep on the couch." He exited his car and opened the back door to retrieve some brown paper bags containing groceries. "I hate to do this, but would you mind helping me carry these inside? There's only a few more left and the damn stairs in my classroom are starting to get to my knees."

"Oh, for sure," Simon nodded and quickly walked over to take the bags from the professor.

Sam grabbed three more while the professor carried the last two and opened the front door. The first thing they saw when they walked into the entrance hall was the wooden floor that connected to a grand sweeping staircase which curved against the wall, with intricate iron baluster bars under the wood railing. On the ceiling hung an iron and crystal chandelier with electric candles. Next to the foot of the staircase, on a navy blue and cream patterned rug, sat a small grand piano and stool. To the left of the staircase, was a room containing a dark wooden dining table with antique chairs and a door (which Sam assumed led to the kitchen), and to the right was a parlor where antique white and wooden couches were positioned around the focal point of the ornate white fireplace.

"…Did you buy a museum instead of a house, professor?" Simon squeaked out.

Dr. Stewart laughed, "You would think so, wouldn't you? This house was built in 1883, very nearly torn down in 1962, with the threat of businesses coming in and demolishing the area to make parking lots, and then abandoned in 1987. History is my life, agents, so when this house was put on the market in 1989, I couldn't pass up an opportunity to make it my own."

Even Sam had to admit that he was impressed by the stately home's majesty. "Wha' di' it set ye back t' fix it up?"

"Nearly a half a million dollars over the course of ten years. Thankfully, my expertise has allowed me to make quite a bit of money identifying artifacts and antiquities. Now, if you'll just follow me to the kitchen, and I can take these groceries off of your hands."

The professor led them through the door in the dining room into a large kitchen that matched the rest of the house in style, despite the obvious upgrades that had been made to it: Light wood cabinets with ornate moldings and sandy colored granite counter tops surrounded a gas range that had a double oven beneath it. In the middle of the kitchen, was an island with a sink and dishwasher and plenty of glass cabinets revealing antique painted china inside of them. Aside from the enormous double refrigerator that stood against the opposite wall, there were French doors leading onto a deck.

Sam allowed himself to admire the rich room for a moment when he detected a faint smell of toasted butter and cheese in the air. Glancing into the large sink, he noticed a plate and a pan were sitting in it that had been freshly used. He turned his attention back to the professor, who was putting away his groceries. "Do ye have any children or grandchildren, professor?"

Dr. Stewart laughed. "No, I'm afraid I have never been married."

"Well, you've got an awful lot of food here for just one person," Simon huffed as he put his bags on the counter. "And why would you be staying here in the middle of the week if your semester is so busy?"

"My niece, Charlotte, is visiting for the next few weeks. I'm planning on making her favorite: French cuisine. I've got all the fixings here for onion soup, sole *meuniére*, and a cherry *claufoutis* for dessert. Judging by the grilled cheese sandwich mess in the sink, it would appear she arrived earlier today." Dr. Stewart retrieved a bottle of white wine from one of the bags and walked over to deposit it into the refrigerator when he glanced through the door outside. "Yup, she's out in the pool having a swim as we speak."

Sam looked out the door to the deck and saw a lush garden that was next to a large pool in the back yard of the professor's house. A figure in a black swimsuit with long hair gliding under the water caught his attention.

"I'm sorry, agents, I'm rambling. What was it you wanted to talk to me about?" Dr. Stewart asked.

Sam couldn't deny the gut feeling he had that the professor might be able to help them again, so before Simon could answer with their phony excuse of taking a survey, Sam asked, "Do the initials C.W. mean anythin' t' ye, professor?"

"In history or in general?"

"In general."

"Well, as a matter of fact, Charlotte's last name is Whitney. Why?"

Sam's curiosity piqued. "Would ye kindly introduce us t' her?"

"Certainly, but may I ask why?"

"Please, Dr. Stewart," Sam said firmly.

Although the professor was obviously confused by the request, he led them onto the deck, and the three of them descended the stairs to the pool. Charlotte had already climbed out and wrapped a towel around herself and didn't seem to notice them, but Sam took notice of her by how her swimsuit did nothing to hide her lovely back. Her long, wet hair was draped over her shoulder as she continued to dry herself off. When she turned to see them approaching, a gigantic smile crossed her face; it revealed the slightest hint of age with the very few wrinkles that surrounded her mouth.

She ran over to them, her eyes focused on the professor. "Hi!"

"Hello, my dear," Dr. Stewart answered as he wrapped his arms around her in a hug, "I thought your flight didn't get in until later this evening?"

"I managed to get an earlier one, and I thought I'd surprise you. Of course, I wasn't expecting you to get home so early, either. Who are your friends?"

Sam stepped forward and offered his hand, his eyes staying trained on her face. "Agent Sampson McKay of the FBI, an' this is Agent Simon Abler."

"FBI? Ooh, how interesting," the shorter woman teased and accepted his handshake. "It's nice to meet you both, I'm Charlotte."

"Charlotte Whitney?"

"Yes."

"Wha' do ye do fer a livin, Ms. Whitney?"

"I'm an image consultant, which is really a glorified traveler of sorts," she chuckled.

Her voice seemed so familiar to Sam; he continued, "Wha' brings ye t' town?"

"A client, and I thought I'd stay and visit with Spencer for a while before I go out on the road again."

"How di' ye arrive?"

"By plane."

"From where?"

"Miami, and before that I was in Sacramento."

"Wha' time di' yer plane land?"

Charlotte's cheery smile began to disappear, and her eyebrows furrowed in confusion. "Around 2:30 p.m., I think. Do you always have conversations this way, Agent McKay?"

Ignoring her question, Sam continued to bombard her. "Wha' airport?"

"Midway International."

"Wha' airline?"

"I'm sorry, am I being interrogated?"

Dr. Stewart nodded his agreement and asked, "Is there a reason for this, Agent McKay?"

Sam turned to Simon and said, "Check Midway International fer a passanger named Charlotte Whitney."

"You got it, boss," Simon nodded and quickly pulled out his trusty laptop and began typing as fast as lightening.

"Can somebody tell me what I did wrong?" Charlotte demanded.

"Do ye have an interest in art, Ms. Whitney?"

She shrugged, "Sure, I've seen the *Mona Lisa* and the Sistine Chapel. But I'm not really an expert, if that's what you're asking me."

"Where were ye' this las' Saturday evenin'?"

"In Miami, like I told you."

"Were ye with anyone?"

"No, I stayed in my hotel room alone."

"Wha' hotel?"

"The Kimpton. Would you like me to give you the name of the concierge, too?"

"Really, Agent McKay, what is the reason for this harassment?" Dr. Stewart asked, very perturbed.

Simon cleared his throat, "There's a Charlotte Whitney registered at the Kimpton Epic in Miami, checkout time was this morning. And a Delta flight landed at Midway at 2:40 p.m. with the same passenger."

Sam kept his eyes trained on Charlotte, who didn't look away for a second. "Are ye stayin' a' a hotel, Ms. Whitney?"

"No, she's staying here at my house," Dr. Stewart answered for her. "Her old room, actually."

Sam faced Dr. Stewart and asked, "Would ye mind lettin' us look through the room?"

Charlotte scoffed, "Do you have a warrant?"

Her reaction had Sam convinced he would find something in it. "Why? Do ye have somethin' t' hide?"

"No, but I'm not feeling very generous towards somebody I just met who's convinced I'm some sort of a criminal."

Sam turned to Dr. Stewart again. "Professor, this is yer house, an' yer niece is right: I cannea perform a search without a warrant or yer permission. Bu', if ye le' me search it now an' I donnea find anythin', I promise we'll never bother ye again."

"And if I say you need a warrant?"

"Then I'll go ge' one, an ye'll never ge' rid of me."

Dr. Stewart pursed his lips as he thought about the options before he nodded, "Alright, but *just* her room. Is that clear?"

"Spencer!" Charlotte protested.

"Sweetheart, you've got nothing to hide, right? Well, then let's let him look around really quick, then he's out of our hair."

Charlotte grew pale, and Sam smirked.

The professor began to walk towards the house, but Charlotte hadn't moved. Sam faced her and asked, "Aren't ye comin'?"

Begrudgingly, his suspect started walking towards the house, still dripping wet.

Simon came up and whispered, "I thought you said the woman you saw at the gala had short, silver hair and glasses? Looked like she could have been sixty years old?"

"Our thief also looked like a cop," Sam whispered back "C.W.'s a master of disguises, I'm certain of it. Charlotte has the same initials, tha's good enough fer me t' check her out."

"Okay… what should I do?"

"Stand by the door, an' donnea le' her ge' past ye."

Sam and Simon caught up to Charlotte as Dr. Stewart led them back to the sweeping staircase and up to the second floor where there was more hardwood lining the long hallway adorned with oil portrait paintings. Sam noticed six doors and another staircase leading to an upper floor, but the professor led them to the door at the end of the hallway. The room had an old four-drawer dresser next to a large, draped window, a sitting chair next to a small bookshelf filled with books, and a smaller fireplace in front of an antique four-poster bed. The sheets on the mattress were messy and tussled, so Sam walked over to inspect them.

"Ye say ye go' in early this afternoon? Looks t' me this bed has been slept in."

"I took a nap when I got here," Charlotte answered. "I was tired."

A faint scent lingered in the air next to the sheets; Sam inhaled and thought he could smell green apples. He smirked to himself, recognizing the perfume from the gala. He walked over to the dresser, opened the first drawer, and briefly ruffled through the silk panties sitting inside it before moving on to the next drawer.

"An' ye unpacked yer suitcase already?"

"Yes, then I had my nap."

"Where's the suitcase?"

Charlotte nodded towards the closet.

Sam retrieved the suitcase and opened it to find another smaller suitcase inside, but otherwise both were completely empty.

"Why d'ye need two suitcases? Ye dinnea pack enough clothin' fer two."

"You should always travel with a second suitcase just in case you buy more than one suitcase can handle," she answered simply.

He patted it around the sides and checked each pocket, but there was nothing to be found. When he had finished with it, he continued his search around the room, even under the bed and behind the bedpost but found nothing.

"Are you satisfied, now?" she asked.

Sam grew annoyed at the lack of evidence; he was positive there was more to the professor's niece than just her name. He reluctantly stood up, ready to humble himself and apologize to the woman, when the fireplace caught his eye.

"Dr. Stewart, are the fireplaces still bein' used?"

"Only the one downstairs. The ones up here are mainly for decoration."

The hat an' necklace... t'was in a bag in the garbage shoot... Sam looked towards Charlotte, but her emotionless face made him a little bit nervous that he would only make more of a fool of himself. Still, he knelt down in front of it and began to feel around inside of the flue. "Di' ye have them capped an' filled?"

"Yes, otherwise all of the heat would escape."

Sam's hand brushed against something that felt like plastic and he quickly pulled on it. Several small plastic bags fell onto the floor. Each of them held different items: pieces of clothing, jewelry, wigs, even skin colored prosthetics and makeup. But the one that he was the most interested in held a silver haired wig, a pair of glasses, and a tube of lipstick in it. He glanced up at Charlotte and smirked; her eyes were as wide as dinner plates.

"Charlotte?" Dr. Stewart said softly, "What is this all about?"

She glanced at the professor nervously, but she couldn't answer him.

"I'll call Julie and Rivera and tell them to get their butts over here," Simon said as he whipped out his phone.

Sam stood up, the bag of evidence in hand, "Perhaps we should le' the lady ge' decent before she explains herself, professor."

Chapter Seven

By the time the others had arrived at the house, Sam and a dressed Charlotte were sitting at the professor's dining table. Despite having evidence that clearly proved she impersonated the curator at the gala, she appeared calm and reserved; her hands were folded, and she kept eye contact with Sam. Simon was sitting in the parlor with Dr. Stewart, who was demanding an explanation as to what was going on.

Rivera walked over and cleared his throat, "Sam, a word?"

Sam followed him into the kitchen while Julie took his place at the table.

"Wha'?"

"Don't you think headquarters would be a better place for an interrogation? We're on her home turf."

"This isnea her home turf; i's the professor's. Besides, I have a feelin' she'll talk t' us."

"What makes you so sure?"

"We've go' the disguise a' the apartment; there's bound t' be physical evidence on it belongin' t' her. We've also go' the 911 call, an' I'll bet ye $100 we'll be able t' match her voice t' the one on the tape."

Rivera sighed, "Right. Okay. Of course, that's assuming she didn't disguise her voice when she made the call."

"I listened t' tha' tape me-self, Rivera, I'm tellin' ye the woman on it is Charlotte. Watch."

Walking back into the dining room, Sam noticed how Charlotte had turned her attention to the bewildered professor, a guilty expression in her eyes. The professor was still talking to Simon, muttering how he didn't understand anything that was going on, and Charlotte looked at her hands sadly. When Sam took his seat across the table from her, she looked into his eyes again.

"Why di' ye pose as the curator?"

Charlotte smirked, "I thought it'd be fun."

"Di' ye also think it'd be fun t' steal a paintin'?"

"I'm sure I don't have any idea what you're talking about."

Sam leaned back in his chair, "Alrigh', wha' about a ring?"

"What ring?"

Sam pulled out his phone and brought up the picture of Annabelle Matheson's switched ring. As soon as Charlotte saw it, her smirk disappeared. Knowing he was getting warmer, he then showed her the photo of Annabelle Matheson lying dead on the floor. Charlotte paled and looked away from the phone.

"Please put that away," she said quietly.

"Do ye know who this is?"

"Put it away," she said more sternly.

"Her name's Annabelle Matheson; she was killed. She owned the ring."

"I'm telling you, right now, put that picture away."

"Why? Too ashamed t' look a' yer handiwork?"

"I would never hurt h—anyone!"

Her little slip caused Sam to smirk. "Ye knew her, didn't ye?"

Charlotte's mouth formed a thin line, and she glared at him. Sam then pulled up the enhanced photo of the woman in the lobby of the Natty Towers apartment with the black beaded necklace and showed it to her. "We found tha' necklace an' hat in the garbage chute of Mrs. Violet Winston, who owns both of these items. The problem is, the ones we found were knock-offs, they couldnea have belonged t' her. This is you, isn't it?"

"I don't have any idea what you're talking about."

"We found a broken bead from tha' necklace in Annabelle's apartment, an' there was an anonymous 911 call askin' somebody t' check on her. Based off the M.E.'s time of death, we know it was made the same day she died. We know ye were there."

"Oh really? Because as far as I can tell, no one can see the face of whoever that is. And you can search through my whereabouts all you want, Agent McKay. But I promise that you'll never find any connection between me and wherever you think I was. So, as anyone can plainly see, I've never met that woman in my life."

Sam then brought out his phone and pulled up the 911 recording he'd listened to at least a dozen times before. He kept an intense stare on Charlotte and pushed play:

"911, what is the address of your emergency?" said a male voice.

"Send somebody to check on Annabelle Matheson," a female voice that sounded just like Charlotte answered.

"Ma'am, could you tell me your name please?"

The line went dead.

Charlotte stared at Sam's phone but remained quiet.

Sam leaned back in his chair and folded his arms across his chest, refusing to look away from her. "No' only can we compare the voice on tha' tape t' yers, bu' we have yer necklace, yer wig, an' the hat. The funny thing abou' DNA, Charlotte, is I' only takes the tiniest spec t' make a comparison. All it takes is one bi' of proof fer us t' make a conviction."

Charlotte remained silent. Sam pressed on.

"Here's the thing, I donnea think ye're a killer. In fact, I think ye hate violence. Why else would ye call the police after findin' Annabelle? An' why would ye take the chance of leavin' behind DNA? Ye know all tha' can be used as evidence against ye, an' ye're a clever thief: Ye've always made sure nothin' can be traced back t' ye. I think the sight of Annabelle's body put ye in shock, an' ye slipped up. Truthfully, we donnea care tha' ye're a thief. We're tryin' t' find who killed Annabelle Matheson, an' I believe ye can lead us t' who did it. If ye help us, then we'll be lenient with ye."

When she still refused to answer, Sam began to lose his patience. "Alrigh', fine. Here's wha's gonna happen: We'll take ye back t' our headquarters an' prove the evidence we found is yers. Then we'll arrest ye fer obstruction of justice, makin' a false statement to a Federal officer, an' the murder of Annabelle Matheson."

"Alright!" Charlotte shouted, throwing her hands up in defeat. "You're right: I'm the one who called the police."

"Why?"

"...Because I did find Annabelle dead in her apartment."

Julie leaned forward. "What were you doing there in the first place?"

Charlotte sighed, "I was supposed to meet her for drinks that night. When she didn't show up, I went to check on her."

"How did you get in if she was already dead?" Rivera asked.

"You figured out that I'm a thief, kudos to you. So that should tell you that I have my ways."

"Such as?"

"...Let's call it a special key. I keep one on me at all times just in case, but I didn't need it until that day. Annabelle and I had become friends."

"What would an 85-year-old woman and a fifty-year-old woman have in common enough to be friends?" Julie asked.

"Forty, thank you very much. Honestly, she wanted a friend that didn't make her feel like an old woman. Her kids treated her like she couldn't take care of herself; that's why they hired the maid. She may have been 85, but she certainly didn't act like it. She liked to attend special events, eat at fine restaurants; she really didn't need to be looked after. She may have broken a hip, but she didn't even have a walker, for God's sake."

"Was she yer target?" Sam asked her directly. "Because there's no mention of ye in any of her family or friends' statements. I donnea think they even know ye exist."

"That's why I'm good at what I do: I don't get involved with anyone I don't have to. I admit it, she was my target. I was after her ring, just like you said. But... I liked her. She was spunky and funny; she just wanted a friend."

"Do you always make friends with the people you plan to steal from?" Julie asked skeptically.

"I usually don't have to, no. I specialize in not even being seen, agents. But this was different: I had to steal an heirloom that was on somebody's finger at all times; that's not an easy thing to do. So, I figured the only way to get close to the ring was to get close to her. But after getting to know her...I just couldn't do it." Charlotte looked at her hands sadly.

Sam sighed, "I believe ye, Charlotte. So, answer me this: why were ye after the ring, an' why di' ye steal tha' paintin' from the gala?"

"What if I was to tell you that there's somebody out there obsessed with George Jamesone? That they've been hiring people for years to steal every piece of artwork connected to him?"

"Somebody is killing people just for specific paintings and rings?" Rivera asked.

"It's not as crazy as you think, agent. Why do people steal art in the first place?"

"Money?"

"The thieves may make the money from the stealing, but who buys the stolen paintings? The ones with the obsession to own them. I'm sure even you can think of a few famous artists: Pablo Picasso, Monet, Rembrandt, for example. Do you really think that every piece of art you've seen has a clean legal history of ownership? If you do, you're naïve."

Sam smirked at her attitude. "So, somebody hired ye t' steal Annabelle Matheson's ring an' the George Jamesone paintin'?"

"Yes."

"An' ye stole three more paintin's of the same artist, aye?"

"Maybe," She answered in a nonchalant tone. "But before you ask, I don't know who for. We've never met."

"You don't even know who you're stealing for?" Julie asked incredulously.

"There's a reason I'm the best. My line of work thrives on a certain level of anonymity, otherwise somebody could point fingers at the other, if someone gets caught."

"Well, obviously whoever you work for doesn't think you're their only option, if they're willing to hire complete amateurs to try and steal the painting."

"The thing about chasing down certain artifacts, agent, is it's not a one-time job. It's ongoing. Sometimes the clay pot you buy at a garage sale for $5 isn't just a piece of home décor, it's a priceless antiquity. But if you don't know or care what you're looking at, how does anybody else know? George Jamesone assignments have been on the market for years, I already know I'm not the only one working for the buyer."

"So, what's the attraction?" Rivera asked. "Money? There's got to be easier jobs to take in your line of work that pay just as well, if not better."

Charlotte leaned back into her chair and folded her arms. "I have my reasons, and we'll leave it at that. Look, I don't know who my competitors are, but I promise you that one of them is your killer."

"Aye, we agree with ye. Which is why ye're gonna' help us catch them."

Charlotte scoffed, "No I'm not. If anybody catches wind that I'm working with Feds, career suicide is an understatement."

"An' goin' t' prison doesnea count as career suicide?" Sam challenged.

"You're going to put me in prison anyway; I can recover from that."

"Perhaps we'll lose track of ye before this is over."

"…If I help you catch the killer, you'll let me disappear?"

"Aye, we will. Do we have a deal?"

Charlotte stared Sam down as she considered his offer. Finally, she smiled and gave him a wink. "Alright, McKay, deal."

"I don't believe what I'm hearing," Dr. Stewart said from the other room. Everyone turned their attention to him, including Charlotte. "I've known you since you were a kid. I took care of you. And then I find out…"

A tear escaped from Charlotte's eye. "Spencer… I couldn't—"

"I'd like you to leave. All of you, now." Dr. Stewart marched to the front door and yanked it open. "Out, now."

Rivera, Julie, and Simon obeyed the professors wishes while Sam handcuffed Charlotte before following. As she was escorted out of the house, Dr. Stewart refused to look at her. When the door slammed shut, silent tears were rolling down Charlotte's face.

Sam turned to Julie, "Think ye can handle havin' a professional thief as a roommate?"

She smirked, "I can take first watch, but Derrick gets second."

"Fine by me," Rivera said.

They had barely gotten into the SUV when Sam's phone began ringing. "McKay."

"Agent McKay, this is Director Bronson. We've got a problem: Aiden Marcus and the Franks brothers have escaped."

"How?!"

"The convoy was attacked on the bridge over the Chicago River during their transfer to MCC this morning, they disappeared by boat. Not only were there dozens of civilian casualties, none of my agents survived."

"How could this have happened?" Sam demanded.

"If I knew how, it wouldn't have happened. Ten good men and women were killed this morning because of your investigation, McKay, and one of your prisoners could have been a valuable asset to my agents. My tolerance for you and your ragtag team is growing short because of all of your blundering. I suggest you get a move on this and find out what the hell is going on immediately. Is that understood?"

"Yes, sir," Sam answered just before the director hung up on him. Turning back to his team (who were watching him curiously) he growled, "Aiden Marcus an' the Franks brothers escaped a' the riva'."

"What? That's impossible!" Simon blurted out. "FBI prisoner transfer schedules are one of the best kept secrets in the world! Nobody can get their hands on that knowledge unless they're supposed to, not even *me!*"

"What the hell is going on here?" Rivera asked, "Since we took over this investigation, every step we make runs into a brick wall!"

"I dunno, bu' whoever wants these paintin's, obviously donnea want us t' find them, else they wouldnea be goin' t' this much trouble t' cover their tracks." He glanced back at Charlotte, "So we can probably assume somebody'll be comin' after ye, too."

"I doubt I'd be so lucky," she answered quietly.

"Wha's tha' supposed to mean?"

Charlotte didn't answer; she turned her head and kept looking out the window as Rivera drove them back to their cheap little motel.

Gathered in Sam's room around another pizza, the team kept going over everything they knew so far: Any and all artifacts related to George Jamesone were being targeted, but there was no way to track the buyer, yet. Charlotte's instructions were always the same: Every painting she recovered was taken to a random abandoned warehouse and placed inside of a waiting truck with no driver. A bag of money was always waiting for her, so she would make the exchange and leave. At least that is what Charlotte had told them, and they had no choice but to believe her.

Sam picked up the evidence bag with the ring that had caused so much trouble for everyone; he glanced back at their prisoner, who was sitting in a chair in the corner, the pizza on her plate completely eaten despite the handcuffs. Charlotte caught him staring and gave him a playful wink, and he turned his attention back to the ring again. Then she cleared her throat, and everyone looked over at her. "You know, if you want my help, I think I deserve a little bit of trust."

"Trust goes two ways, Ms. Whitney," Rivera answered. "And so far, you haven't given us any real reason to trust you other than your word."

She chuckled, "Funny, neither have any of you."

Simon scoffed, "I think, out of the five of us, the people who have sworn to protect and serve can be trusted more than the woman who lies and steals for a living."

"You make a fair point," she nodded. "But keeping me handcuffed to a radiator in a cheap motel is a little extreme, don't you think?"

"It never hurts to be prepared," Julie answered.

"Right, because there are four of you with guns and me with only my wits, knowledge, and chlorine-bleached hair. I'm very dangerous."

"Ye're in our custody," Sam grumbled as he continued to stare at the ring. "An' as long as ye're in our custody, ye'll continue t' cooperate or else be treated as a prisoner."

"Well then, since I've done nothing *but* cooperate so far, I think it's fair to say I'm above prisoner treatment, don't you? If I'm supposed to trust that you'll let me go, don't you think you can trust me enough to stick around while I help you?" She lifted her cuffed hands in the air and fluttered her eyelashes.

Sam looked to his team for their opinion: Julie subtly shook her head, Simon rolled his eyes, and Rivera shrugged his shoulders. Sighing, Sam walked towards her and opened the handcuffs. "Fine, pull up a chair an' tell us wha' ye see."

"Much better," Charlotte sighed. Doing as Sam instructed her, she pulled over her chair and rubbed her wrists as she looked over everything. "Wow, you guys don't have much, yet, huh?"

"We caught you," Julie said shortly, "It's only a matter of time before we catch the next piece of the puzzle."

Charlotte smiled, "Settle down, honey, it was just an observation. Is that Annabelle's ring you've been staring at, McKay?"

Sam handed the baggie over to her, "A fake tha' was switched in evidence somehow. I donnea suppose ye'd be able to tell us how tha' happened?"

She opened the bag and pulled the ring out, examining it closely under the light as she twisted it. "Sorry, tampering with police evidence is not my style. But..." She brought the ring to her nose and sniffed it, then she licked it (which earned a disgusted look from Simon) and smiled, "I can tell you who made the fake: Chase D'Angelo."

"And how could you get that from licking it?" Rivera asked skeptically.

"Chase D'Angelo is not only known as a jewelry forging genius in underground circles, but also for using a special solution during the gold plating process."

"Of what?"

"Rose water."

"And you can taste that?"

"If you're not looking for it, you'd miss it. Lucky for you guys, I know what to look for."

"Alrigh', so where d' we find this Chase D'Angelo?" Sam asked.

"You don't; I do," Charlotte smiled. "Chase doesn't trust anyone unless they're practically family. You have to know a guy who knows a guy who knows a guy just to get an appointment."

Julie smirked, "So how did *you* get one?"

"I got myself invited to my fair share of family dinners. You don't even want to know how many different versions of Cannoli I had to sample at my first one, not to mention how many gym hours I had to put in just to work them off. But thanks to my vigilance, Chase knows me and trusts me. I can find out who had this ring made for you."

Sam looked to Simon, who was entering all of Charlotte's knowledge on his laptop. "...I can't find a record of *anyone* named Chase D'Angelo."

Charlotte laughed, "Well, you wouldn't. Chase is old school, doesn't like new technology. Everything is via word of mouth. Only person in the world that I know of who doesn't even own a cell phone."

"Then how are we supposed to find him?"

"*Her*, actually, and she runs a little antique shop in Logan Square. It's too late to call now, but I can take you there first thing in the morning."

Sam sighed, "Alrigh', then fer now le's all ge' some rest an' we'll start again in the mornin'. Julie?"

"You got it," the fiery redhead nodded and walked over to Charlotte, "You're with me tonight."

"Ooh, girls' night! We're gonna' need some vodka, nail polish, and you can tell me which of these three you're most likely to sleep with."

"Or you could just go to sleep, *quietly,* with the knowledge that my gun is always under my pillow," Julie replied. "And if you give me any trouble, I'll handcuff you to the headboard."

Charlotte turned to the others and smirked, "Well, now you'll have something to dream about tonight, boys."

While Sam rolled his eyes, Simon and Rivera cleared their throats uncomfortably. After securing Charlotte in Julie's room next door, the rest of the team separated into their own rooms for the night. Finally alone, Sam picked up his phone and decided to text Oliver: *Are you being good for your mum?*

He stared at the screen, hoping his teenage son wouldn't ignore him, and sighed in relief when he saw the little text bubble start to reply.

Good enough, the boy answered.

Sam smirked. *I'm in Chicago, the pizza's not bad. Want me to bring you some when I come home?*

Again, he waited for a reply, which didn't come. Five minutes later, he texted again. *Do you?*

Finally, the bubble appeared followed by another text: *If you want to.*

Sam shook his head and sighed at his son's attitude. Knowing he wouldn't get anywhere that night and too tired to pick a fight, he texted back, *I'll bring you sausage and bacon when I come home. Love you.*

Though he didn't expect a reply, he waited for one anyway until his eyes grew tired. Setting the phone on the nightstand, he shucked his shirt and pants and crawled into the too-small bed for a night of uncomfortable sleep.

Chapter Eight

Julie always woke up bright and early on an assignment, but she was surprised to see her roommate/prisoner already awake, apparently showered and putting on makeup.

"Morning, sunshine," Charlotte said nonchalantly.

Julie looked at Charlotte's bed and saw a set of unlocked handcuffs sitting on top of the covers. "What the—how did you—"

"Please, handcuffs are child's play."

"You said you couldn't get out of them last night!"

"Did I say that?" Charlotte smirked. "Don't worry, I won't tell the tall one on you."

At a loss for words, Julie rolled her eyes and started to get ready. Picking her usual attire of black slacks, a white silk button down, and black boots, she pulled her hair back into a ponytail and motioned towards the door. "Come on, I bet everyone's already waiting for us."

The two women made their way to the lobby of the motel where, sure enough, Sam, Rivera, and Simon were already sitting around a table, eating the skimpy breakfast of powdered eggs and toast. As soon as they walked in, the three men kept their eyes trained on Charlotte while she poured herself some coffee and grabbed a little package of jam for her own toast before walking over to join them.

"Relax, guys," Charlotte snickered. "It's not like I have anywhere to go."

Julie just stuck to the coffee with a little sugar and joined the others at the table. "So, what's the plan regarding Chase D'Angelo?"

"Simple: You take me to the shop, I go in, and I find out who made the ring for you."

"And how do we know you won't just skip out on us?" Simon asked.

"How do we know you're even telling the truth?" Rivera added.

Mocking a pained expression, Charlotte clutched her chest. "After all we've been through? That hurts."

Sam grunted, "If ye were expectin' us t' le' ye go in there alone, ye're dafty."

"So, one of you lucky boys' club members is going to join me, huh? Okay, sure, then we'll just have to wait until we get invited to another meal before we find out who had that ring made. That should take about... oh, six months? Eight, tops. I hope you guys are prepared to make the motel bed your home for a while."

"This isnea funny, Charlotte, we need t' find out who switched Annabelle's ring quickly."

"I agree, which is why you should just let me go in and ask. Look, Chase is the all-original independent woman, you honestly think she's going to trust one of you two?" she nodded towards Sam and Rivera.

"Hey!" Simon protested, "I'm right here!"

"Please," she scoffed, "You're the behind-the-scenes guy, anybody can see that."

"I'm coming with you," Julie said. "I'm independent, and I'm not a man."

"Yeah, and you're also stiffer than wood. I'm telling you guys, just let me handle this. I'll be in and out."

"No," Julie said sternly. "We've already established that we don't trust you, so I'm coming. Period."

Charlotte looked her over for a long minute. Finally, she rolled her eyes and replied, "Okay, fine, but first we'll need to take you to get some decent clothes. Anyone can smell cop on you a mile away while you dress like that."

Looking down at her business attire, Julie argued, "What's wrong with the way I dress?"

"It screams 'army bitch' and not 'career troublemaker.' Eat up, guys, the girls need to go shopping!"

As soon as their tense breakfast was over, the team escorted Charlotte to the nearest mall, where she practically dragged Julie inside of a very feminine boutique. After what seemed like hours trying on various outfits, jewelry, and emphatically saying no to the lacey underwear, Charlotte finally settled on a tight pair of jeans, a wraparound olive-green blouse that barely hid Julie's middriff, heels, and a couple silver bracelets.

Charlotte walked around her. "Hmmm... let your hair down."

Julie rolled her eyes but did as she was told. As soon as the curls were free from the tie, Charlotte wasted no time in tussling her hair about until it was draping her shoulders.

"There, if I didn't know any better, I'd think you were out to destroy a couple hearts," Charlotte giggled.

"Are you saying I need to *flirt* with Chase?"

"No, I'm saying you look less cop and more swanky. I think we *might* just be able to fool Chase. Oh, you've got the company card, right? I left my wallet at home."

"Of course, you did," Julie grumbled.

Once everything was paid for and Julie was dressed, the two women walked out of the boutique towards a bench where the men were waiting. The three of them did a double-take when they saw her, and Julie suddenly felt very self-conscious.

Simon was the first to speak. "Wow! You look hot, Jules!"

Rivera's eyes were as wide as dinner plates, but eventually he shook himself out of it and cleared his throat, "Damn!"

Julie could feel her cheeks turn pink at the praise and did her best to hide the smile that was threatening to show.

Sam didn't say anything but nodded his head before turning to Charlotte, "An' ye're certain Chase'll talk t' ye both, now?"

"I think so," Charlotte smiled. "Let's go find out."

The next stop was the tiny corner store called *Andamo Antiques;* while Sam and the others stayed in their SUV a few blocks away, Julie followed Charlotte down the quiet walkway towards the entrance.

Just before opening the door, Charlotte turned to Julie and said, "This is your last chance to turn around."

"I didn't go through 'The Makeover' for nothing," she argued, "I'm coming with you."

Charlotte snickered, "Alright, if you insist. But stay behind me and let me do all the talking. Try smiling a bit. And give me the ring."

Although apprehensive, Julie handed over the ruby antique. Shaking herself loose, she brought her lips up into a thin smile.

"Good enough," Charlotte laughed and entered the building.

Julie followed their only lead through the little glass door; the first thing she noticed was the strong smell of espresso that permeated the air, as well as cookies. But the lovely aromas didn't completely mask the staleness that came from the old furniture throughout the store. Wooden cabinets were positioned all around them with glass trinkets and porcelain dolls on display inside of them. Wherever there wasn't a cabinet, different sets of wooden tables and chairs were gathered with antique tablecloths and china dishes set up for a tea party. There was hardly any room to walk, but Charlotte led her to the back of the shop. Julie felt the hair on the back of her neck raise when she saw a porcelain doll with piercing blue eyes sitting on the counter next to the register. For a moment, she thought the doll was staring right at her. She reminded herself that was ridiculous as she continued to follow the apprehended thief.

Charlotte reached the register and tapped the little bell that sat on the counter. Not a moment later, a frail old woman wearing black cat-eye glasses, another set of gold-rimmed glasses hanging by a gold chain on her chest, and an apron appeared from behind a curtain.

"*Buongiorno, come posso aiutarla?*" she smiled. Julie's interest was piqued by the Italian language, but she kept her distance as she watched Charlotte's interaction.

"*Buongiorno, bella mattina, non è vero?*"

"*Si, molto bello. Sta cercando qualcosa di speciale?*"

"*Si,*" Charlotte turned and gestured to Julie, "*io e il mio amico stiamo cercando* Chase D'Angelo. *Sai dove possiamo trovarla?*"

The old woman turned her gaze towards Julie and looked her over with skepticism, which did nothing to help her nervousness. But she held her ground, kept her posture as relaxed as she could, and smiled coyly while the old woman sized her up. Finally, the shopkeeper turned back to Charlotte and the two of them continued to converse.

"*Questa sconosciuta, ci si può fidare?*" the old woman asked.

"*Si,*" Charlotte nodded.

"*Sai* D'Angelo *non vedrà nessuno. Perché dovrebbe fidarsi di questa bambina?*"

"D'Angelo *si fida di me e posso garantire personalmente per questa bambina. Ma, se vuoi che si dimostri, lo farà.*"

Once again, Julie became the object of the shopkeeper's attention as she looked back at her. Julie suddenly understood why Charlotte was so apprehensive about bringing her; she didn't know what to do. *If I'm this nervous around a little old lady, how the hell will this Chase D'Angelo talk to us?*

Finally, the frail old woman turned towards the curtain and shouted, "Nikola! *Vieni qui e guarda il negozio!"*

A young teenage girl walked through the curtain and took the older woman's place behind the counter. Then the older woman hobbled towards the curtain and gestured to Charlotte to follow. One look from the lady thief, Julie followed her. Behind the curtain was a backroom where three other women of different ages were sitting around a table enjoying small cups of espresso; although they appeared curious about Charlotte and Julie, they immediately returned to their coffee and Italian gossip with one look from the old shopkeeper. Julie carefully looked about; the counters were lined with different antiques: some were broken, some were old and faded and sitting in a pile. Other surfaces had different salves and solutions and different tweezers and tools; Julie assumed all of this was for business needs, but she couldn't tell legitimate or not.

The little old woman led them through the workshop to a door at the back. Opening it, Charlotte walked through with Julie right behind her. It appeared to be a waiting room of sorts. There was a floral couch up against the wall, a long coffee table in front of it, a comfortable looking chair against the other wall, and a corner table. Other than an espresso pot and a plate of cookies, nothing really stood out to Julie. But then the door shut behind her.

The old woman locked it before turning back to the two of them, a wide grin stretching across her face and her arms open wide. "Charlotte, *mia cara! Ciao bella!"*

"Ciao, nonna Chase," Charlotte smiled and leaned into the old women's embrace.

Julie was stunned. *This is Chase?!* Quickly composing her facial expressions, she kept her distance behind the two women until she was properly introduced. Finally, the old woman released Charlotte and looked to Julie with a sly smile, "And who have you brought today?"

"Chase D'Angelo, meet Julie Russell, my friend and protégé."

Julie stepped forward with her hand outstretched but was immediately pulled into a tight hug; the old woman was certainly stronger than she looked. Between that and the fact that she actually could speak English, Julie couldn't help but continue feeling surprised.

Chase finally released her but kept hold of Julie's hands. *"Ciao, Julie. Bellissima, bella ragazza!"*

Despite how uncomfortable she felt with the strange woman holding her like a grandmother would her grandchild, she couldn't help but blush at what felt like a compliment. She smiled and muttered, "Thank you, Mrs. D'Angelo."

"Mio Caro, I insist that you call me *nonna.* Charlotte tell you, only people I do not like call me Mrs. D'Angelo. That name only remind me of my late husband, Antonio. *Amore mio, riposi in pace,"* she muttered and made a cross in front of her before kissing her fingers.

"Right, um... thank you, *nonna,"* Julie nodded uneasily.

"Good! *Molto bene!"* Chase smiled and turned her attention back to Charlotte, "Protege, eh? Don't tell me you think of retirement, *bella donna.* Far too young for golf and chess in the park."

Charlotte laughed, "Never, *nonna."*

"That's good! Don't let anyone, especially a man, tell you that you should stop being you, eh? My Antonio tried that once, and you know how I responded, eh? I threw his dinner out the window and said, 'If you think God put me on this earth only to serve you, then I'll be serving you outside with the rest of the *suino!'"*

The two women laughed heartily before Chase turned to Julie and said, *"Suino,* they...they make noise go 'oink! Oink!'"

Julie laughed uncomfortably, "Pigs. You told your husband you would serve him with the rest of the pigs, huh?"

"Si! Si, the pigs! Ah, *amore mio, riposi in pace,"* she crossed herself again, "Antonio had his faults but he was a good man. Now, why didn't you tell *nonna* you were 'a comin', eh?" Chase chided Charlotte, "I would have made your favorite: steamed mussels and tagliatelle pasta!"

"Oh, Chase, if you did that, then I would never leave."

"Well, it'sa been too long! Come, I just brewed some espresso to go with my biscotti! Come, come! Sit, sit!"

Chase gestured towards the couch. Charlotte took a seat without any problem and Julie followed her lead while still watching the strange old woman. An array of small white mugs hung on the wall behind the refreshments; Chase grabbed three and poured each of them an espresso before she also grabbed the cookies.

Lifting the plate up, Chase gestured to Julie, "Have a biscotti, *miei cari.*"

Doing her best to not appear rude or nervous, she took a cookie, dipped it in the espresso, and took a small but crunchy bite; the licorice and vanilla flavor was subtle against the coffee but very delicious. She then took a small sip of the hot drink and had to admit it was the best espresso she'd ever tasted.

"Mmmm... *Nonna,* no one can make a biscotti like you," Charlotte hummed.

Julie smiled genuinely and nodded her agreement. "I agree, this is the most incredible espresso I've ever had. Thank you."

"It's because it's not from those instant pod things they try to sell you. *Ridicola!* No, no, this is how *real* espresso is made," the old woman's eyes twinkled as she took a sip of her own coffee. "Now, tell *nonna, affari o piacere?*"

"Business," Charlotte answered and withdrew the ring from her pocket, handing it to Chase. "I was on a job and I found this. Beautifully done, *nonna,* you nearly fooled me."

Chase lifted her cat eye glasses onto her head and put on the other set attached to the gold chain before she looked at the ring. *"Si, si,* I made this ring. I could not forget such a beautiful ruby-color stone."

"Ah! I thought so," Charlotte smiled, "Could you tell me who you made it for?"

"A *bruto,* very disrespectful. He's not allowed to call me *nonna."* Chase's face twisted in disgust and Julie had to stifle a giggle. "His name William Finn."

While Julie had never heard the name before, out of the corner of her eye she saw Charlotte flinch and looked over to her; she had suddenly paled.

"Are you sure? It was really William Finn that had you make this ring?"

"Si, I never forget such a *bruto.* He said his name is William Finn, and he show me a photograph of this ring. Said he would pay much for an exact copy. I did not like his attitude and I told him no, but then he tried to... *minaccia nonna;* said he could have me taken care of. I told him I would make this ring, and he must never come back. He agreed. I make the ring; he comes two weeks later and takes it."

Julie didn't even know the old woman, and yet she couldn't help but feel angry at the thought that someone would think to threaten

93

her. Before she could give her sympathies, Chase rose her hand in a fist and exclaimed, "*Se viene di nuovo qui, mi prenderò cura di lui stesso!*"

Charlotte chuckled, "I know you would, *nonna*, I have no doubt you'd take care of him. But he's got what we want."

"*Hai bisogno anche di una copia dell'anello?*"

"No, we don't need a copy of the ring. I just don't like people taking my stuff, nor do I like it when somebody threatens my *Nonna*. So, when we find him, we'll be sure to remind him not to."

"Yeah," Julie nodded.

Chase chuckled. "Do not trouble yourself, *mieie cari; nonna* can take care of herself."

"Oh, we don't doubt that at all," Charlotte smiled. Finishing her drink, she stood up from the couch and leaned over to hug the old woman. "We know you're busy, so we won't keep you. Thank you for the coffee, biscotti, and information."

"Oh, anything for you, *mia cara.*" Chase rose from her chair and walked over to Julie, wrapping her in another embrace, "*Arrivederci, bella ragazza!*"

Though still a little uncomfortable, Julie accepted the hug and smiled, "*Arrivederci, nonna.*"

Walking out of the shop and back towards the SUV, Julie kept glancing at Charlotte; she was still a little pale, but she looked much better than she had when the name William Finn was first mentioned. Before she could broach the subject, Charlotte spoke first.

"Chase likes you," she smiled.

"I think it helped that you were there."

"Maybe. But either way, you've made a very good impression on her."

"I didn't say anything."

"You can call her *nonna;* not just anybody gets to do that after just meeting her. If you weren't so black and white, you'd make a pretty good criminal."

"That will never happen."

Charlotte laughed, "Take it easy, I'm only saying. Accept the compliment, Julie."

Feeling a small sense of pride, Julie nodded. When they were closer to the car, she asked, "So, who's William Finn, and why are you scared of him?"

"The short answer: a deranged psychopath. And we're going to have to tread very carefully because he's involved."

Though Julie wanted to press her for more information, they were already back at the SUV, and Charlotte had climbed in without another word.

"Well?" Rivera asked.

"We got a name," Julie answered. "William Finn."

Sam turned around, a curious look in his eyes. "William Finn? As in 'The Redcap'?"

Charlotte nodded, "Yup, that's him. You know him?"

"I've heard of 'im," Sam answered shortly. Turning to Rivera, he growled, "Back t' the motel."

Once they were back in the room, Simon began clacking away on his laptop as soon as the name of the ring buyer was mentioned. While the young man focused on finding everything he could about this man Sam referred to as 'The Redcap,' Julie kept her eyes on the troubled Charlotte.

"Wow," Simon said, "I definitely wouldn't want to be anywhere near *this* guy on a bad day. William 'The Redcap' Finn: born October 31, 1953; he's the only son of Joseph Finn who was known as 'Big Joe,' head of the Finn clan. Good God, Big Joe was known as quite the hell raiser. But from what I can see here, William is the devil incarnate compared to him."

"I wasn't kidding when I said psychopath," Charlotte muttered.

"You can say that again," Simon agreed.

Curious about the nickname, Julie asked, "What's a Redcap?"

Sam answered her. "I's a monster: looks like a goblin tha' wears a long cap, known fer lurin' strangers an' travelers t' their lairs t' brutally murder them before stealin' everythin' they own. When their victims are dead, the Redcap dips its cap in their blood t' keep the stain red."

"And William Finn certainly lives up to his moniker," Simon agreed. "He's been charged with assault and battery, rape, arson, theft, even extortion, since he was fifteen. Never convicted, though. Surprise, surprise. Mafia dealings aren't exactly anything new, but it's like this guy has absolutely no code of honor."

"You think every mob boss does?" Rivera scoffed.

"I've seen *The Godfather;* I thought that was supposed to be the standard."

"Sicilians an' Scots are no' the same people," Sam said. "Wha' else can ye find?"

"According to the files from Chicago's Town Hall, he owns most of the business district. He married a girl named Audrey Jaimes in 2000; they had a son in 2010."

"Di' ye say Jaimes? As in the Jaimes Clan?"

Simon typed on his computer for a moment before he answered. "Yup: Audrey Jaimes is the daughter of Bruce Jaimes, a wealthy philanthropist and the known head of the Jaimes clan, former Godfather of the Scottish Mob."

"Aiden Marcus had ties to the Jaimes Clan," Julie piped up, "That can't be a coincidence."

"What do you mean by 'former'?" Rivera asked.

"Bruce died of a heart attack in 2011, a few months after Audrey and William's son Malcolm was born. William is now the Boss of all Bosses." Simon answered. "But what does the Scottish Mob want with a bunch of paintings from a random artist? I mean, from an economic standpoint, established mobs are well-oiled money-making machines. It really can't be that hard to just buy or steal paintings that would be considered *much* higher in value."

"Don't forget the ring," Rivera added. "Dr. Stewart said that ring is priceless, but only someone who truly knew its history could have wanted it. It could be just as Ms. Charlotte said: obsession."

"Donnea assume anythin' yet," Sam said, "Fer all we know, 'tis just a coincidence."

"It probably isn't," Charlotte said and everyone looked to her. "Aiden Marcus has a reputation of being a former student of William Finn's, until they had a little falling out. Then he went to work for the Jaimes clan. When Finn married Audrey, the bad blood couldn't be ignored, and he disappeared. I honestly thought he was dead."

"How does one just 'disappear' from the mob?" Simon asked.

"It's not impossible," Rivera said. "Just difficult."

"So, what is a former student of the Redcap doing trying to steal a painting? Making a name for himself?"

"That would be my guess," Charlotte nodded and sat down on the motel bed. "But the real problem here is William Finn."

"You met him?" Julie asked.

"No," Charlotte shivered, "but I've seen his work first-hand. Your little FBI files only give you the stripped-down version of what kind of monster he is..."

Before Julie could probe her further, Sam had already pulled up a chair in front of the shaken Charlotte. He folded his hands together and asked her gently, "Wha' can ye tell us?"

"...All I know is that whenever somebody crosses him, he doesn't give second chances. In 2016, I was doing a job that required a lot of research on a guy named Holden Gray, a business man. One night, he was having dinner at The Oriole with his wife when suddenly, a package was brought to the table. He opened the package, his wife began to scream, and he threw up."

"What was in the package?" Rivera asked.

"I didn't get a good look at it, but I remember seeing blood..." Charlotte practically turned green and covered her mouth. After taking a few deep breaths, she blurted out, "It was a fetus."

Sam and Rivera appeared impassive at the answer, but Julie felt as though she might throw up herself. Simon had already rushed for the bathroom, leaving her to breathe deeply until the nauseous feeling passed.

"How did you find that out?" Rivera asked again.

"An' how do ye know it was Finn tha' did it?" Sam asked further.

"A guy throws up all over his $300 dinner, wouldn't you want to know why? I'd been tracking Mr. Gray for a while, so I already knew he had a side chick he was screwing around on his wife with. They found the girl the same night the package had been delivered. A source at the morgue told me she had been cut open and died from bleeding out. He also said that she was four months pregnant, but there was no baby. Given the bloody package, I pieced that part together. As far as figuring out it was Finn... well, I didn't get a chance to finish that job before Finn sent his lug, Robert McGail, to take care of Mr. and Mrs. Gray a few days later. I didn't stick around for the butchering, but I did hear him say to them: 'Finn sends his regards.'"

"That still doesn't technically prove it was Finn that sent the package," Rivera countered.

"Maybe not, but I sure as hell didn't want to make an appointment with him to ask."

Simon finally emerged from the bathroom again, looking pale from the heaving, and sat down next to Julie. "I wouldn't either."

"Ye said the girl died from bleedin' out," Sam said, "Was i' from the stomach?"

Charlotte shook her head, "No, they figured out that her throat was slit first, the baby was cut out long after she was dead."

"Wha' abou' the couple?"

"I didn't bother finding out about them."

Sam turned to Simon, who was already at his laptop again and typing furiously, "Way ahead of you, boss. I've found a news report that the home of Mr. and Mrs. Holden Grey had mysteriously caught fire, but the police report says there was an anonymous 911 call and it was stopped quickly. I take it you were the good Samaritan in this instance?"

Charlotte nodded, "I called 911 the second I saw their throats being cut. I didn't stick around for the fire."

"Well, according to the M.E. report, the bodies were saved in time to ascertain the true cause of death: they both died with their throats slit... Hey, the report says it was a straight-edged blade, but there seemed to be some jagged skin marks, which made them note that the murder weapon might have a broken tip. And get this: the cuts had traces of carbon steel. The heat from the fire must have sealed the chemicals on the skin."

Julie narrowed her eyes, "Slit throats, jagged skin marks, carbon steel, that's exactly how Annabelle Matheson was murdered...But didn't Darris and Remy say there weren't any connections to other cases?"

"Finn sets his victims homes on fire, and part of the carpet was burned. There's no way this is a coincidence," Rivera nodded his agreement. "And even if our PD buddies couldn't find the connection, somebody else would have. Maybe Chicago's PD isn't as clean as we've been led to believe."

"Aye," Sam nodded. "An' I'll be' someone owes William Finn a favor. Simon, I donnea care who or wha' ye need t' hack, bu' I wanna know everythin' abou' Darris, Remy, everyone in the PD."

"If any of them even downloaded music illegally, I'll let you know, boss," Simon smiled and returned his attention to his laptop.

"And what should we do?" Julie asked.

"Ye'll be stayin' with Charlotte while Rivera an' I go speak t' Mr. Finn."

"We're not going to get anything out of him, Sam," Rivera said.

"Anno, bu' this is abou' sizin' him up. I want to know exactly who it is tha' we're dealin' with before we delve any deeper inta this."

Shocked, Julie got up from the bed and stood directly in front of her Scottish boss. "Hold it, why does Rivera get to go? I can do more than play dress up and babysit!"

"Aye, anno. An' tha's why the two of ye will be goin' t' speak t' Dr. Stewart togetha'. Perhaps he may be able t' give us insight on whoever it is tha's been lookin' fer these artifacts."

"Wait, what?" Charlotte asked. "Why? Spencer is a historian, not an expert on thieves and mobsters."

"No, bu' he's passionate abou' his work. Ye said yerself tha' only those with an obsession go to this trouble, perhaps he might be able t' give us a clue on who t' talk to next."

"I doubt that. And anyways, I thought you were trying to solve Annabelle's murder. It seems to me that William Finn is definitely who murdered her."

"Aye, bu' we have nothin' more than a name an' circumstantial evidence. Tha's no' enough fer a warrant, le' alone goin' up against a mobster. An' this investigation accidentally pointed us a' you because of Annabelle's ring. If we're righ' tha' William Finn killed Annabelle fer her ring, then tha' means he's yer competitor."

Charlotte's eyes opened wide, "Oh my God...you might be right. But Spencer's not going to want to talk to me."

"He migh' now tha' he's had some time t' cool off." Sam stood up from his chair and looked down at Julie. "I trus' this interview will no' be a problem?"

Despite his towering advantage, Julie refused to feel ashamed for her outburst; she knew Sam well enough to know when he was benching her. She glared and huffed out a low, "Yes, sir."

***

It was late afternoon by the time Sam and Rivera's Uber pulled into the stone driveway in front of an enormous white Colonial-style house on Glencoe beach. Given the two tough looking men standing in front of the door, Sam felt comfortable assuming that Simon had given them William Finn's correct address.

"Listen, buddy, there's a $50 tip in it for you to wait here for a few minutes, okay?" Rivera said to the driver.

"Sure," the kid nodded and turned off his car.

Satisfied, Sam and Rivera exited the car and walked up to the door, where they were immediately stopped by the two enforcers.

"Relax, fellas," Sam said and withdrew his badge, flashing it to them. "We're no' here t' cause a rowe, we jus' wanna' talk t' Mr. Finn."

"About what?" the stockier one grunted.

"Tha's between him and us. I'm sure he can make time, aye?" Sam walked onto the final step and asserted his height advantage over the guard; he smirked inwardly when he saw the little flash of fear flicker across the man's eyes. Finally, they opened the door, and Sam and Rivera were escorted through a foyer bigger than Sam's apartment. Without a word, the enforcers led them to the back of the house.

While the walls were a bright creamy marbled color, red wooden beams and bannisters lined the ceiling and accents. With the stained glass windows they passed casting blood red light onto the marble floor, nothing about the house seemed friendly to Sam. Every step made the hair on the back of his neck rise. A brief flashback of when he was a child was called to mind: Ben Abernathy, Sam, and the Lawder twins were playing in the hills of Rosneath's forests when they came across a deep, dark cave. Being children, their first thought was that it belonged to a Redcap, and on a dare, Sam went inside of it. He didn't make it very far when the sound of a branch being broken somewhere in the dark sent him running for his life; he had refused to walk alone in Rosneath's woods for a long time after that, terrified that the Redcap would be looking for the victim that had gotten away. Walking through William Finn's house now, with the blood red hues seeming to stain everything they touched, he couldn't help but feel the same prickle of fear in his bones.

Finally, they arrived in front of an enormous redwood door, and the stocky enforcer rapped on it.

"Entar," a gravelly voice answered, and the grunt opened the door.

They were greeted by a younger man with a large bruise around his nose that stood slightly taller than Sam; between his lack of advantage and the glare on the stranger's face, even Sam felt a little intimidated by him.

"Ach, le' them in, Robert," the gravelly voice said again. The right-hand man moved to the side, and Sam and Rivera entered the den of The Redcap.

William Finn's office wasn't any less foreboding than the rest of the house. The entire room was constructed of redwood from the ceiling to the floor; the desk that Finn sat behind made of redwood as well. Other than a family portrait hanging on the wall to the left, every other wall was a bookcase or a cabinet. The only chair was the one Finn sat in, another stained-glass window of red hues behind him. The man himself was old and heavy-set with white hair and a beard, but his eyes were curiously, and frighteningly, black and doll-like: lifeless. Sam couldn't help but agree that he certainly lived up to his monstrous nickname.

"Do I know ye?" Finn asked.

"We havenea had the pleasure," Sam answered and flashed his FBI badge to him. "I'm Agent McKay, this is Agent Rivera of the FBI."

For a brief moment, Sam would've almost thought he saw a glimpse of happiness in the old man's eyes. Finn smiled, revealing a set of disturbingly yellow teeth. "Always a pleasure meetin' a fellow Scot. FBI, eh? I've met every agent evar assigned t' watch me, bu' I donnea remember evar seein' you two before."

"We're not here about any previous misconceptions," Rivera answered calmly. Pulling out a mug shot of their escaped thief, he laid it on the desk in front of Finn. "We were told that you know this man."

Finn picked up the photo and smirked. "Aye, Aiden Marcus. Wha' di' he do t' ruffle yer feathers?"

"Tried to steal a painting."

"Tried to? So ye caught him."

Neither Sam nor Rivera answered him beyond a silent stare. Finn chuckled.

"He got away? Shame, tha' must've been embarrassin'. Isnea theft a li'le below yer paygrade, lads?"

"When's the last time you saw him?" Rivera continued.

"I cannea recall."

Sam stepped forward, "Mr. Finn, i's no secret tha' Aiden Marcus was a student of yers once."

"I donnea deny tha' we used to be close, Agent. Bu' tha' was a long time ago, before he started thinkin' with his prick instead of his brain."

"A woman come between ye?"

Finn's eyes glanced towards the wall with the portrait for only a split second. Looking back at Sam, he continued. "If I see 'im, I'll be certain t' give ye a call. I'd like t' be helpful."

"We appreciate that, Mr. Finn," Rivera nodded. "One more question before we go: Do you know anyone by the name Annabelle Matheson?"

"I cannea say tha' I do."

Rivera then produced a photograph of the mysterious ring and handed it to him. "And what about this ring? Does this look familiar?"

Again, Finn looked at the photograph thoughtfully before shaking his head. "I'm afraid no', I'm not much of a jewelry man. Ye'd be bettar off askin' me wife."

Sam took the opportunity to glance at the gloomy family portrait on the wall; none of the subjects were smiling, just painted in a way where they were staring at the admirer. In the center of the portrait was William Finn sitting in a red chair; the dead black eyes staring back were no less frightening than his real ones. It was obvious the portrait was done recently, but Finn's hair was flaming red instead of white (which Sam guessed was a special request). Standing to his right was a lovely woman with short blonde hair who reminded him of the late Princess Diana; despite the change in hair color of the portrait, anyone could see that William Finn was at least thirty years older than she was. On his left stood a young boy with jet black hair and freckles with his hands in his pockets.

"Is yer wife available, Mr. Finn?" Sam asked.

"She's out of town, agent, an' won't b' back until the end of the month."

"I donnea suppose she has a cell phone we can reach her with?"

"My wife doesnea like t' be disturbed when she's on vacation," Finn answered simply. "Was there anythin' else?"

"No, sir," Rivera answered. Sam felt him put his hand on his arm and tug, encouraging him that it was time to leave the Redcap's lair, and Sam reluctantly turned to follow him. "Thank you for your time, Mr. Finn."

"Of course; I'm always happy t' help law enforcement, especially durin' these troubled times. By the way, Agent McKay, yer name is verra familiar. I donnea suppose ye know anyone by the name of Hamish McKay?"

Sam felt his blood freeze. Keeping his poker face trained, he answered, "No, Mr. Finn, I do not."

"Interestin', the man I'm thinkin' of looks a hell of a lot like ye. Are ye sure?"

"McKay's a verra common name, bu' I'm sure I donnea know anyone by the name of Hamish."

Finn smiled again, the yellowing teeth sending chills up Sam's spine. "My mistake. Robert will show ye the way out."

"Have a good day, Mr. Finn," Rivera responded and turned to leave with Sam right behind him.

Just as promised, the tall right-hand man followed them all the way to the front door and waited while they got into their Uber. Once they were far enough away from the Redcap's house, Rivera cleared his throat. "So, what do you think?"

"I think Charlotte's righ', an' we're dealin' with a maniac. We're gonna' have t' tread verra carefully, bu' we'll keep lookin'."

"I agree. So what now?"

"Now, we go talk t' Darris an' Remy again. If we're right, an' they're less than honest, then we'll find the next piece t' this puzzle. If we're wrong an' they're jus' bampots... well, we'll ge' t' tha' point first."

Rivera chuckled, and the drive fell into a heavy silence. The driver remained quiet and continued driving in oblivious ignorance, but Sam could feel his partner's stare.

"Hamish," Rivera said pointedly. "Finn said 'Hamish.'"

"Anno," Sam nodded, "I heard 'im."

"He's still in Statesville, isn't he?"

"The las' I checked."

"Do you think he might know something?"

Sam shook his head and kept his gaze trained on the road, as they were taken back to Chicago. "Tha's no' a road we'll be goin' down, Derrick."

103

"Sam, he could help us. And right now, we're so far up shit creek without much of a paddle."

"I said no. I'll no' be givin' me brother the satisfaction of askin' him fer help. No' when we donnea need it," Sam growled.

He could practically hear Rivera roll his eyes by the way he mumbled, "Damn stubborn Scotsman."

Chapter Nine

With neither of the detectives answering their phones, Sam and Rivera stopped by the Chicago PD. That proved to be both useless and frustrating; no one had seen Remy or Darris, and a very grouchy Captain Knight informed them that they had both called in sick. The man himself wasn't any more helpful than before, he even went as far as to mutter, "You feds know everything; find them yourselves."

It was of no consequence, though, as Simon got both of their addresses within seconds of opening his laptop. "Remy and his girlfriend, Britney Holistair, share an apartment in Brighton Park, while Darris lives alone in Little Village."

Darris was closest, so the two of them went there first. Sam pounded on the door, "Detective John Darris, this is the FBI! Open up!"

They were met with no answer, so Sam kicked the door down. The apartment was in shambles: what little furniture there was had been overturned, curtains were ripped, various items thrown about and broken.

"Looks like there was a struggle." Sam looked to Rivera quizzically. "Ye think he's tryin' t' throw us off?"

"If he is, he's definitely going for realism; I found a little blood spatter over here. It looks recent."

"Call the PD an' have them send somebody over; le's ask aroun' an' see if anybody saw anythin'."

A quick interview with the neighbors wasn't any more enlightening. Darris hadn't been seen around his home for almost two days, and nobody heard or saw anything suspicious. With nothing else to go on, Sam and Rivera headed to Detective Remy's home a few blocks away.

Remy's neighborhood was much nicer, despite the tiny building he lived in. Climbing the tight stairwell, Sam felt almost claustrophobic the closer they got to the top. Finally, they reached the third floor, where there was only one apartment, and discovered the door slightly ajar. Rivera already had his gun in hand, and Sam quickly withdrew his before the two of them entered the premises. But they lowered their guns almost as soon as they walked in; in the middle of the floor, with an enormous bloodstain stretching out, were the bodies of Detective Remy and a woman that Sam could only assume was his girlfriend.

"I'll check the rest of the apartment," Rivera grunted before he began his sweep.

Sam nodded and leaned down to examine the bodies a little closer; both Remy and his girlfriend's necks were slit, the skin at one end of the cuts slightly jagged. The smell was already enough to know they'd been dead for some time, but the ice-cold feel of their skin told him it had been at least a few days.

Rivera came back to the living room, his gun holstered. "Nobody else is here."

"Ach, there wouldnea be. These two have been dead a while. Ge' Knight's people over here, too."

"With the exception of a fire, that looks like the work of The Redcap. What the hell is going on here?"

Sam shook his head, "I donnea know…"

* * *

Between taking statements and dealing with the wrath of the loathsome Captain Knight, it was nearly midnight by the time Sam and Rivera finally got back to the motel. Sam was eager to collapse into bed and sleep some of his problems away. Stripped down to his boxers, he was just about to turn in when an erratic knock at the door stopped him.

"Who is it?"

"The thief," Charlotte's voice answered slightly slurred.

"Christ," Sam mumbled to himself; quickly pulling his pants back on, he rushed to the door.

Charlotte was leaning against the door frame with Julie barely holding her up by the waist.

"Wha' the hell happened?"

"The visit with Dr. Stewart didn't go well, that's what," Julie said shortly. "And you drew the short straw tonight."

She practically pushed Charlotte towards Sam, and he barely caught her. Before he could say a word, Julie had already left.

Sam could smell the vodka on Charlotte since the moment he'd opened the door, and her behavior confirmed she'd had a bit too much. Grumbling, he hoisted her over his shoulder and carried her to the only bed in the room. Setting her down, he repeated his question, "Wha' the hell happened?"

"You were wrong," Charlotte answered him. "Spencer won't forgive me. He never wants t'see me again."

"I meant how di' ye end up like this? Julie donnea drink on the job."

Charlotte blew a raspberry and giggled. "I'm a thief, and a damn good one. I can make booze appear out of thin air. See?"

Like magic, she produced a mini bottle of Smirnoff from her jacket pocket and started to open it. Sam quickly got it away from her and took off her jacket.

Shaking his head, he sighed, "Alrigh', lass, ye've had enough t'night. Ye're in fer a hell of a hangover in the mornin'. Ye bes' sleep it off."

"No," she whined. "Still too sober to sleep. Give me back my bottles."

Sam pulled back the covers and awkwardly tucked Charlotte in, "I donnea think so."

"What if I promise to share them with you?"

"Nope."

Charlotte giggled, "The guy from Scotland doesn't drink. Wow. Now I've really seen it all."

Despite the annoying situation, Sam had to stop himself from chuckling. "I donnea drink on duty."

"Maybe not vodka, but what about stout?"

"Aye, I like a good ale. Bu' ye donnea have one so the point is moot."

She giggled again and pointed to her jacket; she said in a sing-song voice, "Check the pockets..."

Rolling his eyes, Sam did as she asked and wasn't surprised to find a few more small bottles of Smirnoff and one bottle of Guiness. He sighed again. "Where'd ye ge' these?"

"I'll never tell."

"Right, t' sleep with ye."

"Where are you from?"

"Sleep."

"Why did you come to America?"

"I'm no' playin' with ye, lass. Sleep."

"I've been told I'm an annoying drunk; I can keep this up all night."

"Ye'll fall asleep soon enough."

"You donnea know," she answered in a poorly imitated brogue. Giggling again, she said, "I'm not a lightweight."

Sam had his fair share of drunk nights and regretful mornings when he was younger, and they still happened occasionally, but having a drunk suspect was a completely different animal he didn't feel like taming that night. Sighing, he sat down on the edge of the bed and narrowed his eyes at Charlotte. "Alrigh', I'll make ye a deal: Ye ge' t' ask me five questions, an' I ge' t' ask ye five questions. Then, ye go t' sleep. Deal?"

"I already asked you two questions that you haven't answered. That's cheating."

Sam allowed himself a small laugh at her antics. "Aye, alrigh'. I'm from a little village in Helensburgh called Rosneath. And I came t' America t' ge' married."

Charlotte awkwardly sat up and leaned against the headboard. "You have a wife?"

"Had a wife, we're divorced now."

"Oh, sad. Did you have any kids?"

"Aye, she had a son, an' I adopted him when we married."

"Awe, that's so sweet. What's his name?"

"Oliver."

Charlotte smiled. "Like *Oliver Twist? Oliver and Company?* "

"Aye, I suppose. Now, ye've had yer five questions, is my turn."

She folded her arms and pouted, sticking her lower lip out and grumbled, "Fine."

"Ye mentioned earlier tha' ye have yer reasons fer chasin' these artifacts. Wha' are they?"

"I had a George Jamesone painting a looooong time ago. It was stolen."

"An' ye're tryin' t' ge' it back?"

"Nope, I didn't really care about that painting. It's the guy who stole it I want."

"Who is he?"

"I don't know." Charlotte threw her hands to her side and shook her head, "I don't know who he is."

"Okay. Why are ye lookin' fer him?"

"Because he's a baaaaad man. Very, very bad."

"Wha' do ye mean? Ye steal paintin's. Doesnea tha' mean ye're bad too?"

Charlotte's expression quickly turned; she frowned and growled at him, "No, I don't kill people. I just steal stuff."

Sam furrowed his eyebrows and scooched a little closer. "Ye've seen him kill people?"

Tears had suddenly formed in Charlotte's eyes. Choking back a cry, she answered, "He killed Claire."

"Who's Claire?"

"Claire... I'm so sorry," Charlotte slinked back down into the bed and turned her face to the pillow. Suddenly her body began to rock as she sobbed out, "I'm so sorry, Claire. I'm sorry."

Realizing that their little game was over, Sam rubbed Charlotte's back as she cried into the pillow. It wasn't long after that her wracking sobs had turned into even breathing, so he grabbed the unused pillow and walked over to the armchair sitting in the corner. Pulling it round so he could prop his feet up on the bed, he turned out the light. He hardly slept that night; the chair was far too small for him to even be remotely comfortable. So, he thought about everything Charlotte had revealed to him and what it could mean: Who was Claire? Why was she killed? And why was Charlotte chasing whoever it was that did it? Eventually the curiosity was starting to get the better of him, so he tabled the questions and tried to close his eyes again.

He woke up at 5:30 a.m. the next morning after a very fitful night, which did nothing to help his grumpy disposition. Charlotte was still completely passed out on his bed, much to his relief. Deciding she could be trusted enough not to run away during a hangover, he quietly got dressed and went to the motel lobby for breakfast, where he wasn't surprised to see Rivera already showered and ready for the day. After toast, coffee, and cereal, he sent his partner up to his room to keep their thief company while he drove to Chicago University to have a word with Dr. Stewart.

There were a few students still in their pajamas holding steaming cups of coffee as they wandered like zombies through the enormous study hall towards their classes; all of them too tired to even care about Sam, who was making loud and resounding footsteps as he walked towards the glass doors in the back. Thankfully the professor's annoying assistant Noah Porter wasn't at his desk, so Sam had no problem walking down the hall towards the office. Sure enough, there was a light shining underneath the doorframe. Sam could hear the sound of papers being rustled, confirming Dr. Stewart was on the other side, so he knocked loudly.

"Office hours don't start until 9:00; come back later," Dr. Stewart said through the door.

"I's Agent McKay, professor."

A few moments later, the door was opened. Despite being dressed in his usual garb of slacks and a button-down with no tie, Dr. Stewart looked as though he hadn't a better night than Sam had: dark circles were under his eyes, and his silvery-brown hair was unkempt, just like his wrinkled shirt. He scowled at Sam. "I thought I told your agent very clearly yesterday that none of you are welcome at my door without a warrant from now on."

Ignoring him, Sam pushed his way past the professor and into the office. "Wha' do ye know abou' someone named Claire?"

The question had caught Dr. Stewart off guard; his eyes opened wide. "Charlotte told you about Claire?"

"After a few too many vodkas, aye. Who is she?"

Dr. Stewart sighed and walked back to his desk. "Claire was Charlotte's older sister. She's dead."

"Murdered?"

"No, no, there was a house fire; it was an accident."

"Wha' abou' her parents?"

"Linda and Bob died in a car crash when Claire was nineteen. Charlotte was only four at the time; she doesn't really remember them. I'll go ahead and fill you in on a secret, Agent McKay, I'm not her real uncle. Linda and Bob were dear friends of mine; they made me Godfather of the girls. After they died, I offered to take Charlotte with me so Claire could focus on her studies... she loved art. But she insisted that Charlotte would be better off with her. The only thing I could do was manage their inheritance, which wasn't much. I sent them all that I could as my career progressed."

"She mentioned tha' she used t' own a George Jamesone paintin'?"

"No, not really. Claire was an artist, she particularly loved everything from the Renaissance era. She was working on her master's dissertation involving a replica self-portrait of George Jamesone. Charlotte was only ten; I think she's always assumed the painting was a family heirloom. But it was lost with Claire."

"How di' Charlotte survive the fire?"

"The firemen found her in a closet, passed out from smoke inhalation. She had a couple of burns, but nothing too damaging. She was in a coma for almost two months before she finally woke up. But when she did... the poor girl was catatonic. It was nearly a year before she could speak properly again, and every night she would wake up screaming from these horrible nightmares. I took her to every specialist I could find; I did everything the experts told me to do. But any time I brought up the fire she would just... freeze, get very angry, or completely break down. The doctors didn't really know what to call it back then, but we know what it is now: PTSD.

"It only got worse as she got older, too. She was a recluse at school, didn't really have any friends, and at least twice a month, I was called to the principal's office because she had broken into some kid's locker or stolen some girl's makeup. Naturally, I brought this up to the doctors, but they all said the same thing: She was still very confused. But one day she would come to terms with everything. I just had to be patient. That day didn't come for almost six years. But when it did, they were right: It all just stopped. The nightmares, the unresponsiveness, the lying... she became this happy girl again. I thought it was all over... but the day your team came to my house, I realized she had only perfected her skills."

Dr. Stewart leaned back in his chair and rubbed his face. "Perhaps it's my fault, though. I should have paid more attention. I was just... so relieved, I couldn't even think that she was still holding on to her sister's death."

"She tol' me she saw somebody kill Claire."

"She told all the doctors the same thing, but she saw the fireman who saved her. The police kept the investigation open for as long as they could, just to be sure. They couldn't find any signs of a break-in through the rubble, and Claire's body was too burned for them to ascertain anything other than accidental electrocution. Some burned bits of brushes were found around her body, they determined that she was drying a painting with a faulty dryer that got too wet in the socket. The residual paint from the brushes started the fire, and her body was part of the path."

"An' Charlotte dinnea see or hear anythin'?"

"It was late at night, and Claire had just gotten home from work. She was a waitress at a place called Gigi's. Charlotte would have already been in bed. The doctors said that sometimes children will cling to their version of a story in order for it to make sense to them, especially if they're convinced it might be their fault. I told her the police couldn't find any signs that there was somebody else with Claire. I told her that none of it was her fault; it was all an accident."

Sam pondered all of the information carefully. Clearing his throat, he asked, "Professor, why do ye think Charlotte became a thief?"

Dr. Stewart sighed again, "She remembers a painting, and the fireman's shadow has her convinced there was somebody else in that house the night Claire died. Honestly, I think she has committed her version of what happened to be the truth. Maybe looking for this painting is her way of coping with all of it. But if that's true... then I'm scared to think of what could happen to her if she finds one just like it."

"Do ye think cuttin' her off is th' bes' way t' help her now?"

"I don't know, Agent McKay. I just... I'm not a young man anymore, I don't think I can do this."

Sam nodded, "Believe me, I understand. I have a son, meself. He go' into a wee bi' of trouble after his mum and I divorced. He ended up tryin' t' rob a gas station, an' a' the time, I was facin' bein' deported back t' Scotland. No matter wha' I tried, I couldnea ge' through t' him."

"So, what did you do?"

"Jus' kept at it, an' at it. Things are no' perfect, bu' they're bettar. An' he's no' getting' inta trouble anymore. Granted, my son's a teenager, an' Charlotte's an adult. Bu', the point is, she may need ye now more than ever."

"And I'm just supposed to ignore the fact that she's repeatedly breaking the law?"

"No, of course no'. Bu' I will say this: Forensic science is no' the same as it was thirty years ago. If she's held on t' her version for this long, then perhaps there was somebody in tha' house after all."

"Or it really could be a story she's put together, right?"

"Aye, perhaps. Bu' tha's no' my problem right now. I need t' find whoever killed Anabelle Matheson, an' I need yours an' Charlotte's help t' do it. I promise ye this: When my team an' I catch our killer, I'll personally look into the fire an' settle it once an' fer all."

Dr. Stewart pressed his fingers together under his nose as he considered Sam's offer. Finally, he mumbled, "I will think on it, Agent McKay. But for now, you'll have to excuse me. I've got a class to teach."

Sam gave Dr. Stewart his card and left without another word.

Chapter Ten

S am returned to his motel room and was pleased to see the whole team awake and investigating: paper trails, evidence logs, anything they could get their hands on that related to William Finn, Aiden Marcus, John Darris, or Hank Remy and their victim Annabelle. Charlotte was nursing a cup of black coffee and an ice pack amidst all of the chaos, but that didn't stop her from trying to help any way that she could.

Simon was the first to speak with a loud, dramatic sigh. "You're not gonna' like this, boss, but there hasn't been any fishy movement from the detectives or anybody in Chicago PD for as far back as I can see: no suspicious money movement, no history of police abuse, nothing. And Chase D'Angelo may be pointing us in William Finn's direction, but I can't find *anything* in Annabelle Matheson's life to tell us why he'd want to kill her. Honestly, he was making money because of her."

"Wha' do ye mean?"

"Remember how the detectives said she donated regularly to charities and stuff? Since we've now determined that they're not the most trustworthy sources of information, I checked into who she was making donations to. For the last few years, she's been donating to the C.A.R.E.S. Foundation."

"An' wha's the C.A.R.E.S. Foundation?"

"Chicago's Abuse Rehabilitation Ecological Solutions, it's a non-profit. According to the website's mission statement, their main mission is to provide more habitable housing and living for Chicago's poor and underprivileged by creating better homes and jobs. Not exactly anything new, it's been around for nearly forty years. But, get this Bruce Jaimes was the founder."

"The Jaimes Godfather," Rivera confirmed before Sam could ask. "The head of the Jaimes Clan founded a non-profit to help the underprivileged. We can all agree that's totally a bullshit cover for something, right?"

"Obviously," Sam nodded, "bu' if Jaimes is dead then who's runnin' it now?"

"According to the website, it's being run by his daughter Audrey," Simon answered. "Considering we know who her husband is, I think we know who's *really* running the cover now."

"We've been looking over all of his business dealings too, but we've come up with squat," Rivera added. "Literally the only connection Annabelle had to Finn is her donations. From what we could piece together from her life, she never attended any of the seminars or galas."

"So tha' begs the question how Finn knew she had the ring in the first place," Sam said. Joining them at the table, he rubbed his face and sighed, "Christ, we cannea catch a break, here."

"What I can't figure out is why Finn would go after this ring," Julie said suddenly. Lifting the fake into the air, it glinted under the dim light. "From what you guys said, Finn doesn't seem like an art connoisseur, let alone a jewelry guy. So why would he even get involved in this?"

"I told you guys this job has been on the market for years," Charlotte mumbled. "Whoever wants the George Jamesone stuff doesn't seem to care who gets it or how they do it, as long as they deliver, and they can't point a finger at them. Annabelle was a fairly low-profile person, so it's not like there'd be too much attention put on her murder. Maybe that's why Finn took the job; just because it was convenient."

"Ye've go' a point," Sam nodded his agreement. "Bu' here's wha's really been botherin' me: Aiden Marcus. Why would he ge' involved in somethin' tha's completely outside his talents? His history doesnea suggest he's a notorious art thief type, an' there's no love between him an' Finn so why would he risk mixin' in The Redcap's business? An', finally, who would go t' the trouble of freein' him?"

Simon raised his hand in the air and began to wave it around. "Pick me, teacher! Here's a crazy idea: What if it was Finn who got Marcus out? An assassination/rescue in broad daylight seems like The Redcap's style. He doesn't seem to care about the collateral damage he causes."

"I'd actually buy that theory," Rivera nodded. "Finn does seem like the type to get a man he hates just to kill him."

Sam stood back up and began pacing the floor, "Aye, he does... I suppose i's a possibility. Bu' tha' still donnea explain why Marcus would try t' steal a paintin' in the first place. He disappeared aftar Finn was brought inta' the Jaimes fold, ye'd think he'd leave Chicago, or a' least nevar do anythin' t' cross paths with the Redcap again."

Charlotte nodded, "The fact that he even tried coming into this game is almost an insult. Honestly, that gala was so easy, even a blind man could have robbed the place. Marcus and his little troupe were practically the Three Stooges in there."

"Exactly. Whoever wants these artifacts obviously donnea want anythin' t' lead back t' them, so how would Marcus even know abou' the job unless he was told? An' if he was, why would the mystery buyer hire somebody who donnea know wha' they're doin'?" Sam could feel a headache brewing from all of the questions; he closed his eyes and rubbed his temples, continuing to pace the floor. "Nothin' abou' this makes any sense... no' t' mention nothin' explains how Annabelle's ring go' switched in the first—" Sam's eyes shot open and he stopped pacing the floor "—Christ! I'm an idiot! Remy an' Darris!"

Simon practically jumped at his outburst, Charlotte hissed in pain and groaned out, "Do you *have* to yell, right now?"

"What about them, Sam?" Rivera asked.

"They switched Annabelle's ring while t'was still in evidence!" Everyone in the room looked up curiously, so Sam continued his theory. "Since we reopened this case, we've hi' nothin' bu' dead ends an' dead bodies. The first day we go' here, everybody's been tryin' t' ge' rid of us, bu' no' them. Then Remy turns up dead, an' Darris has disappeared? They're workin' fer Finn, an' Finn's cleanin' up the loose ends."

Rivera looked as though he wanted to argue but stopped himself and began to think about Sam's theory.

Julie started to pace the floor. "It makes sense; they couldn't find any connecting details to The Redcap's other victims, which means they're either really bad at their job, or they're crooked. It's got to be the latter."

"Aye, I agree. So wha' are the odds tha' crooked cops wouldnea switch the verra ring tha's bein' overlooked in the investigation in the first place? Nobody'll think t' question the lead detectives checkin' on the evidence, an' who's gonna worry abou' a ring tha's been in plain sight the whole time?"

Finally, Rivera began to argue, "This is an interesting thought, but without Darris we can't prove it."

Sam turned to Simon and barked, "Can ye find him?"

"I've been trying, boss, but he hasn't made any card charges or anything that I can track. Of course, that's assuming he's still alive. Look, it's not exactly a secret that The Redcap is a murderer. Can't we just go in and have him arrested for suspicion of Remy and Annabelle's murders until we find something more concrete?"

Rivera shook his head, "The way Annabelle was killed is circumstantial. It's not enough to prove Finn did it. Hell, it's not even enough probable cause for a search warrant. For all we know, it could be a copycat hit."

"Are you kidding?" Simon asked, "There are at least three other bodies on ice that have their throats slit *exactly* the same way."

"And only Charlotte stumbled on that being the way Finn dismisses his problems. A jury isn't likely to take the word of a professional liar. No offense."

She waved her hand and mumbled, "None taken."

"Without a murder weapon, we can't prove anything. Like I said, all circumstantial and no probable cause."

"What exactly would you need to be considered enough probable cause?" Charlotte asked, forcing everyone to turn their attention on her.

"Anything physical to prove he killed those people," Julie answered her. "The broken tipped knife, for example, would be great."

"You *know* he keeps its hidden location to himself at all times," Rivera added. "And the guy owns most of Chicago; there's no way we'd be able to look at *every* place in his name."

"Well, couldn't you look into his businesses? You know he owns most of the district; not *everything* is going to be clean. Surely you could arrest him for *something*."

"We'd have to get somebody to roll on him and tell us what we're even looking for. Our Chicago buddies are too busy with this turf war business, plus they don't like us, and the PD wouldn't even light a cigarette for us. The only guys who might have given us a hint are dead and most likely dead. Let's face it, Sam, we've got squat. I really think we should —"

"No," Sam growled, "We're no' goin' t' Statesville."

Rivera was about to argue when, suddenly, a loud ping sounded from Simon's laptop. The lanky man started typing furiously and smiled with glee. "Darris just used his ATM card! And thanks to my kick-ass facial recognition program, I've got him on candid camera only two blocks away from here! If you hurry, you might catch him!"

"How, genius? He'll duck into a corner faster than we can get there."

"Rivera, Rivera, Rivera, when will you learn to never doubt me?" Simon chuckled and turned his computer towards him, showing the traffic camera and ATM feeds. "I'll track him through the cameras and guide you, so stop whining and move it!"

Sam was already out the door with Julie right behind him, Rivera jogging to keep up. Placing their siren on top of the SUV, they raced through the busy streets of downtown Chicago until they got to the ATM where Simon received the notification. Thankfully, Darris was on foot and hadn't gotten too far. Within minutes, Sam and his team had found him about to enter a restaurant.

"Darris!" Rivera barked, earning a panicked look from the detective.

He turned to run but was stopped by Sam pulling the SUV in front of him.

"Donnea even think about it," Sam smirked, his gun pointed directly between Darris' eyes. "Ye've go' some explainin' t' do."

***

Sam sat across from John Darris in the FBI's interrogation room; while Rivera led the interrogation with his preferred heated, yelling manner, Sam watched their suspect with a cool and calm demeanor. Darris tried to remain impassive during the interrogation, but the way the man fiddled with his fingers told Sam how nervous he really was.

"We know that you conveniently left out some information about Annabelle Matheson's murder," Rivera barked at their suspect. "There are at least three other bodies with their throats slit exactly like hers. Do you know what the penalty for obstructing justice is? Hmm? It's two years in prison."

Darris muttered, "I don't know what you're talking about."

"You know what happens to cops in prison, don't you Darris? They don't last a week unless they agree to be a fat guy named Bubba's bitch, and then you only last two months. Not to mention what will happen if William Finn just happens to get word that we have you in custody, and you talked to us."

At the mention of the Redcap, Darris's posture changed from nervous to terrified. His fidgeting hands were now completely still, and Sam could see a bead of sweat appear on his brow just below his greying hair.

Sam took the opportunity and leaned forward, placing his hands on the table. "Darris, if ye donnea help us, we cannea help ye. We know tha' ye tipped off Finn abou' Annabelle Matheson, an' we know i's no' the first time ye've helped him. We even know abou' the ring."

Sam kept his eyes trained on Darris through his bluff. Truth be told, they couldn't prove anything other than Darris and Remy were incompetent in their investigation of Annabelle Matheson, but his fear of William Finn was obvious. Sam knew if they could find the right button to push, he would help them.

"Did you know that your partner Remy is dead?" Rivera continued. "We found him and his girlfriend; both of their throats were slit, just like Annabelle's. How much do you want to bet Finn did it, Sam? Better yet, how much do you want to bet that Darris here won't survive the night once word gets out—"

"You don't understand what's going on here!"

Sam felt a small sense of triumph. They were finally cracking him. Calmly, he probed further. "Then tell us, Darris. Yer bes' chance is with us; ye understand tha', don't ye?"

Sam wasn't sure what Darris would do, but tears certainly weren't what he was expecting. "It's my fault that Remy's dead... I tried to stop him; he was getting too close. But he just... he knew we hadn't investigated that woman's murder to the best of our ability, but I was able to convince him to let it go. When you guys started poking around, he dug a little deeper... I tried to stop him, I tried. He just wouldn't stop... all I had to do was keep him from poking his nose in Finn's business... I failed my partner..."

"We've seen your apartment," Rivera continued. "Tell us everything."

Darris rubbed the tears away and sighed. "...You're in for a long story. Trust Darris Furniture and Appliances—that's my old man's shop. He put his heart and soul into that store since he was a kid. But he's always been too damn nice. Sometimes people would come in and not have enough but really needed the bed or the washer, whatever, and he'd just take what they had and call it even. And when the pandemic happened... a lot of people were affected, my dad included. The banks let him hold on as long as they could, but then it was time to face reality: Small businesses were closing all over the country. My dad was already $200,000 in the hole; he'd never be able to reopen if he got shut down."

"So, he went t' the Redcap fer help?" Sam probed.

"Yeah. Dad and Finn go way back. I told him it was a bad idea, but he was so damn stubborn! He got the money, said Finn told him 'He's happy t' help an ol' friend.' Then one day, I get a call from The Redcap..."

"Wha' di' he want?"

"...He told me my dad wouldn't owe him a cent if, occasionally, I looked the other way on some of his affairs. I tried to refuse. I even said that I would pay him back myself. He just laughed and told me that if dad didn't come up with what he owed, plus 30% interest, by the end of the week, then he was going to kill him, my mom, even my sister and her kids... You'd think there'd be a sense of loyalty among friends, but Finn doesn't know the meaning of the word. He even said he'd make me watch while he took care of them. I didn't have any choice!"

"So, when Annabelle was murdered, you knew it had to be The Redcap's doing," Rivera pushed further, "and that's why the case went cold."

"Yeah, and then he came to me with a copy of her ring and told me to switch it out with the real one, once all of the tests were performed, like you said."

"So, what happened at your apartment?"

"Once word got around about you guys catching Aiden Marcus, and Annabelle's investigation being reopened, I knew it was only a matter of time before he'd come after me. Finn's not a second-chance kind of guy. I managed to get my mom and sister out of here... but dad wouldn't leave. Finn killed him, and then set the store on fire. I stayed away until I thought I might be able to sneak in and get a few things, but Finn's guy was already waiting for me. I only just managed to fight him off and escape, I even got in a good punch to the nose."

Sam suddenly remembered the enormous bruise on Robert McGail's face; he looked to Rivera, who nodded his agreement that it had to have been him that attacked Darris.

"I tried to get to Remy and warn him, but Finn had gotten to him first."

"So ye went inta hidin'. Bu' then ye ran out of money an' went t' yer ATM, where we found ye."

Darris nodded. "Finn's going to kill me. And then he'll find my mom and my sister —"

"We won't le' tha' happen; ye have my word."

"What can you do to protect me? I made a deal with the devil, and now I've got a target on my back the size of the damn Wrigley Field."

"We'll get you and your family into witness protection," Rivera answered. "You'll get a whole new life; Finn will never be able to find you."

Darris scoffed, "This is Chicago, agents: Gangster Central. The Redcap is in bed with everyone who's anyone; you're not the first ones to think you can stop him. Why do you think nobody has ever been able to take him down before, hmmm? Because he doesn't give anyone the chance to."

"We're no' interested in takin' down a mob syndicate; we're interested in solvin' Annabelle Matheson's murder," Sam growled. "Bu' unless ye saw him slit her throat yerself, we cannea do tha' withou' a murder weapon. If ye help us, ye'll be a completely different person by this time tomorrow."

"Look, you want me to say William Finn did it? Okay sure, he did it. But I don't have a clue where he keeps his tools. I don't know how he does anything!"

"You're telling us the only thing he used you for was to fudge the paperwork?" Rivera sneered.

Darris wiped the sweat from his brow, "...Look, I did hear a rumor that he does a little smuggling on the side, supposedly through one of his shipping companies."

"Of what? Drugs? Stolen goods?"

"How the hell would I know? All I ever did was keep my department off of his trail. But, believe me, I'm not the only one that's been shanghaied into working for him. I told you: He's in bed with everybody. Hell, I wouldn't be surprised if there are a few people in this building that William Finn calls for the occasional favor."

"How long have you been looking the other way for Finn?"

Darris sighed, "Eight months. At first it was just whenever Remy and I were on a case, then he started having me look into customs for his shipping —"

"Wha' shipping company?"

"Any of them; whichever one he felt like using at the time. There wasn't any pattern."

"Can ye remember the dates?"

"...Yeah, I think so. Why?"

Sam stared at Darris, weighing his usefulness to their situation. Tapping Rivera, he told their suspect to sit tight as they walked out the door towards the observation room where Julie was watching the encounter.

The three of them stared at their crooked cop through the screen, but Julie was the first to speak. "You can't seriously be considering letting this guy go free? Who knows how many people have died because he's looked the other way for Finn?"

"He's a little fish, Jules," Rivera said. "If we want the big one, we let the little one go."

"Yeah, and then the little fish swims away and becomes a bigger fish later on. What about all the families who won't get justice for their dead loved ones?"

Sam answered, "Ye heard him; he dinnea have a choice. If somebody threatened yer mother, wouldn't ye do anythin' t' protect her?

Julie didn't answer him.

"Look, we ge' William Finn; everyone ge's justice," Sam declared.

"And how are we going to do that? Darris doesn't have any useful information for us."

"Perhaps no' abou' the murder, bu' he does know enough abou' Finn's business dealin's. Frankly, the only way I can see us gettin' our fish is if we hit him where it hurts: the wallet. We'll have t' intercept a shipment."

Julie scoffed, "You want to steal whatever Finn's smuggling?"

"No, I want t' catch him in the act. We catch a dirty shipment; we ge' a warrant t' search his facilities. A' minimum, we force everyone t' pu' him under a microscope an' stop him until we ge' our proof tha' he murdered Annabelle Matheson."

Rivera nearly laughed, "You really think he'll keep the knife that killed Annabelle and the others at his office? He's more likely to keep it in his home somewhere, if it's not in his pocket. And even if we do get the chance to look around his businesses, we'll be putting ourselves and Annabelle Matheson's children in danger."

Sam angrily turned towards Rivera, his height advantage giving him much more menace to his tone than he meant as he growled, "So wha' do ye suggest, then? We call Copper an' tell her we know who killed Annabelle, bu' he jus' so happens t' be the head of the Scottish Mob, so we'll no' risk it?"

"I'm just being realistic, Sam," Rivera growled right back, ignoring the fact that he was still a foot shorter than him. "It's not just us we're risking here; we need to be careful."

"An' we will be. We keep Darris out of the light until this all blows over, then we send him t' the other side of the country where Finn cannea touch him. Finn will never know t'was Darris tha' tipped us of his operation."

"I still say that bastard is just as guilty," Julie grumbled. The way she folded her arms across her midsection reminded Sam of Oliver when he was a child. He would pout when he didn't get his way.

Sam rolled his eyes and answered, "Only of tryin' t' protect his family, an' he's no' who we're after. Ye bes' accept tha' if we're t' ge' the Redcap. Now, are we ready or no'?"

Rivera and Julie shared a final glance between each other before nodding their agreement.

"Good. Call Dower an' have him start arrangin' things w' witness protection," Sam grunted. Grabbing a pen and a pad of paper, he marched back into the interrogation room. Taking his seat across the table from Darris again, he said, "I want ye t' write down every date an' detail ye can remember abou' the times Finn asked ye t' look inta' customs. Can ye do tha'?"

"Yeah, but what good would it do? I already told you, there wasn't any pattern on how he used his companies. Believe me, I tried to find one."

"Ye le' us worry abou' tha', Darris, an' we'll ge' ye an' yer family far away from here in the next twenty-four hours."

"...Fine, but I'm not going to tell you where my mom and Sheila are until Finn's in custody, got it?"

"Fine," Sam nodded.

"And what do you intend to do with me until this is over?"

"We'll get you to a safe house," Rivera answered. "I'll take care of it personally. Believe me when I say this is the safest option."

Detective Darris took a deep breath, nodded, and began to write down everything he could on the pad of paper; there were nearly two full pages of dates and shipping companies by the time he was done.

"Good man," Sam nodded. "Until we can ge' ye' t' the safe house, we'll put ye in a private cell here. Alrigh'?"

"Fine," Darris answered quietly.

Sam and Rivera joined Julie in the observation room again as Darris was led away. Whipping out his phone, Sam sent pictures of the list to Simon. Within seconds, his phone was ringing.

"Okay, boss, what is this and what do you want me to do with it?" Simon asked perkily.

"I's a list of William Finn's shippin' companies, an' the dates an' the times he go' them through customs withou' anyone lookin'. I want ye t' find a connection between all of them."

"You can do that?" Charlotte's voice said over the phone.

"Please," Simon scoffed. Everyone could hear his fingers moving across his laptop keyboard like lightening, but they remained quiet as the young man worked his magic. "...Boss, you never cease to amaze me! You're right, there is a connection!"

"Wha' is it?"

"Every one of these companies was acting on behalf of the C.A.R.E.S. foundation!"

Rivera snapped his fingers, "I *knew* that phony non-profit was a cover for something!"

"Aye, an' now we can find ou' wha' exactly. Simon, can ye find ou' when Finn's makin' another shipment on behalf of the foundation?"

"Way ahead of you, boss," Simon snickered. "Trust Jaimes Shipping had a recent load come through New York customs a few days ago. It's expected to be shipped to the warehouses in two days."

***

Sam, Julie and Rivera marched directly to Director Bronson's office for permission to go to the next step: surveillance and the search of Trust Jaimes Shipping. After handing over their guns to Heidi again (which Sam knew was merely the most subtle way the Chicago office could insult them), they walked in to the Director concentrating on a pile of paperwork.

After explaining everything they had, Bronson couldn't even be bothered to look up from his desk. "You want me to authorize a search of The Redcap's warehouse based solely on the word of a crooked police officer? I'm beginning to think you're not as bright as Copper led me to believe."

Sam bristled at his comments but did his best to remain calm. Folding his arms across his chest, he continued, "Sir, we know he murdered Annabelle Matheson, bu' we cannea prove it. Bustin' him fer smugglin' will ge' us into his facilities, where we can have a bettar look an' possibly find the actual murder weapon."

"Mmm, and Finn's lawyer will tear that evidence apart in seconds, stating how it had nothing to do with his business dealings, and you'll end up with nothing. Really, McKay? Any rookie cop knows the basic rules of search and evidence collections."

"True, bu' bustin' him fer smugglin' would a' least be enough t' ge' him off the streets until we find more. There's a' least three other people tha' have been killed with their throat slit, the same way as Annabelle Matheson."

"Has Finn ever been found guilty for these deaths?"

"If he had, he wouldnea be where he is now."

"So, what you're saying is you don't have any real proof, other than William Finn's reputation and the rumors that your suspect heard."

The back-and-forth game finally brought Sam's blood to a boil. Rivera stepped forward, but Sam stopped him from saying anything as he slammed his hands down on the Director's desk and bellowed, "Fer Christ's sake, Bronson, we're the goddamn FBI! If somebody donnea toss their rubbish in a bin, we can arrest 'em fer it! Ye know there's enough suspicion against Finn t' go after him!"

The Director stood up from his chair, slammed his own hands on the desk, and bellowed back in his nasally voice, "You're talking about going up against one of the most dangerous men in the country, McKay! So, unless you've got something concrete that will guarantee we can put him away, I'm not going to sacrifice any of my people during a turf war, in the hope that you might get lucky. Nor will I risk any of their lives solely because of your hunch. You ought to be ashamed of yourself for even considering putting your own team at such risk."

"Ye donnea know my team, Bronson; They'd walk into hell itself t' ge' the bad guy if I said tha's where he was. Ye may be Chicago's FBI director, bu' my team has bigger balls than ye or this whole buildin' combined."

Sam's insult hit exactly where it was intended; Director Bronson's eyes opened wide, and his nostrils flared. The balding man snarled, "Get out. You and your ragtag delinquents can go back to Cleveland; we'll be taking over this case. I'll expect to see all of the evidence you've gathered on my desk first thing in the morning. You're dismissed, McKay."

Sam thought he might break the desk with his bare hands, and he had to resist the strong urge to do it. Taking a deep breath, he backed away from the Director and deliberately stomped out of his office, Julie and Rivera right behind him. He practically snatched his gun out of Heidi's basket before he marched towards the elevator, not caring in the slightest that every agent in the building was watching him. Sam was used to the funny looks, thanks to his height, but the angry scowl on his face was enough to scare certain people out of his way as he walked. Julie and Rivera didn't try to say a word as he stormed out of the building; they just followed him to the car and got in. Even the drive back to the motel didn't give Sam enough time to cool off, and he burst through the door to his motel room.

Both Simon and Charlotte jumped at his outburst, but Charlotte was the first to comment. "Is he always this charming?"

"Only when somebody says he's not allowed to do something," Simon answered her. "Bronson said no, right?"

"He's takin' over the case, an' we're no' longer allowed t' use the facilities," Sam growled.

Rivera sighed, "Well, I'm sure insulting his family jewels had a little something to do with that last part."

"Please, Derrick, you would have said the exact same thing to the smug prick," Julie countered. "Bronson may be a coward hiding behind his rank, but his word is final. Right, Sam?"

Sam paced the room and breathed deeply, trying to get his temper under control as he thought about their options. "...Maybe, maybe no'. Technically Copper is the one tha' put us on this case, so she's the only one with authority t' take it away from us."

"Yeah, but I bet Bronson has already called her to bitch about us."

"I donnea think so; he didnea seemed too pleased tha' we came here in the first place. I highly doubt he'd call a woman fer permission, after she forced him t' accept our bein' here. He may no' be willin' t' le' us search Finn's trucks, bu' Copper will."

"You really think she'll let us go digging around Finn's dealings that easy?"

"Aye, bu' we'll have t' move fast. The shipment comes in two days."

Rivera smiled and turned to Simon, "Figure out what trucks we need to bust; I'll give Copper a call."

Julie cleared her throat, "I don't want to be a black cloud here, but those trucks could make a stop anywhere from New York to here and unload whatever it is they're smuggling."

Sam turned to Rivera, "Ye still have a few friends based in New York, don't ye?"

The short, Latino man nodded. "I'll get those containers tailed."

Chapter Eleven

Rivera had called Copper to update her and get the green light they needed to stop the trucks. After passionately arguing their stance, Copper approved the search and sent them the authorization to enlist the Chicago PD for the bust, as well as promised to keep Bronson at bay. Before hanging up the phone, she sternly said to the team, "Just make sure it's the right trucks; we only get one shot at this." Simon was able to hack into Trust Jaimes Shipping's schedule and discovered that there were at least four trucks scheduled to deliver 'humanitarian aid' on behalf of the C.A.R.E.S. foundation at 6:00 a.m. The truck numbers to look out for were 128, 543, 919, and 245. Rivera called in every favor he had to keep a tail on those trucks all the way to the border of Illinois, but everyone came through and followed them all the way from New York. With every stop, they all confirmed that the containers had not been touched nor tampered with since they left the shipping yard.

It was 5:50 a.m. the day the trucks were scheduled to arrive, and the streets were just starting to fill with the sounds of loud horns and engines as Chicago's residents started their typical work day. Sam, Rivera, and Julie were positioned in their SUV by the Western edge of the Loop on West Van Buren, the other side of the river, for their stakeout. While the three of them sat alert in the car, they had Simon keep his eyes on the ATM and traffic video feeds back at the hotel all through the night to remain absolutely sure that the containers weren't switched. Though, everyone knew the real purpose he was left at the motel was to make sure Charlotte would stay out of trouble.

Once again sitting in the driver's seat, Rivera lifted his radio and said, "Is everyone in position?"

The familiar, disdainful voice of Captain Knight answered, "I've got units surrounding the whole block; three of them on Lower Wacker ready to move in, *agents.*"

Rivera smirked and radioed back, "We appreciate your cooperation, Captain."

Julie snickered and said in a hushed tone, "You should have seen his face when I gave him Copper's order. I thought his head might pop off from how red he was getting!"

"I bet *that* felt good, sticking it to the chauvinistic pig."

"*So* good."

Though Sam kept his face stony, he couldn't help but feel a mix of relief and excitement at their luck; once they got their hands on whatever Finn was smuggling, he would be put in prison for a long time. His life would be torn completely apart, and it was only a matter of time before they found the blunt-tipped knife that killed Annabelle Matheson. So many murders would be solved, and a truly dangerous man would be off of the streets. It was a fantastic goal that required all of his attention, but his mind was preoccupied with Oliver. Sam hadn't heard another word from his son since they last texted each other, and he knew the only time the boy would truly talk to him again was when he was back home, and they were face to face. Though Meredith hadn't painted Sam in the best possible light, he knew that she did her part in insisting to Oliver that Sam loved him more than anything. It was better than nothing.

Not a minute later, Simon's voice sounded through the radio and interrupted his thoughts. "Heads up, guys! They're ten minutes away!"

"Which way are they coming, Abler?"

"...They're breaking up. Two of them are headed north on Wacker, one's going south, and the last one is heading towards you!"

Rivera barked into the radio, "Everybody split up, I want three units per truck!"

While everyone else got into position, the trio stayed in their position. And they waited. Despite the ambient noise in the streets, the air in the SUV was so thick it could have been cut with a knife. Suddenly, an enormous semi pulled onto the road just behind them with *Trust Jaimes Shipping* printed on the side of the container. Sam had to grab the roof handle as Rivera wildly drove through the crowded street and directly into the path of truck number 128. Two Chicago PD cars pulled up behind them, and every officer jumped out of the car with their guns raised.

"Turn off the engine!" Sam bellowed to the driver and passenger of the truck, who did so and kept their hands raised in the air. "Out, now!"

The two men shakily exited the cab and were tackled to the ground by the police while Sam, Rivera, and Julie marched to the back of the trailer and opened the door with zeal. Inside were crates marked *perishable* and *non-perishable*, bedding items, and even sparse wooden furniture pieces.

Sam wasted no time in climbing into the trailer and breaking open each crate; the non-perishable box contained canned and boxed food, bags of rice, beans, salt, and pepper. The perishable crates were ice chests full of milk, cheese, and various lunch meats. He began to feel more than nervous as he tore into the bedding, even going so far as to tear apart a few pillows looking for something, anything, that was remotely illegal, but he was met only with cotton down and fluff. He smelled the packages desperately, hoping to catch the scent of drugs, ammunition, anything at all, but the scent of cheap laundry detergent was all he could make out. He kicked the furniture to splinters only to be met with more disappointment: there was nothing illegal about the shipment; it was exactly as it was described as humanitarian aid.

Rivera yelled into his radio, "Does anybody have anything?!"

"Truck number 543 just has boxes of blankets and food," a female voice answered.

"Same for 919 and 245," Captain Knight's voice confirmed. "There's nothing wrong in any of these crates."

Sam turned towards the destroyed cargo and kicked the biggest piece of broken rubble near him into the wall of the trailer. "Shit!"

"What the hell is going on?!" the truck driver yelled. "All of that stuff was for West Side!"

Julie turned to the PD and barked, "Let them go. And don't worry, sir, everything will be replaced."

"You better goddamn believe you'll replace everything! Do you know how many families were expecting food and blankets on their doorsteps this weekend?! What the hell is the matter with you people?!"

Ignoring the driver, Sam jumped out of the trailer and started walking back towards their SUV. Snatching the radio away from Rivera, he growled, "Simon, is there any other trucks tha' we missed? Di' any of them make any stops once they go' through customs? Anythin' a' all?"

Before he got his answer, another cop car pulled onto the scene and out stepped Captain Knight with his growling, red face. The man didn't scare Sam, despite how his eyes were raging, though that was mostly due to the fact that he wasn't as tall as Sam. Knight growled, "Well done, McKay, not only have you held up traffic, given William Finn the right to sue us, but you've also managed to publicly humiliate every law enforcement official in front of most of lower Chicago!"

"Anno, an' I'll take full responsibility."

"You're damn right you will! The minute I get back to my office, I'm giving the FBI a call! How dare you make a mockery of us!"

Sam knew there was nothing he could say that would excuse this blunder, but that didn't stop the annoyed anger he felt as Knight stood there berating him in the middle of the street. A small crowd had already gathered, and Sam could feel each stranger's questioning, judgmental eyes on him. He clenched his fists and took deep breaths, as he listened to the onslaught for only another moment before he snapped. "Instead of worryin' abou' how stupid we look, why donnea ye help by gettin' this mess under control, Knight?!"

The Captain's face turned even redder and for a moment, Sam thought the man's head might pop off. Then he huffed and turned away to get back in his car.

Sam turned to Rivera and Julie, who were already trying to smooth over the current situation: The Trust Jaimes truck was already making its way back to the main building; curious drivers were ushered through the scene as quickly as possible; and the rest of the Chicago PD set to work breaking up the grumbling spectators. Sam did his best to tune out the ramblings of the masses, but the embarrassment of their failed operation made it significantly more difficult to do so.

Finally, everything was moving normally again and Sam, Rivera, and Julie retreated to their SUV. While Rivera was still driving, Sam lifted his radio and said, "Di' ye find anythin' yet, Simon?"

The radio was silent.

"Simon, do ye copy? …Charlotte? Are ye there?"

Again, nothing but static replied.

"Somebody answer me!"

Sam began to feel a sense of panic rise in him.

Rivera seemed to have already read his mind as the SUV lurched forward. They sped down the road recklessly; Rivera ducked, weaved, and blared the horn at every car on the main highway. When their exit came up, he practically forced the car to jump the rail by the way he swerved into the lane and ran through every red light, until they finally pulled into the parking lot of the motel.

Sam wasted no time in jumping out of the SUV and sprinting towards his room; he practically shoved the key card into the lock mechanism as he barged through the door, when he saw Simon lying on the ground under the table. Looking around the room, he cursed himself: There was absolutely no sign of struggle, and Charlotte was nowhere in sight. He hadn't noticed that Julie was right behind him until she placed her fingers on Simon's neck. Coming to her side, he looked down at their young companion with concern.

"...He's got a pulse, and he's breathing!" she sighed in relief.

Sam looked up at the table where he saw two coffee mugs sitting next to Simon's laptop; one of them black and practically full (which he guessed was Charlotte's) while the other was a creamy blonde color (full of cream, just the way Simon liked his coffee) and already nearly empty. Picking up the empty mug, Sam ran his finger along the inside of it and tasted it: milky and sweet with a hint of something he couldn't quite place, but the sudden but mild tired feeling he got only confirmed what he suspected.

"Charlotte drugged him," Sam growled, slamming the mug back on the table.

"That bitch!" Julie snarled, "Hold on, Simon! We need to get him to a hospital!"

Rivera had walked in sometime when Sam wasn't looking and quickly knelt down next to Julie. "He'll be okay, Jules. Don't worry."

"Rivera, ge' his laptop," Sam barked as he leaned down, grabbed Simon under the arms, and swung their young companion over his shoulder. Ignoring the pointed but confused looks from some of the other motel residents, he walked back to the SUV and placed Simon in the backseat. Julie had already climbed in and gently placed Simon's head in her lap while Rivera clambered into the passenger seat, the little computer in his lap. Satisfied that everyone was secure, Sam jumped into the driver's seat, slammed his foot on the gas pedal, and took off down the road towards the nearest hospital.

***

Sam practically power-slid the car into Chicago Hospital's parking lot, and he wasted no time in flashing his badge and demanding for the closest doctor to start examining their young companion. The staff tried to insist that due to the pandemic, the trio were not allowed to go back with Simon, but Sam wouldn't hear anything about it; not even Security wanted to tangle with the large, angry Scotsman, and an exception was made for the rest of the team. After what seemed like an eternity, they were finally in their own room, and their young companion was laid on a bed with a heart monitor hooked up to him. Julie sat in a chair next to him with both of her hands clutching his right; Rivera was leaning against the wall on the other side of the bed with his arms crossed, and Sam was pacing the tiny room with fury.

Doctors and nurses, clad in facemasks or hazmat suits, were bustling through the corridors with charts and equipment in their hands, and yet not one of them had said a word about Simon's condition for almost an hour. Despite flashing their badges proving they were law enforcement, the only thing that had been done was a nurse had come in to draw a few vials of blood, administer some liquid charcoal through a feeding tube, and then she left without another word. But that was forty-five minutes past, and everyone's patience was wearing thinner by the second.

Although concerned for their young companion, Sam's mind was actively flooding with questions. He continued his pacing as he pondered why Charlotte would drug Simon. The answer: to escape. But again, why?

"What the hell is taking these tests so damn long?!" Rivera barked aloud, interrupting Sam's thoughts.

"The pandemic has instituted a lot of new procedures, including wearing more gear for blood tests," Julie said softly, "There's nothing we can do but wait."

"It can't take that long to run a tox screen. And we have priority since we're law enforcement!"

"Look, I want answers just as much as you do, Derrick. But they're doing their jobs as best as they can. At least Simon's heart is beating steady and strong, and he's breathing on his own. Maybe this isn't as bad as we think, and we're all over-reacting."

Rivera scoffed, "And you're not the least bit pissed at Charlotte for drugging him in the first place?"

"Shut up, you idiot! Of course, I am!" At the insistent shushing of a passing nurse, Julie lowered her voice and continued, "But she didn't kill him, so that makes me a little bit more forgiving."

"Yeah, she didn't kill him *yet*. For all we know, she slipped him something that's shutting down his organs one by one."

Sick of their bickering, Sam interrupted them by growling, "She didnea do tha'."

"And what makes you so sure of that, Sam?"

"Ye saw the way she reacted when she saw Annabelle; she hates violence and death. I donnea think she'd kill Simon; jus' knock him out. Bu' why? Why would she do tha'? Why would she escape when she knows we'd let her go anyway?"

While Rivera remained as quiet as Simon, Julie answered without hesitation, "Because she did something we can't forgive...like tipping off Finn!"

Sam stopped his pacing and turned to Julie, and the fiery redhead continued her theory. "Think about it, we were set to bust him; Simon had made doubly sure of the connection; and the trucks were watched carefully all across the country. The only way we could have been wrong is if the containers never left the shipping yard with the Trust Jaimes trucks in the first place!"

A wide grin spreading across Sam's face, "Ach, ye beauty! Yes! Tha' has t' be why the bust failed!"

"But why would she do that?" Rivera asked. "I got the impression she wanted to get Finn as much as we did. Siding with him doesn't make sense...unless she's been working for him all along. She could have been helping us just to keep us away from whatever it is Finn wants."

Julie sighed, "Considering she's a master at disguises, that would make sense."

Sam's phone suddenly began to ring; looking at the screen, he winced to see it was Copper calling him, and he knew it wasn't going to be pretty. Taking a deep breath, preparing himself for the reprimand, he answered with a, "Hallo, Belinda."

"I thought my requirement of keeping me in the loop was very clear, McKay," Copper answered with her level yet authoritative tone. "I'm sure you can imagine my embarrassment when Bronson called me this morning to give me the news: The Chicago PD had destroyed a humanitarian aid shipment for Chicago's citizens in need at the order of *my* agents."

Sighing, Sam rubbed his face. "Finn was tipped off; tha's the only explanation fer it."

"I don't care *what* the explanation is, McKay. The point remains: The four of you fouled up a simple murder investigation. And now, we'll most likely never get another chance to find the weapon that murdered Annabelle Matheson."

"Wha' are ye sayin', Copper?"

"Bronson got a call from Finn accusing you and your team of harassment, misconduct, and destruction of property. He intends to sue. And, if that wasn't bad enough, I just got through a very heated phone call from the Attorney General. The four of you will have to be put on probation while an investigation is carried out. So, all of you better pack your bags and get your asses back here pronto."

Though he wasn't the least bit surprised by the charge, that didn't stop Sam from clenching his fist together and looking around him for something to punch. Taking another deep breath, he calmly replied, "Well tha' won't be fer some time; we're a' the hospital. We found Simon knocked out, he's been drugged."

"With what?"

"We donnea know yet, we're still waitin' on the results from his blood test."

"Fine, then you can stay until he recovers. But I warn you, McKay, as of this moment, you, Rivera, Russell, and Abler are officially on probation. That means you are not allowed to set a foot near the Chicago FBI building, is that clear?"

"Yes, ma'am."

"I mean it, McKay, don't go *anywhere* near the FBI."

Per the norm, Copper hung up with the last word. Sam felt as though he could squeeze his phone to dust with his bare hands, but he quickly placed it back in his pocket before kicking the closest thing next to him, which happened to be a swivel chair. His outburst made his companions jump, but the air remained heavily quiet as Sam did his best to control his temper.

Rivera's voice broke the silence. "You don't have to tell us what she said; we can pretty much guess."

Right at that moment, a short, stubby man wearing a doctor's coat over the hazmat suit walked in carrying a little stack of papers. "Okay, so the good news is your friend is going to be fine. It took a little bit of deducting, but we figured out he's got gamma-hydroxybutyric acid in his system."

Julie's eyes opened wide. "GHB? As in Liquid X?"

"Those are only a few of the names for it, but yes."

"What's the bad news?" Rivera asked.

"He was given a pretty large dose. The charcoal we gave him will absorb however much is in his stomach, but there's no way to tell how much has already gotten into his bloodstream."

"Will he wake up?"

"Yes, we just don't know when."

Sam stepped forward and asked in his gruff voice, "Wha's yer best guess?"

The little man tried to not appear intimidated, but he visibly flinched when he looked up at Sam. Clearing his throat, he answered, "GHB doesn't stay in the system very long, and as long as he didn't have any alcohol with it, I would say...anywhere from 12-24 hours. But I should warn all of you: When he does wake up, he'll have a bit of amnesia. And it could be very serious. GHB is notorious for erasing recent memories, even when taken recreationally in smaller doses; it's quite possible that a large dose will leave behind a big dent in his memory."

"How big of a dent? Big enough that...he may not know who any of us are?" Julie asked, completely horrified.

The doctor swallowed uncomfortably and answered, "It's possible."

"But amnesia can be cured, right? Like with time and doing things he's familiar with, one day he might just snap out of it?"

"Sometimes an amnesia patient's memory comes back, but other times...I just want to prepare you all for any of the outcomes. Honestly, it's impossible to predict what will happen. This drug has differing effects for everyone, we really won't know the damage until he wakes up."

Rivera then stepped up, "Come on, Doctor, isn't there anything else you can do?!"

"There isn't a proven antidote for GHB. All we can do is hope that the charcoal absorbed most of it and keep a close watch on his vitals." The doctor began taking a few steps backwards, trying to slink out of the room. Just before he ducked around the corner, he finished with, "I'll send a nurse around to re-fill his IV in a minute. I'm sorry, I wish I had better news for all of you."

With the doctor gone, Sam turned his gaze back to Simon; though he kept his face stony and impassive, he desperately wished there was a bar in the hospital where he could get a glass of scotch. Maybe two. Glancing to the rest of his team, he could tell they were having similar feelings. Julie had tears forming in the corner of her eyes, but she quickly wiped them away before they could fall. Rivera walked back to the hospital bed and took a seat next to Simon before he leaned down and whispered, "You better remember me when you wake up, smart ass. Who else am I going to fight with?"

Julie snorted at his comment and walked over to join his side. She placed her hands on his shoulders, but Rivera quickly shrugged them off and growled at her, "If the doctor's right, and he wakes up without knowing who we are, do you still think you can forgive Charlotte?"

Julie snarled back, "Do you have to be such a bastard?"

"Oh, honey, I haven't even gotten started yet."

"When did this become *my* fault?!"

Sam stepped forward and bellowed, "Haud yer wheesht! Both of ye!"

Another passing nurse leaned in to hush him, but with one glare from Sam she quickly scurried away.

Turning back to Julie and Rivera, he continued, "Yer bickerin' won't help Simon, nor does it help our case."

Rivera scoffed, "Ha! What case? Copper told you we're off of it, right? Besides, our only lead has joined the enemy, and we don't even know where the hell she is. What are we supposed to do, Sam?"

"Fer starters, the two of ye can go back t' the motel an' look fer clues tha' migh' actually tell us wha' happened. Perhaps we're wrong, an' there's another explanation. An' while ye're there, take a nap."

"Are you serious?" Julie argued, "You really expect us to sleep right now with Simon lying in the middle of a hospital?"

"Ye heard the doctor, he'll wake up. An' if he wakes up without his memory, do ye really think seein' a bunch of angry bampots is gonna' help him? Ye have yer orders, go!"

Though Rivera and Julie were glaring at him, the two of them reluctantly did as they were told and walked out of the hospital room, leaving Sam alone with Simon. Truthfully, he couldn't listen to their fighting and bickering when he knew it was his fault that Simon was laying in that hospital bed. Sitting down in the closest chair (which was too small for him), he rubbed his face with his hands. *I should've known bettar than t' leave him alone with her,* he thought to himself. *She's a master thief, we knew she couldnea be trusted! An' she played us... played me...* He sat in that chair for what felt like hours stewing over his blunder, swearing up and down to himself that if Simon didn't emerge from his coma as his normal self then, if he ever saw her again, he would shoot Charlotte on sight.

Suddenly there was a knock at the door. Sam dropped his hands and looked up to see a redheaded female nurse clad in blue scrubs, heavily made up, and wearing a face mask, carrying an IV bag.

"I've come to replenish his IV," she said sweetly, "Unless this is a bad time?"

"No, please. Donnea le' me stop ye."

Without another word, the nurse walked in and set to work switching the bags. "Is he your son?"

Sam shook his head and muttered, "No."

"Nephew?"

"My employee."

"Wow, aren't you a nice boss?"

Ignoring her, Sam rubbed his face with his hands again. But that didn't stop the chatty nurse from continuing. "Just so you know, the cafeteria makes a really good chicken salad. Why don't you go get something to eat while your friend rests?"

"Thank ye, bu' I'm no' hungry," Sam answered, though his stomach argued otherwise by growling right on cue very loudly.

The nurse chuckled. "Alright, but you should keep your strength up. If you change your mind, tell them Martha sent you. They give you double portions when you know a nurse, and you look like a guy with a big appetite."

Sam did his best to smile at her politeness, but he quietly answered, "Thank ye, I appreciate tha'."

"Now, I just need to give him a little vitamin shot and...done. Let us know if you need anything." Without another word, the nurse walked out of the hospital room.

Leaning back into the too small chair, Sam did his best to get as comfortable as he could. Deciding to try and close his eyes for just a minute, he felt himself ready to drift off to sleep when a loud gasp made him jump from his chair.

Simon was awake and gasping for air, then he suddenly started shaking.

Rushing to his side, Sam did his best to hold the young man still and soothe him, "Easy, pal, is alrigh'. Ye're alrigh'."

Turning onto his side, Simon pushed Sam out of the way before he began to violently throw up onto the floor. Not knowing what else to do, Sam reached for the nearest bowl and held it out for the young man while he continued to retch. Looking around him, he snatched the communication remote and shouted, "Simon Abler, GHB overdose in room 543 is awake! Somebody ge' in here!"

A few nurses appeared within seconds and rushed to the bed.

"What happened?" one of them demanded.

"One minute he was in a coma, an' then he suddenly started gaspin' fer air."

Simon continued to retch everything in his body until it turned into dry heaves. Another nurse suddenly produced a syringe, which she injected directly into the IV, and the heaving began to slow down. Finally, it stopped, and Simon fell backwards into his bed. Panting, he opened his eyes and turned his head. The young man smiled and croaked out, "What's up, boss?"

Although Sam was more than relieved to see him awake, the young man's bloodshot eyes made him look as though he was close to death. "How do ye feel?"

"On a scale of a very bad hangover to being hit by a truck...somewhere in the middle."

Though Sam couldn't help but laugh at Simon's never-failing comedic wit, he turned his attention back to the nurses and demanded, "Wha' di' ye give him?"

"5 milligrams of Zofran to stop the nausea."

"No, I mean the nurse before ye. The one tha' came an' changed his IV. She said she gave him a vitamin shot."

The nurses looked at each other, the confusion in their eyes evident, before one of them began to type into the computer next to the patient bed. "...I don't see any notes made that the saline was refilled or that any shots were given. Any and all medicines have to be recorded, even the saline."

Sam's eyes opened wide. "Martha, she said her name was Martha! She had red hair!"

"I'm sorry, I don't know anybody named Martha or anyone that matches that description."

"Neither do I," the other nurse nodded. She quickly added, "I'll call security. Gina, get a blood sample and rush it to the lab."

The nurses hustled about the room in a frenzy, but Sam's mind was on the imposter that had magically cured Simon; There was no questioning the red-head nurse had been Charlotte. While he was impressed that she had managed to fool him again, he was equally livid with her trickery. She had talked to him face to face, and he didn't recognize her for the second time. Humiliated didn't begin to cover how he felt, and he was happy that Copper wouldn't find out about this, or she'd most likely fire him on the spot.

How in the hell does she do this?! He yelled at himself inwardly. *Ye'd think tryin' no' t' be caught, one would stay away from the verra man tryin' t' catch ye. Bu' instead, she has the balls t' talk t' me abou' chicken salad? If I ever see tha' blasted woman again, I'll*—Sam's eyes opened wide. *Wait... she wasnea makin' small talk, she was sendin' a message.*

Before anyone could ask what the problem was, Sam raced out of the room and down the long, white, and winding corridors looking for the hospital cafeteria. Ignoring every patient and staff member that demanded he slow down, he didn't stop running until he found his destination. Walking through the door, he was hit with a wall of delicious smells: soups, salads, hot and cold sandwiches, and even main meals like fried chicken and Salisbury steak were being served with various side dishes. His stomach growled loudly in protest at the lack of food, but he ignored it and walked over to the sandwich bar in the far-left corner. Three staff members (all in face masks) were putting together meals in assembly line form behind the counters lined with clear glass guards, but they quickly turned their attention to Sam as he marched over.

"What can we get for you, sir?" one of them asked.

"Actually, I believe ye might have already taken my ordar. My friend Martha said she'd ordered a chicken salad fer me?"

"Oh yeah, we've got that right here!" The employee reached underneath the bar and produced a tray with a large, sumptuous looking sandwich, cookies, and an apple juice box. Next to the ensemble sat a pink envelope. "She asked us to say sorry she missed you and happy birthday. Enjoy!"

Taking the tray, Sam walked to a table in the farthest corner where he was away from prying eyes. Completely ignoring the meal, he ripped open the envelope and found a birthday card with a message written inside that said: "2500 South Christiana Ave, 7 p.m., reservation in your name."

He stared at the note, completely ignoring the tempting sandwich on his tray, as he decided whether or not he should meet her. Despite the fury he felt towards Charlotte, Sam couldn't help but feel intrigued at the cloak and dagger meeting she'd set up. His thoughts were at war. The fact that she had brought Simon out of his coma made him a little bit more forgiving, but that didn't completely quell his rage. Still, she must've had a very good reason to do what she did, if she was willing to meet him face to face after doing it. But he still couldn't think of any reason why she would drug Simon and tell Finn anything, and his curious nature just wouldn't let him leave it alone. Sighing, he pocketed the note and got up from the table. Throwing the tempting sandwich into the trash on his way out, he made his way back to Simon's room and called Rivera and Julie to update them on their young companion's condition.

Chapter Twelve

It was 6:50 p.m. when Sam arrived at the address on the note; he pulled the SUV in front of a tiny bistro that appeared to be closed and wondered if his GPS had gotten him lost. But looking at the little restaurant, he decided to chance it, as he felt confident that Charlotte wouldn't just send him somewhere for no reason at all. The door was locked, but a short, portly woman rushed over to open it before he could knock.

"*Hola!*" she smiled as she opened the door. "Please, come in!"

Though still a little unsure of the situation, Sam crossed the threshold without a word. While the outside of the building resembled an old cathedral (as did most of older Chicago's architecture), the inside was an eccentric myriad of colors and paintings: abrasive orange and yellow walls that were lined with gold painted banisters. The onslaught of color was only soothed by the sky-blue ceiling. Everywhere Sam looked, he saw wooden crosses of different sizes and colors. He took note of the door in the back of the little bistro and guessed that it led to the kitchen and perhaps was the only other way out of the place. When he heard his hostess re-lock the door, he turned to see her gesturing to a set of stairs that led to a second floor.

"You are Sam? I'm Juanita. Your table is waiting upstairs."

Sam didn't hesitate in following her, but he kept his hand on his gun grip to reassure himself, just in case he was walking into a trap. When he saw a single table set for two, he relaxed somewhat. Taking a seat in the corner (where he could keep an eye on everything surrounding him), he tentatively accepted an offered menu from the little old woman.

"Charlotte said you like drink? I have beer, wine, tequila—"

"Water, please," he answered her gruffly. "Ye know Charlotte?"

"*Si,* she's a good friend of mine. She helped me a while back, now I help her."

"Is she here?"

"She said you'd ask me that and to tell you she'll be here. Until she is, I make you whatever you like."

Sighing, Sam reluctantly nodded his head and glanced at the little menu. "Donnea be offended, bu' I'm no' much fer Mexican food. Is there anythin' ye migh' recommend tha's no' on the spicy side?"

"*Si,* I make you steak *fajitas* with beans and rice, not spicy."

"Alrigh', I'll take it," he nodded and handed his menu back.

The portly little Juanita scurried away, leaving Sam sitting awkwardly alone at the small table in the eerily quiet room on the second floor. He began to regret not telling any of his team where he was going when he left them with Simon; both Julie and Rivera were relieved to learn that Simon was awake and his memory was completely intact, and they rushed to the hospital. While everyone bombarded Simon with questions regarding what had happened in the little motel room, Sam had kept his eyes on the clock on the wall, anxiously awaiting the time to meet the professional thief that had been so much trouble for them. Everyone wanted to know where he was going when it was time to leave, but he simply answered that he needed to think, and he would be back later. His thoughts were interrupted when Juanita returned with a cup filled with ice water and some chips in a basket.

"I go make your *fajitas* now, say 'Juanita' if you need anything."

"Aye, thank ye," he nodded and tentatively nibbled at a chip as his hostess walked away again. He sat at the table for a long time, and still there was no sign of Charlotte. The time was 7:23 p.m., and he began to wonder if he'd been played yet again. He began to smell the tempting scent of beef wafting through the air towards him, and his stomach grumbled in protest; he hadn't eaten all day. Looking towards the stairs where the scent was coming from, he nearly jumped when he heard the sound of two women's voices laughing and talking to each other. Reaching for his gun, he quietly hurried down the stairs towards the source of the voices. They were coming behind the door that led to the restaurant's kitchen. There was a little window the size of a sticky note on it, so he quickly ducked to the side and peeked through it: Charlotte was inside, sitting on a metal prep table, eating a piece of pepper while Juanita was concentrating on the stove. He watched the encounter carefully, curious as to what Charlotte's game was, when Juanita suddenly turned towards him. Sam ducked behind the door and waited for her to pass by, but was surprised to see Charlotte walking right behind her carrying her own plate of food. Raising his gun, he cleared his throat to get their attention.

Both Charlotte and Juanita turned around, and while Charlotte remained completely unphased by his actions, Juanita began screeching in a rapid-fire manner, "¡*Dios mío, nos va a matar! Por favor, solo cocino comida, no tengo nada*—"

"Juanita, *cálmese, cálmese,*" Charlotte said soothingly. "It's okay, he's not going to hurt either of us. Right, Sam?"

Sam continued to glare at Charlotte, but the whimpering Juanita softened him a little, and he holstered his gun.

"¡*Oh Dios, gracias!*" Juanita practically slammed the plate she was carrying on the nearest table and crossed herself emphatically. "You didn't tell me he would be violent!"

"Sorry, I didn't think he'd be *that* mad at me," Charlotte answered her with a smile. "But, then again, I probably should have known better. I promise, he won't use the gun anymore tonight. Right, Sam? Now, let's eat, I'm starving!"

Despite the fact that she was still visibly shaken, Juanita picked up the little plate of food she had been carrying and continued up the stairs.

Sam kept his eyes hard and trained on Charlotte, wanting to explode on her the first moment they had alone. But she had already begun following their hostess as if nothing in the world was wrong. Reluctantly, he ascended the stairs again. Once Juanita had finished fussing over his plate, she hesitantly passed him and raced back down to the main floor, leaving Sam and Charlotte alone.

Charlotte broke the silence first by turning to face him with a small little smile on her face. "Let me just start by saying I'm sorry for the way I disappeared on you guys, but believe me, I wouldn't ha—"

Sam didn't give her the chance to finish; closing the distance between them in two mighty steps, he swiftly brought the back of his hand down against Charlotte's cheek with a loud crack. "Ye poisoned Simon. Ye poisoned him, ye bitch!"

He couldn't help but feel satisfied to see the glimmer of shock and fear in her eyes; he hadn't hit her hard enough to send her to the floor, and that took a lot of restraint on his part. But it was enough to demonstrate how livid he was with her.

144

Charlotte brought her hand up to her cheek and rubbed the reddening spot very tenderly. "I didn't have a choice, Sam."

"Wha' the hell di' ye give him tha' woke him up? The doctor said there's no antidote fer GHB."

"He meant not one that modern medicine accepts. It's called physostigmine, and it can bring GHB overdoses out of comas safely, as long as they're not habitual users. Considering he woke up, I'd say everything worked out alright, wouldn't you?"

Snatching her hand, Sam growled, "Why di' ye drug him in the first place?"

"Because if I didn't, the Redcap's right-hand man was going to kill him!" She growled right back, yanking her hand from his grasp.

"So, it's true, then: Ye did tell Finn wha' we were up to."

Charlotte looked into his eyes defiantly. "Yes, I did. And I can explain everything."

"Why the hell should I believe anythin' ye have t' say?"

"Because if I really wanted to just hurt you and run, I wouldn't be here right now, would I? Now will you please sit down before your stupid steak gets cold?"

Sam didn't release his glaring stare from hers; though his head screamed he should just arrest her and haul her to jail right then and there, his gut told him she really did have a good reason for the betrayal, one that might even help them. Taking a deep breath to calm himself, he walked over to his chair. When Charlotte was seated on the opposite side of him, he growled again, "Alrigh', explain."

***

5:35 a.m., 14 hours earlier that day...

"My God, doesn't the FBI sleep?" Charlotte yawned as she poured herself a cup of black coffee from the motel room's coffee maker.

"We do, the office just decides when," Simon answered. Nodding towards her, he teased, "And isn't it a little early for cocktails?"

He was obviously referring to her form-fitted red dress, and she playfully gave him a spin, "Didn't your mother ever tell you to always dress to impress? I'm ready to celebrate when we catch Finn."

"Mhmm, and I'm sure the boss will love that little number, too."

"That's exactly my point," she chuckled. Charlotte watched Simon type on his little laptop furiously and couldn't help but smirk. Coming to sit next to him at the small motel desk, she asked, "So, the other three get to run off with guns blazing, and you do what exactly?"

"Oh, haven't you figured it out yet? I'm the most important guy on the team," Simon smiled proudly, his white teeth practically beaming against his ebony skin. "Whatever the boss needs to know, I find it for him on my trusty laptop. Heck, I was even able to find you through your burner phone."

Charlotte opened her eyes wide in feigned amazement. "Really? Wow. Big Brother really does have an ear everywhere now, doesn't he?"

"Well, only the best members of Big Brother. And I'm one of the best."

"That part I figured, smart guy. But what I meant was: What exactly do *we* do here and now for this big bust?"

"Well, our job is to keep an eye on the cameras that are lining the streets and follow the movements of the trucks, once they come through the border. Also, should we happen to see any funny business, we give Sam and the others the head's up, so they're not blindsided."

"So... we're basically glorified lookouts?"

Her sarcastic comment earned a glare from the playful computer genius. "Well, if you want to strip it down...yeah, you could say that."

"Sorry," she giggled. Taking a sip of the coffee, she winced, "Ugh, this stuff is terrible."

"Really? I don't think it's that bad." Simon took a sip of his own coffee, which was practically blonde from how much creamer he'd poured in.

"If that's true, kid, then you must think Hot Pockets are gourmet meals."

"Hey, pepperoni pizza pockets are life! Don't knock them!"

She tried another sip of the bitter liquid but winced again. "Okay, I can't stomach anymore. And I need my coffee. There's a little bakery around the corner; they've got to have *much* better wakeup juice than this stuff. I'll be back in five minutes."

"Whoa, whoa, whoa, wait a minute! I'm not supposed to let you out of my sight."

"Come on, Simon, It's literally ten yards away. I'll be back before the action starts. Don't you trust me?"

Simon eyed her skeptically. "Is that a trick question?"

She giggled again. "I promise, I'm not going to run away. Where would I even go?"

"Sorry, Ms. Master of Disguise, but Sam will have my ass if he finds out I let you leave without an escort."

"It'll be our little secret. What if I promise to bring you back a doughnut, too?"

Simon perked up and eyed her over the rim of his laptop. "...Custard filled?"

"And smothered in chocolate," Charlotte winked at him.

"...Fine, but you better be back here in ten minutes! Any longer, and I'll hunt you down and handcuff you to the heater again."

"So dramatic," Charlotte giggled and walked out of the door before the computer boy could change his mind.

Jogging down the stairs of the cheap motel, she ran around the corner to the little mom and pop bakery and was hit with the intense smell of fresh coffee and pastries. Thankfully, it was early enough that the line wasn't very long, and she was able to order two coffees and half a dozen doughnuts (two of them custard filled just for Simon) in practically no time. While she stood to the side, waiting for the fresh ground coffee, she couldn't help but feel that she was being watched. In her line of work, paranoia was a normal sensation, so the feeling wasn't particularly new. But when the hairs on the back of her neck began to rise, she couldn't help but wonder if her senses had a little merit. Reaching into her pocket, she pulled out her makeup mirror and feigned fixing her lipstick while she used it to glance all around her. Nobody suspicious stood out to her in the little bakery, but outside of the window she noticed a little black car sitting across the street from the motel. She couldn't make out the driver, but she had a pretty good idea of who he might be working for.

When the coffee was ready, she made her way back to the motel. With trained expertise, she carefully glanced at the black car again and felt her blood run cold: The driver was none other than Robert McGail, William Finn's second in command.

Shit, not now! She thought to herself as she calmly ascended the motel stairs to the little room; she'd been expecting Finn to pick her up since she'd dropped him an anonymous message two days ago. Knowing his resources, she had no doubt that he'd find her. She just expected it to be after Sam and the others found nothing in the trucks, not right at the moment the operation was happening. At least Sam, goody-two-shoes Julie, and Rivera were safe, but Simon would be beaten to death if McGail came to the room. She had no doubt that's exactly what he was there to do: pick up Charlotte and leave absolutely no witnesses behind. *I've got to do something...*

She barely got a chance to knock on the door before Simon practically yanked it open from the other side. The relief on his face was evident; Charlotte teasingly nudged him as she walked in.

"Such little faith. Here: your extra creamy coffee and custard-filled doughnuts."

Simon reached for the doughnut first and sighed in contentment, a smile stretching across his face. He had barely taken a sip of his coffee when the radio on the table sounded:

"Is everyone in position?" Rivera's voice said.

An unfamiliar but clearly disdainful voice answered, "I've got units surrounding the whole block, three of them on Lower Wacker ready to move in, *agents.*"

Rivera answered back, "We appreciate your cooperation, Captain."

Simon ran back to the table and glanced at his laptop. "Looks like everybody's starting to roll out. In less than an hour, we'll be busting a smuggling operation open! Sam will find the murder weapon in record time after that, I guarantee it."

"And Annabelle will get justice, right?" Charlotte asked tentatively.

"If Sam has anything to say about it, you bet she will. Along with everyone else William Finn has hurt."

She smiled. "He's really that dedicated?"

"Dedicated is the nicest way to put it. Honestly, he's just a dang stubborn Scotsman whose curiosity will most likely get him killed one day....And here come the trucks!" Simon picked up his radio and said urgently, "Heads up, guys! We've got movement!"

"Which way are they headed, Abler?" Rivera answered.

Simon typed on his laptop furiously for a moment before radioing back, "They're breaking up. Two of them are headed north on Wacker, one's going south, and the last one is heading towards you!"

Rivera's voice barked through the radio, "Everybody split up, I want three units per truck!"

While Simon sat back in his chair with a smug smile on his face, Charlotte quickly (and subtly) glanced out of the motel window at the black car; her heart began to beat faster when she saw McGail step out of the driver seat and start making his way towards the motel. There was no way Simon would let her go out again without warning Sam, and he'd be shot on sight if Finn's men saw him. She had to think quick.

"Hey... how's that coffee? Better than this garbage?"

"Yeah, I have to admit, it is pretty tasty."

"Mind if I try a little sip? I usually always take mine black, but it does smell pretty good."

"Don't you remember the pandemic rules? No sharing anything."

She chuckled nervously, "I promise my cooties have been taken care of. May I?"

Simon shrugged his shoulders. "Alright, sure, go ahead."

Charlotte reached into her pocket and pulled out the little bottle she kept on her person for emergencies: liquid X, or GHB. Thankfully, Simon was too preoccupied with his computer to notice her movements, and she quickly slipped a larger than normal dose into his cup before handing it back to him.

"Meh, too milky for my taste after all. I'll stick with it black. But you better hurry and drink, it's starting to get cold."

Simon had already stuffed his face with the second doughnut and muffled out, "I-a-mi-ute, dey're mo-in."

"What?"

He swallowed and answered, "I said in a minute, they're moving in."

Charlotte could almost see Robert McGail's shadow moving through the window; she could almost feel the beads of sweat appearing on her forehead. Her eyes darted around the room in a panicked state, trying to think of a Plan B for Simon, when he picked up the coffee and practically downed it in one gulp. She sighed inwardly. Just as she could hear the door handle being jiggled,

Simon's eyes rolled over and his body dropped to the floor in a heap. Relief flooded her and she raced to open the door before Finn's henchman decided to kick it down.

She yanked it open and felt a chill crawl up her spine as she looked at the hulking mass before her; his face was cold and stony, there was an ugly yellow bruise around his nose, and he didn't bother to hide his leering stare. She had a pretty good feeling he would have no problem shooting Simon regardless of the fact that he was passed out.

"The Redcap wants to speak with you," he said gruffly. "Now."

Gulping down her fear, she did her best to appear sweet as she replied, "I figured, and he was nice enough to send me an escort. What a gentleman."

McGail suddenly looked over her shoulder and nodded his head towards Simon. "Is that a problem?"

Charlotte coolly lied through her teeth. "Unless somebody gets here in two minutes with an antidote for pure rattlesnake venom, I doubt he'll be telling anybody anything."

She had to choke back a laugh at McGail's confused expression. "There aren't any rattlesnakes in Chicago."

All brawn and no brains, a perfect sidekick for William Finn, she chuckled inwardly. "You're right, there aren't. Which means nobody will be able to cure him in time. He'll be dead in about 90 seconds, and there's no mess."

"Of course, you'd choose poison to kill somebody," he sneered. "Women never want to get their hands dirty."

"Finn wants to see me now, right? Shouldn't we get going?"

McGail looked over her shoulder at Simon one more time. *Please don't come in, please don't come in...*

Finally, he snorted. "Follow me."

Relief flooded through her; grabbing her jacket, she followed the brute to the black car. Seated in the back seat, Charlotte glanced out of the window at the motel as the car sped away. All along the drive, she hoped and prayed to any God that happened to be listening that Sam and the others would find the young man before the drug could seriously harm him.

The drive through the streets of Chicago was awkward and terrifying; her escort never said a word the whole way, but he didn't bother hiding turning around to look her over. He didn't seem like the type that would appreciate her flirty banter, at least not without following through, which she had no intention of doing, so she kept quiet. She had nothing else to do but glance out of the window at the buildings they passed until they pulled up to a chain-link gate that was impossible to climb over. On the other side of the gate was an enormous white warehouse with no slogan on it. McGail leaned out the window to enter some digits on a keypad, and the gates slowly opened. The car moved in through rows of shipping trucks poised for departure until they pulled inside of a large garage where there were more trucks up on lifts with dozens of men underneath the hoods. Charlotte couldn't see any sign of another woman in the whole business, and that only made her even more nervous.

Once the car had stopped moving, Charlotte got out and held her head high as she looked down every male in the room that was leering at her with the confidence of a queen; as terrified as she felt, she knew better than to let a man smell fear on her.

McGail walked in front of her and grunted, "This way."

He led her through the garage and the rows of ogling men to the back where a lone door sat closed. McGail knocked three times before a gravelly voice answered, "Entar."

McGail opened it and practically pushed Charlotte through, where she came face to face with the man who lived up to his nickname. Seated in the middle of an office that was made almost completely out of redwood with no windows, William Finn looked perfectly at ease in the middle of his lair. Surrounded by the dark red hues, Charlotte felt as though she had walked into a butcher shop, albeit a fancy one. Relying on all of her expertise as a master of disguises, she cloaked her face with fearlessness as she walked inside.

The Redcap looked her up and down before meeting her eyes with a sinister smile, his yellowing teeth showing through his white beard, giving more weight to his reputation of horror. "T'is a pleasure t' finally meet ye, C.W."

Swallowing her fear, Charlotte returned his smile with a flirtatious one of her own and, without invitation, took a seat across from his desk. "The pleasure is mine, Mr. Finn. Or would you prefer that I call you by your more colorful moniker?"

"Mr. Finn is alrigh' fer the moment, lass. An' while it's no surprise tha' ye've heard of my reputation, I cannea say tha' I've heard of yers until recently."

"Yes, we appear to have crossed our paths a few times only in the past few months. To be honest, the Covid Relief Gala was a surprise."

"How so?"

"I just wouldn't have expected The Redcap to send a disgraced acquaintance to steal a George Jamesone piece. You seem like the kind of man who prefers to do something right yourself, not let it get screwed up by amateurs."

"I'm sure I havenea the faintest idea wha' ye're talkin' abou'."

"Oh, come on, Finn. Any criminal worth their salt knows a little about their competition. Seriously, what was the point of sending Aiden Marcus to steal that painting? Wouldn't it just be easier for you to burn the whole building to the ground?

Finn didn't blink his black, doll-like eyes as he leaned forward onto his desk. Folding his hands together, he said in an unnervingly calm voice, "Careful, lass. I admire yer gumption, walkin' inta' me business like this, bu' be careful. Verra few have had the opportunity t' insult me an' live t' talk abou' it."

Charlotte could hear his right-hand man behind her, walking closer along with the sound of a gun hammer clicking; her urge to run and hide was overwhelming. She slowly crossed her long legs, sure to give the Redcap a wonderful view of them, and bowed her head before sweetly replying, "My apologies, Mr. Finn."

Her actions seemed to soothe the white-haired terror as he looked over her shoulder to McGail; the sound of the gun hammer was lowered again. Finn leaned back into his chair. "If we're bein' honest with each other abou' surprises, then I hafta admit tha' receivin' yer message abou' the FBI certainly surprised me."

"Oh, you did get my note? I was starting to wonder."

"Indeed. Bu' ye have me curious: Why would ye go out of yer way t' warn me abou' the search? An' more t' the point, how do I know ye're no' workin' with the agents?"

Charlotte giggled. "I suppose it is a little odd that I would want to help my rival, isn't it?"

"Aye, t'is rather. So ye won't mind when I say tha' I'd like t' check ye fer wires?"

The intense feeling of panic was coursing through her, but Charlotte remained impassive as she stood up and raised her arms to the T pose. "Of course not, what's a little distrust among criminals?"

Finn showed his yellowing teeth in another smile as he signaled for his right-hand to come forward. Charlotte did her best not to gag as Robert McGail pawed and fondled every inch of her body through the dress, paying special attention to her breasts (which he chuckled in delight about), but she defiantly kept her eye contact with the Redcap. She knew he was trying to gain control in any way, but she refused to lose the upper hand, despite how humiliated and degraded she felt with every passing minute. When Finn finally called McGail off, she almost slipped a sigh of relief that the excruciating inspection was over. But with the way he continued to smile at her, she had the horrible feeling that he wasn't finished.

"I'm afraid anythin' can be hidden under tha' dress, lass. Would ye mind?"

Her confident smile shifted to a scowl. Despite her personal feelings towards violence, Charlotte almost wished she had something to hurt the Redcap with right then and there. Before McGail could get the chance to personally violate her again, she pulled down the zipper of her little red dress and removed it quickly. Knowing Finn's games of control wouldn't stop there, she went a step further and removed the bra and panties she wore. If anything, it would help to speed the process along. With as much confidence as she could muster, she turned herself slowly around so that the Redcap, McGail, and all of the men in the garage who were peeking through the door got a very good look at her naked body.

Finally, she looked at Finn again and seethed, "Satisfied that I'm not here to spy on you?"

William Finn's raspy laugh was even more unnerving than his voice. "Aye, tha'll do. McGail, show the lassy some respect, aye?"

With a disgusting chuckle, Finn's man left the office and shut the door behind him.

Charlotte did her best to calmly replace all of her clothing, but the way the old man leered at her every move didn't help the anxiety she felt. She nearly slipped when she replaced her heels. Finally, she felt armored up again and retook her seat.

The heavyset man suddenly produced a bottle of dark, amber liquid which he quickly poured into two crystal glasses before handing her one. Reluctantly, Charlotte accepted the offering and took a sip. The whiskey burned her throat, but she was grateful for the familiar, grounding pain to help settle her nerves.

"Gumption, indeed," the lecherous old man chuckled before taking a sip of his own drink. "Now, then, back t' business: Why would ye help me?"

Charlotte quickly re-applied her face of confidence and answered, "I wish I could say it's a professional courtesy, but my motives are selfish. They caught me, and I wanted to get un-caught. Considering their interest in you, I thought if I helped you then you would help me."

"T' set ye free?"

"I was thinking along the lines of giving me the ruby ring you stole from that old woman in The Towers."

Finn leaned back in his chair and took another sip. "Ye migh' want'a check yer source of information, lass. I donnea have any idea wha' ye're talkin' abou' now."

"Oh, I think you do. Does the name John Darris ring any bells? He's already confessed to the FBI about your little extortion tactic. They already know that you had him switch the rings in evidence. Very clever, by the way: Who's going to question a respected detective when he goes looking at evidence on his own case? Certainly no one is going to think that he'll switch the real ring for a fake."

"Ye've go' gumption, an' ye're clever. I like ye, lass, bu' ye're bum's oot the windae if ye think I'm abou' t' hand over a pretty thing like tha' ring."

Then he did take it! Charlotte felt a sense of triumph at his admission but was careful not to show it as she continued, "Mr. Finn...you know...I think I can call you William now that you've had a chance to admire my tits. William, I've been collecting George Jamesone pieces for a long time, and I know that you don't just wake up one day and decide to go after a certain, relatively unknown artist unless it's for a very good reason. You and I both know that we're working for the same man, the one that's been paying us to collect these pieces over the years."

"Even if ye're right, I'm still no' about t' hand over a priceless ring t' ye."

"Just because it's priceless doesn't mean you haven't accepted a price for it. How much will you get for delivering the ring? Five million?"

Finn's demeanor changed instantly from assured to curious.

"And how much are you planning to sue the FBI for? I'm going to guess somewhere close to one... maybe two million for four truck's worth of destroyed aid and all of the aggravation they've caused you. Am I in the right ballpark?"

"Enough!" Finn suddenly snapped at her.

Charlotte flinched, but held her head high as she continued. "Here's what I'm proposing: You give me the ring, and I will give you the five million you were promised plus another million. I just want credit for the retrieval. My reputation has been built on collection and delivery in the cleverest way possible. And, considering I've already outsmarted your men once, it wouldn't be too hard of a stretch for anyone to think I've outdone The Redcap twice. That would almost certainly cement my reputation. Six million dollars seems fair, don't you think?"

Finn eyed her coolly for several long, uncomfortable moments before answering. "I want ten."

Charlotte snickered, "And after I saved your business this morning, how greedy. But, as an apology for my less-than-ladylike behavior, I will meet you halfway and give you eight."

Finn's face hadn't moved from the terrifying scowl since his outburst, but Charlotte refused to look away. Finally, he answered, "Aye, eight million seems fair indeed. Bu' I want the money before I give ye the ring."

"Then I want proof that you actually have it first."

Finn's scowl slowly formed into a smile again, and Charlotte was almost certain he was going to kill her right on the spot. "Verra well, perhaps I can take ye t' lunch while my men retrieve it?"

Charlotte gave him a flirtatious smile in return and stood up from her seat as if preparing to leave. "Distrust among criminals, remember? So, you'll forgive me for denying the invitation. However, if you're free Monday evening, I'd be happy to meet you for dinner, and you can show me the ring then."

Finn's black eyes twinkled as he chuckled again. "I like ye a lo', lass. Alrigh', t'is a date."

Charlotte cringed at the word, but she bowed her head respectively and answered, "It's been a pleasure, Mr. Finn."

Turning on her heels, she opened the door and sauntered through the garage without another word. The cat-calls and whistles from the men came unbridled, but she ignored them as she walked to the edge of the property and hailed a taxi, which she practically jumped into and ordered the driver to get going. Sitting in the back seat, grateful to be out of the Redcap's lair, she wrapped her arms around herself and closed her eyes. Forcing her mind to focus on the one thing that always helped her when she was distressed, she breathed deeply through her nose and visited an old memory of a lake. She had no idea where anymore, but that didn't matter because she knew she could never go back anyway. The last time she had been to this lake was when she was nine, and Claire had taken the weekend off so they could go camping together with some of her friends—a night of s'mores, scary stories, and stargazing with her sister. It had been perfect. Charlotte had a lot of happy memories with her sister, but this was the one she treasured the most. She honestly didn't know why, but she did. And it never failed to soothe her in times of panic.

The taxi driver brought her out of her memory when he cleared his throat. "Do you know where you want to go yet, ma'am?"

With no way to get to her money and not knowing where else she could go that didn't lead to her FBI caretaker's wrath, she gave the driver Spencer Stewart's address. The drive was long, and every minute of it, she dreaded the thought of what he would say when he saw her. At minimum, he would pay for her cab fare, she knew that, but more than likely he would tell her to leave again.

When the taxi pulled into the drive of Spencer's beautiful home, Charlotte hoped with every fiber of her being that he wouldn't shun her like the last time she talked to him. Of course, Julie had accompanied her the last time. That had made the situation a little more than awkward. Perhaps alone, he might be willing to speak to her. The taxi driver agreed to wait for an extra $20, so Charlotte tentatively approached the door of the stately plantation style home and knocked. Spencer answered the door within moments, and Charlotte felt the blood drain from her face when she saw him.

"Spencer... I... I..." her bottom lip trembled; she couldn't finish her sentence. He answered with a gentle smile and a warm embrace. Leaning into his hug, she felt safe for the first time that day.

Chapter Thirteen

Charlotte finished telling Sam the whole story with tears brimming in her eyes; after explaining everything to Spencer, he promptly forgave her and agreed to help her finish the situation with William Finn. Of course, he made the condition that she must permanently give up this lifestyle of crime, which she agreed to.

Sniffling, she continued, "He told me that you went to talk to him. Sam... I really do appreciate that. And after that, I found out which hospital Simon was in and checked in on his condition. When I heard how those idiot doctors hadn't woken him up yet, I knew I had to stop by and give him the antidote myself. I don't expect you to forgive me. Hell, I don't even expect you to understand. But I wanted you to know I really didn't have a choice; it was either temporarily poison him, or let him get killed. I thought the former was the better option, wouldn't you have agreed?"

Sam didn't let any of the hardness leave his eyes. "Tha' doesnea explain why ye warned Finn abou' our operation."

"Because it was the only way we were going to get anywhere with Annabelle's murder case."

"Or ye decided ye'd have better chances of getting wha' ye want by sidin' with the enemy."

Charlotte's eyes were suddenly clear again; she straightened herself and answered, "That hurts, Sam. You can believe whatever you want, but let me spell out the situation for you: William Finn has most of your resources bought and paid for or threatened and terrified. If you want to catch him, then you need to think outside of your little box of cop rules. I can help you with that, so I did. Tipping off Finn has given me a 'seat in his court'; I'll be able to get more information faster than any of you can now."

He scoffed, "Yer mastar plan has a flaw: We're off the case now. We've been ordered t' turn everythin' over t' tha' idiot FBI Chicago Directar an' return home the minute Simon is released from the hospital. Yer intentions may have been admirable, bu' ye dinnea consider the consequences."

Charlotte looked like she was going to say something but quickly shut her mouth and looked at her hands. "...I guess I hadn't considered your boss might stick it to you."

Sam didn't answer her beyond his angry stare, the guilty expression on her face softening him only a little. But the more he thought about her actions, the less angry he became; truthfully, he knew he would have done something similar if the only choices offered to him were death or impairment. He admitted inwardly that she was quick on her feet, albeit misguided in her execution.

His thoughts were interrupted by Charlotte's quiet voice. "So, are you going to arrest me?"

"Aidin' an' abettin', escape from custody, no' t' mention all the sleep I've lost because of ye are jus' a few of the reasons I should. But..."

His hesitance caused her to look up, a glint of hope in her eyes. When he couldn't continue, she smiled and threw him a playful wink. "But you like me too much, don't you?"

Something in the way she said that brought Sam to complete attention; something about her was so familiar, like a dream he'd forgotten but could still see glimpses of. Before he could say anything, his phone began to ring. Rivera's name was on the screen, which told him it had to be important, possibly about Simon's condition. "Wha' is it?"

"I've only got a minute," Rivera answered in a hushed tone.

Sam was instantly on alert. "Wha's wrong?"

"Shit just hit the fan: Chicago FBI's here at the hospital to take all of us into custody."

"Wha' does Bronson think we've done now?"

"Sam, Bronson is dead. And so is Darris. Chicago's people think we had something to do with both of them."

Sam's eyes bulged open. "Wha' happened?!"

"Darris was found in his cell just now, it looks like he hung himself. And apparently Bronson was shot at point-blank range early this morning, right outside of his house. Considering everyone in the building heard the yelling match, I think we can guess why they're looking at us for his murder."

"They cannea arrest us fer tha'!"

"They pulled a slug from Bronson, and they're claiming that it matches one of our guns, Sam."

"Tha's impossible! We've go' an alibi fer las' night!"

"Yeah, but these clowns aren't going to listen to that. Either way, we don't have a choice. We've got to go with them, until this gets worked out."

"Christ!" Sam rubbed his face. There was only one answer to all of this: William Finn. "The Redcap really is in bed with everyone. First Aiden Marcus escapes, Bronson is killed, an' then our only lead kills himself. An' all of this happened in the FBI buildin'...there's only one person tha's had access to our guns: the directors assistant, Heidi! Christ! A mole's all we need righ' now."

"Sam, I know what you're thinking, but don't! Don't come back to the hospital, and don't go anywhere near the PD or the FBI. If you do, they'll arrest you the second they see you."

"I cannea leave the three of ye!"

"You have to! I've already called Copper, and she's on her way. If you're right about Heidi working for Finn, then we might have a little leverage. But that won't stop him. With you on the outside, you've got a chance at figuring out what the hell he's up to. I have to go, they're coming. Lose the phone!"

Before Sam could argue, Rivera had already hung up. He sat in his chair completely bewildered: His team had been arrested, and he was now a fugitive hiding from the FBI for the second time within a year. Suddenly, Charlotte snatched the phone out of his hand, threw it on the ground, and stomped on it with her boot heel. Before he had the chance to argue, she grabbed him firmly by the collar and yanked him to his feet.

"You need a place to hide, right? I've got one, but we need to hurry."

"Where? Hidin' from the FBI is no' tha' easy. Trust me, I know."

"So do I," she smirked. "Listen, I'm leaving right now. If you want a chance at saving your friends, you're just going to have to trust me."

There wasn't any other choice; Sam followed her out the kitchen door of the little restaurant (where the still frightened Juanita was cowering) and into the night. Charlotte led him through the winding streets of Chicago until he felt lost. Finally, she hailed a taxi and told the driver to go to an unfamiliar address. By the way the cabbie reacted, he could tell it was somewhere far out of town. Sam didn't feel particularly safe not having any sort of control over the situation, but he knew that his only option was to trust her judgement.

The ride was long, and that gave Sam plenty of time to stew and boil over everything. It all came back to one question for him: Why? What was so important that the Redcap would go to such lengths to assure he couldn't be touched? What in the world had they gotten themselves into? Was this really all because of Annabelle's ring? Was Finn really that insane? Sam scoffed thinking about that last question: There was no doubt the man was a psychopath. But for Finn to arrange the chessboard the way he had took money and resources, and somehow Sam couldn't help but think the man valued the almighty dollar enough to have a really good reason for his actions. He just had to figure out what that reason was and then, perhaps, he could make the man pay for everything he had done.

Finally, the cab stopped in front of an old apartment building. Charlotte paid the driver and led Sam up five flights of stairs to the third apartment down the hallway. It was nicely furnished, but it was easy to tell that hardly anyone lived there. Dr. Stewart was sitting on the couch, much to Sam's surprise. "Wha' are ye doin' here?"

Charlotte answered him, "You really think I'm going to give Finn the chance to find Spencer and kill him? I made him come."

"Wha' is this place?"

"My home away from home."

"I didn't even know she had her own place until this morning. Damn near got lost on the way here," Dr. Stewart said. "Are you alright, Agent McKay?"

Sam sighed, "No' even close. An' I donnea know where t' begin."

"As a historian, I have found that the beginning is always a very good place to start," the professor replied kindly.

Sam chuckled and took a seat on the couch. After explaining what he knew, Dr. Stewart immediately took over and began to treat the dire situation like a teacher would: plenty of pens, notebooks, and markers to get the entire series of events out on paper for them to physically see. Sam had to admit, it was interesting to try and look at the case from the professor's fresh perspective, but it had yet to prove anything helpful. For hours, the three of them went over all that they knew and theorized any possible reason they could think of for Finn's actions, but nothing stood out. Eventually the professor began to fall asleep, and Charlotte insisted that he get some rest. Sam was feeling the fatigue, too, but his attention was focused on the dozens of papers that formed a web scattered all over the tiny living room floor, and at the center of it all was William Finn. If it were up to him, he'd love to go straight to the murderous Redcap, shoot him on sight, and be done with it. But until he knew exactly how deep Finn's claws were into his team, that wasn't an option. His team came before his own personal feelings. But looking at everything he knew, there was no way to possibly trace any of it back to William Finn. The man was good at not leaving behind any loose ends. At that moment, Sam wished he had something to break, and a nearby lamp was starting to look like a good candidate.

Suddenly Charlotte appeared in his peripheral vision. She held a plate with a large sandwich on it and handed it to him insistently. "You didn't touch your fajitas at the restaurant."

"Thank ye, bu' I cannea eat now. I've go' t' solve this."

"Which you can't do on an empty stomach. Come on, a big guy like you needs to keep his strength up."

Sam's stomach growled, and he chuckled; knowing she wouldn't quit pestering him now, he accepted her offering and took a large bite.

"There, isn't that better?" She smirked. Taking a seat on a chair out of the way, she nodded towards the myriad of papers and asked, "So, what is the next step?"

"Tha's wha' I cannea see. Wha' I know fer certain is tha' Annabelle was murdered the same way William Finn murders his victims, an' thanks t' ye, we know he stole her ring. Aiden Marcus escaped FBI custody, bu' I donnea know how or why. Director Bronson was murdered las' night, an' Darris seems t' have killed himself this mornin'. All three of them are connected t' this case somehow, an' suddenly the FBI has concrete evidence tha' we're involved with the death of Bronson. I'm convinced the Director's assistant is involved with tha'; tha's the only explanation fer how one of our bullets ended up in Bronson's brain."

"Okay, well you've got a candidate for who framed you, that's something. So, what's your problem here?"

"I cannea understand wha' the hell Finn is up to! He obviously thinks we're onto him abou' somethin' important, or else he

161

wouldnea have gone t' all this trouble t' ge' rid of us. Bu' fer the life of me, I cannea see wha' it is!"

"Could it just be the smuggling ring?"

"Perhaps...bu' this all started because we looked inta' Annabelle's murdar; me gut is tellin' me tha' wha'ever is goin' on here, Annabelle is somehow the key t' the answar."

"So, what you're saying is, you've got no idea what to do."

"Aye, tha' sums I' up."

"Then I guess, basically, all we've got is my meeting with Finn in two days."

"No, because ye're no' goin' to it."

"Ha! What are you going to do, handcuff me to the bed? As enticing as that idea is, right now we've got to get to Finn."

Not in the mood for her teasing, Sam rounded on her and argued, "Ye mus' know it's a trap, lass. Ye've witnessed firsthand wha' the Redcap is capable of. Do ye really think he'll jus' give ye the ring?"

"For eight million dollars, yes I do. And you don't have to worry about me, Sam, I'm a master thief remember? I've always been able to get out of sticky situations."

"Charlotte, I'll no' be havin' ye risk yer life against a madman...no' when there's another way."

"Which is?"

"...Ye've gotten yerself inta places ye shouldn't be many times. Do ye think ye can ge' me a new identity fer a visit t' Statesville prison?"

She furrowed her eyes, "Yeah, but who's at Statesville that can help us?"

Sam sighed; this was the one thing he really did not want to do, but he knew there wasn't any other choice. Turning back to Charlotte, his voice laced with shame, he answered, "Me brother, Joshua."

***

Monday, 4:45 p.m.

Sam sat in the waiting room of Statesville with a suitcase in his lap, his eyes focused on the door connected to the visitation room hallway. Charlotte had gotten him a disguise and an identity within minutes of their conversation and had even gone as far as calling the prison to make an appointment for him. Claiming that Joshua Hamish McKay was under the new representation of Harold McFaddin, Esquire, her prickly and persistent acting persona had managed to get Sam the last visitation appointment of the day. Despite his annoyance with the ridiculous name she had given him, Sam was impressed with her skills, as well as shocked at how easy it was for their ruse to be pulled off. But, just to be sure, he had called Dower with instructions to keep his fingerprints out of the system for security checks. The enthusiastic agent was thrilled to be involved and had the request taken care of immediately, but that didn't lessen the anxiousness Sam felt. With the best poker-face he could muster, he breathed the sweat-smelling air and waited. The hair on the back of his neck was alert at the situation he was in: He was technically a fugitive, and he was sitting in the middle of a maximum-security prison. Blank white walls surrounded him; there were prison guards on practically every corner if they weren't behind the glass windows at the reception desk. He felt like a cornered animal. Dressed in a nice blue suit and tie, wearing thick-rimmed glasses, he was doing everything he could to remain authoritative and calm as he waited for the appointment with Josh.

Finally, a buzzer sounded, and a guard walked through the door. "Harold McFaddin? A room is ready for you."

Sam rose from his chair, suitcase in hand, and straightened his suit jacket before he followed the guard through the door, down a long hallway lined with white painted steel doors until they came to one marked number four. The guard opened the door and allowed Sam through to a small table with two chairs on either side of it, a bar under the table, and a camera in the corner. Ironically, he suddenly felt a little more comfortable being in a somewhat familiar environment.

"Please take a seat, your client will be here in just a second," the guard said absently.

Sam did as he was told. Not a moment after he'd sat down, the door opened again, and he watched with a cold expression as his brother was led to the table by two guards and handcuffed to the bar underneath. Josh nearly did a double take when he saw Sam, and an unnerving smile creeped across his face.

"Thank ye, officars," Sam said politely. "Now, I need a few minutes with my client, if ye please."

The guards nodded and pointed to the camera. "We'll be able to monitor you through the cameras. Don't worry, we won't hear a word. When you're finished, press the button on the wall behind you."

"Understood," Sam nodded.

The guards locked the door, leaving Sam alone and face-to-face with the brother he had not seen nor spoken to in nearly ten years. Aside from the ragged, unkempt beard he must have let himself grow, he looked exactly the same as the last time Sam saw him: just as tall as Sam, muscular, and cold dark eyes. If it weren't for Josh's ragged appearance, it might have been easy for anyone to tell that he and Sam were brothers.

"So ye're my new lawyer, Harold McFaddin, aye?" Josh jeered at him with a chuckle, "Ye're tha' ashamed of me, ye donnea even use ye're real name fer a visit."

"If I had my way, I wouldnea be here a'tall," Sam answered as levelly as he could muster.

"Ah, so ye need my help, is it? I seem t' recall a promise tha' ye'll never come t' me, no' even if yer life depended on it."

"I's no' my life I'm here on behalf of."

"Really? Who's then? The bitch in heat? Her wee bassard?"

Sam had to resist the strong urge to jump from his chair and wring his hands around Josh's neck at the mention of Meredith and Oliver, the only thing stopping him being the camera in the corner watching the two of them closely. Squeezing his fist together, he took a deep breath to calm himself before replying, "I'm no' here t' play games with ye, Josh. Ye've go' information I need abou' The Redcap."

At the mention of William Finn, Josh's jeering smile disappeared. "Wha's he done t' deserve ye?"

"Tha' doesnea mattar."

"It does t' me, Sam. If ye want my help, I deserve t' know wha' I'm helpin' with."

"...Fine. He murdered an innocent."

"He's murdered lo's of innocents, an' worse. Ye'll have t' do bettar than tha'."

Sam leaned across the table and folded his hands together. "She was a harmless old woman, an' he stole a ring from her. He also had an FBI director an' my witness killed....An' now my team has been arrested fer suspicion."

The jeering smile returned to Josh's face; leaning back in his chair, he said, "An' ye donnea know wha' t' do next?"

Reluctantly, Sam nodded his head.

"...Ye donnea even know wha' yer up t' yer arse in, do ye, Sammy?"

Sam bristled at the hated nickname. Still, he kept himself calm and answered, "Obviously no'. If I did, I wouldnea be here. I know ye were Finn's right-hand man fer years, Josh. I know ye can tell me wha' I'm missin'."

"Aye, I might know somethin'. Bu' ye havenea tol' me wha' ye'll give me in return."

"Call it a favor from one brother t' another. I'm in the FBI now, so I might be able t' help ye be a little bit more comfortable here."

"Ha! Is tha' all ye've come with? Ye're a right bampot fer thinkin' I'll give me only card against The Redcap fer a good haggis every week."

"Hannah doesnea know why ye're here, Josh," Sam growled.

His younger brother suddenly sobered at the mention of their youngest sister. "Don't she?"

"As far as she knows, ye're servin' time fer possession. Believe me when I say tha' was fer her sake, no' yours. She thinks ye've jus' made some bad choices in life, bu' ye can still be a good man."

Josh held Sam's gaze, but the confidence in his eyes suddenly diminished. "...An' ye donnea believe I can be a good man?"

Leaving the question unanswered, Sam continued with a growl, "If ye donnea help me, tha's yer choice. Bu' I swear on our father's grave, when I leave here, I will tell Hannah the truth abou' everythin'. Every murdar, every woman, wha' happened with Paige, all of it."

Bringing up their stepmother was a low blow even for Sam, but he had to chance it. It was the only way he could be sure that his disgraceful brother would agree. He knew that telling Hannah what kind of a monster Joshua was would hurt her, and he was counting on the last little bit of humanity Josh had left to convince him to help.

Sure enough, Josh growled out, "Finn's no' the true head of the clans."

Sam's eyes opened wide. "Wha'?"

"The man's gone t' many lengths t' make sure nobody knows the truth, bu' no' everythin' stays buried. Especially when there's parties interested in takin' over his position."

Josh's cryptic answer had Sam furrowing his eyes; suddenly it clicked. "Christ! The turf war! Tha's wha' this is all abou'?"

"Aye," Josh nodded, "The other clan leaders are comin' forth t' remove Finn from his seat. Ye've met him, aye? As ye can imagine, there's no' much love between him an' the other leaders. The Redcap's been losin' his assets one a' a time, even his house is on the block, an' he's gotten desperate t' keep a hold on everythin'. Even gone as far as t' pick up odd jobs he hasnea done since he was a young man."

Everything was suddenly falling into place for Sam. "Tell me abou' his smugglin' ring."

"Like I tol' ye, he's gotten desperate; so much so he's startin' t' branch out fer fundin'. I heard he was dabblin' into illegal arms usin' ol' man Jaimes' C.A.R.E.S. cover, bu' I assumed t'was a rumor."

"Who tol' ye the rumor?"

Josh's lips curved into a tiny smile. "Le's jus' say an interested party."

"Wha' do ye know abou' Aiden Marcus?"

"Finn recruited 'im when he was a young man, 'til a woman came between them. Last I'd heard, he'd gone t' work fer a rival t' Finn. The McNallys, I think."

"An' he's one of the rivalin' parties, aye?"

Josh's tiny smile stretched into a full-on grin, "One of many. The Redcap has made lo's of enemies, an' thankfully I know all of 'em."

Sam narrowed his eyes. "…Ye'd betray Finn? Surely even you are no' tha' crazy."

The grin disappeared, and Josh snarled, "The Redcap's taught me only one thing: no second chances. He donnea ge' one from me, either."

Sam didn't break eye contact with his little brother, but the hostility Josh had for The Redcap rivaled his own, and he couldn't help but understand that part. "Can ye tell me anythin' else?"

"I think ye've go' everythin' ye need, Sammy," Josh jeered again.

Sam wanted to press him further, but he could tell their time was coming to an end by the way the guards peaked in through the window.

"Now," Josh continued, "I helped ye. So ye have t' keep yer part of the bargain: Ye won't tell Hannah anythin'.'"

Sam squarely nodded his agreement before he reached behind him and pressed the button the guards had mentioned. Within moments, the door opened, and the guards re-entered. One final glower was the only goodbye they shared as Joshua was led out of the room, and Sam was escorted to the prison entrance. Dr. Stewart was waiting in his beautiful grey Mercedes Benz.

The professor waited patiently for Sam to get into the back seat before driving away. The moment they were out of range of Statesville, Sam removed the fake glasses with a sigh of relief. "How Simon can stand t' wear these damn things is beyond me," he muttered to himself.

"Did you get the information you needed, Agent?" Dr. Spencer asked.

"Aye, an' now I think I know wha' we can do next."

"Spectacular! Then back to the homestead we go!"

"Aye, an' after I collect wha' I've go', t' the FBI headquarters."

"But I thought you said you'll be arrested if you go anywhere near there."

"I will, bu' now I've go' the answer t' savin' my team. I'll be fine."

Dr. Stewart shrugged and replied, "Alright, Agent, I suppose you know best when it comes to these things."

Along the drive back, Sam felt a mixture of elation and foolishness: Suddenly, everything pieced together perfectly. There was no doubt that Copper was fighting for his team as hard as she could, and it was only a matter of time before they were proven innocent. And yet, he felt foolish for refusing to see Joshua for as long as he had. He wondered if all of this turmoil could have been avoided, if he hadn't been so stubborn in regards to his brother. As Dr. Stewart parked in the shady garage of Charlotte's building, Sam quickly pushed the dilemma to the side.

Sam expected to see Charlotte as soon as the two of them walked inside the apartment, but it was empty.

"Charlotte? We're home, sweetheart," Dr. Spencer called, but there was no answer. "Charlotte? Where are you?"

Sam was instantly on alert; he ran to her room at the end of the hall and burst through the door. She wasn't inside, not that he expected to find her, and nothing appeared out of place. Still, he desperately tore through her room.

Dr. Stewart appeared moments later, a panicked expression on his face. "You don't think she'd still go to the meeting with that monster, do you?"

"Of course, she did," Sam growled. "When has tha' woman ever listened t' wha' anyone tells her t' do?"

"Not once her whole life," Dr. Stewart answered quietly.

Sam looked through her clothes, the dresser, the nightstand, but found absolutely nothing that even gave him a clue as to where she would go to meet the Redcap. He raced through the apartment, looking for a note she might have left, a takeout menu, a page in a book, anything at all that gave a hint as to where she might suggest to go for this meeting. There was nothing there.

"Goddamn tha' woman!" he bellowed, slamming his fist on the dining room table. "Apologies, professor."

"No need to apologize, agent; believe me, the feeling is mutual. But Charlotte's been doing this sort of thing for a long time. She'll be alright, won't she?"

"I donnea trus' the Recap's honor as far as I can throw him. My gut tells me she's in danger, an' she'll need help whether she admits it or no'."

Dr. Stewart paled at Sam's response. "Then what do we do?"

"We have t' think where she'd meet him. Somewhere familiar, where she's go' a home turf advantage. Somewhere public, so he cannea hurt her with witnesses abou'. An' knowin' her practice of always keepin' the upper hand, I'd say somewhere classy...expensive...so she can stick him the bill. Think, Dr. Stewart! Is there any place she'd go like tha'?"

The professor brought his hand to his lips and paced the room for a moment. "...There's only one place I can think of, La Crique des Sirènes. It's this French restaurant I take her to every year she visits."

"Then we'll try there." Sam made for the door with Dr. Stewart right behind him.

Deep in the heart of Old Town Chicago, the professor turned onto a busy street teaming with traffic and stopped in front of one of the shortest buildings Sam had ever seen in the city; it was barely as tall as a two-story house. With a line of roughly a dozen people waiting next to the door, Sam had a good feeling that this was where Charlotte would choose to have the meeting with Finn. Before he could even get out of the car to check, he saw her being led out of the restaurant on Finn's arm with the large, surly Robert McGail right behind them.

"Damn the woman, I knew t'was a trap!"

"What are you talking about? She's right there, she's safe!"

"Ye donnea understand, professor: Travelin' decreases her odds tha' she'll survive. He'll take her somewhere with no witnesses. We have t' follow them!"

"Wait, McKay! Shouldn't we bring backup? What about going to your boss?"

In the panic of trying to stop Charlotte from becoming the Redcap's next victim, Sam had forgotten all about getting his information to Copper. "Christ! We cannea do both. An' ye donnea know the first thing abou' bein' undercover, so I cannea send ye after her! Give me yer phone!"

The professor had barely gotten his cell out of his pocket before Sam yanked it from his hands. Dialing the memorized number, he growled when it went straight to voicemail. He tried two more times, still it went to voicemail.

"Her phone mus' be off. I'll have t' leave a message an' hope she ge's it in time."

"What are the odds that she will get it in time?"

"...No' great," Sam growled. He kept his eyes on Charlotte, weighing the options before him: save his team before Finn's mole could have them killed, or save the woman who refused to listen to him. When Finn's man opened the door to the car, he knew he was out of time.

The sound of the car's door opening and slamming got his attention: Dr. Stewart had jumped out of the vehicle. "Agent McKay, save my niece! I'll get to the FBI building and tell this Copper what's going on. Go!"

Sam glanced back at Finn's car; it had started to move. Sliding over to the driver's seat, he practically yanked the shifter into drive as he set off after Finn's car, doing his best to remain far enough away that they wouldn't suspect he was following them, but close enough not to lose them. Thankfully, the car was staying on crowded streets for most of the trip, so it was easy to not appear conspicuous. Within moments, they had gotten onto highway 64 before merging onto I-90 westbound, then finally onto I-94 heading north. Sam barely blinked as he followed them for over an hour, determined not to let Charlotte out of his sight. The traffic was getting thinner and thinner, making the element of surprise less likely to be in his favor. He tried to slow down a bit and remain a few cars behind, which thankfully appeared to have worked, as the car kept going. It was starting to get darker, so he turned off his lights. Finally, Finn's car took an exit which led into the city of Glencoe and continued through winding streets, further and further away from the urban areas and deeper into a factory district, until it came to a tall chain link fence. Parked far enough away to not be seen, Sam watched keenly as a hand stretched out from the car to touch an erected keypad before the gates opened. Once the car was through, the gates closed behind it, and the car stopped. Sam watched as Finn, Charlotte, and McGail got out of the car, and they escorted her into a building that appeared to be a garage of some sort.

Sam carefully got out of his car and withdrew his gun before he stalked his way towards the gate, keeping his eyes open for a camera or a point man. Relief washed through him that there wasn't anything of the sort, but there was still the problem of getting on the other side of the gate. He jogged around it, looking for anywhere that might be a little bit easier to climb but had no such luck. Coming back to the erected keypad, he knew the best option he had was to use it as a jump point for as much height as he could before he'd have to climb it the rest of the way. Holstering his gun, he prepped himself for the jump. *I'm getting too damn old fer this shite!* Thinking of all the times he and Thomas and Ben Abernathy climbed trees and fences as boys, he summoned every bit of muscle memory he could as he ran for the keypad and jumped onto the gate. He'd managed to get three-quarters of the way up and didn't stop climbing until he reached the top, swung his leg over the barbed wire that was painfully cutting through his pants into skin, and dropped to the ground. His feet gave out beneath him so he landed on his rear; he grunted in pain but quickly got to his feet, withdrew his gun again, and ran to the opened garage door. *Hold on, Charlotte, I'm comin!*

Chapter Fourteen

Sam snuck through the dusty, enormous garage with his gun pointing into the dark. The still air and motionless machinery inside the spacious building gave him the eerily familiar feeling that he was walking through a graveyard, causing the hair on the back of his neck to rise. It was only the smell of oil and gas that kept him grounded to the fact that he was inside of a mechanic's garage, an environment he was familiar with. Other than the sound of his heart pounding, all was quiet. Too quiet, in fact. A garage as big as this one certainly had the right acoustics to hear a pin drop on the other side of the room; he should be able to hear talking, whimpering, anything at all, instead of just silence. The moonlight barely cast enough of a glow to give the shapes and obstacles in front of him an outline but not nearly enough to see clearly. The chill in the air didn't help either; he could almost see his breath. Knowing that he had surprise on his side stopped him from turning on any lights as he slowly waded through the garage, careful not to touch any of the tables just in case there were any precariously positioned tools sitting on them. Sam's ears strained to hear anything at all as he wandered, but he was met with stale silence. For a brief moment, he wondered if he'd accidentally followed the wrong car all the way out into the middle of nowhere. Suddenly he heard a short and sudden, muffled shriek sound through the darkness. His grip on the gun tightened as he quickly, but stealthily, made his way towards the location of the noise.

At the back of the garage was a door which Sam carefully crept up on. He had to press his ear to the wood to hear anything, but he could definitely make out a muffled voice talking and a light whimpering through it. There was no doubt that it was Finn and Charlotte he was hearing, but he couldn't tell if the big henchman was in there with them or not. Straining to make out anything Finn was saying, Sam desperately tried to think of a plan. If he broke the door down and Finn's henchman was in there, then he would be in for a hell of a fistfight, and Charlotte would most likely already be dead before he could help her. If the big brute was hiding somewhere when he went in, then Finn had the element of surprise, and Sam would be easily overpowered. Both scenarios gave him a tactical disadvantage. The only answer he had was to draw them out and make them come to him.

Sam turned and looked into the dark garage; with how difficult it was to hear anything through the soundproof door, he knew it would take more than knocking over a few tools to get the Redcap's attention. There were two trucks sitting in the stalls; surely, they were loud enough for everyone to hear if he could get one started. The only problem was he might be heard trying to break into them, and he'd lose the surprise element. There were also some extremely tall shelves with heavy looking drums on them, a fall from one of those would be really loud. But Sam didn't want to waste any more energy climbing things. Grateful that his eyes had finally adjusted to the dark, he peered through the garage, looking for another answer, when he spotted another vehicle on the other side: a lone forklift that held some crates. Sam holstered his weapon and ran to it. He breathed a sigh of relief to find the keys still in its ignition as he forced the thing to start. It roared to life, and the eerily quiet garage suddenly turned into an ear-splitting theater.

Sam didn't wait to see whether or not the Redcap came out of his lair as he yanked the shifter on the vehicle. It jerked forward and, before he could stop it, smashed into the wall below the shelves. The impact nearly sent Sam toppling over the wheel, but he managed to stop himself from flying out of his seat. He heard a loud groan of metal and looked up to see the drums teetering on the edge of the shelves from the forklift's collision. The erected poles beneath were beginning to bend under the weight, and Sam didn't waste another minute, running before it crushed him. He barely made it behind a stack of crates sitting in the back as dozens of metal drums crashed to the ground with deafening force. When the sound began to subside, Sam could hear something that sounded like a hose spraying. Before he could determine what it was, he heard a door open, and a bright light suddenly illuminated the garage.

"Wha' the hell happened?!" he heard WIlliam Finn's voice demand.

Running footsteps got closer to Sam and he withdrew his gun, holding his breath. Suddenly they stopped.

"The shelves must have broke. Ah, shit, they're leaking! I've got gas on my pants!"

"Then ge' out of there, ye damn numpty! Miss Charlotte has our attention a' the moment."

Sam heard a faint cry in the background and relief washed through him. Charlotte was still alive, but his rescue plan was growing shakier by the moment. While he looked all around for something he could use, the huge idiot continued to talk.

"But...there's gas all over the place, boss. If we start a fire here, we'll lose the garage! The trucks!"

"The insurance will cover the damages, ye nyaff. It'll be fine. Now ge' over here an' finish this bitch off!"

Sam glanced upwards at the lights and a crazy idea came to him. *I' works in the movies, it has t' work now if I aim right. Right?* Sam acted fast. He stood up and aimed his gun directly in the center of the lamps at the lightbulb and fired. The bulb shattered in a flash of sparks and Sam began to run. Finn's henchman was already walking back towards Finn but had turned around at the sound of gunfire. The next thing Sam saw was wild flames racing across the diesel-soaked ground and climbing McGail's pants leg just as instantly. The bloodcurdling screams that followed were terrible. Sam watched in horror as the brute wailed in agony, the scent of burning flesh beginning to overwhelm the scent of the fuel. He knew he needed to get to Charlotte before Finn could kill her, but the horrible screams coming from McGail made his stomach turn. He aimed his gun for the head and fired. He didn't miss. The enormous brute suddenly stopped screaming and dropped to the ground. Sam looked all around for Finn, but the gangster had disappeared. *Shit!*

Not knowing where else he could look, Sam ran back towards the office and burst through the door; Charlotte was duct taped to a chair, a rag shoved in her mouth, her dress ripped and exposing her breasts. There was a small cut at the base of her neck, but she was alive. Relief washed through him to see he'd stopped her murder just in the nick of time, but the feeling was short-lived as the heat from the flames grew closer. Sam wasted no time in ripping the tape off of her.

"Come on! We've go' t' run fer it!"

Charlotte didn't move; her eyes were glazed over in panic as she stared at the rising flames that were quickly engulfing the garage. "No, no! Not like this!"

Ignoring her whimpers, Sam grabbed her wrist and tried to pull her to the door. "Charlotte! We donnea have time! Move!"

"NO!" Charlotte screamed.

Sam didn't know which came first: the hard crack sound or the sharp pain on his face; Charlotte had hit him with more force than he thought she was capable of. Rubbing his cheek, he watched her race behind the enormous desk in the room. Fear coursed through him as he looked out into the garage again: The drums of fuel and the semi-trucks were already engulfed in flames, and it was only a matter of moments before all of the tanks would burst. But with Charlotte too petrified to move, there was no way he could get the both of them out of impact range in time. *Bu' I cannea leave her here t' die!*

Panic surged through him, but he slammed the door shut and barricaded it with the chairs. Satisfied that it was barricaded as much as possible, he raced around to join Charlotte under the desk. Her legs were curled up under her chin as she held herself tightly. Her eyes closed, she wept in a barely audible voice, "Not like this, not like this, not like this..."

Sam crawled in next to her, his tall frame making sitting in the tiny space extremely uncomfortable. Pulling her close to him, he did his best to rock her and soothe her as the room began to grow hotter and hotter. He hoped with all of his might that the thick door would protect them from the explosion just long enough for help to arrive, but at that moment he wasn't certain of anything.

"It'll be alrigh', somebody will find us," he whispered soothingly, but even he couldn't hide the fearful crack in his voice.

She finally turned to look at him. Her voice hoarse and quiet, she replied, "I wasn't supposed to die like this."

Holding her tightly in his arms, Sam squeezed his eyes shut and replied, "I know. I wasnea supposed t' die like this either."

The next thing Sam heard was the loud thunder of an explosion, followed by a shockwave that forced the desk to the back of the room with Sam and Charlotte still under it. Even with the cover to help, it wasn't enough to stop the forceful gust of flames that suddenly flooded the room. Charlotte turned her face into his chest and sobbed. Sam held her as tightly as he could, trying his hardest to shield her from the terror they were faced with. The flames weren't close enough to touch them yet, but the radiating heat already gave him the sensation he was burning. Smoke filled the room and stung his eyes. Though he tried his best to cover his mouth and nose, he couldn't stop the noxious fumes from invading. Everything began to swim in front of him. Closing his eyes, he could feel himself slipping out of consciousness. He summoned up an image of Meredith and Oliver, back when they were a happy family. But the image didn't last very long.

***

Pain was the first thing Sam felt when he awoke; he couldn't move his arms, and something large and uncomfortable was covering his face. *Bu' I'm alive,* he reasoned with himself, *Tha' counts fer somethin'.* He slowly opened his eyes and was nearly blinded by the bright light shining above him. After a few blinks, his eyes adjusted. His right arm was wrapped in gauze and suspended above his body, but the obtrusive mask that covered his face was what really had his attention. A tube ran from the end of the mask and he felt the air being forced into him. Despite the aches and pains, he tried to at least remove it to no avail.

"Whoa, hold up there, boss!" Simon suddenly appeared in his peripheral vision. "Let me hail a nurse to get that for you."

"Sam, we all know that you're a tough bastard to kill, but do you really have to prove it by being in a burning building?" asked Rivera in a cheeky tone.

Turning to his right, Sam felt relief to see Rivera sitting on a couch. Julie was asleep with her head on his lap but she quickly came to once Rivera spoke.

A nurse appeared within minutes and removed the mask, to which Sam responded by taking his first real breath of air with gusto. His throat felt raw and abused, but his pride felt better.

"Christ, tha' thing's uncomfortable!" He was momentarily surprised by how hoarse his voice sounded.

"Well, it did keep you alive, so..." Simon answered quietly.

Sam nodded to his arm, "An' wha's this abou'?"

"Second- and third-degree burns," Rivera answered. "You had a little work done while you were out, but the doctors said you won't need any skin grafts. Just a pretty nasty scar on your right arm, there."

Julie rushed to Sam's side and sat on the bed next to him. "You've been out for almost two days because of the smoke inhalation. The doctors didn't think you would pull through."

Simon snorted, "They tried to tell us that, but we told them you're too stubborn to die just because of a fire. That nurse owes me a cup of coffee!"

"Seriously? You made a bet on whether or not he would die?" Julie asked with disgust.

"Hey, I knew he wouldn't! I just said he's too stubborn to die!"

"I wonder what you promised her if you lost," Rivera commented wryly.

Interrupting them, Sam asked very croakily, "Where's Charlotte?"

"Still in intensive care; she hasn't woken yet."

"Is she alrigh'?"

Rivera sighed, "Her burns weren't as bad as yours, but they think she inhaled more of the fumes than you did. The last I checked, her vitals were normal, but they're keeping a close watch on her. Dr. Stewart's with her, and we've got two guys outside of her door, just in case."

"And we caught Finn!" Simon added happily. "Caught him right in the act, just as we were rescuing you!"

"How?" Sam asked.

Simon scoffed, "After all this time, you still question me? That hurts, boss! When Dr. Stewart showed up to headquarters, he told Copper how you were chasing Finn, and she got me to my laptop within seconds. I was able to pull addresses for every one of Finn's business dealings, both legal and illegal. The guy has most of Chicago wired! Somebody called 911 about a fire, and it pinged on my search as his garage. We figured that was the best place to try and find you. Honestly, if it weren't for the fire, we wouldn't have known where to start."

"In a sick way, Finn saved your life," Rivera added.

"I'd agree with ye, if he'd been the one tha' started the fire," Sam answered.

Julie narrowed her eyes. "That was *you?*"

"Aye, Copper's gonna be pished when she ge's *tha'* bill."

Perfectly on cue, the woman herself walked through the door. "I'll consider it your Christmas bonus for the year."

While Sam was still laid up in bed, the rest of his team stood to attention and nodded their heads with a respectful, "Ma'am."

"I'm glad to see you're awake, McKay," she continued.

Though touched by her concern, Sam's focus was still on Finn and his accomplice. "The mole, Heidi, di' ye catch her?"

"Relax, boss," Simon smiled, "the minute Copper walked in the door, we were proven innocent."

Sam coughed, his hoarse voice protesting him using it. "...Why? Wha' reason' would she have t' help Finn?"

"Mr. Abler discovered that Ms. Tombs has a younger brother. He was in a tragic climbing accident ten years ago, which made him permanently quadriplegic. Ms. Tombs had trouble attending to his medical needs up until seven years ago."

"Finn took over the payments an' blackmailed her."

"Precisely. She confessed to switching your weapons and killing Bronson with Rivera's gun, as well as planting hair follicles on his body. And, considering the rather loud discussion you and Bronson shared, the rest of Chicago's house was more than happy to put two and two together without much thought of an investigation."

"Wha' abou' Darris?"

Julie answered him. "It turns out that he really did kill himself. An autopsy confirmed there was no ligature marks on him or any drugs in his system to suggest he was coerced into it. After the failed sting, he was just too afraid of the Redcap finding his family to take the chance of staying on our side."

Disappointed, Sam shook his head. "The bloody fool. Well, a' least Heidi'll be able t' testify against Finn fer extortion. An' wha' abou' Annabelle's murder? I caught him attemptin' t' slit Charlotte's throat, he had t' have his knife on him."

"We've already started processing it," Rivera answered, "The lab boys are being careful to collect every microscopic piece of evidence they can get off it."

"Bu' wha' abou' the trucks? How di' we miss—"

"Seriously, boss, relax!" Simon said. "You're going to hurt your voice even more if you keep using it like this. After Finn got the tip from Charlotte, he hired a different shipping company to pick up his stuff, and his own trucks were the decoys. We've already cracked them, and they admitted to helping Finn with illegal arms smuggling. We got this!"

Before Sam could argue with him, Director Copper waved her hand. "McKay, I assure you that your team is capable of tying up all of the loose ends; you've taught them well. And you can comb through their findings with a microscope all you like when you've completely recovered. But for now, allow yourself to heal, and let your team get to work. I have already informed your ex-wife of your condition, and she said to tell you that she expects you at her house the moment we return to Cleveland."

"Awe, Christ, ye called Meredith? She'll no' le' me out of her sight, now!"

"Considering your incurable tenacity, that's exactly why I called her: to keep an eye on you. Now rest; that's an order."

Copper turned on her heels and left.

"Ach!" Sam grunted in annoyance, "I'll be damned if tha' woman donnea ge' the las' word!"

"You don't know her as well as I do, Sam," Rivera chuckled. "*That* wasn't her last word."

"Wha' do ye mean?"

"You're going to be on leave as soon as we get back until you make a full recovery, pass a psych eval, target test, the whole nine yards."

Sam closed his eyes and sighed, "An' I thought things couldnea ge' any worse."

"You were nearly burned to death," Simon countered. "It's not just your arm that needs to heal. Your mind does, too. Think of it this way: You get to spend some quality time with Oliver during your recovery."

As much as Sam wanted to argue further that he was perfectly capable of taking care of himself, the thought of more time with Oliver did make the situation a little more appealing. Not to mention, the soreness from his abused throat was the only thing at the moment that could convince him to drop the subject. Well, at least to stop talking about it.

Julie added her input, "And like she said: You need to rest, so we'll get going now that we know you're okay. Is there anything we can get for you before we leave?"

"Ach! Away with the lo' of ye! I've go' morphine an' Jell-o t' keep m' occupied. Bu' before ye go, ye should know tha' Finn's losin' control of the clans."

The three of them looked at each other quizzically.

"How do you know that?" Rivera asked.

"...A jailbird tol' me."

His team chuckled in reply; just as they turned towards the door, Dr. Stewart walked through it. By the slowness of his movement and the bewildered look on his face, Sam knew something was wrong. Before he could ask, the professor muttered, "...Charlotte's dead."

"What? When? Wha' happened?"

Rivera caught the professor as he stumbled and swayed before helping him into the nearest seat. "I just...I stepped out to get a drink...when I came back, they wouldn't let me into the room with her. They were using one of those defibrillator machines on her..."

Sam didn't waste a moment in using his one good arm to push himself up from his reclining position. He started ripping off all of the offending wires and pads that were connected to him and machines started beeping. Simon quickly attempted to stop him.

"Whoa, whoa, whoa! Boss! What are you doing?"

The noise didn't go unnoticed; a nurse came through the door. "Mr. McKay? You need to stay in bed!"

"I want me badge an' me pants," he answered gruffly. Ignoring the sharp pain in his damaged arm, he lifted it out of the sling and swung his legs over the side of the bed. "I'm goin' t' see the woman tha' was brought in with me: Charlotte Whitney."

"Sir, I have to insist that you get back into bed. I can find out the status of the patient for you and tell you."

Sam stood to his full six-and-a-half-foot glory, not caring at all that the hospital gown was too short for him, and limped past her. The nurse continued to shout, insisting that he return to his hospital bed but he paid her no mind as he walked. Rivera had to keep a jogging pace to stay with him despite the limp, but he led him towards the room Charlotte was in without argument. A team of medical staff surrounded her, but from one look at her deathly pale skin and her already blue lips, Sam could tell it was already too late. The maddening but intriguing Charlotte Whitney was already gone.

Chapter Fifteen

Two Days Later

Back at Chicago's FBI headquarters, in much more accommodating conditions, Rivera stared at the forensics report before him in disbelief. "This...this can't be right."

"The guys in Forensics ran the test twice, and there are absolutely no traces of Annabelle Matheson's blood on the knife William Finn had on him when he was arrested," Julie answered disdainfully.

"Was there any blood on the knife?"

"So far they've got at least dozens of different DNA profiles in trace amounts. He never even bothered to properly clean the thing after he used it."

"That part doesn't surprise me. He burned all useable evidence for everyone else, but of course he'd want to keep a trophy for himself. The blood on the knife was his trophy."

"Sick bastard."

Simon suddenly burst through the door, carrying a manila package that was already opened. "If you thought this case was already messy, it just got a whole lot messier."

"What's that?" Julie asked.

"A bike messenger just delivered it with the instructions to give it to the officer in charge of the Annabelle Matheson case, and he insisted he has no idea who hired him." Simon dropped the stacked contents onto the table before them and separated the papers. "This one is copies of Finn's business accounts, both legal and not, his federal tax records; there's a copy of Bruce Jaimes' Last Will and Testament, and then there's this." He handed a lone paper to Rivera; there was nothing except a list of directions. "I already took a look: these directions lead to a pretty big stretch of land quite literally in the middle of nowhere Wisconsin."

"What does any of this have to do with Annabelle Matheson's murder?" Julie asked.

"Absolutely nothing, this whole package is purely a death sentence for William 'The Redcap' Finn." Simon picked up the last will and testament of Bruce Jaimes and started flipping through its pages. "Listen to this: 'I, Bruce Alistair Jaimes, being of sound mind and body, do leave my entire estate and all that I possess to my grandson Malcolm William Finn.'"

Julie gawked, *"Everything?"*

"Everything: The Jaimes fortune, businesses, the house, pretty much all of Chicago that Finn has his hands on! Absolutely everything was left to his son and only him. Audrey and Finn were named trustees of the estate until Malcolm came of age, but if the boy dies before he turns twenty-one, then everything gets auctioned off and goes to the C.A.R.E.S. foundation."

"Jaimes obviously didn't like his son-in-law, but why would he blackball his own daughter like that?"

Simon took a seat at the table in front of his laptop and typed furiously. "...Aside from being the head of the Jaimes clan, I'm going to guess that Brucey had a masculinity complex that he channeled into a fetish for domestic violence: His late wife went to the hospital several times for broken bones, bruises, the works. She died when their daughter was twelve, then the hospital visits transferred to Audrey until she married Finn."

"And absolutely *nobody* thought to do something to protect Audrey or her mom from Jaimes?"

Rivera answered her with a sigh. "It was the seventies, Jules. Not only was abuse a very taboo subject, people believed in minding their own business, no matter how horrific the truth might be. Plus, who was going to fight Bruce Jaimes?"

"I know I wouldn't," Simon agreed, "So not only did Brucey hate Finn, but Audrey was useless to him, until she suddenly gave him the son he never had. The poor woman was nothing more than a brood-mare to him."

"The only way he could keep his fortune in the family was to make sure it went to family blood," Rivera nodded his agreement. "Finn only gets to control the clans until his son is twenty-one. After that, everything he built will be snatched away... If you knew that your whole empire was going to be taken away from you in a few years, what would you do?"

"Spend as much money as you possibly could on fun toys?" Simon suggested.

Julie smirked. "No, dummy, you'd prepare. Set aside a nest-egg away somewhere for yourself."

"And, if you like the taste of power as much as Finn does, you'd start arranging a way to solidify your position in case anything might happen to it. Like, for example, a turf war."

"And when word gets out that you have absolutely no claim to any of the Jaimes fortune, your 'right to rule' gets challenged by other clan members with their own stakes. Good God, it's like we're reliving one of the professor's history lectures."

Rivera nodded his agreement, "And in the end, The Redcap is figuratively beheaded. That Will alone is enough to destroy him; the rest of this just makes sure he's put in prison. Sam's source was telling the truth: Finn really isn't the true leader of the clans."

"We could have used this earlier," Julie scoffed. "Then maybe some of this crap wouldn't have happened. But here's the question: Who sent it? Could it be a rival clan leader?"

"Most likely. But I'm curious about this piece of paper with the directions on it. You said it's just land in the middle of nowhere?"

"Yup," Simon nodded, "about ten acres of it. According to the county records, it's been in the Jaimes family for fifty years, but it doesn't look like there's anything particularly important about it. It's not a business; there haven't been any land excavations; it's just there. Maybe it's a vacation spot."

"Well, if whoever sent us this package gave us the directions to it, then there must be something there that also incriminates Finn, so we might as well go take a look."

"Okay, you guys do that, and I'll see if the lab can get anything useable off this package. Listen, guys, I know you're tough and can handle yourselves, but please be careful. Finn's had everybody that's even slightly inconvenienced him killed, and he nearly took out Sam. Who knows what could be hiding at this place?"

While Julie nudged Simon with sisterly affection, Rivera scoffed and pushed past him towards the garage.

Nearly three hours of driving later, Rivera and Julie were led off of the main highway and deep into the woods of Northern Wisconsin. When the road suddenly transformed from pavement into dirt, the two of them were holding tightly onto their SUV's grips as the car jumped along the bumpy road.

"Are you sure you didn't take a right instead of a left at the cow four miles back?" Julie asked very perturbed.

Rivera ignored her jab and looked back at the directions on the paper. "According to this, we should see a fork very soon that we're supposed to take a right at. Then it shouldn't be too much longer until we find out whatever it is the anonymous tipper wants us to see."

Suddenly the aforementioned fork appeared, and Rivera took a right. The road suddenly got smoother, despite the shrouding trees that still surrounded them, and almost immediately they came to a small clearing where they saw a log cabin. Even from a distance, it was obvious that it had been neglected and was not often used: The roof had visible holes; the two windows were matted with dust and cobwebs; and the logs were warping from the elements.

Rivera turned to Julie and asked, "Do you get the vibe that we're walking into a trap?"

"After seeing *Cabin in the Woods,* you bet," she nodded. "I suggest we do a sweep surrounding the shack first and make sure there aren't any other surprises before breach."

Withdrawing his gun, Rivera nodded his agreement and said sternly, "Stay close to me, Jules."

The both of them exited the SUV with their guns poised in front of them. Sticking together at all times, they walked around the single-level home, checking for all points of entry. There appeared to only be the one door and two windows in the front of the shack. Circling back towards the front, Rivera held his gun up as Julie kicked the door down, and the two of them rushed in. Just as soon as they breached, they were hit with the smell of decay followed by the intense sound of buzzing flies. While there wasn't a body anywhere to be seen, it was obvious they were walking into a brutal crime scene: Blood spatters coated the walls; there were large stains of it on the floor, and what little furniture was there was toppled or destroyed.

Rivera leaned down to inspect the blood: it was at least months old by the brownish coloring and the dryness of it. "The anonymous tipper wanted us to find this crime scene, but whose murder is this?"

"I'll text Simon and tell him to get forensics up here ASAP, then I think we should check around the cabin again," Julie answered.

Leaving the cabin, the two of them stuck together as they walked deeper into the woods behind the little shack. They had continued to wander for a good ten minutes before Julie pointed to their right and hissed, "Look!"

Rivera followed her gaze and saw two shallow mounds in the earth with crude stick crosses planted above them. Walking closer to them, he leaned down to inspect the dirt. "...They weren't buried recently. In fact, I'll bet these are the bodies of whoever was killed in that cabin."

"I don't suppose you have any guesses as to who they are?"

"No, but I'm not going to wait four hours for forensics to get here and tell us somebody just buried their dogs." Rivera holstered his gun, squatted in front of the smaller grave, and began to move the dirt out of the way with his hands. He didn't have to dig very long when tufts of black hair started to appear. He continued to dig faster until he uncovered a pale, shriveled face that belonged to the short black hair.

He didn't notice that Julie was standing over his shoulder until she whispered in horror, "Oh, God...that's a kid!"

Rivera turned his attention to the other grave and began to dig just as urgently. The other victim's body wasn't in any better condition, but as soon as he saw the blonde hair, he knew exactly who they were looking at. "These are the bodies of Audrey and Malcolm Finn, William Finn's wife and kid."

***

It had been two days since Charlotte's death, and Sam hadn't had any rest since the moment Dr. Stewart came to tell them; shame and guilt wracked his brain for not being able to protect her. With Copper ordering him to recuperate and let his team wrap up the murder case, he had nothing else to do but watch television. He was already becoming annoyed with the lack of productivity, so he instructed Simon to dig up the files on Charlotte's sister Claire Whitney and bring them to him. He was scheduled to be discharged that day and return to Cleveland, where he would be under the watchful eye of Meredith for the next few weeks. Knowing his ex-wife, she would have him laid up in bed all day long if she could, and the thought bored him tremendously. At least with a cold case, he'd have something to keep his mind occupied.

Sitting in the chair, waiting for a nurse to give him the final discharge papers, Sam scratched at his healing arm through the bandage; the doctors had insisted he needed to keep it in a sling until the wounds had totally healed up. He already knew it was going to be a long process for him to not use his good arm. After flipping through the channels for the twentieth time that day, Sam sighed in relief to see Simon walking through his hospital door carrying a very small case file. "You know, technically you're not supposed to be working right now."

"This isnea related t' Annabelle Matheson, therefore I's no' work. I's a hobby."

"Yeah, and Copper will absolutely buy that justification," Simon chuckled. "And I'll have you know that it wasn't easy finding this because Claire Whitney isn't dead."

Sam furrowed his eyebrows. "Wha' do ye mean?"

"I mean there's records of Claire Whitneys all over the country still alive and well, albeit a few of them are eating applesauce in a home or a daycare somewhere—"

"Simon, the point."

"Yeah, yeah, the point is this isn't Claire Whitney's file. According the parameters you gave me, the only tragic fire with a DOA and a rescued ten-year-old girl from thirty years ago is the case of Isobel Claire Winter."

Sam's eyes opened wide. *Winter...* snatching the file from Simon, he hurriedly opened it and scoured the contents. "Donnea tell me: Charlotte's no' Charlotte."

"And that's why you get paid the big bucks," Simon smiled, "Her name was actually Mary Robin Winter. She officially changed her name in 2005. How did you know?"

Memories from twenty years before came flooding back to Sam: going to a daft concert in the crowded city of Aberdeen with Thomas, meeting the slender and flirtatious woman that managed to use him in her robbery scheme, being arrested and proven innocent within a three-day period...*It cannea be her, i's no' possible...*Too curious to leave the question unanswered, he turned his attention to

Simon and barked, "Go find the doctars tha' attended Charlotte an' ask if she had any tattoos on her."

Though surprised at his outburst, Simon nodded and hurried away, leaving Sam alone with the case contents: The cause of the fire appeared to be electrical, there were no signs of forced entry into the home, and there wasn't anything concrete regarding the victim, so it was speculated that she was burned alive. Though he already knew that the original report wouldn't be able to tell him much, as fire forensics was not as advanced thirty years ago as it is today, he still checked all of the findings against the series of photos that were taken. Everything appeared to be in order, so Sam moved on to the newspaper clippings which read:

"Berwyn, Illinois. August 24, 1979, house on Clarence Avenue destroyed in accidental fire. The home belonged to the late Robert and Linda Winter, who had died in a car crash six years prior. At present, their daughters Isobel, 19 and a waitress at Gigi's, and Mary Winter, 10, occupy the home. Sources say the eldest daughter Isobel was the only casualty, while young Mary was taken to MacNeal Hospital and placed in intensive care."

No' much coverage on a random house fire, Sam thought to himself. Turning his attention to the police report, he continued to read as he carefully examined each of the details:

"8-24-79   23:57: 911 received call about a house fire at 567 Clarence Avenue, caller's name is Gina Bitts, a neighbor to the victims. Berwyn Fire Department arrived on the scene at 00:06, fire was extinguished at 01:23. One body discovered DOA, young child rescued from closet in north bedroom.

"8-25-79   01:47: Detectives Farber and Knight arrive at the scene and are met by Fire Chief Inlion. No witnesses other than Gina Bitts, who reports she stepped outside her house for a cigarette when she saw the fire and called 911."

Other than the fact that one of the detectives shared the same name as the ever-so-jolly Chicago PD's chief, there was nothing else particularly curious about the details. By all accounts on paper, the death of Charlotte's sister Claire (or Isobel) was truly an accident. Sam stared at the file and thought about Charlotte. She had clearly still suffered from the fire even thirty years later. Just as Dr. Stewart

187

had mentioned, she desperately needed a good therapist to have committed her version of what happened to be the truth. And yet, by all other intents and purposes, Charlotte had functioned incredibly well despite her fear of fire.

Sam picked up the autopsy report of Isobel Winter:

"8-30-79   10:26: Subject Isobel Claire Winter found DOA. Cause of death: burning by accidental fire. Identification made by state dental records."

Sam turned his attention to the faded Polaroids: Isobel's body was burned beyond recognition, but the fire hadn't completely incinerated her. *No bloody wondar they had t' use dental records.* At the bottom of the page was a sticky note with Simon's handwriting that said: "her final resting place is at Mount Olive Cemetery." *Tha's where Charlotte had tha' boy take the bump key... she was committed t' rememberin' her sister. Too committed fer this t' jus' be a fantasy she concocted...* Sam's thoughts were interrupted as the lanky young man came back into his hospital room, a triumphant smile on his face.

"Okay, someday you're going to have to tell me how you know the things you know, boss. Charlotte had a tattoo on her hip that said "Memento," and according to the doctors, it was put over an old burn mark."

Simon had confirmed Sam's suspicion: Charlotte and Mary were one and the same, and Sam almost sighed in relief. *No wondar she seemed so familiar t' me...an' twenty years later, she was still able t' take me fer a fool.* Despite all of the trouble that infuriating woman had caused him twice in his life, he couldn't help but chuckle and admire her cleverness. The confused expression on Simon's face only made the situation more amusing.

"Okay, I guess you're not going to tell me what the joke is. And hey, Rivera wanted me to tell you that the knife we got from Finn doesn't have any traces of Annabelle Matheson's blood on it. But, considering Finn had his henchman do some of his dirty work, we can safely assume that somebody in his organization took out Annabelle. It was probably the big ugly guy that followed him around everywhere. Forensics has already turned his house upside down, but there's still no sign of Annabelle's ring. I bet he's already sent it off to the buyer, though. We can kiss that thing goodbye. Oh!

And, believe it or not, we got an anonymous package that incriminates him even more."

Sam's head snapped up. "Wha'?"

"Oh yeah, this package is gold! It's got all of his business records; he'll be in prison for a *long* time just for the tax evasion. It even had a copy of Bruce Jaimes' Last Will and Testament, in which—get this— Finn gets absolutely nothing. All of it goes to Malcolm or charity. That's why the turf war has been happening! And the last thing it had was an address where Julie and Rivera found two bodies."

"Whose?"

"His wife and kid."

Sam's eyes grew even wider. "Wha'?"

"Oh, yeah. We already matched their hair follicles to some samples we found at Finn's house; it's definitely them. And with Malcolm dead before he turned twenty-one, Finn's entire empire has been stripped from him." The triumphant smile returned to Simon's face. "His ass is grass, boss. In fact, it would appear that the turf war has pretty much stopped because of all this info."

Sam heard the young man, but too many questions flooded his brain. "...This donnea make sense. None of it does!"

"Come on, boss, you know there's no making sense of what a psychopath will do. And we can all agree that Finn's definitely not somebody we even want to try to understand."

Sam began to pace the tiny hospital room. He continued to voice his thoughts aloud. "We've been stopped a' every corner tryin' t' take down Finn, an' suddenly we ge' an anonymous package with everythin' an' more t' stop him? Tha's too convenient."

"Before you ask, I already had the lab boys check the package, but they couldn't find any prints or anything. There was some DNA on the envelope that says it's a male, but it doesn't match anyone in the system. And anyway, who cares if it's convenient? We got him! That's what we set out to do, right?"

Ignoring him, Sam continued to engage his curiosity as he spoke. "Why would Finn go t' the trouble of killin' Annabelle Matheson an' no' steal her ring?"

"...I don't know how we got back to that but okay. He *did* steal her ring, remember? Darris switched it for him."

"When has Finn ever shown tha' kind of plannin'?"

"What do you mean?"

"Finn operates like a storm; he donnea care wha' kind of damage he leaves in his wake. We know his signature: He slits their throats brutally an' then he burns the evidence. Whenever he's sent his henchmen out t' take care of things, they operate in the same way, aftar accomplishin' Finn's goal. Like the couple tha' Charlotte tracked: She said she saw Finn's man, McGail kill them, an' then he burned the house. Bronson was killed with our guns, thanks t' Finn's mole. Tha's the point: He finishes a job the first time the right way. So why did he make stealin' a ring from a harmless ol' woman a two-part job?"

Simon's confused expression didn't slow Sam down any; he continued his onslaught of theorizing. "An' there's still one person's involvement tha' hasnea been answered: Aiden Marcus. Marcus used t' be Finn's student, then suddenly they hated each other."

"Yeah, that is interesting. Why would Finn let a former henchman live? He never struck me as the forgive-and-forget type of guy."

Sam continued to pace the room, his mind flying in different directions furiously. "...Ye said the bodies Rivera an' Julie found belonged t' Finn's family? Ye're sure abou' tha?"

"There's no arguing with hair follicles."

"How di' they die?"

"Rivera said it looks like their throats were slit, Finn's usual M.O. They bled out."

"Ye said the entire Jaimes fortune would go t' Malcolm Finn, an' The Redcap donnea ge' a cent. Why would Finn kill the only people tha' he can keep control of a fortune through, unless..." Sam summoned up his very first meeting with the Redcap, and the family portrait hanging on the wall was immediately where he set his focus. Finn's wife had blonde hair, and she reminded Sam of the late Princess Diana. Finn's hair was painted red to look like his younger self, but the boy had black hair—jet black hair. "Unless Malcolm Finn is no' William Finn's son."

"Wait, what?" Poor Simon's eyes grew wider with confusion.

"Aiden Marcus has jet black hair; Malcolm Finn had jet black hair. Finn's a' least thirty years older than Audrey Jaimes, so we can safely assume there was no love in tha' marriage. An' t'was a woman tha' came between Finn an' Marcus. The Redcap donnea share anythin. Why would he share his wife? Hell, Marcus went t' work fer the Jaimes clan aftar their fallin' out, an' then he's suddenly banished when Finn marries Audrey?"

"So, you're saying Finn killed Audrey and the kid because his wife fell for Marcus? Why wouldn't he kill Marcus, too?"

"The Redcap enjoys cruelty, he left Marcus alive t' punish him. Hell, he dinnea even burn the bodies, probably jus' t' torture him even more. Bu' back t' Marcus: The bampot tries t' steal a George Jamesone paintin'; we catch him, an' then suddenly he ge's away? How?"

"Um..."

"We assumed a' the time t'was because he was workin' fer Finn. Bu' Finn wouldnea go t' the trouble of freein' a man from FBI custody if he wants 'im t' suffer."

"Then Marcus was trying to stake his own claim in the game! If he got a George Jamesone piece, he'd be competition with Finn and therefore, get closer to his revenge!"

"Or he was doin' somebody a favor. This somebody knew Marcus would lead us t' Finn, so he was put in our way on purpose. Ye said yerself there was nothin' sophisticated abou' the robbery; catchin' them was too easy! And Marcus was far too calm fer the position he was in! Then he escaped from FBI custody before we could go down the wrong path tha' dinnea lead t' Finn."

Simon looked bewildered; rubbing his temples with his fingers, he sighed, "Okay...so...who's left? Who would want to free Aiden Marcus? Could it be one of the rivaling clan leaders?"

"Aye, they must have helped; they have a vested interest in getting rid of Finn. Bu' there's someone else involved in this, someone who's obsessed with George Jamesone paintin's an' artifacts, an' their interests align with Marcus an' the clan leaders in destroyin' The Redcap. Another player tha's been usin' us all along t' help accomplish their goals: the buyer." Deciding he couldn't wait for the blasted nurse any longer, Sam grabbed his little packed bag and brushed passed Simon with determination. "We need t' find Aiden Marcus."

"For what? Charlotte told us she'd never met the buyer; why would Aiden Marcus have met him?"

"Because the buyer convinced him t' start this investigation in the first place."

"How?"

"By killin' Annabelle Matheson an' framin' Finn fer it."

Chapter Sixteen

Getting back to Chicago's FBI headquarters and finding Rivera and Julie was easy for Sam. Explaining his theory about Aiden Marcus, however, wasn't as well received. Thankfully, Director Copper had already departed back to Cleveland, so he had one less obstacle in his way as he barraged his team with information.

Rivera immediately balked. "Whoa, whoa, whoa, how in the world could you possibly draw *that* conclusion? Other than catching Marcus during a botched-up coincidental robbery, there is absolutely nothing else that suggests he's involved."

"We've still go' Marcus' hair an' DNA samples when we arrested him, an' now we have the bodies of Audrey an' Malcolm Finn. The lab is comparin' them both. If I'm right, an' Malcolm is Marcus' son, then tha' proves he has motive t' kill Finn, ergo he's involved."

"According to you, Sam. All it physically proves is that Audrey Finn and Aiden Marcus had a fling, not that he killed Annabelle Matheson. Forget finding him, we have absolutely squat for a warrant to look for any sort of weapon."

Julie jumped in. "Here's what I don't understand: How does Annabelle's ring fit into all of this mess, if Finn isn't the one who had her killed?"

"Finn was losin' control of his empire an' needed t' make any money he could. He saw the ring as a moment of opportunity; tha's why he had Darris switch it while it was still in evidence. I'm no' sayin' he wouldnea have gone after it himself, jus' tha' he hadnea found it yet."

"But how would he have known to look for it in the first place?"

"Simply, somebody tipped 'im off. I's no' the first time he's done it." Sam turned to Simon. "When was the las' time a George Jamesone paintin' or artifact was stolen, aside from the gala?"

Pulling out his laptop, Simon typed furiously. "... About five years ago from a museum in California."

"Any indications on who stole it?"

"The place wasn't burned down, and nobody's throats were slit, if that's what you mean."

"Aye, tha's wha' I mean. Now, when's the las' time there was a reported loss an' Finn's MOs showed up?"

Again, Simon typed. "2017 in Peoria."

"An' before tha', same MO?"

"... Fifteen years ago in St. Louis."

"An before tha'?"

"… 1983, Rockford."

Sam turned back to the others. "See a pa'ern yet?"

Rivera sighed. "So, he stayed local and didn't go all over the world. Again, Sam, you're grasping at straws here."

"And if anything, that only adds more weight to Finn being the one that killed Annabelle," Julie nodded. "He just switched the ring later so nobody would think to look at him."

Sam shook his head and argued. "No, Finn donnea work like tha'. When he does a job, he does it the first time. Forge' abou' Annabelle's ring for a moment and look a' her murder: Why was she murdered?"

Rivera answered. "There's absolutely no reason that she was murdered: She wasn't robbed, and only her family had any gain from her death. But all of them have been ruled out as suspects."

"Exactly, her death makes no sense. If it was a random act of violence, why wasnea she killed behind a dumpster or somewhere more accessible? Why was she killed in her apartment? An' a heavily guarded apartment with some of the finest security tha' money can buy, a' tha'?"

"Why do serial killers go after innocent people, Sam? Because they can get their sick jollies off of it," Rivera argued. "You know there's no possible way to make sense of why murderers do what they do."

"Ye're missin' the point! Annabelle Matheson was killed in her home in a brutal way verra specific t' how Finn delt with enemies, right down t' the knife! Bu' accordin' t' the physical evidence, he dinnea do it. Hell, the scene wasn't even complete: Annabelle's body wasnea burned. There's nothin' tha' connects Finn t' Annabelle's murder, because he's no' the one tha' murdered her. T'was staged t' look an' seem like he did, so tha' we'd dig deeper inta Finn an' find

193

somethin' t' arrest him fer. We can all agree tha' Finn's list of allies is short, an' the only way he'd keep them in line is through fear an' blackmail. He's called The Redcap fer a reason. Nobody is stupid enough t' go up against him; they'd have too much t' lose. Aiden Marcus had nothin' left t' lose when Audrey an' Malcolm were murdered, so he set out t' ge' revenge on the man tha' took everythin' from him. An' he me' the people who wanted the same thing t' make it happen."

Rivera, Julie, and Simon shared a glance; Sam could see the wheels slowly start to turn as he spelled everything out for them.

Julie was the first to speak, "Okay...so Finn stealing the ring is just a coincidence."

"In this instance, aye, bu' i's still the clue t' the key player: the buyer."

"What makes you so sure that Marcus didn't do all of this himself?"

"The man was Finn's protégé fer years; he learned violence an' fear from the best, no' plannin' an' cunnin'. I have no doubt he was plannin' revenge on Finn, bu' he would have jus' gone in an' killed the man a' the first chance he go', no' go t' the effort of makin' sure his empire is taken away first."

"But why would this mysterious buyer want to kill Finn, if Finn's worked for him before?"

"I donnea know, yet," Sam admitted.

Right at that moment, the door opened and a tech from the forensics lab walked in with a report in his hand, which he immediately handed over to Simon. "...Gold sticky star for the boss: Malcolm Finn's DNA and Aiden Marcus' DNA match: The kid was Marcus' son."

"Di' the DNA on the anonymous package match Marcus' too?"

"No," Simon shook his head, "I already told you that at the hospital, remember?"

"Right," Sam nodded. "Then i' has t' belong t' Marcus' partners, probably the buyer. I jus' donnea understand why he'd send it to us now..."

Rivera held up his hand to interrupt. "Hold on, before you can push this theory any further, let's go back through the apartment security tape. If Aiden Marcus really did kill Annabelle, then we'd be able to see him somewhere in it, now that we know to look for him."

"Already working on that now," Simon squeaked as he opened his laptop, "I've got an algorithm running facial recognition through the whole thing, and it should be done right about...now!"

Like magic, three pixelated images appeared on the screen and Simon set to work furiously cleaning them up; Sam smiled triumphantly as the side of Aiden Marcus's face showed clear as day in one of them right within Annabelle's time of death window, wearing a uniform for a pizza delivery service of all things.

"No...there's no possible way it was *that* easy for him to get in!" Rivera argued. "She never called for pizza that night; her phone records say so! And every witness statement backs that up!"

"Because tha's no' her pizza. Somebody else in the buildin' ordered it. Marcus shows up an' pays the delivery guy off an' delivers it himself. Then he calls Annabelle Matheson, says her daughter sent a pizza fer her, she lets him in, an' he kills her."

Before Sam could tell him to, Simon already had his hacking program up and was clacking on the keys furiously for the answer to who made the order. "...Yup, Mrs. Lila Brown in penthouse number two ordered a chicken and spinach pizza that night."

Julie jumped in. "But the doorman wouldn't have let him in without confirming the order with the tenant. So, Marcus just waited until somebody ordered the pizza and then used that as his way in? That's leaving an awful lot up to chance. If the buyer really is working with Marcus, then they wouldn't have done something that simple."

"Sometimes the mos' genius thing ye can do is the simple things nobody thinks t' look a'. Bu' ye're right, our mysterious buyer has been far too clever an' calculated t' jus' leave all this up t' chance...I'll be' ye $100 tha' Mrs. Brown's been bugged." Sam turned to Julie and Rivera. "The two of ye go back t' the apartment an' talk t' her, an' check the apartment fer bugs. Simon an' I will concentrate on findin' Marcus."

"How?" Rivera asked.

"By examinin' the evidence found when Marcus was freed from FBI custody. Simon—"

"Get the FBI files up, I'm on it," the lanky young man smiled and began clacking away. By the time Julie and Rivera had left, he was done typing and beaming with pride. "Here we go: So, ballistics found Colt .45 shells at the scene, and the shells belonged to a gun that has a noted history in Chicago's system."

"Of wha'?"

"Mostly property destruction cases and a few bodies that were determined to be 'hits.' There's definitely mob connection to this gun, but unfortunately there's no name attached to it."

"Then perhaps Heidi can fill us in," Sam muttered before turning on his heel and marching directly to the Chicago Offices' prison cells beneath the building.

Director Bronson's former assistant Heidi Tombs had her own private cell far away from the usual myriad of dangerous criminals, but from one look at her, Sam could tell she wasn't faring very well. Her usual friendly, freckled face looked worn and faded. Not that he expected her to look healthy after her indiscretions were brought to light, but he still couldn't help but feel sorry for her. His good arm still wrapped tightly in the sling, he used his left to scan his badge for access and walked in to take the single metal seat across from her bed where she sat.

"Mr. McKay," she said quietly. "What brings you here?"

"Only Bronson would have known the details of Aiden Marcus' prison transfer," he stated softly, but clearly. "Which means ye would have had access t' them as well. Why'd ye help Marcus escape, an' who di' ye tip off t' free him?"

"Bram McNally," she answered simply, much to Sam's surprise, "Head of the McNally clan. He owns a string of dry cleaners downtown. He's usually at the one on 16th and Wabash during business hours, but if not then you can find him having lunch at Big Scotsman around one."

"…Thank ye," Sam answered, dazed by how cooperative Heidi was being. "…I'll arrange t' have a sentence recommendation—"

"Forget it, I'm prepared to serve my time for what I've done."

He narrowed his eyes. "Lass, ye were coerced. I donnea blame ye for doin' wha' ye had t' do."

"Well, I do," she stated, finally meeting Sam's eyes. "I didn't just break the law, McKay, I killed my friend and boss, and I let one of the worst men possible get his hooks into the FBI… I put my personal feelings before my duty to this office. Law Enforcement has never looked the other way for the criminals who acted out of love. Giving me a slap on the wrist just because I was with the FBI is hypocritical, to say the very least."

"Ye dinnea intend t' give Finn power, tha's the difference."

"Not to me. I broke the law, and I put the people of Chicago in more danger. I've accepted the consequences for my actions."

"An' wha' abou' yer brother? What'll happen t' him?"

"He's not any of your concern, Agent McKay. I've told you what you need to know. Now, please, go away."

Stunned and bewildered, Sam slowly stood up from the tiny metal chair and left Heidi Tombs to her fate. Taking one last look at her, he resisted the urge to go back in and try to convince her to fight for her freedom once more. He knew it was pointless; he could see in her eyes that she had given up the fight. And he knew that once someone had given up, there was no convincing them to do anything anymore. He shook his head in disappointment before he made his way to the garage for a car, his next destination: a dry cleaner on 16th and Wabash.

***

Bram McNally wasn't at the dry-cleaning store Heidi had directed Sam to, and none of the employees wanted to disturb the boss, so Sam was forced to find Big Scotsman and wait for the man himself when he went to lunch. Big Scotsman was a pub and grill located in Near South Side that had Scottish flags and football team photos hung all over the brick walls. Sam felt strangely at home when he walked in. He got there at 12:50p.m., ordered himself a stout, and (after giving the pub keeper a $20 bill for the heads-up) waited for Finn's main rival, Bram McNally to show up. Right at 1:00 p.m. sharp, a tall, middle-aged, bald man with a silver goatee wearing a suit walked in with two younger men behind him.

Sam didn't need the confirmation from the pubkeeper to know that he was looking at Bram McNally. He waited for the clan leader to take his seat and place an order with the waitress before he walked over. "Mr. McNally?"

While the two grunts stiffened in their chairs, the clan leader merely cocked his head to the side. "Do I know ye?"

"My name is Sampson McKay... I believe ye may know me brother, J —Hamish."

"Aye, I thought ye migh' be familiar. Other than a few more wrinkles around the eyes, ye're the spittin' image of Hamish."

Sam bristled at the comment, resentful at any idea that he and his brother were easily relatable, and asked politely, "May I sit?"

"Please," McNally said simply, gesturing to the chair directly across the table from him. "Wha' can I do for ye, Mr. McKay?"

"Sir, I donnea want' t' start our conversation on the wrong foot so I'll be honest with ye: I'm an agent of the FBI, an' I'm interested in takin' down yer rival: The Redcap."

"Las' I'd heard, The Redcap was done for."

"Aye, he is. I'm lookin' fer his old associate, Aiden Marcus. I heard a rumor tha' ye were involved in his escape. I though' perhaps ye migh' be able t' tell me where he is."

Bram McNally folded his hands together on the table, and an amused smile crossed his face, "Wha' do ye need Marcus for? Ye've go' all ye need t' ge' rid of Finn, aye?"

His direct comment piqued Sam's interest. Carefully, he took a sip of his ale and asked, "I donnea suppose ye know anythin' abou' a package the FBI received regardin' Finn's dealin's, do ye?"

"Hypothetically, I might know someone tha' does."

"Then, hypothetically, ye might know tha' I'm lookin' fer someone else involved in this. Someone tha' helped Marcus ge' his revenge on The Redcap, an' used yer resources t' make i' happen. Marcus came t' ye fer help, didn't he? Bu' he had a plan too well-thought-out t' come up with himself."

McNally chuckled before answering. "Ye McKays are smart, arn't ye? Le's jus' say someone came t' me t' ask fer money, resources, an' a rescue when the time was right. Tol' me I'd be contacted when i' needed doin'. In exchange, I'd ge' the first claim t' the position of clan leader once Finn was removed. Seemed like a fair trade, so I agreed."

"Then wha' happened t' this someone aftar ye rescued him?"

"We le' him go his own way once events were set in motion fer Finn's downfall."

Sam narrowed his eyes, "Where'd he go?"

McNally looked to the man to his left and Sam followed suit.

"There's a hotel called The Primrose Inn in St. Louis; you might want to check out there," the man grunted.

Sam nodded and turned back to McNally, "I donnea suppose ye know who Marcus was workin' with, do ye?"

"I nevar asked," McNally answered simply.

"No? Ye took a hell of a risk trustin' the plan of somebody ye nevar met."

"Aye, t'was a gamble, bu' in the end i' paid off, didn't it?"

By the shifting of the two grunts, Sam could tell that the conversation was over. Pulling out his wallet, he set another $50 on the table in front of McNally and stood up. "Thank ye fer yer time Mr. McNally, enjoy yer lunch."

"Aye, t'was a pleasure. Good luck, Agent McKay."

Sam walked out of the pub with confidence, but immediately rushed to the car once he was clear of McNally's sight. Pulling out his phone, he dialed Simon and barked as soon as the young man answered, "Be outside of the buildin' in ten minutes, we're goin' t' St. Louis."

***

The drive to St. Louis passed by almost instantly; Sam couldn't help but feel optimistic as they pulled into the parking lot of the Primrose Inn. The concierge confirmed that not only was Aiden Marcus a guest, he was still in his room on the fifth floor. With a staff member in tow, Sam and Simon quickly got on the next elevator and raced to catch their fugitive.

Standing outside of room 516, a Do Not Disturb sign hanging on the knob, Sam pounded on the door. "Aiden Marcus! I's the FBI! Open up!"

Silence answered them. Sam nodded to the staff member to open the door for them and withdrew his gun; he was a terrible shot with his left hand, but he might be able to make anyone think twice about anything. The young woman shakily pulled out her key card and just as soon as the little light on the door flashed green, Sam burst through it with Simon right behind him. But just as soon as they barged in, they lowered their guns in bewilderment. The young lady screamed and ran back out to the hallway, while Sam and Simon walked closer to the body of Aiden Marcus. His throat was slit, and the weapon that appeared to have caused it was in his hand: a hunting knife with the tip broken off, similar to that of William

Finn's. Next to his body was an empty bottle of Jack Daniels and a piece of paper.

Sam, careful to only touch the corner, picked up the paper; the scribbles were barely legible, but he was able to read it aloud:

"Congratulations, pigs, ye finally figured it out. I killed the ol' lady, bu' Finn would have sooner or later. I had t' make sure ye'd look inta The Redcap, t'was the only way I could ge' justice fer Audrey an' Malcolm. Tha' bassard took everythin' from me, so I took his empire from him."

Simon let out a low whistle. "Damn. You really don't survive going up against a Redcap, do you?"

Sam shook his head, but mumbled his agreement, "No, ye don't."

"I'll get forensics over here ASAP." Simon pulled out his phone and headed towards the door, where he tried to calm down the distraught young hotel worker.

Sam carefully placed the suicide note back where he found it before standing over Aiden Marcus' body; without him, there would be no way to find out the mysterious mastermind buyer's identity. Although he knew that wasn't what they had been set on the case to do in the first place, knowing that the final player in this sordid game was still out there somewhere left a bad taste in his mouth. *Annabelle Matheson an' her family can rest. An' ye go' The Redcap! He has nothin' t' help him now.* Try as he might to rationalize that he had done everything he could do, Sam couldn't shake the unpleasant feeling of being a pawn in the twisted power play the buyer had control of. He knew exactly what his team would say to him, particularly Rivera: Does it really matter so long as they caught their man? The politics of crime and justice was not a dance Sam was interested in learning, especially when he was the one being used.

The forensics team arrived within minutes of Simon's call and set to work processing the hotel room: checking everywhere for prints that should not be there, looking for anything peculiar on the body, and taking thousands of pictures of any and all relevant evidence. Some dirt was found in the rugs, another smashed whiskey bottle, a small black rubber button; the tiniest things were being assessed. Sam stayed out of their way, but he kept his eyes on Aiden Marcus. As a husband and father, he understood the man's need for revenge; if anything ever happened to Oliver or Meredith, Sam knew he would not hesitate to go after the man responsible with everything he could. But to kill himself after it was all over —he couldn't understand how a man like Marcus could feel that was the only option left to him. Despite being Annabelle's murderer, Sam couldn't help but feel sorry for him.

Simon suddenly appeared, interrupting his thoughts. "You were right, boss, there was a bug in Ms. Brown's apartment. Marcus and the buyer really did their research, too. Julie said Ms. Brown received a "Thinking of You" card that had a gift card inside of it for the pizza place. She assumed it was from her sister and didn't think anything of it, and she went ahead and ordered pizza that night. And when they went to talk to the delivery guy who was supposed to be on duty, he confessed to letting Marcus take over the delivery for $500. That's seriously just crazy with how simple, but also how genius of a plan it was! All of that just to get Marcus into Annabelle's apartment without being detected!"

Sam nodded his agreement. "Aye, we're so used t' seein' new an' complicated crimes, sometimes i's easy t' forge' tha' the old tricks are the bes' tricks."

"No kidding. Well, the others are on their way back to headquarters. We should get going and pack up; we're due back in Cleveland tomorrow morning."

"Aye, alrigh'." Sam took one final look at Marcus's body, and his thoughts turned back to Charlotte; with the capture of William Finn and all of the evidence stacked against him, not to mention Sam himself would testify about the traumatic night in his shop, the woman would get justice for her murder and all of the humiliation Finn put her through. And now that Annabelle's murder was solved, he could take a deeper look into Charlotte's sister's death. It didn't matter that Charlotte was gone; he had made a promise, and he intended to keep it. Plus, there was Dr. Stewart to consider. The man deserved answers as well.

Back at the FBI office, Sam read over Isobel Claire Winter's case file again. He called Captain Knight and asked if he remembered anything unusual about the fire, but he was answered with the man's typical surly attitude and absolutely nothing that was helpful. While everyone else around him packed up their things to make ready to leave, he kept his thoughts focused until Rivera nudged him.

"What happened to the whole 'We're equals, we each take part in doing the work' bit? Because as far as I can see, we're doing all of the grunt work while you sit and read."

Julie was walking by and smacked his arm. "Leave him alone, Derrick. His arm is still in a sling, for God's sake."

"If he's well enough to work a murder case, he's well enough to carry some boxes. What is it you're looking at, anyway?"

"An open and shut accidental housefire," Simon grunted behind the heavy box he was holding. "Our former thief's sister's death, to be more precise."

"Why?" Rivera asked in an annoyed tone. "What does her sister have to do with any of this?"

"Nothin'," Sam answered. The single word reply was enough to convince Julie and Simon to leave him be, but Rivera kept pestering him.

"Then what's so important about it? What do you hope to figure out? Whether or not Charlotte's sister was murdered? What good does that do her now that she's dead?"

"I's no' fer her benefit, Rivera, i's fer mine. I promised I'd look inta' it, an' I am."

"Well, it looks like any and all evidence to look at doesn't exist anymore."

Sam shut the case file and stood up. "Tha's no' true, there's still Claire's body. An' we know where she's buried."

Simon piped in. "Don't you need permission from the next of kin to do that?"

"No' if the next of kin is dead, which Charlotte is." Sam walked out of the little room before anyone could argue with him further. Once he was in a quiet corner of the building, he pulled out his phone and called Copper directly.

Ring... Ring... Ring...

"I thought I specifically said that you're on leave, McKay?" The director's tone, level as ever, had that slightly irritated cat-like feel to it, and Sam couldn't help but smirk.

"We both know a little thing like bein' hospitalized isnea gonna' stop me, Copper. An' I solved Annabelle Matheson's murder without breakin' a sweat. Tha' has't count fer somethin', aye?"

"Don't get cute with me, there's only so much of your insubordination that I can take. Now that the case is officially over, I expect you to go back to your home and get proper rest and recuperation until you pass the physical and psych evals."

"Aye, an' ye have my word tha' I will do tha', bu' first I need yer permission t' exhume the body of Isobel Claire Winter."

Copper would never laugh, but Sam could almost swear he heard her snort. "Why on earth would I grant you that?"

"'Cause then I'd owe ye a favor, Belinda. I think tha' holds a little weight, aye?"

The Director's silence gave Sam some hope that she was considering his offer. Just when he was starting to wonder if the call had been disconnected, she answered him. "Alright, Evan will get you the paperwork within the hour."

Ever true to keeping the last word, the woman hung up before Sam could respond. Rolling his eyes, he pocketed his phone and made his way towards the car, then towards Mount Olive Cemetery.

Chapter Seventeen

Digging up Claire Winters body proved to be the easiest thing Sam had done since coming to Chicago; he had barely shown the authorization Copper had sent him to Mount Olive Cemetery's director, and the groundskeeper was called over within moments. While her final resting place was being excavated, Sam took note of the familiar spot and decided to look around him. Not more than a couple hundred feet away was the gravesite where the young and stupid boy at Chicago University was required to make his delivery: the gravesite of Mr. and Mrs. Lopez. Sam wasn't particularly shocked to see how close Charlotte had made the drop site to her sister, but it further fueled his growing belief that she really did witness her sister's murder. Every move she made seemed to revolve around Claire; surely there had to be some truth to the theory. He didn't want to celebrate prematurely, but he was almost positive that Finn would get another murder charge on top of the others. Finally, the casket was free from the ground, and Sam carefully took it back to Chicago's headquarters.

Copper apparently wanted his little pet project to be over and done with as soon as possible, so she had also sent him the correct priority authorization that forced the forensics lab to drop everything else and examine the very few remains of Isobel Claire Winter. Sam sat in the closest chair and patiently watched the medical examiner, a woman by the name of Matilda Ghee, conduct a thorough autopsy. She examined every inch of the charred remains, scraped off anything organic from the bones, put petri dishes under a microscope, all the while comparing her findings to that of the original case file. Her movements were quick, graceful, and efficient, so Sam made sure to stay out of her way. Finally, after examining what seemed like the twentieth glass slide, she turned her attention to Sam.

"You are very lucky," she said with a courteous smile, "Between the fire and time destroying most of any evidence, there was just enough flesh left for me to examine. I couldn't' find any traces of accelerants, which matches the initial report: The fire was caused by electrical failure."

"Can ye tell me if she was dead before the fire?"

"As a matter of fact, I can. And yes, she was."

Then Charlotte wasnea imaginin' things; she saw her sister murdered. I' must've been Finn! Sam smiled triumphantly, but the feeling was short-lived with what Ghee said next:

"She was electrocuted."

His smile disappeared. "Wha'? How can ye tell?"

"The tissue surrounding the bones was burned, but not the same way as by a fire. Electrical burns manifest in tissue differently than fire burns do in the form of metallic traces. On the skin of her fingertips, I found trace amounts of a metallic residue called nichrome. The report says the fire was started by electrical failure caused by a hair dryer and a damp wall socket. Hair dryer plugs are made of a metal alloy mix of nickel and chromium: nichrome. So, based off of the evidence found and what I could physically find now, I can confirm that she died of accidental electrocution. Then, according to the report, the fire started from the sink where they found pieces of what looked to be paint brushes: Sparks from the faulty socket must have caught onto the brushes, which then caught the paint on the walls and started the fire. It was a mercy that she died quickly and didn't have to suffer being burned alive."

Sam stared at Claire's charred remains unconvinced. "Could ye be able t' tell if somebody slit her throat an' she bled out or no'?"

"If the cut was made deep enough to nick the bones, yes. But there would be some indication of that in the flesh samples if she'd died of blood loss. Things like spots or marbling. But with a sample this old and decrepit, I couldn't honestly tell you whether or not there is."

"Can ye check the bones, jus' in case?"

"Sure, just a moment." Ghee turned around to grab a magnifying glass and immediately began to examine the neck bones under Claire's skull. Sam didn't blink as he watched her, but the excited feeling he'd had had all but disappeared when she stood up straight again. "Sorry, but I can't find anything that suggests she bled out through her neck, nor anywhere else. My professional opinion based off of the physical and circumstantial findings is she was accidentally electrocuted, and then her remains were burned by the housefire."

Sam slumped against the chair. He began to think about Finn and mentally reviewed all of the facts of what The Redcap's signature was: He always slit his victims' throats, relished in the time it took for them to die of blood loss, then he'd use some sort of accelerant he could find on hand to set the whole crime scene ablaze. Not once had electrical failure been a method he'd use, and there wasn't anything to support that Claire Winter had bled to death first. *Then wha' Dr. Stewart tol' me was true: She really di' die by accident, no' murdar.* Feeling confused and a little defeated, he thanked the medical examiner and left while she replaced Claire's remains in her coffin for re-burial.

As Sam made his way through the office to his team, he kept thinking about Charlotte: While her traumatic experience definitely explained her obsession with her sister, it didn't explain her obsession with George Jamesone, nor how she concocted that the two were related. If he learned anything from her during their brief and interesting time together, it's that you don't just walk around asking people about art thief jobs; you have to build your reputation through time, research, and dedication (with dedication being the biggest factor) until you get hired. He had promised that he would confirm or debunk Charlotte's story that she had been clinging to, and he had. But her dedication to George Jamesone art holding whatever key she was looking for had him more than curious. And, as everyone knew, he did not like being left curious.

Sam walked into the office room to find Rivera carrying the last of the boxes while Julie and Simon were enjoying a cup of coffee. The scowl on his face must have given away how the search of Claire's body didn't provide him with anything useful, as Rivera wasted absolutely no time in goading him.

"So, now that you're done playing around with random dead people, we can go home."

"I told you, boss," Simon added, "There wasn't anything at all that suggested foul play in Claire Winter's death. It was just an accident."

Sam didn't answer beyond sitting down at the table; his eyebrows pursed together as his mind rapidly ran in different directions.

Julie chuckled, "Hold on, guys, he's got that look in his eyes again: Sam McKay is still curious, which means we're not going to be done until his curiosity is satisfied."

"Why would Charlotte dedicate her life t' stealin' paintin's tha' had absolutely nothin' t' do with her sistar?" Sam mumbled to himself.

Simon answered flippantly. "As a coping mechanism?"

He shot the young man an irritated stare.

Rivera set his heavy load down on the table and heaved a sigh. "But it *did* have something to do with her sister, remember? Dr. Stewart told you that Claire was an art student. George Jamesone was her pet project for her thesis. Charlotte was just a kid when the fire happened, and it's obvious that she and her sister were close, so she probably remembered the artist and pieced the two together. Any head-hunter would say the same."

"Aye, tha' would be the obvious answar, bu' I'm no' convinced. There's more than we know goin' on here."

"According to *you,* Sam. There's no way to tell how people will cope with anything. Sometimes the answer that makes zero sense to us makes perfect sense to somebody else."

"Ye may be right, Rivera, bu' tha' still donnea explain who would go t' the trouble of assurin' The Redcap's downfall."

The short, chiseled man scoffed. "So *that's* why you're so bent: It's not about Charlotte and her sister; it's about the buyer."

Sam always admired Rivera's bravery in calling him out whenever he couldn't seem to let something alone, but that didn't make his lack of tact any less frustrating. He narrowed his eyes at his friend and growled, "No, i's abou' both: I want t' know why Charlotte go' inta this in the first place, an' who's been usin' us as puppets t' accomplish their goals."

"Derrick, you have to admit this whole thing does smell kind of funky," Julie nodded her agreement. "Since we started the case, we've been running around in circles. Finn didn't kill Annabelle, but it was made to look like he did by Marcus."

"Who was the real killer," Rivera argued. "And we've got the proof of that in his note and the knife. Case closed. Taking down The Redcap is icing on the cake, not to mention lucky."

"Aye, bu' I'm no' convince tha' Marcus would jus' kill himself aftar takin' down Finn. He's no' the type. An' besides, arrestin' Finn was a little too easy," Sam argued.

Simon snorted. "Boss, if that's your definition of 'easy,' then I'd hate to think of what you mean by hard. You were almost barbecued because of him!"

"Only because I was chasin' Charlotte. Every crucial piece of evidence we found since we've been here has one thing in common: Charlotte."

"Well, duh. It was her resources that helped us."

Sam shook his head, "No, no, i's more than tha'. When we first arrested her, she tol' us tha' George Jamesone jobs have been on the market fer years, bu' she also tol' us tha' ye have t' be hired by this person in ordar t' ge' the job. I donnea think we were the only ones bein' used. Charlotte was another pawn in the game, jus' like us. Tha' tells me tha' she has the key t' the buyer's identity, an' i's somehow connected w' her sister."

Julie stepped forward. "Um, so how do we find it? They're both dead. And Charlotte also told us that she's never met the buyer before, remember?"

"Aye, bu' the buyer obviously knows who *she* is. How else could tha' woman cross paths with me again?"

Rivera gawked. "Wait a minute, what do you mean *again*?"

Ignoring him, Sam started to pace the room as he continued to voice his thoughts. "Somethin' must've happened tha' really set Charlotte on this path. Somethin' triggered it, whether she knew it or no'. Bu' the first question is why...Simon, pull up everythin' ye can on Claire Isobel Winter: places of work, college admissions, financials, all of it."

While Rivera continued to roll his eyes skeptically, Simon practically yanked his trusty laptop out of his bag and immediately let his fingers fly across the keyboard. For what seemed like an eternity, the room was filled with heavy silence (other than the sound of Simon's typing) until, finally, the young man sighed. "Please remember that you asked me to hunt for information in a time before computers were a thing, when I tell you I couldn't find much."

"Wha' *di'* ye find?"

"Just the birth and death records. Anything else is hidden on paper somewhere, and nobody has taken the time to put it in a database." Simon shivered as he groaned, "Ugh, paper..."

Sam furrowed his eyebrows. "Wait, Dr. Stewart tol' me tha' Claire was an art student a' university. Wouldnea the college have updated her information int' a database?"

"Legally, schools can only keep records of students for up to six years. And unless you're a famous person, and the college publicly claims you, the only proof of your attendance is a diploma and resume."

Sam started pacing again; his hand covering his mouth, he thought back to the newspaper article in Claire's file. "She worked a' a restaurant called Gigi's. Can ye see if i's still around?"

Again, Simon worked his magic; just moments later, a triumphant smile was on his face. "Not only is it still around, it's still in its original spot in Lincoln Park. Owned by the same family since 1922, it's considered a landmark."

"Then somebody's bound t' remember Claire workin' there," Sam nodded. Turning on his heel, he marched towards the garage. Julie and Rivera were right behind him.

***

Lincoln Park had a variety of 'hole-in-the-wall' options to choose from, and right smack in the middle of them was Gigi's. Red brick walls, hanging lights, and small tables packed with people filled Sam's view as he looked around the tiny restaurant. Along the walls were a few paintings that brought a lightness to the copper red. The smell of tomatoes and fresh bread made his stomach rumble; despite how hungry he felt, he ignored the pangs and searched for the owner. He was just about to walk to the back where a completely visible kitchen was when a young man rushed over.

"Sorry to keep you folks waiting. Just the three of you?"

Sam brought his badge up. "Actually, we're here t' speak t' yer oldest staff member. Someone who's been here the longest."

The young man, though startled at first by the badge, nodded. "Um, Alonso is the original owner's grandson. He's in the back."

"Fetch him, please."

The waiter rushed away and within moments, a portly middle-aged man with curly, greying hair wearing a white apron over a blue t-shirt appeared. Wiping his hands on the apron (which was splattered with stains), he walked towards Sam, Julie, and Rivera. "I'm Al, can I help you?"

Sam, too preoccupied with finding an answer, completely skipped the introduction portion of the conversation and asked, "Di' ye ever work with an Isobel Claire Winter?"

Shock appeared on Alonso's face. "God, I can't remember the last time anybody's talked about Claire. Yeah, I knew her really well. She was a waitress here a long time ago. When we found out about the fire, everyone around here was heartbroken."

"Wha' can ye tell us abou' her?"

A nearby booth suddenly opened up; Alonso gestured to it and escorted the three of them. Once everyone was seated comfortably, he folded his hands together and sighed. "...She was gorgeous, funny, sweet, one of the best waitresses my dad had hired. Also, a very good friend of mine...You might say that we were pretty close."

"How close?" Julie asked, her tone implying what she really meant.

"Close enough to share a few secrets with each other, but we never slept together. Actually, it's because of her that I had the guts to come out to my dad. She was a one-in-a-million person."

"D' ye know where she went t' university?" Sam asked.

The owner furrowed his eyes. "Who told you that? Claire was an incredible artist, but she wasn't interested in college. She only did the waitress thing for a steady income in between gigs, at least that's what she always told me. I always thought one day she'd make it big as a painter. Hell, she even recreated a Botticelli painting for my dad when he mentioned we needed to add some more culture to Gigi's."

Alonso pointed to the wall across from them towards a large, 5'x4' painting hanging on it. In the middle was a naked woman with long, flowing red hair standing in an open shell in the middle of the sea. On both of her sides were other figures on land and in the air watching her, celebrating her.

Julie was the first to speak, her voice laced with the obvious amazement. "...Is that—"

"Yup, *The Birth of Venus*. Well, not the original, of course. But an amazing knock-off," Alonso nodded. "My dad jumped over the moon when he saw it and kept insisting to everyone who asked that it's the real deal. Like I told you, she was incredible."

Rivera finally spoke. "Did she ever do any original pieces? Have you seen any of them?"

"...Now that you mention it, I don't think I did. Not once. I asked, of course. I wanted to showcase a few of her pieces, along with the Botticelli, to hopefully bring some attention to her talent. Any time I asked her, though, she would always say that she wasn't ready to show her work to the world yet."

Another voice rang through the air yelling, "Al! Are you done, yet? We're swamped back here!"

The older man chuckled. "That would be my husband. I'm sorry, agents, I've really got to get back to work. I'm not sure what more I could tell you about Claire. But if you need anything else, please let me know."

"Thank you for your time," Julie answered with a smile.

"Before you go, can I interest you in some of our famous focaccia? A brand-new batch has just come out of the oven. On the house. Law enforcement has had to deal with enough crap the last few years, I'd like to at least show you some of *my* appreciation."

"Thank you," Rivera nodded. "We'd love some."

As Alonso walked away from the table, Julie and Rivera turned their attention to Sam. They could tell that the giant Scotsman was deep in thought by the way his furrowed eyes were staring into the space before him, but at nothing in particular.

Rivera was the first to clear his throat. "Alright, I admit it, there was something more to learn about Claire."

"Yeah, she was a working art forger," Julie scoffed. "And from the looks of that Botticelli, a pretty damn good one."

"Now everythin' makes sense," Sam mumbled. "Charlotte saw her sister frequently paintin' famous works of art. She was workin' on a George Jamesone paintin' when the fire happened, an' tha' was part of wha' se' her on the path of bein' an art thief. She though' the two were connected."

"Just from one painting?"

"Maybe... bu' mos' likely from multiple," Sam sighed. "Remember, Simon said three George Jamesone pieces were recently discovered t' be forgeries. They had t' be Claire's forgeries."

He stopped himself from continuing when the friendly Alonso suddenly reappeared with three small loaves of delicious smelling bread on a plate. The owner said a final "Enjoy" before walking away again, and Sam brought his cell phone to the table. Dialing Simon, he pressed the speaker button and waited for the young man to answer.

"You guys are going to bring me back a pizza, right? I'm starving, and the thought of a real old-school Chicago Deep Dish is making me salivate."

Sam ignored him and growled, "Simon, go back t' the forged George Jamesone paintin's ye mentioned a while back. Can ye find ou' when they were registered t' public record?"

"Um...yeah, just a second." The sounds of keys clacked away for a moment before he answered, "In 1988, why?"

"Good work, now can ye cross reference Dr. Spencer Stewart against Charlotte an' Claire's parents? Robert an' Linda Winter."

Again, the sound of a keyboard came through the phone. "No, I don't see any connection between the professor and them."

"Di' ye find *anythin'* on the Winters?"

"Robert and Linda Winter owned a catering company called Taste of Winter, which is still operating today. According to the founder's page on the website, the both of them grew up in Englewood and were high school sweethearts. Both died in an accidental car crash in 1984. But Dr. Stewart was born in New York, attended Harvard, and didn't move to Chicago until 1989."

Sam could feel his blood starting to boil with rage as everything began to piece together in front of him. "Di' the Winters ever travel t' New York? Are ye absolutely positive there's nothin' connectin' them t' the professar?"

"Yeah, boss, I'm positive. From what I can find, they never even left Illinois for a vacation."

Sam closed his eyes and breathed a heavy sigh. "Alrigh, thank ye, Abler."

Before Simon could comment, Sam ended the call and rubbed his temples. Composed, his brogue got stronger as he growled out, "The professor lied t' me. He's no' the girls Godfather, he was Claire's fence."

Rivera, true to his nature, was the first to argue. "Hold on, just because he lied about how he knew the girls doesn't mean he's—"

Glaring, Sam interrupted and continued. "He tol' us himself when we firs' met: Only someone who *knew* abou' the history of this painter would know wha' t' look for. An' when we first spoke t' him, he knew exactly wha' Annabelle's ring was an' i's worth. The George Jamesone job has been goin' on fer decades, an' ye', only five of the dozens of pieces have been reported stolen in the las' thirty years. Claire Winter was a brilliant art forger; she recreated tha' Botticelli when she was 19. Why couldnea she recreate George Jamesones a' 18? Dr. Stewart commissioned Claire t' paint the George Jamesone pieces. An' when she accidentally died durin' her recreation of one, he decided t' care fer her younger sistar."

"But why would he take care of a kid of somebody he hardly knew?" Julie asked.

Sam sighed, "The report says the fire started because of electrical failure, then i' caught onto some paint which se' the house ablaze. Charred bits of paint brushes were found next t' Claire's body, she had them in the bathroom. Probably t' clean them. My guess, she was usin' the hair dryer t' help dry the piece she was forgin' then accidentally go' electrocuted. Dr. Stewart, bein' the man tha' he is, felt guilty abou' an innocent child bein' left behind because of the accident an' decided t' care fer her, rather than le' her ge' lost in the system."

Rivera sighed. "Fine, you're obviously going to stick with this theory, so I'll bite. So how do you really think Charlotte concocted her version of what happened?"

"Dr. Stewart was lookin' inta' other forgin' artists bu' couldnea find one tha' matched Claire's caliber. Charlotte must've accidentally happened upon one of his dealin's with a paintin' tha' looked exactly like the one her sistar was forgin'. After tha', she se' herself along the path of followin' her sistars footsteps as bes' she could, hopin' t' make sense of everythin'."

Rivera and Julie's stunned faces were almost amusing, but Sam couldn't be bothered to chuckle.

After a moment, Julie said, "...But, if Dr. Stewart's the fence, then he might know the identity of the buyer."

Sam nodded. "Aye, he must."

"...Or he *is* the buyer," Rivera countered.

Sam sighed. "...Aye, he might be."

Chapter Eighteen

Back at the University of Chicago, Sam marched through the enormous library with his team right behind him. The professor's assistant, the insufferable Noah Porter, practically jumped out of his seat when Sam burst through the glass doors towards the lecture hall.

"Agents, the Professor is busy with a student. I don't suppose you'll come back in twenty minutes?"

Not even bothering to acknowledge the young man, Sam never broke his stride as he made towards the office in the back.

"How dare you! Listen, you ignorant G-men, you can't just come in and interrupt him any time that you want! This is Chicago University, and Dr. Stewart is one of the most—"

Rivera interrupted him. "Spare us, brown nose. He's got some explaining to do."

While Rivera stayed with the prickly young man, Sam continued down the hallway with Julie and Simon right behind him. Before long, he could hear the familiar sound of Dr. Stewart's soothing voice speaking. Not even bothering to knock, he barged into the tiny room. Dr. Stewart was sitting comfortably behind his desk across from a young man holding a notebook. When he turned and looked up to the doorway, Sam caught the noticeable flinch when their eyes met. And sure enough, the professor's friendly demeanor suddenly turned solemn.

"...I'm afraid we're going to have to cut this meeting short, Liam. I will have Noah email you the rest of the notes. Thank you for stopping by."

The poor young man appeared confused, but he stood up with his books in hand and left without a word. When it was just the four of them, Sam walked towards the desk and took the now vacant seat. Meanwhile, the professor had not moved from his spot as he and Sam continued to stare each other down.

"Ye dinnea know Charlotte an' Claire's parents a'tall, did ye? The only reason ye were in their life in the first place is because of Claire an' her talent fer forgery. Ye hired her t' re-create the art tha' was targeted, an' when she died, ye took it upon yerself t' raise her sistar. I'm right, aren't I?"

Dr. Stewart finally showed some emotion in the form of a sad smile; everything was out in the open. He nodded, "Yes, you're right."

Julie suddenly appeared in Sam's peripheral vision; looking directly at the professor, she asked, "Tell us the truth: Are you the one who's been collecting all the George Jamesone artifacts? Are you the buyer that Charlotte was working for?"

He surprised them with a gentle shake of his head, "I'm afraid not, my dear. I'm only the middleman."

"But you do know who the buyer is?" Simon asked.

The professor didn't answer, but Sam didn't miss the flash of fear behind his eyes at the question.

"I don't understand," Julie continued. "You're such a nice man. A good, decent man. You're the most brilliant and respected academic in your field. You *had* to know about William Finn's involvement with these jobs and what he would do to people when he was done. How could you possibly go along with that? How does a man like you end up in the mix of thieves and gangsters?"

"You answered your own question: respect and knowledge. As I'm sure you're aware, we no longer live in a world of black and white, agents. We, unfortunately, live deep within the many hues of grey. Every decision we make is either on the lighter or the darker side, but grey none the less. To get to the position that I am in required making many decisions, and acquaintances, on the darker side. Oftentimes, not of my own choice."

"You're a college professor," Simon countered. "Not Indiana Jones."

Dr. Stewart chuckled, but continued his sad soliloquy. "I don't expect you to understand, but I love history. Despite its blood-soaked reputation, it is a love affair that I have never been able to part with, and one that I have always desired to know more and more about. I have seen and discovered so many things that were thought to be lost with time. To bring a piece of the past back from the dead, to understanding the times and the cultures... I have gone from

215

observing history to living it. Digging up the past means wading through the blood of others, both old and new. But you're wrong in thinking I have not lost many a night's sleep over some of the things I've been a party to."

Sam leaned forward. "I jus' have one question tha' I want answered: where is Charlotte?"

Dr. Stewart looked at him blankly, but Sam refused to back down from his theory.

"Ye know the game is up, bu' ye won't tell us who ye're workin' for. I can only think of one reason why: Charlotte's no' dead. Ye were the only one in the room with her, an' ye love her like a daughtar. Ye tol' me so yerself. Ye'd do anythin' t' prevent harm comin' t' her. All tha' aside, I know she's a clever woman, an' this wouldnea be the first, or even the second time, she's tricked me. She's no' dead, is she?"

Sam kept his hard gaze on the professor, daring him to lie to him once more, until finally the gentle man chuckled. "She was right about you, Agent McKay. You're a little slow on the uptake, but you are in fact brilliant. No, she's not dead."

"You're shitting me!" Simon balked.

"Where is she?" Julie asked.

"I honestly have no idea. But even if I did, I wouldn't tell you. It's the only way I can be sure that she'll stay safe."

Hearing the professor confirm what he had already suspected gave Sam a great deal of relief, but that didn't make the lack of cooperation any less troubling. "Ye realize tha' if ye donnea help us, ye will be charged with theft, an' conspiracy t' murdar? Ye jus' confessed t' knowin' abou' all the illegal activities, includin' wha' happened t' Annabelle Matheson. Ye'll go t' prison fer a long time. How can ye help Charlotte if ye're behind bars?"

"The alternative wouldn't help her. You told me yourself, Agent McKay, that you would do anything to protect your child. Charlotte may not be mine, but I will protect her until the day I die. Perhaps that day is coming sooner than I thought." Dr. Stewart calmly rose from his desk, turned around, and folded his hands behind his back.

Sam watched Julie produce a pair of handcuffs and proceed to take the older gentleman into custody without a second thought. He inwardly sighed; he liked Spencer, and the thought of arresting him wasn't something he wanted to do. But it was clear that the man had already made up his mind, as Julie led him from the office and out into the hallway. Rivera was still arguing with the professor's insufferable assistant, but the young man finally stopped talking when he saw his teacher being escorted as a criminal. With Julie leading the troupe, Sam walked behind and kept his eyes trained on Dr. Stewart; while he may not have committed any of the actual crimes, there was no doubt that there was blood on his scholarly hands. His bleak outlook and justifications left a very bad taste in Sam's mouth. And yet, despite his poor choices, Sam couldn't help the respect he felt for him. But the feeling was quickly lost with the hard fact that without the professor's help, there was no way they would discover the mysterious buyer's identity. Sam was raging with unsatisfied curiosity, but that was nothing compared to the rage he felt knowing that Copper wouldn't let him indulge in his curiosity any longer. They had to, finally, drop the case and go home.

After a grueling eight-hour drive (and a quick stop at Gigi's at Sam's behest), the team was back in Cleveland. The first thing each of them declared that they wanted was a good night's sleep in their own beds far away from each other. Sam couldn't have agreed more, but the first thing he wanted to do was see Oliver and deliver the deep-dish he had promised more than a week before. His large frame cramped and ached from being cooped up in a car for so long, but when he arrived at Meredith's house, he plastered a cheerful smile on his face as he walked up and rang the doorbell.

Meredith answered. The sweat on her face, tank top and leggings, and jet-black hair pulled into a messy bun informed him that he had interrupted her evening workout, but he presented the pizza anyway and asked, "Is he asleep?"

"At 9:30 p.m.? You're kidding, right?" Meredith chuckled. Moving to the side, she motioned for him to come in and called up the stairs. "Oliver! Dad's back! And he brought your favorite all the way from Chicago!"

Sam had to strain to hear, but he could make out the faint sounds of the TV in the background coming from Oliver's room. At first, he wondered if the boy hadn't heard them, and he'd have to walk up to hand deliver the food.

"Oliver!" Meredith called again, "Come down here, please!"

Eventually, the TV shut off, and the sound of feet falling came from overhead until the teenager appeared at the top of the stairs; his hair was a mess and, while he may not have been sleeping, he was preparing for bed by the state of his pajama pants and wrinkled t-shirt.

Sam smiled when he saw him. "Sausage an' bacon, as promised. True Chicago deep-dish, courtesy of a new friend I made a' a place called Gigi's."

"Cool," Oliver huffed as he descended the stairs.

"Perhaps, if I's alrigh' with yer mum, I'll take ye t' Chicago on a weekend. There's an' interestin' art gallery I'd like t' show ye, an' we'll ge' the pizza fresh."

"Yeah, sure."

The box was practically yanked from Sam's hands, but Oliver didn't spare the angry look he gave him before turning around to go back up the stairs and return to whatever program he was watching. Sam had half a mind to bend the boy over his knee and give him a good wallop for his ridiculous, angsty attitude. But before he could say anything, Meredith had stepped up.

"Hey, get back here! You know better than to be rude, especially to your father."

Oliver was hidden by the shadows, but Sam could practically feel the boy's eyes rolling as he scoffed. "Whatever. He left me early, so I'm leaving him early."

"Alright, you know what? That's it!"

Both Sam and Oliver watched with interest (and a slight twinge of fear) as Meredith marched to the kitchen and returned only moments later with a sharp set of scissors in her hand. Brushing past Sam, she ascended the staircase, past the bewildered boy, and around the corner towards his room. Sam watched, and listened, as the situation unfolded.

"What are you—Mom? Mom! Hey, that's mine! Mom, don't—what the hell did you do that for?! How am I supposed to watch *Stranger Things* now?!"

"Read a book. I've let you be a moody little snot for long enough. Your dad is downstairs trying to make up for the time he's had to be away."

"He's *always* away, mom!"

"Yeah, I know that. But you know what? That's because he has to be. I don't like the crazy schedule any more than you do, Oliver. I never have. But that doesn't change the fact that your dad is a great man. He helps people; he saves people. You may not like how often he has to be gone, but you should be proud of him. Give me that pizza, and you stay up here and think about that until we come talk to you."

"Wha—a time out?! Seriously?! I'm not a kid!"

"You're *my* kid, and you will listen to me! Or else that TV cord is only the start of the many unfair things I can do."

A door slammed shut, and Meredith suddenly appeared at the top of the stairs again holding the take-out box. Running down quickly, she turned the corner and headed for the kitchen. "Come on, we're going to eat this just to spite him."

Sam watched her walk away and felt both impressed and a little bewildered; from the beginning of their relationship, he had always been the one to discipline or otherwise teach Oliver. Not to say that she let the boy get away with whatever he did wrong, but she avoided fighting and scolding him whenever possible. This was the first time she had ever stood her ground, and it was in Sam's defense. Admittedly, he wished she was a little less disapproving in her delivery, but he quickly pushed his criticism to the side. With a sense of amazement (and gratitude), he followed her to the kitchen.

***

For the next three weeks, Sam did as he promised and rested and recuperated. Meredith had offered him the spare bedroom so he would not be alone during that time, but he insisted that he would be fine in his apartment. The only way he could convince her was if she could call him daily to check on him, to which he reluctantly agreed. Her paranoia ceased when he was finally allowed to remove his arm from the sling; a large, angry red scar scaled his forearm, but he was otherwise completely back to normal.

While he was technically not allowed to work during medical leave, that couldn't stop his insatiable desire to figure out the identity of the mysterious buyer. Nearly every moment during those three weeks, he went over everything that he knew: from every interaction they'd had with the professor to anything they'd picked up during the investigation, trying to decipher any and all hints that might have been dropped about the mysterious buyer. But nothing stood out. When Simon told him that the anonymous package's DNA didn't match Dr. Stewart, that only further fueled Sam's anger from being used to accomplish the buyer's goals, whatever they were. If there was anything Sam hated more than being left curious, it was being used.

Finally, enough time had passed for Sam to complete his physical and psych evals, which he passed, and could return to work. Despite the other cases that were sitting on his desk, it wasn't enough of a distraction for Sam; Dr. Stewart's trial was only a month away, which meant that the team and he would have to travel back to Chicago to deliver their testimonies. He didn't doubt that Charlotte would most likely be somewhere in the crowd in disguise, and he intended to look for her.

His thoughts were interrupted when Julie appeared carrying a stack of papers. "It's good to have you back, boss. We've missed you. And we have a new case. Once you deliver your evals to Copper, we can scratch that off the to-do list and get to work. Do you want me to get the boys in the conference room?"

His evals in hand, Sam stood up and mumbled, "Aye, thanks."

Despite his dismissal, Julie hadn't moved. Realizing that she wouldn't, Sam looked up. She eyed him knowingly, and her hands were on her hips. "You're doing it again. That brooding/beating yourself up thing you do whenever things don't turn out the way that you want. You're still thinking about the buyer, aren't you?"

"Spare me the lecture, Julie."

"Maybe one day, when you actually listen to it, I will. Look, we solved Annabelle's murder, found a main source of the George Jamesone art theft, The Redcap is going to prison for the rest of his life, and Charlotte's not dead. All of the loose ends are tied up, aren't they?"

Leaning back in his chair, Sam growled, "Aye, except one."

"Boss, if you don't let this go, you're going to make yourself sick. Or have an aneurism."

"An' while we jus' move on, the buyer still roams free an' goes unpunished fer his crimes."

"Yeah, I agree it sucks. But the only person who *might* know is Dr. Stewart. And without his cooperation, we have nothing. You remember what he said: He's determined to take the fall for this, so nothing happens to Charlotte."

"Anno', bu' tha' donnea mean i's finished!"

Julie didn't flinch from Sam's outburst; she was too tough for that, but the way she looked at him disapprovingly and turned on her heel to walk away made Sam regret his actions. Taking a deep breath to calm himself, he called to her, "I'm sorry. Ye're right."

She continued walking without looking back, and Sam felt horrible. Regardless of their professional relationship, Sam truly saw Julie as the daughter he never had. Hurting her hurt him. Alone again, his frustration got the better of him, and he slammed his fist on his desk and hissed "dammit!" to himself. When he finally felt composed, he picked the file up again and headed towards Copper's office.

As he got closer to her office, Sam thought he could hear laughing. *Unusual fer Copper.* But what made it even more peculiar was the large man standing outside of her door; he was obviously private security, which made Sam believe that the boss was with someone very important, or very rich. He furrowed his eyebrows and tentatively knocked on her door.

"Come in," she answered in an airy, unfamiliar tone.

Sam walked in to see Director Copper and an old, white-haired man he didn't recognize sitting across from each other. By the way they were smiling at one another, and each of them holding a glass of the Director's cognac, he could tell that they were close.

"Excuse me fer interruptin', ma'am, bu' I came t' give ye my evals; everyone says I'm capable t' work again."

"Thank you," she answered politely. Taking the file from his hands, she nodded towards the stranger. "Edward, this is Agent McKay, one of my best men. McKay, Edward White."

"A pleasure, Mr. White."

The gentleman had already stood from his seat and offered Sam his hand. "So, you're the famous Sam McKay that solved Annabelle's murder? I'd like to personally thank you, agent."

Sam shook it and answered, "Aye, ye're welcome."

"I'm sure they have already thanked you as well, but let me also give you gratitude on behalf of Annabelle's children. They deserve peace and closure; thank you for working so diligently to give it to them."

Sam shifted awkwardly, "Well, I'm afraid I havenea given them *complete* closure. The ring is still missin'."

221

"Yes, that's a real shame. But, in time, I'm sure they'll come to understand that you did your best."

Sam bristled at the patronizing comment but tried to be polite on his boss's behalf. "How well di' ye know Mrs. Matheson?"

"Annabelle and I met many years ago at a charity organization, and we bonded over our love of heritage. Belinda told me that her murder was staged in order to frame the infamous Redcap? You're a very clever man indeed to have figured that out, Agent."

"Thank ye, sir. I donnea want' t' interrupt yer reunion any longer, an' I have t' ge' back t' my team—"

"Oh, of course. Forgive me, Belinda," Mr. White turned his attention back to the director and leaned down to kiss her cheek. "I won't take up anymore of your precious time."

"Thank you for the book, Edward. Have a safe flight."

"Thank you again, Agent McKay." Mr. White walked past Sam and nodded towards the bodyguard, "We're ready, Porter."

The large man nodded and followed without a word.

Turning his attention back to Copper, Sam took Mr. White's seat across from her. "So, he's the friend who cashed in the favor, eh?"

"Not that you need to concern yourself about it, but yes."

"Wouldn't a phone call have sufficed t' say thank ye?"

"He promised me a first edition of his newest book and wanted to personally deliver it. I'm glad you showed up when you did; he was anxious to meet you."

"I cannea say the same," Sam answered her quietly, ignoring her pointed stare. "Wha's the book abou'?"

"It's his autobiography with some genealogical history. You might like this: his ancestors came from Scotland. According to Edward, it was his great-great-great grandfather Bram Whitehorn who immigrated here with his wife, their two children, and his mother to make their fortunes."

Sam rolled his eyes, "Ye American's love t' boast abou' yer heritage, don't ye?"

Copper answered by walking around to the other side of her desk and turning her attention to his evaluations. With a pen in her hand, she read over every line. "Yes, it appears you are more than fit. Was there something else?"

"...I want t' talk t' Dr. Stewart again."

"To what end? I thought it was very clear that he is unwilling to cooperate with us. And besides, he has his own crimes to answer for."

"If I can jus' find the righ' button t' push, I believe he'll tell me who the buyer is."

"You mean you *want* to believe he'll tell you who the buyer is. Request denied; you'll only be wasting your time, and our resources, for your obsession. And there are plenty of other cases on your desk that need your attention."

"An' I' doesnea bother ye tha' somebody out there used us fer their own ends?"

"Here's a free lesson in law and politics, McKay: There is always somebody pulling the strings, and sometimes we must live with that. If I were you, I'd make peace with that fact before your immovable morality jeopardizes your career."

"Is tha' a threat?" Sam growled.

Director Copper stopped making notes, set down the pen, and met Sam's eyes in a staring match. "Let me be absolutely clear about one thing: We are not enemies. Your job is to follow my orders, and my job is to make sure you remain safe and healthy in this dangerous line of work. If you are so certain otherwise, you are free to leave the FBI. Understand?"

Her unflappable attitude only fueled Sam's growing anger, but he curtly nodded.

"Very good. Your next case is waiting." Copper turned her attention back to the file.

Dismissed, Sam left her office feeling even more annoyed. There were days he almost wished his curiosity could leave him be and he could accept partial outcomes, but today was not one of them.

***

For the next two weeks everything went back to normal: Sam and his team worked and advised on cases sent to them by local police departments, and as soon as he clocked out, he would go to Meredith's for dinner (per her invitation, in an effort to get Oliver to stop being so angsty). As hard as he tried to follow Director Copper's advice about the buyer, he couldn't shake the annoyance he felt by the whole situation. Meredith seemed to sense his frustration when she made an unusual suggestion: the three of them go out fishing on the boat one weekend. Sam was puzzled to say the very least: Meredith hated doing anything outdoorsy in nature. She insisted she would learn to like it and admitted it was mostly for his and Oliver's benefit. Amused (and curious as to how she would react to putting a worm on a hook), Sam agreed.

The next Saturday at 5:00 a.m., the three of them were out on the small fishing boat in the middle of Lake Erie. Oliver's and Sam's fishing lines were already in the water, but Meredith struggled just baiting her hook. While Oliver remained quiet and non-conversational, Sam was particularly amused at how hard Meredith tried to hide her disgust during the activity.

"Ew...ew...ugh, I can't do it!" Meredith shrieked, tossing the squirmy worm in her hands over the side of the boat.

Sam laughed harder than he had in a long time, "I's jus' a worm, lass, i's no' gonna' hurt ye!"

"It's gross, slimy, and wriggling everywhere! How the hell do you find this fun?!"

Chuckling, he took the rod from her hands, "Alrigh', I'll bait the hook for ye. Bu' ye'll have t' reel in whatever ye catch."

"Thank you," Meredith sighed.

"You do know how weird the two of you are, right?" Oliver asked.

Although surprised that the boy had strung more than three words together for the first time in weeks, Sam remained calm and answered, "We're parents, ye'll always think we're weird until the day ye become one."

"Which won't be for a very long time, by the way," Meredith added.

"Exactly as yer mother says."

Oliver turned around and looked at the two of them straight in the eye. "I'm not kidding. The two of you seem to get along just fine, but you want to stay divorced. Mom—you refuse to go out with anybody, but you're always inviting dad over for dinner. And you're not even my real father, so why do you do it? Why do you stick around? You don't have any responsibility to Mom or to me."

Sam felt relieved that Oliver was finally speaking again, even if it was about such a touchy subject as their family. He turned to Meredith for guidance, but she appeared just as lost for words as he was. Taking a deep breath, Sam asked, "Are ye sayin' ye donnea want me t' come around anymore?"

Oliver appeared shocked by the question, and Sam held his breath. He could feel his heart in his throat, petrified at what the boy's answer might be. Still, he remained silent, so Sam pressed further. "I may no' be the man tha' fathered ye, bu' ye're my son no matter wha'. I've tol' ye tha' before, an' tha' hasnea changed. When ye say I donnea have a responsibility t' ye or yer mum, ye're wrong abou' tha'. Ye're no' my responsibility, ye're my privilege."

Meredith jumped in, "Sweetheart, I know all of this is confusing. But don't take it out on your da—on Sam. I should have told you the truth a long time ago. It's just that I was afraid to. But…if you want to know about your real father, I'll tell you."

Meredith was shaking; Sam wrapped his arm around her and pulled her close, which she accepted without hesitation. Oliver appeared just as bewildered as ever by their tender embrace, but Sam held his breath as he waited for the boy's reaction.

Finally, he answered, "…No, I know that you're my dad. It's just that…I don't understand why you can't get back together. I mean…you get along just fine."

"Aye, we do. Bu' right now, bein' together is no' really an option either of us are ready t' try yet."

"But maybe that will change in the future," Meredith added. Looking up at Sam, she asked quietly. "Maybe?"

The look of hope in her eyes never failed to melt Sam. He didn't want to give Oliver false hope, but he knew he needed something to cling to in their twisted familial tree. Nodding, he answered, "Aye, maybe i' will. We jus' want'a be good parents t' ye, son. An' we're doin' the bes' tha' we can with everythin' tha's happened."

Oliver looked back to his fishing pole and nodded, "I know that…I'm sorry for being such a jerk lately. I know your job is important. And I am proud of you for going out and catching the bad guys."

Sam breathed a sigh of relief; the tension in the air finally dissolved, and the three of them were able to sit in comfortable silence. Then, suddenly, Meredith's pole started jerking.

"Oh my God!" She shrieked, "What do I do?!"

"Start reeling it in, Mom!" Oliver laughed. "Dad, get the net!"

Doing as he instructed, Sam stood at the ready, as Oliver helped Meredith catch her first fish. For the first time in weeks, he felt content and happy.

A few hours later, with the boat secured in the shed in Meredith's backyard and Oliver over at a neighbor's house playing video games with a friend, Sam was standing over the kitchen sink cleaning the fish they'd caught while Meredith sat at the kitchen table with a cup of tea. It was obvious she was doing her best not to throw up by how green around the gills she looked; Sam found it amusing as well as cute and just continued to filet every fish until they were done.

"Just so you know, I am never, *ever,* going to do that with you two again," she croaked.

"Ach, t'was only yer first time. Ye've go' t' give it another go until ye can a' least catch a ten pounder."

"I'll stick with my little two-pound sardine I caught today, thank you."

Sam chuckled and loaded the filets into the freezer before he set about cleaning up the mess. Once he was done, he joined Meredith at the table and took her hand; she had put on a good show for their son during the entire discussion on the lake, but he knew the truth: She was still shaken. "Are ye alrigh'?"

"I don't know…I guess I should have known this day would come, since he figured out that you're not his dad a year ago. It just doesn't make the thought of telling him the truth any less nauseating."

"He's a good kid, Meredith. An' strong. I think he'll understand why ye've never tol' him."

"But what will he think, Sam? How will he react when he learns that I was raped? He's struggling as it is trying to figure out our twisted family situation. If he finds out that he's the product of a rapist…" tears started to fall from her eyes, and she began to shake.

Sam wasted no time in getting out of his chair and pulling Meredith into his arms; she sobbed into his chest, but he didn't let go. "Shhh… i's alrigh', darlin'. I's alrigh'."

Finally, she pulled back and wiped her face with the back of her sleeve. "It's funny, you'd think after sixteen years and all the therapy I've been to, I'd have finally come to grips with this. You deal with victims all the time, so tell me: Will I ever stop crying about what happened?"

He sighed, "My opinion, no' until ye finally admit everythin' t' everyone involved. An' tha' includes Oliver. But tha's yer decision t' make, no' mine."

She nodded sullenly. "I know you're right…you're always right."

"I am?" He teased.

She giggled and kissed his cheek, "Don't let it get to your head."

They were interrupted by a ping on her cell phone; Meredith removed herself from Sam's arms.

"Huh, here's something you might find interesting: Somebody killed your gangster while he was in prison."

Sam's eyes bulged. "Wha'?"

"Look, it's right here: "William 'The Redcap' Finn found dead in prison cell.""

Sam practically yanked the phone out of her hands and raced to pull up the article. A video clip with two anchors showed up and he clicked play.

"Only days after the trial of William 'The Redcap' Finn, and the notorious gangster has been found dead in his prison cell. The cause of death has yet to be confirmed, however it is rumored that the 78-year-old was murdered. The Redcap was found guilty of murder, rape, arson, extortion, and racketeering and sentenced to life imprisonment in Statesville Prison."

The short video ended and Sam felt strangely relieved; with the Redcap dead, he could sleep better at night. But up until now, he didn't know where he'd been sent and to find out it was Statesville made his hair stand up: Statesville was where Josh was. He had no doubt of the horrific things his brother was capable of doing, and murdering his former boss was certainly not beyond the imagination. He couldn't help but wonder if McNally had something to do with it, too.

Meredith interrupted his thoughts. "This is a good thing, right? I mean, you said the guy was a walking nightmare."

"Aye…I suppose it is." Just as he was about to close the feed down, another video in the news clip caught his eye. The title read: Former Redcap Property bought by Chicago Historical Society. Curious, he clicked on the article and read it.

"Chicago's Historical Society has been trying their hardest to keep architecture and landmarks preserved for many years, and

it is only now possible due to the conviction of the infamous William 'The Redcap' Finn. The will of Bruce Jaimes has been discovered and authenticated, stating that any and all property and assets were to be left to his grandson, the late Malcolm Finn, whose body was discovered only weeks before. With the death of the Jaimes heir, the entire fortune was to be liquidated and donated to the C.A.R.E.S. Foundation, which has been revealed to be an illegal arms dealing cover, and therefore has been dissolved. With no other claims to the properties, Chicago Historical Society was able to purchase them with the generous donations made by its citizens and the help from its President: Edward B. White, the real estate mogul of Illinois."

Sam did a double take as he re-read the name of the Historical Society's president: Edward B. White. Quickly pulling up the staff members, his suspicions were confirmed when he saw the photograph of the same elderly gentleman he'd met in Copper's office only weeks before.

"Christ! Tha's it!"

His outburst made Meredith jump, but he ignored her and yanked out his own phone. He quickly dialed Rivera's number and practically yelled when he answered, "Ge' everyone togethar, a copy of Edward White's book, an' everythin' abou' the Matheson case. I know who the buyer is!"

Chapter Nineteen

Within moments of arriving to the office, Sam was in a frenzy of connecting the final pieces together. Suddenly, everything was making sense, and he was determined to have every duck in a row before he presented his findings to Copper. He knew she wouldn't like what he knew to be true, but he would make sure it was indisputable.

"McKay, even if Edward wasn't a friend of mine, I would still find this theory hard to believe."

"Everythin' fit's, Copper. William Finn was fightin' t' keep everythin' Jaimes left t' Malcolm, even goin' so far as t' bury the will so nobody could question Finn's control. Thanks t' Simon, we checked the Historical Society's records: White's been workin' w' the Historical Society society since 1986; he was only made president five years ago. They've been tryin' t' purchase the Jaimes estate fer thirty years, bu' Finn wouldnea budge. So, White bides his time an' collects any an' all evidence he can against The Redcap, waitin' fer the moment when he could push somebody t' go in an' arrest him."

"But that moment never came; The Redcap was quick to remove a problem," Julie continued. "So White hired Finn's former protégé, Aiden Marcus, to kill Annabelle Matheson and make it look exactly like The Redcap did it."

"So, we investigate, discover the Redcap's connection, an' suddenly ge' an anonymous package tha' convicts Finn of everythin'. He even provided the location of Audrey an' Malcolm's bodies, so there was no possible way we couldnea convict him."

"Why didn't he send the package to the police?"

"Because he knew The Redcap had either bought or threatened everyone tha' could do somethin' abou' it; all of tha' evidence would have been burned as soon as i' was found."

Ever unflappable, Copper kept her demeanor cool as she probed, "Why would he kill Annabelle Matheson? She was close friends with White."

"They *were,*" Rivera interjected, "until two years ago when Annabelle stopped donating to the Historical Society and instead started donating to the C.A.R.E.S. foundation—Finn's foundation. Maybe she grew tired of historical preservation and decided she wanted to help people instead, we don't know. But either way, she was a pretty large benefactor, other than White. That'd certainly make *me* mad if I lost that much money. Plus, there's the matter of Annabelle's ring: It's worth a goddamn fortune! With that in his possession, there'd be more than enough funding to make up for Annabelle's diminished donations."

"Then I assume that you've found evidence connecting White to Marcus?"

Sam sighed, "No, we have no'. White's too good t' leave evidence behind. Hell, t'was damn lucky I even saw the news abou' the real estate deal. One blink, an' we'd have missed tha'."

"Then all of this is conjecture."

"I's enough t' ge' a warrant fer a DNA sample, Copper! I'll be' me life the saliva on the anonymous envelope is White's!"

"And, even if it is, what exactly would that prove, McKay? Only that he made a hobby of collecting newspaper clippings and stalking The Redcap. The case would be thrown out of court, and White would be a vigilante hero for assisting in bringing down one of the most dangerous criminals in Chicago. Besides, you have yet to give me any real reason to believe this theory."

Sam wanted to argue further, but he knew that she was unfortunately right about the lack of tangible proof. Her still being on White's side made it sting even more. Suddenly his phone pinged with a text message, and he looked at the screen. It was an unknown number that messaged him a heart emoji and the words 'probable cause' next to it, and he had no doubt it was Charlotte giving him another tip. Clicking on it, he couldn't help but chuckle to see a photograph of Annabelle Matheson's ring sitting in front of a frame that had a picture of White with his arms around two younger people. Giving his phone to Copper, he said triumphantly, "Here's yer proof."

Copper's face didn't budge when she saw the picture, but when she looked back up at Sam, he could see the disappointment in her eyes. She took a deep breath and said quietly, "Everyone, get ready to go back to Chicago. I'll have a warrant within the hour."

* * *

Despite the warrant clearly stating that Sam and the team were allowed to completely tear the Historical Society apart if they needed to, that didn't stop the staff members from protesting their every move. But that did not deter them, as they investigated every inch of the building. Their hopes were quickly fading as they couldn't appear to find anything at all relating to the Renaissance artist George Jamesone; every painting and sculpture had the correct paperwork for proof of ownership. Finally, they came to the basement where dozens of crates were lining the walls, and they wasted no time in tearing them open. When Rivera called them over to one, everyone was beaming to see the painting from the Chicago art gala they'd been tracking packed away and insulated with straw. This was all the proof that Copper needed to know that White really was the mysterious buyer, and she insisted on being present for the arrest.

Practically minutes later, Sam and Director Copper were walking up to the door of Edward White's large estate; the rest of the team, and an FBI escort courtesy of the Chicago office, were standing in front of their cars, waiting for their orders. Copper remained passive with absolutely no hint of emotion, but by the way she had remained silent for the entire trip and the Historical Society search, Sam could tell that she was hurt. Trying to be sympathetic, he asked, "Are ye sure ye want' do this? I can arrest him meself."

Copper answered by ringing the doorbell. Within moments, the same quiet security guard Sam saw outside of her office had answered the door. Copper flashed her badge and said sternly, "FBI, we are here to speak to Mr. White."

Like magic, the man himself appeared from around the corner. "Belinda? This is a surprise; I wasn't expecting you. Let them in, Porter."

While Copper had already marched past the large man, Sam took a moment to size him up before following her. Looking around himself, he nearly let out a low whistle; if he thought that Dr. Stewart's house could be compared to a museum, White's home was like stepping into the parlor of a nobleman: Richly ornate trimmings lined every doorframe, and all along the walls of the foyer were paintings and busts on display. Copper had mentioned that White was eccentric, but that was putting it mildly.

Curious as to how Copper would handle the situation, he quietly remained behind her and watched the situation unfold.

"I just got off the phone with Minnie from the Society, something about an FBI search? Do you know what's going on?"

Copper didn't blink. "Edward White, you're under arrest for murder, conspiracy to murder, and theft."

Her cold, quick answer surprised even Sam, but he remained quiet and watched the stunned gentleman.

"...What? Belinda, what's going on here?"

"If I were you, I would save your questions until we get to headquarters. We searched the Historical Society and found the stolen painting. I'm sure that we'll find more once we search the house."

"How could you possibly think I'm capable of murder?! We've known each other for thirty years—"

"Edward, we know that Annabelle stopped donating to the society years ago. We know that you set Aiden Marcus up to kill her, and this warrant allows me to tear your house apart until we find her ring and everything else you have stolen. Stop lying to me, it's over."

White was struck dumb. Copper wouldn't blink. Sam stayed quiet.

The tension in the air was stifling, then White finally sighed, "...Finn would have killed her sooner or later. He's had his murderous claws in this town for too long; no one would stand up to him. Even the other clans couldn't seem to break The Redcap. And anyone that did would end up dead. You've seen the list of victims; there's dozens. Innocent people, cops, FBI—that monster didn't discriminate. And not once was he ever convicted!"

Copper remained statuesque, but Sam desperately wanted to probe further. He didn't have to wait too long before White continued.

"And the art... well, look for yourself who I liberated it from! Ignorant yokels that had no idea what kind of treasure they had in their possession. To them, it was just a historical piece they'd gotten from a dime store, and they wanted to use it to attract attention to their 'modern art.' Modern art indeed, ha! A bunch of scribbles and paint splotches that a five-year-old could do in their sleep. They didn't deserve to have their hands on such exquisite pieces of history...pieces of *my* history."

Sam's eyes widened, and Lisa Matheson's tale of the jealous sister of her ancestor came rushing back. Unable to contain himself any longer, he stepped up next to Copper and said, "This was never abou' the loss of Annabelle's donations; t'was abou' the ring given t' George Jamesone by King Edward himself. Ye recognized i' the moment ye saw it. Annabelle's daughter tol' me how her ancestor...wha' was her name...Alison! Alison was so jealous abou' no' inheritin' the ring tha' she cut all ties t' the family...ye spoke of yer ancestry in yer book. Alison Whitehorn was the sistar of Lisa's ancestor, Mary Jamesone!"

White chuckled. "You really are the best, Agent McKay. No wonder Belinda puts her faith in you."

Ignoring the jab, Sam continued. "Annabelle wouldnea give up tha' ring so easily, t'was the only thing tha' truly connected her t' her husband, an' her daughtar was so in love with it. So ye had her killed t' point the way a' The Redcap, knowin' somebody in yer little network of thieves would make a move on tha' ring, an' then ye jus' bided yer time until ye could collect. Then, once the dust had settled from the readin' of Bruce Jaimes' will, ye moved in an' bought the house in The Redcap's possession. And ye used us t' accomplish it all. Ye're nothin' more than a common thief."

"A common thief that's kept the historical value of this town alive for decades. That house, that painting, the ring...all of it would have been destroyed if it wasn't for me. It was only a matter of time!"

The ever-level Copper finally spoke. "I couldn't care less about your twisted reasons for your obsessions, Edward."

"You know I wouldn't have if I had any other choice. Forget about the George Jamesones; think about the innocent victims of The Redcap—"

"You murdered two people."

"I did what I had to in order to stop The Redcap!" White didn't break his gaze from her as he walked forward. "Belinda, you of all people know that sometimes making the hard choice is the only way anything gets done for the greater good."

"I agree, which is why I'm here to do this myself."

Her cold, authoritative voice put a chill in Sam's spine; White stared at her with bewilderment. Finally, the old man sighed and offered his hands. Sam watched Copper handcuff Edward White and lead him to the FBI entourage without a single word. Following her lead, he turned and handcuffed the bodyguard, who hadn't even bothered to move during the entire confrontation. With the two of them securely in the custody of Chicago's house, Sam, Copper, and the team watched as the car drove away, and the remaining agents entered White's domain to continue their search. Sam looked at his team and cleared his throat.

Rivera caught the hint and said, "Come on, guys, let's get in there and make sure our Chicago buddies don't miss anything."

Julie turned to follow immediately and grabbed the clueless Simon by the sleeve before he could ask why. When the three of them were out of ear shot, Sam turned to Copper. "...Are ye alrigh'?"

She didn't answer.

"Listen...I know wha' i's like t' be betrayed by somebody ye trusted. I's alrigh' t' feel angry. I'm an authority on tha'." He chuckled at his own joke, but the attempt to lighten the mood did nothing for the situation: Copper remained enigmatic as no emotion was shown on her face. Sam, feeling much more awkward, cleared his throat again.

Before he could say anything further, the Director finally spoke. "Take care to search the house from top to bottom, McKay. I want that ring found."

She walked away, but Sam couldn't find it in himself to be annoyed at her getting the last word again. Not this time. Obeying her orders, he walked back inside of the estate and began to help with the search: Every painting and sculpture was removed for cataloging and authenticating ownership by a few agents, while everyone else began to practically tear the ornate house apart down to the studs. Sam felt a small twinge of regret to see something so beautiful be so quickly destroyed, but he shook the feeling off as he helped his team continue the search of the large house.

Taking it upon himself to investigate White's office, he took his time looking around and examining every inch of the room. It was eerily similar to William Finn's in design, with all of the woodwork and antique furniture, but it was the enormous bookshelf that spanned the entire wall that caught his eye when he saw a familiar photograph sitting on the middle shelf. He walked closer to examine it and discovered it to be the same photo in Charlotte's text: Edward White standing in the middle with his arms around two younger folks (which Sam could only assume were his children). Excitement surged through him; he was close to the ring. Wasting absolutely no time, he practically tore every book, decoration, and frame from the shelves as he searched for Annabelle's ring until the shelves were empty and the floor was disastrous.

"Dammit!" he cursed to himself. "Where is I'?! She wouldnea have taken it…"

He looked all around himself again, trying to think of where White would store something as precious as that ring, when he noticed the same photograph sitting on White's desk. When he picked it up, he heard a little tinkling sound. He practically tore the back of the frame off to discover an old fashioned, faded gold key hiding behind the photo. He couldn't help but feel silly for going after the wrong photograph and creating such destruction, but that feeling was quickly replaced with annoyance to know there was yet another piece of a puzzle he would have to solve.

Julie's voice suddenly rang through the air.

"Guys! Come look at these shoes I found!"

Pocketing the key, Sam left the ruined office and ran up the stairs. Rivera and Simon were already standing next to Julie when he arrived, and she handed the large, clunky work shoes over to him. Slowly turning them over in his hands, he couldn't see what was so important, until Julie pointed at the missing tread in the middle of the sole.

"Remember that black rubbery thingy forensics found next to the hotel bed with Aiden Marcus? How much you want to bet it fits perfectly in that little hole? And what's even better, there's the teeniest drop of blood on the leather."

"If it matches Marcus' blood then White's ass is grass," Simon said enthusiastically. "Once again, boss, you were right: Aiden Marcus didn't kill himself."

"He was just another loose end fer White," Sam nodded, "Bu' we're no' leavin' this house until we find tha' ring."

One of Chicago's agents stepped out from a bedroom and said, "Hey, we've got a wall safe here."

Sam handed the boots over to the Chicago boys with strict instructions to keep him updated on the evidence results before following the other agent into the room.

"It was hiding behind a painting, but it's not like any safe I've ever seen before. Usually, wall safes are new and state of the art with a code, this one requires a key. We can still break into it; it shouldn't be a problem."

The moment Sam saw the elaborate gold faceplate of the keyhole, he began to laugh. While everyone around him wondered what was so funny, he withdrew the newly found key from his pocket and inserted it into the keyhole with ease. With one twist, the safe was unlocked, and the door opened without any problem. There were papers and little trinkets inside, but right in the middle sat a white leather ring box that had Sam's attention. He opened it and smiled: Annabelle Matheson's ruby ring was perched perfectly in the middle. A rarely seen smile crossed his face as he turned to his team and said, "The beer's on me tonigh'."

***

Sometime later, after a long and arduous debate with Chicago house's evidence keeper, Sam was sitting across from Lisa Matheson, watching her stare at her mother's ring that was finally found. He couldn't tell her every detail, but he was allowed to tell her who was really responsible for her Annabelle's death. It was no surprise that the news came as a real shock to her.

"I just…Ed and mom were really close. He's done so much for our family; he even came to our college graduations."

"Anno', i's a lo' t' process."

She tried to scoff, but that couldn't hide the sob she was trying to stifle. "That's putting it mildly. It's not every day that you find out that your step-in father figure kills your mom over a ring…you want to know the ironic part? If he'd have just asked me if he could preserve it, I think I might have been able to convince Mom to say yes. Maybe the curse on this ring is real after all."

"I had a feelin' ye migh' think that, so I had my man do a little diggin'. Alison Whitehorn had two sons, one tha' she moved t' America with, bu' the other stayed in Scotland. His grandson later immigrated here: John McNichols."

236

Lisa's eyes opened wide with astonishment. "…That's Michael's granddad. Are you sure?"

"Aye, lass, positive. If ye ask me, tha' ring is back where i's always belonged: with Alison's blood relative, an' someone who will take bettar care of it."

Lisa gave him a sad smile and quietly slipped the ring back onto her finger. "Thank you, Agent McKay… What am I supposed to do now?"

"Ye move on."

"How am I supposed to move on from this? My mother was killed by a family friend, somebody we all trusted…I don't think moving on is possible."

Sam leaned forward and offered his hand in comfort, which she accepted. Looking at the ring, Sam answered, "Durin' this case, I met somebody tha' seemed t' know yer mum verra well. She said Annabelle dinnea like bein' treated like an ol' woman, bu' rather she loved livin' life every chance she go'."

"Yeah, that sounds a lot like mom. She never really got over my dad's death, but she refused to let us stay sad and upset about it, either. She would do everything she could to pack our lives with fun."

"Well, ye know wha' tha' tells me? She wouldnea want ye t' spend any more time mopin' about. Ye're allowed t' miss her, bu' ye cannea miss out on yer life jus' because she's gone." Sam reached into his pocket and pulled out a folded-up piece of paper that he had Simon print out for him earlier. "This isnea somethin' anyone can do alone, bu' there are plenty of good grief counselors tha'd be happy t' help ye. I'm sure ye already have a list from the funeral home, bu' I had my man print up a few more for ye t' look into."

Lisa took her hand back and wrapped her arms around herself. "…I just don't know if I can."

"Lass, if there's anythin' I believe in, i's tha' no matter how hard i' gets, ye have t' try."

Lisa peaked out from under her eyelashes at him; new tears started to stream down her face, but she gave a slight nod and gently accepted the paper from him. "Okay, I'll try."

Sam left Lisa Matheson-Nichols' house with peace; he was confident she would start reaching out for help in coping with her mother's death. Thankfully, his lie about her husband's ancestor couldn't be truly confirmed or denied, as there wasn't any record of what happened to Alison Whitehorn's other son, other than his death. But he felt better knowing that she wouldn't hold on to the ridiculous notion that her mother's ring was cursed any longer. Now that Annabelle's murder had been solved, and her children had closure, he could move on from this as well.

Chapter Twenty

Eight days later...

Sitting on a bench in Chicago's District Court building, Sam yanked on the knot of his tie again. This was the one thing he despised about appearing in court: being formally dressed all the way down to the uncomfortable tie that was practically choking him. His disposition wasn't any better with how cooped up he'd felt. In the last week alone, he'd spent more time inside of an SUV than he'd cared to, and all of the travel back and forth from Cleveland to Chicago was enough to drive any regular-sized man crazy, let alone a giant such as himself. He had managed to speak to Dr. Stewart three days before and inform him that Edward White had been caught, and he wanted him to testify against him in exchange for the reduced charges of Misprision of a Felony. He had to practically beg the professor, but eventually he wore the man down enough that he agreed to testify. Sam left feeling relieved; with the evidence they had collected and his testimony, there was no way White would be able to worm his way out of a conviction.

Sam had been at the courthouse for the last hour, waiting for his scheduled appearance as a material witness in the Edward White case. Handing over his gun and his phone, there was literally nothing to do except twiddle his thumbs. He thought he might go insane from just sitting, he couldn't wait for the whole ordeal to be over.

Finally, a bailiff approached him. "Agent McKay? We are ready for you now, sir."

Adjusting his tie for the final time, Sam followed the officer down the hall and into the court room. Other than the judge, an old and distinguished looking man, and the jury, there were a little more than a dozen people seated in the pews observing the case. Sam walked with confidence towards the witness box when he suddenly detected the faint smell of green apples....*Charlotte's perfume*...Doing his best to remain composed, he continued his walk until he was seated in the box.

A clerk approached with the enormous book of God in his hands. "Raise your right hand and place the other on the Bible, please."

Sam did as he was told.

"Do you swear to tell the truth, the whole truth, and nothing but the truth, so help you God?"

"Aye, I do," he grunted and took his seat. Before the prosecution could begin their questioning, Sam glanced at the observing audience for Charlotte or anyone that might resemble her. Lisa Matheson-Nichols, her husband, and a man that he assumed was her brother were there, but he didn't recognize anyone else. He was so focused on the faces of the audience, he nearly missed the first question.

"Would you state your name and position for the court, please?" the prosecutor (a young woman with dark hair pulled into a bun) asked.

"Agent Sampson McKay of the Cleveland, Ohio, FBI, Special Investigative Task Force."

"And what is it that you investigate, Agent McKay?"

"The Special Investigative Task Force looks inta' murderous crimes of all nature tha' have gone cold or otherwise beyond police force resources."

"How?"

"We work with local police t' re-evaluate the evidence collected an' continue the investigation."

"And you were investigating the murder of Annabelle Matheson?"

"Aye," Sam nodded, but quickly said, "Sorry, yes."

The prosecutor continued to ask him questions about every speck of evidence that had been found; with every painfully detailed answer he gave, Sam was growing more and more irritated. He knew this was all part of the process of making it absolutely clear to the jury that Edward White was guilty, but it didn't make it any less monotonous and annoying. Finally, they had gotten to the point of questioning regarding Aiden Marcus, and Sam felt relieved that his portion would soon be over.

"Could you please tell the court what was the end result of your investigation?"

"Annabelle Matheson's murder was staged t' appear as though it was committed by William 'The Redcap' Finn, in the form of her throat being slit with the huntin' knife he normally carries. However, my team an' I deduced tha' she was actually murdered by Aiden Marcus, a former associate of The Redcap's. Forensic testin' also proved tha' the knife Finn carried di' no' have Annabelle Matheson's blood on it. Bu' the knife found with Aiden Marcus did."

The prosecutor withdrew a photograph from the pile of papers sitting on her desk and gave it to Sam. "Is this Aiden Marcus?"

"Yes, ma'am."

"But in this photo, he's dead."

"Yes, ma'am. There was a note found next t' his body confirmin' he'd been the one t' murder Annabelle Matheson, an' i' appeared he'd committed suicide along with the murder weapon. However, there was a small piece of evidence close t' the body which later proved tha' he too was also murdered."

A bag with the small rubber button thing was handed to him. "Is this the evidence, Agent?"

"Yes."

"For the record, this is evidence exhibit 36A. And what is this rubber thing, exactly?"

"I's a piece of the bottom of a shoe tha' broke off, assumedly durin' a struggle with the deceased Marcus."

"Objection," the defense attorney called. "There is no evidence supporting the claim that Aiden Marcus had struggled with anyone before his death."

"Sustained, strike that last statement from the record," the judge grunted before turning to Sam. "Revise your statement, Agent McKay."

Sam sighed and inwardly rolled his eyes. "I's a piece of the bottom of a shoe."

The prosecutor (who also appeared perturbed at the ridiculous objection) continued her questioning. "Did you find the shoe that it belonged to?"

"Yes, we did."

"Where?"

"A' the home of Edward White."

"And it has been forensically proven that that tiny rubber button was in fact a piece of the shoes?"

"Aye, through chemical comparison testin' an' tread examination."

"So, to sum it up, the shoes found in Edward White's possession were present at the scene of Aiden Marcus's murder?"

"Aye-yes, correct."

"Thank you, Agent McKay," the prosecutor smiled. Turning to take her seat, she said to the defense, "Your witness."

Edward White's attorney, an older gentleman with slicked back silver hair, stood up and walked towards Sam slowly. In a condescending voice, he said, "You're a very thorough man, Agent McKay. My thanks to you; law enforcement needs more men like you. Before we continue addressing the shoe, I'd like to ask you a few more questions regarding your task force. You said that you work with the police to solve crimes, is that right?"

"Aye, sir."

"So, your team is usually invited by the police to help solve these crimes, true?"

"Aye, correct."

"And were you invited by the Chicago P.D. to investigate the murder of Annabelle Matheson?"

"Objection," the prosecutor called, "Relevance?"

"Relevance will be made clear soon, your honor."

"Overruled," the judge grunted.

"No, we were no' invited by the Chicago P.D."

"Then why did your task force come in and take over the case?"

"We were assigned by my superior, Director Belinda Anne Copper."

The defense attorney smiled. "Ah, Director Copper. The Director and my client have been friends for years, haven't they?"

"If ye say so."

"Isn't it true that you saw the Director and my client having a friendly drink together at her office?"

"Aye, I did."

"And the Director arrested my client, didn't she?"

It wasn't hard to see where the defense was going with his line of questioning, but Sam remained calm as he answered the lawyer with a solid, "Yes."

"Well, I'm not familiar with Scottish law proceedings, but here in the USA, we call the involvement of friends in a case a conflict of interest, which makes the evidence collected questionable."

"Objection! Badgering the witness!"

"Sustained," the judge grunted again. "Careful, counselor."

"My apologies, your honor. Agent McKay, let's get back to the shoes you found. Whose were they?"

"The shoes belong t' Edward White's personal body guard, Isaac Porter."

"Did you have a search warrant for these shoes?"

"Our warrant stated tha' my team an' I were permitted t' look in any an' all places, both business an' personal, belongin' to or otherwise related t' Edward White. The shoes were found in Edward White's home."

"You didn't answer my question, Agent. Was the warrant for the shoes?"

Sam eyed the lawyer coolly. "T'was fer any an' all evidence in relation t' the case. The shoes are evidence in the case."

"Did you know the rubber thing that was found belonged to a pair of shoes?"

Sam suddenly felt his blood freeze; he knew where the attorney was going and he suddenly felt his anger begin to boil. "…No."

The defense attorney gave him another condescending smile. "I see. Well, Agent McKay, as I've stated before, you're a very smart man. So, I'm curious, how in the world did you deduce that my client is this mysterious mastermind behind Annabelle's murder? What could have possibly prompted a search of his house for evidence that you didn't even know you needed?"

Sam took a deep breath to steady himself before he answered, "Edward White is a self-proclaimed historical an' art connoisseur. I's also been confirmed tha' he knew Annabelle Matheson through Chicago's Historical Society, an' she was a patron fer years. Two years ago, her donations stopped, an' she started donatin' t' the C.A.R.E.S. foundation. Annabelle also possessed an antique ring, which was also found—"

"Agent McKay, let me rephrase my question more directly to the point: What was the probable cause that allowed a search warrant into my client's places of business and residence?"

Sam gulped. "…T'was a picture of Annabelle's ring next t' a family photo on his desk."

"And where did you get this picture?"

"T'was sent anonymously."

"Ah. So, if we're being honest, if it wasn't for the ring, there was really no reason to search my client's house, was there?"

"…No."

"Then it's possible that the ring could have been planted at my client's house, isn't it?"

"…Yes, I's possible."

"Your honor, I'd like to submit into evidence exhibit 36B. It is a receipt from the Primrose Inn, the same hotel where Aiden Marcus' body was found."

The judge looked over the paper and nodded his agreement. "Go ahead, counselor."

"Agent McKay, would you please read the details of this receipt aloud for the court?"

Sighing, Sam snatched the paper away from the lawyer and did as instructed. "… Accordin' t' these records, Isaac Porter checked inta' the Primrose Inn from October first until October third fer two people."

"What room was he assigned?"

"516."

"The same room Aiden Marcus stayed in, right?"

"Aye."

"And what were the dates that Mr. Marcus was checked in for?"

"…October fifth t' October fifteenth."

"And according to the M.E.'s report, Aiden Marcus died on October the twelfth, correct."

"…Yes, correct."

"So, then it's entirely possible that the little piece of rubber shoe you found belonging to my client's security guard could have broken off during his own stay at the Primrose Inn, and he couldn't have been present when poor Mr. Marcus committed suicide?"

"Objection, leading the witness." The prosecutor called.

"No, I'll allow it," the judge grunted.

"…Yes, i's possible."

"I have to say, Agent McKay, you have come up with a brilliant fairytale to try and connect my client to any of this."

"Objection!"

"An anonymous picture, a small piece of rubber, and absolutely no connection between my client and the man who *actually* murdered poor Mrs. Matheson."

"Objection!"

"Your entire investigation smells awfully fishy to me, Agent McKay."

The prosecutor stood to her feet and practically shrieked, "Your honor!"

"That's enough, counselor!" The judge bellowed.

"No matter, your honor, I'm finished with Agent McKay." The defense attorney didn't lose his cocky grin as he walked back to his desk. The look on White's face was enough to make Sam want to flip a table, but he gritted his teeth and clenched his fists to help him hold his tongue.

"Agent McKay, you may step down."

Sam stood up, straightened his uncomfortable tie again, and walked into the pews behind the lawyers. As angry as he felt at the defense attorney's patronizing attack, he relaxed, knowing that it wouldn't matter anyway once Doctor Stewart was called to the stand.

"The people would like to call Dr. Spencer Stewart of The University of Chicago, your honor," the prosecutor said calmly.

The doors opened and the Professor was led into the courtroom. He was wearing an orange jumpsuit, and his hands were cuffed, but his calm demeanor assured Sam that he would do exactly as promised.

"Place your left hand on the Bible and raise your right. Do you swear to tell the truth, the whole truth, and nothing but the truth, so help you God?"

"Yes, I do," the professor answered calmly.

The faint smell of green apples wafted through the air again, and Sam began to carefully look all around him. He knew Charlotte was somewhere in the audience, she had to be. But everyone he could look at didn't even look remotely fake. Not that he expected it to be easy; she had proven her masterful disguise routine before. But that didn't stop him.

At one point Sam spotted a peculiar looking man sitting near the back of the courtroom. Dressed in a nice linen suit and tie, there wasn't anything unusual about him other than he seemed to be swaying on his feet a little. His hand began to reach into his jacket when, very suddenly, he dropped to the ground and began to convulse. The entire courtroom gasped. Sam leapt to his feet and jumped the pews to reach the man.

"Bailiff! Call an ambulance!" Sam bellowed. He pulled the stranger's jacket open to see his hand was on the holster of a gun. It suddenly dawned on Sam what he was there for. Glancing back to the defense, he could see the look of terror in White's eyes, and it was all too clear: The man was there to kill Dr. Stewart before he could testify. But what had stopped him? Sam quickly scanned the body when he noticed a tiny dart sticking out of his pants leg. Pulling it out, he tasted the end of the dart and quickly spat before it could affect him. He felt a little woozy, but only a little. *GHB...* Then suddenly, the man wasn't convulsing on the ground anymore. Sam checked his pulse, but it was already too late.

Jumping to his feet, Sam looked all around him again for Charlotte. Everyone was in a state of panic and the judge was calling for order, so he raced into the hallway, desperately searching for the smell of green apples. But there was nothing. He ran all the way out to the street looking for Charlotte, but he knew it was futile to hope that he would find her.

"You Sam?" a slurred voice asked directly behind him.

Turning around, Sam nearly bumped into an old man that looked about ready to fall over. The fact that he knew his name had him convinced Charlotte was involved. "Aye, I am."

"I was told you'd give me twenty bucks in exchange for a message."

Sam scoffed. Pulling out his wallet, he handed a bill over and waited. A wide, and somewhat toothless, grin spread across the man's drunken face before he slurred again, "Frank's Place on North Orleans at eight. That's all she said. Oh yeah, and to give you this."

A card was thrust into Sam's hands; the initials C.W. were printed on it. Before he could probe further, the messenger had already staggered away with his treasure in his hands. Sam almost wanted to laugh at the cloak and dagger approach Charlotte had once again led him into. Instead, he futilely looked around him for her, to no avail. Not knowing what else he could do, he walked back into the courthouse for the remainder of the trial.

***

At exactly 8:00 p.m. on the dot, Sam stopped his car in front of a large brick building that had a neon sign flashing overhead. A set of stairs were to his right, and the bar he where was expected was at the bottom of them. He had to duck his head to avoid getting hit by the railing. He didn't expect to find Charlotte when he walked in, but was surprised to see her sitting in a booth near the back of the rustic underground pub with a pint and an apple martini in front of her. Wearing a t-shirt and a confident smile, Sam couldn't ever remember seeing her so relaxed before. His curiosity was more than piqued, and he walked over to join her.

"Guiness, fresh off the tap," Charlotte said cheerfully as she slid his glass over to him.

Sam eyed the drink skeptically, determined not to let his guard down this time around her.

She chuckled at his suspicion and took the glass back to take a long drink from it. "See? I'm not here to roofie you unconscious."

Satisfied, Sam pulled the drink back and took a tiny sip before he asked, "Then why are ye here... Mary?"

Her smile suddenly changed from humorous to wistful; she answered, "You know, I can't believe it took you this long to remember. I thought I'd dropped more than enough hints for the great Sam McKay to figure out he'd met me before."

"Well, ye di' leave me in significant trouble aftar me first week on the job. Guess I jus' wanted t' try an' forget me blunder."

"Yeah, I guess I deserved that. Well, to answer your question, I'm here now to make sure you don't get in trouble again."

"Wha' d' ye mean?"

Taking a sip of her own drink, Charlotte answered, "You know why I'm a thief, right?"

"Aye, because of yer sistar. I' took me a little while t' piece yer thought process together, bu' I know tha' ye've been chasin' George Jamesone pieces an' artifacts hopin' t' find out how Claire died." Sam took another sip of his drink before he cleared his throat. "I know ye think she was murdered—"

"No, I don't. Not anymore," she interrupted. "I remember being in bed when Claire got home from work that night. She would always

247

come in to let me know that she was home and say goodnight before she would start painting. I'd usually just go back to sleep. But that night, for some reason, she had the hair dryer going, and I couldn't go back to sleep. I went out to ask her if she could stop. She had this painting in the bathroom with her, along with all of her brushes and paints and things. I remember it was a portrait of some sort; the guy in it looked noble but not quite kingly. Anyways, she had the hairdryer blowing on it and promised she'd only be a few more minutes. So, I went back to bed.

"A few minutes later, the noise had stopped. I remember the lights suddenly going out; I assumed she had just turned everything off and was going to bed. But just when I was about to fall back to sleep, I smelled smoke. There was this flickering light under my door. Obviously, I went to see what was going on, but my doorknob was so hot..." Charlotte, shakily, took another sip of her martini before she continued. "I don't know how I got it open, but I did. And that's when I saw all these flames coming from the bathroom. I yelled and screamed for Claire, but the fire kept getting bigger and bigger...so, I ran back into my room. I tried to get out through the window, but it was too small. So, I hid in the closet. It was all I could think to do. The next thing I knew, somebody was standing over me and then I woke up in the hospital. Spencer was talking to some doctors in the corner before he came and sat down next to me. He took my hand...told me everything was going to be alright."

Charlotte let go of a ragged breath. Sam remained quiet. She scoffed, "Ironic, isn't it? I've spent my whole life trying to stay away from fire, and it's because of a fire that I finally came to grips with what happened. Claire really died accidentally."

Sam cleared his throat. "If ye donnea mind me askin', wha' convinced ye tha' she didn't?"

"Once I started talking again, Spencer told me he worked extremely long hours, and he wanted to make sure I'd always be safe. So, he enrolled me in this boarding academy. Well, I came home early one weekend and saw him talking to somebody. There was a painting in between them, it was exactly the same one that Claire had been working on. Spencer and the stranger started arguing, then the stranger grabbed the painting and stormed off. I remember feeling shock from seeing the exact same painting... and by the way Spencer seemed so angry about it...I just knew that something was off. I ran away and missed school the next week, started stealing things…I was a mess for a long time. Then, one day, it finally occurred to me that Claire had to have died because of this painting. So, I told myself that I would do everything to figure out why. Eventually I found out about The Redcap, and I always suspected he might have something to do with her death, considering his love of burning things. When we found out from Chase that he'd commissioned a forgery of Annabelle's ring, I thought for certain that I had finally found my answer. You know the rest."

"Aye, bu' I donnea know one thing: How di' ye know White was the buyer? How di' ye find the ring?"

Charlotte's eyes lit up with that playful look she always got. She asked him, "How did *you* figure it out?"

Chuckling, Sam answered, "By accident. Once Finn was killed in prison, Bruce Jaimes' will came t' light an' nothin' belonged t' him anymore. White's the president of Chicago's Historical Society, an' they moved in t' buy the house an' other property. I jus' had t' dig a little deeper t' connect everythin', bu' truthfully we wouldnea have been able t' do anythin' were i' not fer tha' text ye sent me. White's too good t' leave behind evidence."

"Oh, good, I'm glad to know that my breaking and entering skills were helpful after all," she giggled. "When I was at dinner with Finn, his nimrod muscle man got a phone call and said, 'It's him again.' Finn cursed and said to tell White if he didn't back off, he'd…well, let's just say it wasn't going to be pretty. I just found it curious how anybody could ruffle Finn's feathers like that, so, after I disappeared, I started to snoop around. Edward White is sneaky, but he's not *that* sneaky. One night I saw him admiring Annabelle's ring; God, you should have seen him, he looked like a dragon crooning over his hoard. So, when he was out, I broke in and searched for the ring. And it wasn't easy finding that key, let me tell you. That's why I made sure that the picture was in the picture, I figured you could connect the dots after that."

Sam was impressed. "Bu' how di' ye ge' past his security? I go' a look a' White's systems; Simon tol' me they're tough t' beat."

"Now, now, I can't give you *all* of my secrets." Charlotte threw him a wink and took another sip of her martini. "Just accept it: I'm that good."

249

"Ye took a hell of a risk; if his security guard caught ye, he'd've probably killed ye like he did Marcus."

"I followed my gut; that's what you would've done." Her smile slowly disappeared as she turned to look at her hands. "…I know that you got Spencer's sentence reduced for his cooperation; thank you for convincing him."

Sam eyed her carefully. "The man a' the courthouse, tha' was you, wasn't it?"

She didn't hesitate to nod.

"I though' ye donnea hurt people? Wha' changed yer mind?"

"My mind hasn't changed; that was only a one-time thing. A lot of people have died because of White, and I suspected that he might try to hurt Spencer. I just couldn't let that happen."

"Ye do know tha' man died, don't ye?"

She continued to stare at her hands as she answered him quietly. "And that's why I asked you to meet me here. I'm prepared to turn myself in. I told you, I got into this because I was chasing an answer for my sister's death. I found it, so I've got nothing left to chase. I'm not innocent in any of this, I accept that. I'm willing to take responsibility for my actions and make everything right. I just wanted the chance to really explain everything to you before you took me in. And not in a closet-sized room cuffed to a table. Just here, where it's just us."

To say that Sam felt shock was a bit of an understatement. Despite his head telling him to get his cuffs out and do as she requested, his gut spoke louder: Charlotte deserved a second chance. "…Technically, I's impossible t' arrest a dead woman."

Charlotte snapped her head up at him.

"If ye really want' make everythin' right, then perhaps ye can put yer talents t' good use."

"How? Rob from the rich and give to the poor? I'll have to change my name to Robin Hood, if I'm going to do that."

"We could only find the one George Jamesone paintin' from the museum, an' White won't tell us where the rest of them are. Perhaps ye can find them an' give them back t' the real owners. Includin' those tapestries ye stole twenty years ago," he winked.

She smiled. "I think I can do that. Then what?"

"Then ye retire. Settle down. Buy yerself a quiet little island an' drink martinis all day."

The two of them shared a laugh. Sam was about to raise his glass for another sip when, suddenly, Charlotte's lips were on his. It was a soft kiss, but a warm, familiar feeling still spread through him as their lips danced together. Finally, she pulled back, and he stared at her questioningly.

"You're an interesting guy, Sam. I think that's why I like you too much."

"Ye know wha' I think? I think I'm jus' a glutton fer punishment w' ye American girls. Ye're jus' as much trouble as me ex-wife."

"Be honest, though, I'm much more fun than Meredith, aren't I?"

"How di' ye—nevermind. Ye're no' gonna tell me *all* yer secrets, anno." Sam rolled his eyes and pulled out his wallet. Retrieving a card from a pocket, he handed it to her, "I suppose i's futile givin' ye this, bu' if ye ever need help, ye can call on me."

"Isn't it supposed to be the other way around? If *you* need help you can call on me. Of the two of us, I'm the only one who actually colors outside of the lines, remember?" She, in turn, handed him another of her famous C.W. cards, but this time there was a number scribbled on it under the initials.

Sam chuckled and pocketed the card. He laid down enough money to pay for both of their drinks before leaning closer to kiss Charlotte's cheek. When he pulled back, he gave her a wink and said, "Jus' promise me one thing: be good."

She smiled and winked back, "Only for you. Goodbye, Sam."

"Goodbye, Charlotte."

He stood up from the booth and walked out of the door of Frank's Place without turning around. Not that there was any reason to; he knew that if he looked, she'd be gone anyway. *She's tha' good,* he smiled.

The End
Sam and his team will return.

References

George Jamesone References:
https://www.nationalgalleries.org/search/artist/george-jamesone
https://www.nationalgalleries.org/art-and-artists/artists/george-jamesone
http://mcjazz.f2s.com/Jamesone.htm
https://www.invaluable.com/artist/jamesone-george-q4135gr1vq/sold-at-auction-prices/
https://artuk.org/discover/artists/jamesone-george-158915901644
https://electricscotland.com/history/other/jamesone_george.htm
https://books.google.com/books?id=f85LAQAAIAAJ&pg=PA71&lpg=PA71&dq=King+charles+1+diamond+ring+george+jamesone&source=bl&ots=P5UCz99OkN&sig=ACfU3U2rwMySt9Fly4Mp881rTofoKPvzaQ&hl=en&sa=X&ved=2ahUKEwj44MCA3OflAhWSvp4KHVVLAAMQ6AEwA3oECAcQAQ#v=onepage&q=King%20charles%201%20diamond%20ring%20george%20jamesone&f=false
EBOOK: George Jamesone: the Scottish Vandyck

Mary Jamesone HIS DAUGHTER

https://www.rootschat.com/forum/index.php?topic=626105.0
http://www.ipernity.com/tag/stiffleaf/keyword/1413101/photos/@/page:5:18

https://schoolhistory.co.uk/medieval/history-of-medieval-england/

https://en.wikipedia.org/wiki/Wars_of_the_Roses

About the Author

K.M. Hardy has held an interest in solving crimes since childhood. Graduating with a degree in Criminal Justice in the top ten percent of her class, she went on to work for the government for ten years. Her experience in Law Enforcement and Corrections has given her invaluable insight to the world of crime and politics, which had earned her a finalist spot in a ghost writing competition for the renowned James Patterson. She currently resides in the mountains of Utah with her husband, their three children, and their faithful German Shepherd.